This Vicious Sea

MEGAN G. MOSSGROVE
SARAH C DAVIES

Paperback ISBN 978-1-7635688-4-6

Cover art by Koti Kamori
Cover design by Sarah C Davies
Editing by Sarah C Davies, Megan G. Mossgrove
and Niki Fixtion
Line editing by Mossgrove Writes
Proofreading by Sarah C Davies, Megan G. Mossgrove,
Niki Fixtion and Noelle Ganem
Ship map design by Author Eddy Rose
Treasure map design by Megan G. Mossgrove

Author Note

Mental health matters, please keep these triggers in mind before you read.

This book contains:

Fighting scenes

Crude words

Adult themes

Loss of family

For the ones running from what's in their veins.

You are more than what they said you'd be.

The Gilded Hart

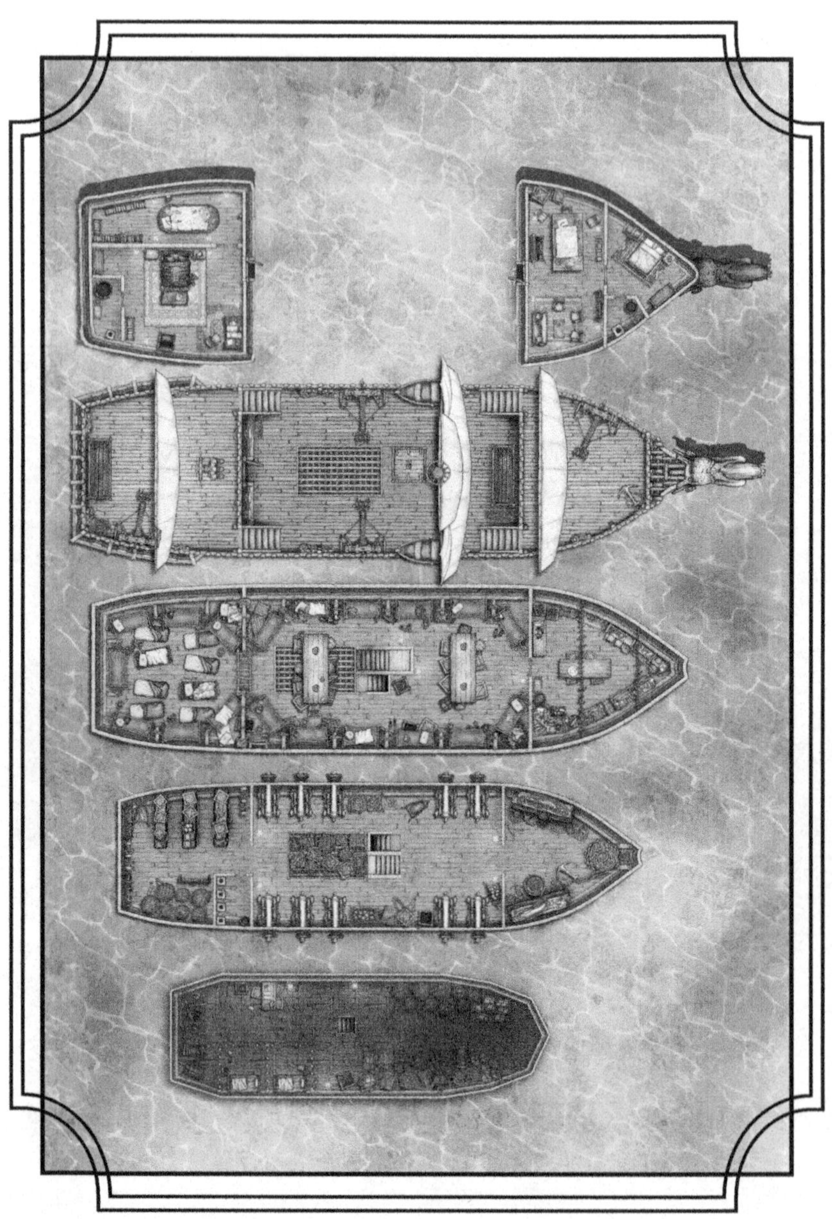

Odelia's Map

The Mainland
The Adamaris Sea
Twin serpent's teeth,
one gaping maw.
Deadly to sleep,
silence a flaw
To step is to leap,
One breath to keep
The beasts are the least
when nature is law.
No greater beast than a man's mind,
and the fear that seeks to claim it.
Balance the scales.
Feather to stone.
Heavier still,
the guilt-sown bone.
One and one may enter.
One and one may die.
Soul the sole preventer,
it and the divide.

Creaking piss pot of a ship

1
ODELIA

A ship's only silence lay in death.

The soft, rhythmic groan of tired wood conceals my steps as she sways beneath me, singing the melody we've danced to a thousand times. Thick fog smothers us both—choking the drenched bones of her sail, soiling the wraps in my boots, wetting my lungs and compounding the fear that threatens to stop me, again.

But we aren't in the water.

Not yet.

The *Sea Bane* is a ghost ship tonight, using the low cloud as cover to approach an ocean village that doesn't know how easily the tide betrays it. By the time it learns, I'll be miles inland, and the captain will have no choice but to go without me, or risk the navy's wrath.

There are few on the top deck, only enough to keep us on target. I stick to the shadows, my cowl low, but it's in vain. The fog works against me, and a man's cough is all the warning I get before heavy steps bring the silhouette of a body too close. *Damn it.*

The mist hides the confusion on his face, but I hear it in his voice. "Captain said no—" The words choke off as he hits the deck. Flipping the knife is a matter of half a thought and muscle memory, and in a blink the kiss of its hilt leaves him unconscious. Long, dark hair spills from the hood of his cloak. Sammie. The meathead in charge of intimidating any random 'recruits' the captain decides to bring on.

Frustrated heat flashes through me—there's no way the sound went unnoticed.

I step over him and manoeuvre towards the stern, dodging coiled rope and crates of glittering weapons prepped for the raid until I reach the rowboats by the captain's office. Their shapes are softened by the foggy gloom and the covers meant to dissuade rain. One of them holds as much supplies as I could stash away as the mainland grew on the horizon.

Behind me, concerned murmurs break out, muted by the damp air. It's beginning to sound like there may not be time to grab the map after all. I haven't let myself imagine what it would be like to get caught, but—after being careful for months, it's not worth it to risk it now.

I reach a hand to pull the cover away, to flee before the disturbance wakes anyone else, but clench my fist instead. No. The map is the key to the entire plan. A foolish plan, to anyone else, but if my hunch is right, I'll sail into a life on soil, with a glittering pile of coin for comfort. They've no reason to think Sammie didn't find his way to the bottom of a bottle and lose his footing. Even if they get suspicious, they won't check the captain's office.

The lock would be difficult if I hadn't been practicing for most of my twenty-four years. The door swings open on oiled hinges. It's the height of vanity for him to silence the creak that might otherwise alert him to intruders, but it helps me now, allowing the heavy wood to open and close without a sound. The polished handle is cool as I twist and ease it back into the frame, preventing the tell-tale click that might alert the man sleeping in the connected room. *That* door would be barred from the inside with a solid length of galanthor bone.

I pull back my cowl and take a breath, trying to ground myself back into this moment. My body always betrays me in here, the scent of waxed wood and barely there salt eliciting memories I'd rather forget. The office is clean and deceptive, wealth hidden in plain sight—plush forest-green carpet, a standing suit of plate mail whose decorative inlay is betrayed by a ray of moonlight that shines in from the round glass window.

Railed shelves line one wall, stuffed with leather-bound books and priceless trinkets scattered between little carved wooden animals that wouldn't go for a copper each.

My attention stalls there, suddenly frozen in indecision. I'd already made peace with leaving behind my own collection—gorgeous leaves, mossy bark, the tiny bits of land I could hide in a pocket or bloody palm—but I'd underestimated the battle of wills it would take to leave my mother's carvings behind. Stealing even one is out of the question. He would notice if any were gone immediately, and I'd be sacrificing time I can't afford to lose. Still, it takes everything in me to move on, gripping the nautilus pendant on my neck. It'll be all I'll have left of her.

It'll have to be enough.

The desk takes up more than its share of space. It's heavy, with intricate ocean patterns burned into the dark wood. The trick drawer slides out smooth, and again I thank past-me for scouting it out beforehand.

Click.

The hidden compartment at the bottom is small, the thin top coated with a thin layer of dust. Three rolls of parchment wait inside. They're all cast-offs. Maps to treasure or the abandoned hidey holes of other crews. All are useless to the impatient or unimaginative.

I take the one with a broken golden seal, but leave the others. The less angry he is, the more likely he'll let me go without pursuit. This map had been exhausted long months ago. We'd wasted days after he tried to cut corners. In his eyes, it's worthless. At least that's what I tell myself as I tuck it into my boot with a trembling hand and clip the hidden compartment back down.

Just then, the ship catches a rogue wave, and it's all I can do to grab for the loose drawer as everything rolls inside. It slaps itself closed, and my strained heart kicks into overdrive, shooting me out the door and down the double step in relative silence.

Holding my breath against the pounding in my veins, I choose a shadow across from the rowboats and sidle in, waiting.

Nothing.

Nothing but the *Sea Bane's* song and the slow whine as the sail adjusts in the wind.

I pull my cowl up and breathe, letting the moment bring my mind back into blade-sharp focus before I start the next phase. If the panic takes over, pushes too fast, the pulley for the rowboat will draw attention, and there's a crate's worth of acid bolts not ten steps away that'll have me in open water with a single shot.

The thought drags the panic up again and I shove the image away. The fear stays, though, tight in my neck, lacing through my gut like a wave viper. Unfortunately, I don't have the luxury of letting it win this time, so I force myself to the rowboat, tangle my fingers into the oiled cover, and pull.

"Nisse."

My father's voice is an afterthought as my heart drops to the waves below, sinking deeper as the moment ticks by. Heavy footsteps approach, but I don't turn.

The rowboat is empty. All my supplies are gone.

A hot weight lands on my shoulder. Heavy. Balanced perfectly between warning and reassurance.

I rip away, hating that I step back as I face him. "How did you find out?"

He sets his shoulders, his huge chest rising and falling as he looks down at me and sighs. The soft sound wraps me in a childish dread, especially as his attention darts to my side, and I realise I drew my dagger without thought. The look in his eye says he'd welcome a challenge, but he waits for a moment, a quiet dare. We both know he's the only one on this ship that could best me in a fight. But he'd win. He'd subdue me and throw me in the brig with no food. The only water offered would be spilled onto the cell floor to mix with old piss. Days without sunlight—without the wind on my skin.

I can't fight him. The certainty seizes me and suddenly I'm eight years old again, crying, begging him not to make me use the weapon he put in my hand.

"You're my daughter. And you've been scurrying around, hiding like a bilge rat for days."

"As if I'd want to be noticed by the new *recruits* you picked up in Thornreach." The whole lot were a thumbless handful of unwashed, leering criminals who've wasted their chance at a normal life. Piracy lends itself well to the type. I won't watch another round of pointlessly cruel cannon fodder get their dicks hard by doing more harm than is necessary. Once, we'd have taken what we needed and gone. But as soon as my father brought in fresh meat, it was clear he'd planned another massacre. I'd argued—of course I'd argued. But it's always the same answer.

Our reputation is what protects us. Keeps the others too afraid to risk a fight.

His grey eyes deaden as my voice carries. Embarrassing him is a worse offense than lifting my blade, but I need time. Need to think. The map is still in my boot and the mainland isn't far now. I could beg for supplies, or forage in my shifted form, maybe, though I haven't given into that side of me for years. I feel it, just under my skin, all smothered instinct and jagged-edged fear.

Run.

I could—should—leap over the side. Should take my chances with the waves and pray to whatever god might listen to a woman with enough blood on her hands to have survived in this life.

"Nisse." The threat in his voice draws me back. "If you'd have made it off this ship, you'd have died a slow, lonely death. Is that what you want?"

I swallow, letting my eyes fall to his stainless frock coat. The black linen is strangely crisp, despite the time and the fingers of wet fog that curl around him, dulling the gilded buttons. Once, I would have let his doubt become my own, but this time the words numb me, extinguish me. Exhaustion rushes in, tucking itself into the empty spaces the frustration leaves behind.

"It's the same fate I face here." I sheath my blade and give him my back, issuing a challenge of my own as I tug the rowboat cover the rest of the way and let it fall to the deck. No matter how this ends, I'm done with this ship.

Behind me, his blade sings. The waves seem to sense the tension, growing larger, lapping the sides of the ship in uneven pulls. "Do not test me."

I spin to him, the laugh bubbling out of me before I can stop it. "Or what?"

His voice is even as the tip of his blade rises. "I'd rather end you here than allow you to suffer at the hands of another."

Again, the ship shifts unevenly, still caught in whatever strange current that angered the waves. I study the scar on his face, the one that runs from his right eyebrow to the middle of his cheek. I'd been ten years old. Things had gone south after he boarded a merchant vessel. The wound bled so much I thought he would die. Hoped he would.

It was always going to end this way. Foolish hope let me believe I had a chance. But fools only ever find one fate.

"Then kill me, Captain." My voice is soft. "And let all the world know you put Nisse down like a rabid dog."

His eyes flash. I've struck a nerve, and despite my words I back towards the edge of the boat as he moves towards me. "A dog would be more grateful!" he spits, and a twisted sense of triumph threads alongside the fear in my gut as his voice rises.

I laugh again. "For what?" My back hits the ship railing, but I can't keep this inane smile off my face, doubling down on a fight I can't win. His longsword could reach me now. His face is sun-scald red, his shoulders curled under the weight of his anger. Now he's just a man. Not invincible. Not infallible. Just brittle rage.

"For what I have made you!"

"A killer? A cheat. A fraud—" I spit the words, every bottled emotion I've felt in the last sixteen years rising like a tidal wave. Sixteen years since she'd died, and the bladed grief had yet to dull.

His hand snakes out to clench my shirt and my feet leave the ground, then the world tilts and I'm clinging to his fist for dear life, gritting my teeth against the bite of railing on my spine as he pushes half of me over the edge. "ALIVE, Odelia!" he roars. "You're alive because of me." My cowl is a noose, its weight tugging on my neck as the hood dangles towards the water.

The waves crash below, taunting, sending the mist of sea spray to tickle my cheek. Its playfulness isn't tempting—I know what lies beneath. Darkness. Deafness. Breathless, monster-laden death. "My life doesn't pay for hers."

Again, he stills. Again, I'm assaulted by the twin spikes of victory and fear.

He really is going to kill me this time.

But instead of pitching me over the edge, he screams, then hurls me onto the deck. There's a brief moment of weightlessness in which I realise the impact is going to hurt like hell, and brace, trying to tuck in.

My shoulder takes the hit, then the side of my head slams the hardwood and I slide, agony shooting down my arm and neck. Instinct pushes me up, but the world spins and my hand is completely numb. All I can do is twitch my fingers as he stomps closer, shrouded by the fog.

Run.

But my head keeps spinning, starts ringing . . .? Ringing like ship's bells—

My father kneels next to me, his voice low as the ship wakes around us, the bells growing in intensity. "You're the only reason your mother is dead."

He leaves me there. Walks away, his steps blending with the frenzied movements of the others on board. My stomach twists, but I can't stay here. I need to move. The bells—

The first scream comes from the crow's nest. "BRACE FOR IMPACT."

A war horn blares, and I blink. Bodies thunder across the ship.

started. Just as it begins to descend, a rogue bolt shoots from the fog, nearly spearing me.

Go, go, go, go—

A man explodes from the fog, his eyes burning with fury. His scarf is scarlet, his linen shirt bloody, but there's no way to tell if it's his. I dodge the first frenzied swing, but with the boat below the railing now, I'm quite literally a fish in a barrel; he's got the high ground. I leap from one side of the tiny boat to the other, trying to wrap his sword arm, using my bola like a whip. If I can get a hold of him I can pull him overboard.

When he lands the fatal blow, it misses me by inches.

I'd managed to get the long arm of the bola secured around the hilt of his sword, but he rips his arm sideways, refusing to let me disarm him. Instead, his sword impacts the rope securing the rowboat on one side.

And the world tips.

I've only got a moment to realise I'm falling before frigid water swallows me from head to toe. The surface of the water hits nearly as hard as the wood of the deck, and the man above must have cut the other side too, because the rowboat comes down on top of me, twisting the world.

Everything in my body screams in pain, screams for me to swim, but I don't know the way. The darkness is absolute. Every direction takes me farther from air. The waves are still angry, disturbed by the ships that create their own wake as they collide. My lungs burn. My ribs burn. My cowl tries to strangle me and I rip it away, leaving it to the sea.

With one arm, I flail, taking a random, hopeless guess which way is up, but a wave sends me end over end, shoving water up my nose and I panic, fighting the cough that would steal precious air. The loose sleeves of my blouse slow me down, ballooning around my face, imitating any number of creatures that might lurk a handbreadth away, unseen in the pitch black.

Like that one.

Somewhere beyond me. In the indistinguishable gloom. Barely there. The difference between the dark of the night and the dark of a nightmare.

A shadow.

A long fin angling it my way.

That manic laugh bubbles from me again, and I don't mourn the air that leaves me.

It was always going to end this way.

When I wake, it's to the sound of tired wood.

But it's not the *Sea Bane,* no. The brig is different. The cell on this ship is luxurious: straw is spread on the floor, the space beyond is clean, and it doesn't smell like the back up piss pot.

I lift to an elbow. My hair is half dry, but the cold ends brush against the skin of my arm and I shiver. My clothes are stiff with drying seawater. My lips are cracked, my skin tight and dry. I try to swallow, but fail. Water waits in a wooden cup in the corner. I lunge for it, but the moment it coats my mouth, I sputter, coughing, heaving on all fours, my body stuck in the memory of drowning.

"That good, huh?" a man teases, his voice all smooth baritone.

I flinch to my feet, launching the cup like a projectile. It clatters back to me with a splash, rattling the bars between us. How had I not noticed he was there?

His grin only grows as I scowl. The gesture is surprisingly boyish, his sky-blue eyes sparkling in a way that probably gets him all the attention he could ever want. He flips an intricately carved bone dagger back into its sheath and tucks his hands behind his head, making a show of stretching, clearly too proud of the perfectly tailored shirt that betrays every ripple of muscle beneath. Despite the relaxed front, the lopsided smirk, and the effortless beach waves in his long, baby-blue hair, there's a current of quiet intensity beneath his movements.

It's his eyes that give him away. Beneath the charm, they're surgical, doing their best to carve through whatever ruse he expects to find. I glower, letting him know where exactly he can shove his assessment.

If my throat didn't feel like it was lined with shattered sea glass, I'd let him know I intend to kill him the moment I have the chance.

Welcome to the Gilded Hart

2
RUNE

She looks at me with such malevolence. Twin orbs. Dark umber mixed with gold, glittering with violence.

The kind that threatens to carve out my tongue if given the chance. Thankfully, she's securely locked in an iron cell. Could be worse for her—she could be at the bottom of the ocean, her breathless body drifting with the current.

I'd been tracking the Headtaker Pirates for weeks, and all in vain. As our spruce bow had eased through the inky blue waters, I came to find them in a fiery, bloody scrimmage with another ship.

The crew and I had almost rushed in to save the opposing side, but even in the fog it was clear they were the ones with the upper hand. It was no innocent merchant's cargo.

We'd kept our distance, watching the destruction unfold under the cover of thick fog illuminated by flame. I'd seen the woman go overboard, cut down as she tried to flee. No one seemed to notice—or care. It was clear there wouldn't be a lot of living Headtakers left to turn in for bounties, so why not save her and wring out all the information I could?

I didn't want this trip to be for nothing.

It turns out my instinct was right. Not only was it an opposing pirate crew, it was the fucking *Vipers*. Just the name has my fists clenching, knuckles bone white. Captain Vincent Ivor is ruthless, savage, notoriously hard to pin down—but rushing in, underestimating him, would mean a swift death. A younger version of me might have tried to use the Headtakers attack as a distraction to go for Ivor while the odds were in our favour, but my crew already bears the mark of going against him and failing.

I shake my head, banishing the memories. I've hunted the man too long to let him get away clean, but I won't make the same mistake I did the first time. We'll get information from the woman and go in prepared.

As I sit, my skin is drying out, and I'm yearning for a soak in the sea. My thumb finds the smooth surface of the pommel on my dagger. I circle it gently, watching her standing inside the cell, arms limp beside her. Her hair is wavy and long, as dark as charred walnuts, with caramel highlights framing the sharp features of her face. Yet, the warmth of her honey-tinted skin, dusted in a collection of small freckles, softens her edges.

She'd be beautiful if she wasn't a filthy pirate who is most definitely planning my death.

I wait. Like a shark circling at the slightest hint of blood. I'd tread the uncharted water inside my mind until sunup if it meant that she spoke first. Force it out of her by the use of silence. Lucky for me, I don't have to wait long.

"Where am I?" she hisses through clenched teeth.

Slowly, I stand, spreading my arms out wide. "Welcome to *The Gilded Hart*."

If she recognises the name, she doesn't show it.

Wood creaks underfoot as I casually pace back and forth in front of her iron cage, hands behind my back. Outside is quiet besides the gentle lapping of the ocean against the hull. Most of my crew would be sleeping by now.

Finally, the prisoner breaks her gaze as she bends down to reach for something inside her boot.

A slow, deliberate smirk forms upon my lips. "You don't need that."

She doesn't look at me. Nimble fingers continue her search inside her other—what I can only presume—soggy leather boot. "Or that."

With a flick of her hair, she straightens, lips pursed in a thin line. Running her hands around the waist of the trousers clinging to her hips, she continues to look for weapons, going so far as to run her fingers over her inner thigh. The movement is mechanical, muscle memory, but I drag my eyes from her figure, as distracting as it is—she's a wet dog, and it would pay to remind myself of that.

She palms under her arm, along her breast, and I smirk as her frustration really sets in. "Oh and you won't need that one either.

This time, she looks at me. Deep brown eyes, alight with a burning flame, stare straight into my soul. So I stare back.

"You searched me?" she rasps, her voice like barnacles scraping on rock.

I shake my head. "Correction, Tavi searched you. Trust me, she's more gentle than I would have been."

Her hand flies to her delicate neck, and I catch the marking on her wrist. I saw it earlier when I saved her from her watery grave, but seeing it again turns my stomach sour. An intricate serpent, wrapping around the circumference of her wrist. Brackish green ink etched into her sun-kissed skin.

The Vipers are the bane of my existence. Scum of the sea. Just the thought of them makes my body flush with the need for violence, and now I have one of their crew here in the hold of my ship.

How the tides have turned.

"Where is my necklace? Did she take that too?" Her voice is filled with venom.

Of course she'd notice the necklace is gone the moment she wakes. It's likely the most precious thing she's ever stolen. It baffles me . . . her carrying a water elemental's necklace around like a trinket. A thing so sacred can only be gifted from the ocean's guardians, never taken. And every sea-born knows a pirate would take the opportunity to hunt an elemental, they wouldn't befriend them.

Stolen, then. That has to be it. But what unsettles me more is this—the ocean hasn't claimed it back. The moment she slipped beneath the waves, the sea should've stripped it from her.

Perhaps I'd interfered too quickly. Either way, it's safe now. And it's no longer her concern.

I take a few steps towards the cell. She takes a few back. Leaning my forearms onto the iron bars, I arch a brow. "No, but you won't need jewellery where you're going."

Her brows draw together in a pained knot, the space between them furrowed deep enough to hold everything she isn't saying. Then it's gone. The deep scowl returns, one corner of her lip turning up in disgust, but for some reason, my attention catches on a freckle over her right eyebrow, it's slightly larger than the rest that dust her cheeks. "You know, for a pirate, you're quite clumsy. Can't even seem to stay aboard your own ship."

She scowls at me even harder.

I push off the bars, shoving my hands into my slate-coloured trousers. My fingers brush the delicate, smooth bone carving hiding there. A nautilus shell, no larger than a green grape, strung on a thin loop of worn brown leather.

I'm not certain why I didn't put the necklace with the rest of her things. There are no thieves on my crew, so it would have been safe, but it's safer still where I can ensure she won't find a way to steal it from the sea a second time.

She takes a few steps towards me, asserting her gaze. "Why did you save me?"

Her question stalls me for just a moment, but I lean into the silence, a loud reminder that it was I who held all the power in the room. With little effort, my shoulders lift and fall.

"I'm a curious guy. Have a lot of questions. So we're going to have a long chat. And when we're done, I'll make sure there's one less Viper scum ravaging the seas, and one more name to add to my list of accomplishments," I say, my voice dripping with triumph.

She doesn't waver. "If you plan to kill me, you may as well do it now."

"Oh, no. None depraved enough to join with the Vipers deserves a death that easy."

Who knows, maybe I'll take her to the far side of the continent, where she'll trade her blood-soaked dagger for a pickaxe. She'd spend her days underground, never see the sun or water again. Killing her would be simpler, but not nearly as rewarding. Viper Pirates don't deserve the mercy of death.

Poison cloaked in laughter bubbles from her rose bud lips, her dark brown eyes dragging down to the bone blade I carry at my side. They linger there for a moment before she flicks them back up to meet me and steps closer to the bars. "I understand that your limp seaweed stands a tad taller at the thought of capturing a big bad pirate. But you don't *volunteer* to sail with the Vipers. You survive them. So an overinflated ego will do little to move me."

"A sea snake with a sense of humour. Quaint." My legs move without thought. I've never done well with being idle for too long. Leather soles squeak under the weight of each step as I pace back and forth once again. "Tell me, how does someone *accidentally* find themselves on the most vicious crew on this side of the Adamaris?"

The tips of my pointed ears twitch as I eagerly await her response.

She folds her arms, eyes tracking my every move. "None of your business."

It's my turn to laugh. This woman, this flea—this vermin—has decided she wants to play games. Unluckily for her, I'm a sore loser, and I always win.

"How many are on your crew?"

Silence.

"I'll ask an easier question." I force a grin, my patience waning with every passing second. "Where is your ship headed?"

Her jaw clenches, her eyes saying a thousand words, yet none escape her lips. I could offer her a reward for giving me the information I seek, but that would go against the very fabric of my beliefs. Pirates don't deserve compromise. Not now. Not ever.

I twist on my heel as the ocean gently rocks *The Gilded Hart* to a salty lullaby. Three steps and I'm inches from the iron bars, acutely aware of where her hands are at all times. She could quite easily reach me and snatch the blade at my hip.

"Do you have an island stop where your captain frequently visits?" It's less a question, more of a demand secretly wishing she'll give me something—anything. It's like wishing on broken stars though.

Something in her demeanour shifts. With silent ease she takes another step closer to the bars. "Why should I tell you anything?"

"Because it would be wise, if you value your hands."

Her gaze roams over my face, as if she's trying to read how truthful my threat is. "They're the first thing I'd lose, if I could. And it seems no matter my answers, you've already sealed my fate."

It's true. Information or not. I'm going to hand her into the law, at my earliest convenience. Yet, it doesn't hurt to try and get something from the secrets she holds so closely to her chest.

"How do they choose which ships to ambush?"

Silence.

She's stubborn, I'll give her that. I share that same trait. My mother used to say it was a fine quality. My father would say it was a curse.

The corner of my mouth tugs up in an almost smile. I move to the small wooden table located near the side of the ship. A single cup, carved from whale bone, sits idly by a matching pitcher filled with the finest whiskey I carry on board. I pour myself a serving before turning back to face the woman. She glances down at the cup in my hand, her dry, cracked lips falling open ever so slightly.

I lift the golden liquid to my lips, hesitating before gulping it down. It coats my throat with a sour tang. I wipe the back of my hand across my mouth before meeting her eye. Desperation flickers across her features, then it's gone. Her cup still lays on the floor of the cell. Perhaps the hope of receiving some sort of relief for the dryness clawing at her throat will encourage her to speak.

So I try again. "The ship . . . Do they have someone feeding them information? Do they have a stash of stolen goods?"

Still she doesn't answer. Instead, she twists on her heel, facing the corner of the cell with her back turned towards me. I grip the cup a little too forcefully, at risk of breaking it. This woman is impossible and this approach is getting me nowhere.

Time to get dirty.

I stalk back to the wooden table, placing the cup down with a solid bang. The sound ricochets off the wooden hull. Then I spin to face her. There must be something I can say that will make her talk. I don't want to resort to torture . . . Not yet anyway.

"We can play this game all night if you like—I have all the time in the world. But for you, I'd say you have a few days—if that—without more water before your body begins to shut down," I purr.

Her back straightens ever so slightly, and the smirk on my face widens. That got her attention.

I pace back and forth again, running my fingers along the iron bars, taunting now. "How many people do you think they've killed, hmm?"

Her shoulders square.

I stop pacing, her reaction enough to know I've got her right where I want her. "More importantly, how many people have *you* killed?"

With the lightness of a water wraith, she whips her body around, slipping her arm through the bars. I jerk out of the way just as her finger tips graze the fabric of my navy blue linen shirt. The look seared into her eyes is one of pure hate, but it's hard to say whether it's hatred for me or for herself.

"Answer one question, and I will get you more water, considering you already spilt my generosity on the floor earlier," I say, tucking my hands behind my back.

She folds her arms across her chest, glaring at me through gritted teeth. "Fine. One question."

I stare into the brown eyes that have yet to leave mine, the fire in them burning as brightly as if she were a queen rather than a soaked rat. "What is your name?"

She hesitates. "Odelia," her voice is barely a whisper, but she says it proudly.

"Now, was that so hard?"

Heavy footsteps sound above us, signalling someone coming down into the hold.

When I told the crew I was heading below to interrogate the prisoner, I made one thing crystal clear—no interruptions. So whoever's stomping outside better have a damn good reason.

Black leather boots appear first, thudding softly on the wooden steps. Then come the matching trousers, the dark shirt—clean, pressed, purposeful. Elio ducks through the narrow scuttle, his shaved head catching the low lamplight as he enters. "Rune." His hazel eyes flicker briefly towards Odelia, adjusting to the dim glow cast by the swaying oil lamp above us. "You're needed up on deck."

There is still so much I need to find out, but being the captain of a ship comes with certain requirements—barking orders on deck was one of them. I nod in Elio's direction. He takes the action as my reply before he heads back up the stairs.

I throw a glance over my shoulder towards the woman. "Don't go escaping on me."

Both her hands grip the iron bars, panic etched in her eyes. "You promised me water."

A slow, deliberate smile forms across my face. "Yes . . . but I didn't say when . . . Odelia."

I don't stick around to see her reaction. Instead, I duck my head and stoop through the narrow opening that leads up to the top deck. A stretch of darkness and an empty stomach might do her some good—give her time to sit with that damn stubbornness.

The full moon bathes the deck in a silver, watery light. A striking contrast to the dull yellow glow in the hold. Sea water sprays over on the starboard side of the ship. The salt in the air comforts my lungs as I drag in a deep breath.

Above me, the velvet night sky is a blanket of glittering pin pricks strewn across the vast expanse. My compass stays in my left trouser pocket, where it currently keeps Odelia's necklace company, but so long as there are stars I'd never be lost.

Elio leans over the edge of the ship, his forearms resting on the dark spruce. I join him, both of us staring out into the inky darkness. The only sound is the waves slapping against the bow of *The Gilded Hart* as she plows through the water.

"You said you needed me?"

Elio shoves his hand into his trouser pocket, pulling out a small green cylindrical bottle. He hands it to me but doesn't meet my gaze. I can tell he's pissed. He'd rather I'd left Odelia to her watery grave.

Perhaps I should have.

The cork lid makes a popping sound as I wedge it loose from the narrow neck. Tipping the bottle upright, I catch the hand rolled paper that falls free. It's sealed with a pearlescent wax in the symbol of a trident and a six spoked crown. My father's sigil.

With a soft sigh, I snap the seal, and unfurl the paper. It's from Selene—my sister. Father's pride and joy. The next ruler of Nareth. My eyes scan her perfect handwriting. I swear everything she does is always just so.

"Is it from Selene?" Elio murmurs, his voice low.

I nod. "She is just doing the elderly sister thing, checking in on our whereabouts. Says father is keen for me to visit soon."

The sea breeze tugs at the edges of the delicate paper in my hand, threatening to carry it away. I roll it up with care and slide it back into the glass bottle. I'd been eighteen when I left home. Ten years later and I'm still not ready to return. Someone has to clean the filth off these seas . . . and I won't turn back until I find some clue of what happened to *her*.

Besides, I have a score to settle, with a certain captain. I won't let him slither away this time.

Boots scuff behind me and I twist around to find Killian. I'd sent him out earlier to learn the outcome of the Headtaker's ship. I need to know if there is any point in going after them again in the future, or if the Vipers wiped them out completely.

Killian's short, curly black hair still glistens with droplets of water, clinging to the inky strands. Pale blue eyes take in the surroundings. His pointy, webbed ears poke through, confirming to anyone who might see, that he is indeed a siren. He nods in greeting. "Captain."

"Killian. What did you find?"

He shakes his head, a slight smirk playing on his lips. "It's good—for us. As for the Headtaker's, their ship is wrecked. Destroyed. I'm surprised it's still afloat."

My mouth forms a thin line. "And the Vipers?"

He shrugs. "I stayed long enough to see them celebrate their win. Most of them seemed to sport a few injuries but the casualties were far less than those of the Headtakers."

Beside me, Elio huffs. "Fucking pirates."

I've been idle too long, so I pace with a slow gait, as I ponder my next move. Killian waits, patient as always. So close . . . I'd been so close to the Vipers. I could have attacked from the other side. But the opportunity surprised us. I need to know more—how they fight, what their numbers are, what weapons they've got on board.

"Kil, rest a moment and then take Eithne and follow the Vipers. I expect reports for every movement. Use the inktopus system to send word." Eithne hated trailing our ship anyways. Kelpies much preferred the thrill of the hunt, and I happened to know Killian liked the little inktopus that ferried messages between us.

He nods, twists on his heel and heads towards the galley. Most likely to fill his stomach with Bear's cooking before ranging underwater narrows his options down to, well, food of the raw variety. Who could blame him? I wish I'd done the same thing. Instead, I'd skipped dinner to interrogate my prisoner and what did it get me? Nothing . . . nothing but her name.

Odelia. Who are you?

Watching her fall from the *Sea Bane* had me hoping she was an innocent caught in the crossfire, trying to escape. She's certainly not what I would have expected. Even now, her voice is caught in my head.

"You don't volunteer to sail with the Vipers. You survive them."

I shake my head and turn my attention back to the ocean. Sometimes I wonder if the sea will always call me back or if one day it'll let me go entirely. The thought should be terrifying. Instead, it settles in my chest like an inevitability. So long as I can breathe air, I'll hunt the hunters. Clean the Adamaris Sea one pockmarked pirate ship at a time.

Elio is still leaning against the ship's edge. His silence speaks louder than any words. I need to think. I need to escape the skin I'm trapped in. But I have matters to attend to first. He watches me as I pull the letter from my sister back out of the bottle. Flipping it over, I stride to my quarters in search of an ink pen. Once retrieved, I scribble down a quick response and head back out to the deck.

Elio offers his hand. "Would you like me to take that for you?"

I shake my head. "Thanks, but no. I need to stretch."

He nods as I shove the note back into the bottle.

With a glance in his direction, I leap overboard and let the shift take me as I hit the water.

DON'T BITE THE HAND THAT FEEDS YOU

3
ODELIA

The map is still in my boot.

If they find it, I won't get it back, so I haven't risked pulling it out to see how the water might have ruined it. My stomach twists at the thought. Especially since I'll be escaping tonight.

The room the cell is in is boring. There's a chair and table in the corner, goods secured in waxy rope nets, and a second cage next to me, empty, swept. I haven't seen a single rat—even the chains on my wrist are devoid of rust. The outside sounds are muffled, though I've tried hard to eavesdrop. There's no way to tell how much time has passed and the endless silence makes me fight the urge to grind my teeth.

Once *Rune* finally left, I'd laid down, unable to sleep, unable to deny my aching body the need for rest. The strength in my hand is back, but I feel like a bruise from head to toe, and a thin laceration on my left shoulder is lucky it hasn't started to fester. Seems the captain's good graces doesn't extend to bandages.

Who is he? What could he hope to gain from information about my father's crew? Attacking the *Sea Bane* would only earn him a watery grave. If that's his plan, I hope he waits until after I'm gone. Imagine gaining my freedom—through capture notwithstanding—only to end up back again.

The weapons on his belt were interesting, though. Bone, like the component bolts we'd captured off one of our more impressive hauls. Each of those bundles had proven to have their own attribute. Fire, acid, absurd stickiness. A specialty of the underwater siren kingdom, Nareth, and the creatures of the deep they hunted or farmed for components. The bolts may as well have been magic, their purchase or creation on the mainland being illegal and near impossible. Did the bone mean his sword might have similar qualities? It must have cost a small fortune. Maybe when I leave I'll take it, see if he grins when I hold it to his thick neck.

He probably would, those sharp eyes calling my bluff. He's good, sure, but arrogant. And I've never let a pretty face stop me from what needed to be done.

Still.

Odelia.

I should have lied, should have given him any other answer. I haven't been Odelia since my mother died.

Still, no one would recognize the name, unlike Nisse. As much as I'm trying to escape it, I'm all too aware of my reputation. Admitting who I am would be like tying the weights to my own legs . . . but even the memory of how my real name had rolled off his tongue makes my stomach flip again, toeing the line between butterflies and nausea. The knowledge that he'll likely torture me for information before delivering me to an underground prison should temper the feeling, but it's been so long since anyone has piqued my . . . curiosity. I can't help but wonder which of us would win in a fight. If I would pull back when it came time for the killing blow.

One after the other, I prick my fingers over the bladed hairpin tangled in my matted, salt-crusted hair. *Tavi* had missed that too. Rune said she hadn't taken my pendant, but I'll have to find wherever they're keeping my things before I go. There's no way I'll leave the last of my mother's legacy behind.

Time bears down, feeding my impatience. The seconds beat by with the pulsing ache of my injuries. As far as I can tell, the ship is stalled in open water. The thought makes my skin itch. They can't be far from the mainland if they haven't moved. It's good fortune, but it means my father could spot them and get murderously curious.

With any luck, Captain Ivor believes his poor Nisse went overboard. After all, no amount of natural murderous talent, no penchant for sleight of hand, no vicious tongue, could ever hope to sway the sea.

Hours pass before the door opens again. I stand, and scowl, expecting Rune to have returned to fulfil his promise of water, but the footsteps are light, and it's a kid that makes his way down, carrying a steaming plate of no-way-in-hell-am-I-going-to-eat-that.

His brown hair is short and shaggy. His collared shirt is buttoned to the top, but lightly wrinkled around the forearms like he's constantly pulling up the sleeves. There's a thin ring in his lip and a single skeleton hand earring that bobs around as he descends. I expect hostile silence, but before his foot

surprise. The flavour isn't offensive, though the textures will take getting used to. "It's . . . good," I say.

"I know right! Captain never eats em, he says they're bad luck."

"Your captain is superstitious?" Maybe I could use that against them, somehow. A lot of those who run the sea have their own versions of cautions and myths. Of what waits in storms and of the pendants one might use for protection.

The absence of my mother's necklace washes over me all over again, like a phantom limb.

Bear doesn't give me time to dwell, waving my question away. "Nah, Rune just hates eggs. Birds too. It makes sense if you think about it. Plus he and Elio really just prefer seafood in general."

I try not to let on that the information intrigues me. Rune is their captain. Of course he is, with a sense of self-importance that large.

"Elio has taken a liking to venison though. You know, deer meat?"

He chatters on about rare vs medium rare and I nod, trying not to think about it too hard while I chew my eggs. They're getting progressively harder to swallow. "Do you have water?" Rune never brought it, not that I expected better from him. Men on the sea are all the same: selfish, ambitious, cutthroat—desperate for anyone to comment on how big their ship is.

"Oh sure! Let me take your bowl and I'll bring some back down. The quail will love that duragan meat, if it's not your preference." He tips his head and plate back to scoop the rest of his food in his mouth and I tuck the fork under my foot as I stand, tipping my toe forward to hide it.

"No, thank you," I say, the words foreign on my tongue. I set the bowl back through the bars and offer a tight-lipped smile.

He takes a moment to chew, then swallows before gathering the dishes. As he moves to leave, he freezes. "Sorry, I'm actually going to need that."

I fake a look around and he points to my feet.

He stands by the bars, waiting, while I pick up the utensil and cock an eyebrow.

"Are you going to come in here and take it from me?"

His eyes go wide. "Oh, no. I don't even have the key. I'd have to ask Rune. Or Tavi. Tavi would probably beat him here, honestly. She's fae so she's really fast. And she hates Vipers. She's mad Rune hasn't tied you up and tossed you back into the ocean yet and Elio mostly agrees but he always sides with Rune. Anyways you don't want Tavi down here—once I saw her pop a watermelon with her thighs. She did it on a dare but it seemed strange to waste food. The quail ate it though. She likes the eggs! Hates the quail though because she says they shouldn't be in the galley but I keep the lights out when I'm not in there because she's afraid of the dark so she won't go inside—don't tell her I told you that by the way she'd probably pop my head like the watermelon anyways, can I have that fork, please?"

His expression is so open that I snort and relent, groaning at the pain in my shoulder as I reach down to grab it.

"Oh. And sorry for not checking your injuries. Captain wouldn't let me." I watch him for a moment before tossing it out through the bars. Rune can't be very experienced if this is the crew he keeps. I'm sure if I'd tried to hand it to the boy directly, he'd have made the mistake of getting too close. I don't want that temptation, so I back away, letting my weight settle against the hull wall as he disappears up the stairs.

Sleep stays out of reach, though the ship rocks gently. It's always been strange to know that, down here below deck, water surrounds me on all sides. Nothing but wood stops it from spilling in, filling this cell, crushing me to the top even as I struggle against the inescapable pressure. There is no malice in the sea, but it is vicious all the same. Sweeping, powerful beyond that of kings or gods.

I shake my head.

I'm used to pushing down the fear. But panic has always had a strange way of sneaking in, coiling my muscles into loaded springs, drawing me tight like a crossbow, a hair's breadth away from violence.

When I can take it no more, I stand, preparing to let the shift take me. I'd swept the sand from my skin, ripped away my already-torn sleeves and tied the mess of my hair back with a strip of the fabric. But none of it matters if I can't remove the chains on my wrist. My stomach flips in anticipation, my gut a mess of flittering minnows.

The world quiets as I draw inward, but the sensation makes me panic, instinctively averse to the idea of being vulnerable while the change happens. I shake my head again. There's no one here. There hasn't been anyone here for hours. I try again, breathing deep, letting the air in my lungs be a reminder that in this moment, I am alive, breathing. I'm safer here than I have been for the last sixteen years, since the last time mother took me ashore to doze in soft meadows and sprint through towering forests.

A warmth blooms in my middle, and I hold on to that memory, relaxing into the change in my limbs, feeling the shape of the world mold around my shifting perspective. The bars feel closer now, the cell smaller. The edges of my vision blur, magnifying in the centre. Delicately, I flip my front two feet, flinching away from the clanking of the chains. The movement causes my hind end to bump the wall, and it's an act of furious willpower to stifle the instinct to kick out. It's been too long since I tried this. There's no way I'll be able to control her for long.

The feeling of being caged already has my heart racing, prey drive overriding frustration in this form. I can't stay this way, so I drop down, tucking my legs beneath me, nestling into the straw. This body is bigger and clumsier than it used to be, and much more foreign: thin, delicate legs, short spotted fur, ears that twitch at every sway of the ship. My legs tense, registering the threat—*no,* I can't think of the water now.

Breathe.

Breathe.

It's an effort to tuck my muzzle down, to focus on my breath and the distant irritation of my human mind.

When the scent of the straw fades to normal, I open my eyes. It's a bittersweet relief to see my fingers splayed on the ground. My head still feels heavy, weighted wrong, and when I reach up, a thrill sparks through me. My antlers stayed, a hand's width tall, coated in crushed velvet.

It never happened in the times before, but it's not something I can dwell on for now. Shifting doesn't affect my human form, thankfully, so I keep my clothes, and the bladed pin is still in my hair.

Free of the chains, I snatch it from my hair, then weave my arm through the tight grid around the handle. The pin's narrow end finds the lock. My dry lips threaten to split, but I can't help but grin, imagining the look on Rune's face when he finds the brig empty. Maybe we'll meet on the deck, and he'll finally be forced to realise it wasn't just any Viper he caught. He'll come to see that his arrogance was his downfall. By then, it'll be too late, and that annoying smirk won't be enough to save him.

Time seems to slow, elongate. My wrist aches at the awkward angle, and it only takes me a few minutes to realise this cell is more secure than the one on the *Sea Bane*. A few minutes more, and a light *snick* sends a wave of boiling rage through me before I even look to confirm that the tip of the pin has snapped.

I spin and hurl it with a muffled curse, watching as it bounces onto the straw.

I stare at it for a moment, trying to drudge up some satisfaction that its end is still wicked sharp, even if it'll be no use as a pick now.

Instead, exhaustion settles over me, heavy and insistent. I'm going to need a different plan, but first, I need to sleep. I'll be useless without it—might already be useless, with how I sink down, scooping the small blade and tucking it into my hair. A realization whispers, so soft I barely catch it. I pause, gingerly patting the top of my head. *Hmm.* The antlers are gone.

Butter and Honey Toast

4
RUNE

Morning sunlight is my favourite. I've always enjoyed the early tangerine, and salmon-pink rays that appear above the horizon just as the dawn breaks, sending a kaleidoscope of golden tones across the sea. Especially when the tips of the rippling waves catch the sun, turning the ocean into a glittering playground where light dances with the water.

This morning is particularly beautiful. I watch the ocean begin to wake through the round glass window in my quarters. I barely slept all night. Hard to do when your enemy is chained below you in the hold of the ship.

With a sigh, I run a hand through my hair, trying to decide what I'm going to do with Odelia. My crew will be expecting me to take her to Goldmere. We're a week away at least, so I have time, but I still don't have answers. Before I discard her into the grasp of the law, I need more information, and she is the only one who can give it to me.

But—like most who are brought aboard *The Gilded Hart*—she's being difficult.

A steaming cup of hot coffee rests on my nightstand. Otto brought it to me earlier. That kid always seems to know what folk need at just the right time. I sip the bitter liquid, savouring the taste as it coats the back of my throat, grateful how it warms my insides just right. Mornings are still cold here in the early spring.

After I finish, I grab my jacket, threading my arms through the dark linen. I don't bother fastening the gold buttons down the front. Too many layers make me feel constricted. The worn, brass doorknob is cold under my hand as I tug the door to my quarters. I stoop under the wooden frame, closing it behind me with a solid click.

My boots thud against the main deck. The crew is already going about their duties. We have a system, and so far I've had no problems with it. Some swab, cleaning the wooden planks to prevent rot and slipping, while others climb to adjust sails and tighten ropes.

We're stalled in open water, but that doesn't mean the routine changes.

"Have you decided what you're going to do yet?" Tavi falls into step beside me, her long strides equalling mine. She's dressed for battle—she always is—in her tight black leathers, matching twin blades carved from steel strapped one on each thigh.

Her long, white hair is pulled back into twists and braids, hanging down the centre of her spine. Ears, pointier than mine, are adorned with a collection of silver hoops, and small bone shards. She likes to wear tiny trophies of her kills on her body, in some form or another.

I twist my head, catching the real question in her emerald eyes. What am I going to do with *her* . . . the pirate scum.

Odelia's fiery eyes flash in my mind. Should I admit I have no idea? That for once in my twenty-eight years, I don't know what path to take? There's no part of me that should hesitate to take her to the nearest port, but I need answers. Something about the fear in her eyes when I mentioned Stonegallows bothers me, but I can't put my finger on it. I hate plotting a course when I feel off centre. Would Tavi think I was unfit to be captain because I was stalling? Was that what I was doing?

Seagulls screech above us, while gentle sea breezes tumble over the ship's railing. I stop at the top of the stairs leading down into the hold. Tavi is still expecting an answer.

"I'm going to do what I do with all the pirates we catch." I grin "I'm going to get information, and then I'll dump her ass in prison."

Tavi's lips form a thin line, like she doesn't believe me. I know what she prefers I do, but she doesn't get the final say. I do. With a small nod, she spins on her heel and heads for the ratlines on the mast. It's her turn to take up residence in the crow's nest.

I mentally prepare myself for the prisoner below. Hopefully a night's sleep, and the food Bear took her last night has changed her attitude. Though I could be wishing on those broken stars again.

There's no point in masking my arrival. I need Odelia awake to answer questions, so I make no effort to soften my steps on the wooden stairs, the sound carrying into the dark hold. My eyes adjust as I near the brig, expecting to see the brown-eyed woman scowling at me from the corner. Instead, she's still asleep.

Obviously, I hadn't been loud enough.

"Odelia."

She remains still.

I clear my throat, speaking louder. "Odelia, wake up."

Not even her finger twitches.

Worry pools in my stomach. Unease making itself known via heat travelling through my body. Something isn't right.

In the dim light, I can see that she's ripped the sleeves off her blouse, using some of the cloth to tie her dark, salt-crusted hair up. I know for certain that Otto brought her water. He didn't really give me a say in the matter. Anyone aboard this ship is part of the crew—his words . . . not mine.

Bear, also known as Otto—if he's given me those blasted quail eggs when he knows I loathe them—takes care of the cooking and any healing remedies we might need. He's young, but one of the most valuable members on this ship.

I let my eyes roam over her limp body. Perhaps she's unconscious? Or has she gone and offed herself with a secret poison, or found the nearest sharp object to jab in her throat? It's not like Tavi to miss things, yet it is possible she missed a tiny glass vial hidden somewhere . . . intimate.

My hand finds the hilt of my sword. Silently I unsheathe it, threading it through the bars of the iron cage. "Hey . . . bilge rat." I mutter, poking the edge of her hip.

Still she remains stiff. Heat floods my body, my heart picking up pace as panic sets in.

She's dead.

I shove my blade back into its sheath, making my way to the brig door. Smooth shell brushes against my fingertips as I search for the key to the cell in my trouser pocket—her necklace is still in there. The key doesn't sit right inside the lock, which is strange, because it was fine yesterday. Gritting my teeth, I jimmy the mechanism and seconds later it gives way. Metal hinges groan as the door springs open.

My knee cracks as I crouch down beside her still body. I can't justify the disappointment in my chest—Ivor has a fierce reputation, hell, even his daughter known by name across the Adamaris Sea does. I'd expected anyone on their crew to fight tooth and nail until the very end, but Odelia's chest doesn't rise or fall in the soft exhale of breath. Cautious, I stretch out my hand to press fingers to the side of her throat, checking for a pulse.

A tremor. So faint I probably imagine it. Then chaos.

Minor pain shoots through my forearm as it's slammed to the side, altering my balance. Then, with the gracefulness of a deer darting through the forest, desperate to flee its hunter, Odelia leaps to her feet, bounding off the ground to wrap her legs around my neck.

Normally, I don't mind having a woman like this—her warmth pressed close, breath stolen in all the right ways. But this time? This time's a little different. This time, the woman is actually trying to kill me.

I glance up in time to see her snake an arm out, wielding a slither of a blade—a hair pin. So that's what Tavi missed. She's losing her touch.

Despite the constriction around my throat, I throw my arm up, blocking the thin metal spike from piercing my eye. With the fluidness of years of training in my father's army, I grip Odelia's warm thighs, and throw my body sideways. We both land on the floor in a tangle of limbs and winded lungs. Her dark eyes are ablaze like wildfire ripping through a dry, desolate field of wheat.

Together, we roll across the width of the brig towards the door. Not a good idea. The cell is still wide open, and she still has a blade in her hand. She lands on me with a snarl, knife raised. I catch her wrist, clench my teeth, and buck hard. We roll again, a blur of elbows and breathless curses. I jam my knee between us, twist, and flip her. A heartbeat later, I have her straddled—knife arm pinned, her glare burning holes in my skin.

There's no time for thinking, only acting. I slam the edge of my palm onto the wrist that clutches the hairpin. With a strangled cry of pain, Odelia releases the blade, and with a flick of my wrist, I send it across the floor out of reach. It clatters against the bars on the other side of the brig.

My left brow rises in triumph, but it's not for long. Slender, powerful legs begin to kick and squirm. She's still trying to get away. With my free hand, I reach for the blade in the top of my boot and yank it loose. Its edge kisses the delicate skin of her throat, drawing a bead of crimson to the surface.

"Did you really think you could outsmart me?"

Odelia swallows, her throat bobbing against the edge of the blade. "You men are all the same. You think you have the upper hand all because you were born with a cock."

I grin. "It definitely comes in handy."

A slow smile spreads across her mouth. I can't help but watch her lips slightly part. "Can't argue with you there."

The amusement dancing in her voice is the only warning I get before excruciating pain explodes between my legs, as Odelia's knee connects with my groin. It isn't a direct hit to my cock, but it is close. The ache makes me want to curl inwards as I gasp for air through clenched teeth. She uses the distraction to shove me off, twisting from under me as she scrambles for the iron door.

She's got fight, I'll give her that.

I throw out my hand, grabbing her ankle before yanking her back towards me, boots scraping against the wood, but she doesn't go easy. She twists, kicks, but I'm faster—dropping my weight hard. I straddle her again, ignoring the pain throbbing between my legs as I trap her hands above her head.

Our chests press together, her soft breasts sear heat into my body. I flick my gaze down to her rosebud mouth, our breaths mingling between us as I pin her to the ground. My cock twitches, and I beg to whatever god might be listening that Odelia doesn't feel it.

Her breath hitches, whether it's from rage or fear, I can't quite tell, but hopefully the firm press in my pants hasn't given me away. My free hand slides up her right arm, dragging across her skin. "Tell me, Odelia. How did you free yourself from your chains?"

She squirms beneath me, her lips so close to mine. "Let me go," she says with a hiss.

A deep, low chuckle bubbles from my stomach. "Oh, but I'm not finished with you yet."

Before she has time to react, I swipe the brig's manacles, and snap the cold iron around her wrist, locking it to the iron bar behind her with a harsh *clack*.

I shift back, trying to sit up, but she's faster, legs snapping up, aiming to drive the sole of her leather boot into my chest, maybe even my face. I catch her ankles mid-kick, the force jarring through my arms. With a grunt, I yank hard, dragging her down and twisting. Her body slams into the floor, stomach-first, arms scrabbling for purchase.

Before she can recover, I'm on her again—knee pressing into the small of her back, pinning her down like a wild thing still fighting the trap.

She twists her head, a feral grin on her lips. "*Captain Rune*, how forwards of you. I thought we'd at least have dinner first."

Despite my heart pounding in my ears, and the drag of breath into my lungs, I lean down until I'm a hair's breadth away from her ear. "I'm flattered, but I don't *fuck* sea scum."

I push off her, scrambling backwards to lean against the frame of the cell. All daggers, and hairpins, are out of her reach, and so is my body. Odelia rolls back over, dragging herself into a sitting position. Both of us just stare at each other, chests rising in sync as we gather our breath.

Fucking pirates.

Her eyes never leave mine, and despite how fixated I am, frustration sets in—I'm done playing this game, my patience is like a fraying rope hanging on for dear life. "I'm tired of waiting, Odelia."

"I'll never tell you anything," she spits back.

I grit my teeth, biting back the fury boiling in my veins. I need to move. I hate sitting still. "How many are on your crew? What kind of weapons are on board? Where are they headed? What's their next target? Is someone feeding them their information?"

Obviously, a night down here all alone didn't cure that stubbornness, because she still refuses to answer. "Are you working for someone?" she says, firing the question back like the answer will matter.

I laugh, because every island and mainland navy has a standing contract out for Vipers. It wouldn't surprise me if the other pirates have coin on their captain's head too.

"I'm not that kind of bounty hunter." If she's looking for leverage, she won't find it. We don't work for individual employers. And while hunting bounties on the Adamaris Sea can be thankless work, there isn't a single member of my crew who wouldn't spill Ivor's blood for free. His fate was sealed the moment I saw the viper tattoo on her arm.

Scraping my boots on the weathered floor, I stand. Odelia scrambles up too.

I take a small step towards her, my arms folded across my chest. "We're three days from Goldmere and something tells me this was the best you've got. The inland navy doesn't allow pirates the luxury of disembarking before binding them hand and foot. You're out of options. They'll march down here, chain you up to your teeth, and throw you in a hole so deep, you'll forget what light looks like. You'll eat rocks and stale air for every meal, and any thought of freedom? Gone. Dead. Buried."

Something flickers in her eyes.

I lean in. "No more running. No more chances. You either talk . . . or you're locked away forever."

I take another step. Panic. That's what it is. She's panicking—and she's frightened. A slow smile spreads across my face. She's crumbling, I can feel it—see it in the way her breath hitches. The victory is mine.

Her mouth parts slightly, her eyes wider than before, and I swear I can hear the tremble in her voice. "I have a map. The kind with gold—more than any bounty. We could make a deal."

A sharp huff escapes my lips. "Liar. Tavi wouldn't miss that."

Odelia's brow raises. "She missed my hair pin."

I shove my hands into my pockets. I'd rather she didn't scent my curiosity, and I don't need gold, so I shrug my shoulders while remaining emotionless. "Prove it."

Odelia hesitates for a moment, then without taking her gaze from mine, she slips one boot off. With nimble fingers she reaches down inside her shoe, retrieving a worn parchment. A map, with a cipher strip down one side.

So she wasn't lying. I'm surprised. Doesn't mean the plan has changed.

Black, cursive scribbles adorn one side—instructions maybe, or clues. I reach out, but before I get a chance to graze my fingers on the paper, she snatches it away, tearing the scribbled corner of the map with her teeth before swallowing it down.

There is no time to process what she's just done, because in the non-eaten corner of the map my eyes land on a mark—a symbol.

Everything stops . . . my breath catching in my throat, heart slamming against its bone cage inside my chest before stuttering into silence. The rest of the map blurs at the edges, useless. Irrelevant.

That symbol—etched in quiet ink but screaming in my head—freezes me cold.

The water elemental mark. My mother's symbol.

The one on her chest. The one that I haven't been able to forget.

A rush of memories—her voice, the shimmer of the marking in the watery light as she danced with my father, the way she used to smile before the world turned cruel—comes crashing over me like a wave.

Odelia is talking, but I can't hear a word she's saying above the rush in my ears.

"Rune—"

My eyes lock onto her face. She pauses mid question, then continues. "We can work together to find the treasure. You get half, I get half."

I can't think, let alone comprehend what she's suggesting. I need time.

I snatch the map from her hands and take a few steps back. Her mouth falls open, but she doesn't speak again.

My gaze roams over her figure one more time. "I don't make deals with pirates." Then I go, slamming, and locking the door behind me.

I've got no interest in cutting deals with sea scum—but this map . . . this damned map has answers. At least it did, before a fool decided to swallow them whole. Still, I'm not letting that stop me. If the answers are in her, I'll find a way to get them out. One way or another.

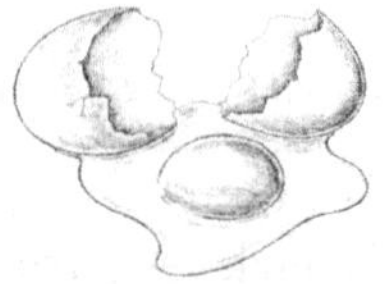

Clear evening skies scattered in diamonds call for feasts under the stars. Soraya insists. Between her and Bear, we'd have a party every night if I allowed it. Otto loves to cook, and Soraya loves to dance.

Who am I to argue with that?

Some of the crew is still eating their meal of garlic-soaked lobster, seaweed salad, and roasted meats and vegetables for those who prefer a more carnivorous diet. I myself prefer white flesh. Others are half drunk with burgundy wine as they listen to Soraya serenade with her siren song.

My mind drifts to the map inside my pocket. I haven't shared it with anyone yet—not even Elio. How did my mother's symbol end up on a map? Does it even mean anything? Better yet, how did the map end up in the hands of a Viper pirate?

Soraya's voice carries on the ocean breeze. I sip my whiskey while watching the crew carry on. Usually I join in on the fun, but tonight my heart is conflicted. It feels heavy, like there is a weight in my chest.

Should I take Odelia up on her offer? Should I say yes to a pirate? One from the *Sea Bane*? The only run-in I've had with Captain Ivor didn't fare well, and only my association with the siren kingdom saved us . . . though Otto had still suffered beyond reason.

If she knew how valuable the map was she didn't let it show. But then again she has the necklace too . . .

A wooden chair scrapes against the deck as Elio sits beside me. "You're quiet tonight. Everything alright?"

I offer him a grin, lifting my cup to my lips. "Splendid."

His hazel eyes squint. He knows I'm lying.

"I've decided we're going to spend some time in Maiden Stone."

Elio leans back in his chair, arms folded across his broad chest. "What's in Maiden Stone? Don't you want to get the prisoner to Goldmere?"

I take another sip of whiskey before answering. "We will—eventually."

His brow pinches together. "Can you tell me what spurred this decision?"

Thoughts churn in my head. I could tell him the truth. I usually do, but I need to buy myself time. I need to clear my head, and maybe having my feet on solid ground will help. Maybe, the secret hope is that when we arrive, Odelia will turn tail and flee. Then I won't have to choose between my mother and the respect of my crew. They'll think I've lost my mind. There's no getting around the fact that pursuing the map would put lives in danger. The uninhabited islands stay that way for a reason. Monsters, deadly flora, you name it. The others wouldn't understand that it could be worth the risk of trusting a Viper. Elio and Tavi might, but everyone else . . . there'd be no way to justify it. But I'll need her to find the answers. She made sure of it.

I shove my hands into my trouser pockets, rubbing the bone-carved nautilus shell pendant between my forefinger and my thumb. "Otto needs supplies, and I know some of the crew are desperate to feel some solid ground beneath their feet."

Elio glances sideways to look at me. "When did you decide this?"

"Earlier today."

"And you didn't think to talk to me or Tavi first?" His voice is laced with a hint of annoyance.

My eyes find him. "Do I need to run everything by you first? I thought I was captain of this ship."

Elio dips his head, brushing an imaginary crumb from his thigh before looking at me. He's pissed, but he doesn't bite back. "My apologies."

I glance towards the skies. Some nights, even the stars feel heavy above me. I've chased bounties from one coast to the next. Handing in pirates that rummage the seas, taking what doesn't belong to them by force. *The Gilded Hart* carries me everywhere but home. Maybe I'm starting to wonder if I even have one. I've never quite fit in my father's kingdom—Nareth. Perhaps I am destined to always sail the oceans.

The night wears on. My body longs for respite, and my mind needs to still. I drag the chair back, standing from the table. I let out a high pitched whistle, and the entire boat turns their attention towards me. "We're heading inland to Maiden Stone. Few stay with the ship—the rest of you, get your supplies, have your fun, but keep your heads. No funny business. You shame this crew, and I'll hear about it."

Someone from the bow of the ship calls out. "Why Maiden Stone?"

The low murmur moves through the crew. It's not like me to go against routine. They like it that way too.

"Maiden Stone don't take bounties!"

"I don't care where we go, as long as I can wet my cock."

"No one wants to see your testicles, Nolan."

Drunken laughter ripples across the deck.

"Shut your goody-two-shoes gob, Corrin! Not all of us have someone waiting at home!"

"Peace, you two. The longer that *wench* stays on board, the worse luck we'll have, Captain."

"Ay! Reid is right. What if she's a decoy and her crew is coming for us. If we're going to Maiden Stone, I say we throw her overboard now. It's impossible to sleep with a Viper on board."

My eyes settle over the crowd. They all look to me for answers. "For those who wish to be captain and make the decisions, feel free to step forwards. Let's see just how fast Tavi can swing her blades."

Unease spreads from crew mate to crew mate. Some might think I'm keeping Odelia longer than I should, yet some fancy the idea of having a few days off. They'll get to socialise, bed women, and men, or both. Some will use the time to send word to family or loved ones.

But there are those who loathe the land as much as they do pirates, and wish to keep their legs on the rocking deck of a ship.

Otto steps in beside me, blue eyes glittering. The young boy has never been afraid to speak out. Not even to fae twice his size. For a human, he's got spark. "I don't know about you lot, but Captain hasn't let us down before, and I doubt he will now. He's a pretty smart guy, even if he doesn't like quail eggs."

A jagged scar—still pink—peeks out from under the collar of his shirt. Heat blossoms in my stomach. After everything he's endured, the way he still greets each day with a smile—it's something to admire.

I offer him a gentle smile. "Thanks, Bear."

Soraya chimes in next. Her different coloured eyes—one brown, one amber—sparkling under the night's sky. She flicks her dark dreadlocks over her shoulder, addressing the crew. "In the end we go where the ship takes us. The captain's the captain after all."

Despite the grumbling of the crew, they'd go. Not all would be thrilled, but it wouldn't be the first time I've dealt with sour morale in one or two—not everyone finds this ship as thrilling as rumour might claim. But they'd follow orders.

There are a few grunts from the crowd, but they'll get over it. Besides, it could be fun?

The night's festivities start up again. They'll likely be at it until the early hours of the morning. I'm grateful the captain's quarters are built with thick wood. Helps to block out the sound.

As I head to my room, I can feel Elio and Tavi, their eyes boring into the back of my head. They have questions, and opinions—who can blame them? I would too. Thankfully, they wait until we are inside my quarters with the door firmly shut before they unleash their thoughts.

Tavi's brow pinches as she angles her head to the side. "What has gotten into you?"

I don't answer straight away, instead I reach into my pocket, pulling out the map and placing it face up on my desk. "She had a map," I murmur.

Tavi's emerald eyes grow wide. "How did I miss that?"

I begin to pace. Letting the news of the map sink in. Elio stalks over to the desk to view it.

"Where's the rest of it?" he asks, his voice tinged with confusion.

A sigh escapes my lips. "Gone."

Odelia ate it. Like it was a crunchy, butter and honey-soaked piece of toast.

Both of them continue to be amazed that there's a treasure map on my desk. I fish into my pocket again, chucking Odelia's hairpin on top of the map. "And she had this."

Tavi's eyes grow wide again. "How did she find a place to keep that?"

I shake my head. It doesn't matter now. At least she's weapon free—I hope. The pacing begins again. The room suddenly feels smaller. Perhaps I should shift, take some time in the ocean to clear my thoughts.

Tavi gasps, drawing my attention. She's pointing to the symbol on the map. "That's—"

Elio's head swivels to me. He's seen the symbol too.

I stop pacing, resting both hands on top of my head. "She wants to make a deal. She wants to find the treasure. Half each."

Elio lets out a crazed laugh. "You said no, right?"

Is there any point responding? Surely the look on my face says it all. How could I not say yes? If there's the slightest chance of finding answers about my mother. I *need* to know.

Tavi takes a step towards me, her voice softer. "Rune—you can't trust her."

My hands slip from my head, and my shoulders lift and fall in surrender. "I can't not try."

RUN

5
ODELIA

He never came back.

It's been two days, if the meals I'm brought are any indication. The pain in my shoulder has faded, though it's blue with bruising. I haven't seen the cook again, only the man with the close-cropped hair who called Rune away that first night. He doesn't sit to watch me eat—doesn't even make eye contact.

The ship moves, then seems to fly and slowly, so slowly, I grow more haunted by the fear. Alone with my thoughts, like Rune intends, no doubt, I can't help but feel the idea of freedom creep away. If the ocean can smother me so easily, imagine stone. Everyone knows of Stonegallows—the inland mining prison—and its endless hunger for wrongdoers and the wrung out corpses it spits when it's done. Escape is unheard of. Being trapped there, underground, would be the same death, only slower. I can't let that happen.

Desperation has me stealing a duragan bone from dinner. The man with the hazel eyes and hair cropped short doesn't notice. By the time the ship is still again—shouts welcoming it in, commotion above as the ropes are tied—I've splintered it in half. They'll either serve as daggers or lockpicks, depending on what comes first: the navy, or the silence of night.

When the door opens again, I feign sleep, hoping to seem pliant. I don't expect to fool Rune a second time, but it's only Bear. He doesn't try to wake me, instead quietly setting the bowl through the bars. He tugs up his shirt collar as he goes, his steps hardly making a sound.

Traitorous hope flutters in my chest as the evening wears on. If they haven't called anyone to retrieve me, maybe Rune is considering the deal after all. I don't eat, but at some point, I doze, the constant vigilance requiring it's due. When I jerk awake, the ship is still. The bowl is gone, but there's no breakfast in its place. It may be my last chance to escape.

My stomach twists at the thought of leaving the map behind. But even if he'd have agreed to work with me, Rune has made his stance clear: He'd just as soon see me at the bottom of the ocean than trust me—a feeling that goes both ways—and working with him might end up being a race to see who goes back on their word first. Between being free and risking getting locked underground, there's no contest.

I shift quickly, not allowing my animal form to stay long enough for the cage to overwhelm it. When I'm back in my skin, the manacles are off, and I hold a breath as I step to the lock.

This time, I'm gentle. The bone isn't quite brittle, but if I snap it inside, I may as well lay down and let them ship me off. Once I've angled everything right, a bit of tension leaves my shoulders. With two picks the lock is a breeze, and a thrill races down my spine as the soft *clunk* of it releasing echoes through my fingers.

This is it. I've memorized the map. And since Rune doesn't know the riddles, there's no way he can solve them without me even if I have to leave it behind. All that's left is to get off the ship and away, into whatever wilderness surrounds this town. Once I touch land, I'll be in the wind. They could search for days—but they won't be looking for a wood nymph deer shifter.

The gate creaks, so I only push it wide enough that I can slip through and then past the neat rows of barrels and crates. When I move up the stairs, I skip the second step, familiar now with the way it protests under weight. The next floor is empty, lined with polished cannons. Muffled voices above tell me the next floor is occupied, but I square my shoulders and stride up, holding one sharpened bone close to my leg. My heart beats hard in my chest as I rise into a room stuffed with mostly empty hammocks. The crew must be out on the town, enjoying it while they can. There's movement, but I don't give the rustling on one side time to register before I've flipped around to go up again and through the already opened door in the floor of the deck.

I keep moving. Trying not to draw the attention of the body in the crow's nest. It's dark, almost pitch black in the shadows of the torches. Only a sliver of moon lights the sky, but the sea reflects the night's stars across from a quiet dock. The warehouses are empty, locked up for the night. A lone figure walks past them, coughing into a rag, shoulders hunched.

Soft murmurs drift down from somewhere towards the front of *The Gilded Hart*. Probably whoever was tasked to stay behind to keep an eye on the ship. It doesn't matter, because if they haven't noticed me by now, they aren't going to. I cross the deck on silent feet, double checking behind me as I go.

Until I crash into solid wood.

An arm snakes around my back, crushing me into an unyielding body, but my gasp is cut short as a hand clamps over my mouth.

"Going somewhere?"

Rune. Golden markings shimmering up his thick neck. Somehow he's bigger out here, as if he'll take up all the space the sky will give him. His eyes glow like blue flame, the playfulness at odds with his rough voice. I fight, trying to knee him, trying to get my arms free, but it's like being encased in marble. He squeezes until my chest feels like it will implode with need for breath, but when I still, his grip loosens, if only a little.

I angle the bone shiv in my hand, prepared to fight to the death as he drags me back down to the cell.

But he doesn't.

Instead, his eyes bore into mine, shining with curiosity. "Did you really think it would be that easy?"

I swallow, seeing no reason to lie. "No."

The edge of his mouth twitches, and when he lets go, his gaze pins me in place, freezing my feet despite how my heart races, and when I don't move, he offers a predator's smile, sending a thrill of something I don't dare name arcing right towards my middle.

His attention flicks over me from head to toe, compounding the issue. For a moment, his attention stalls on the bone in my hand. "It's my turn to set the terms."

I should fight him. Should sink this makeshift blade into his groin and run. But the tension in the air doesn't feel like violence, and if he wants to set terms, it means he's been thinking about the map as much as I have.

"You can try." I don't let my voice waver. Even with my blood pounding in my ears, drowning out the screeching seagulls above. Even with the animal in me whispering, always whispering.

Run.

His smile stretches impossibly wider, revealing canines as sharp as a shark's. "Escape me now, and you're free. On my honour, I won't pursue you. But if I catch you, you return willingly, and then you're trapped here until you prove the treasure is real, or I toss you overboard."

My mind trips over itself, trying to absorb the words. Is it a joke? A trap? Freedom, just like that. They brought me here. And he's letting me go? But he doesn't give my racing thoughts much time.

"I'll give you the count of three." He steps to the side, revealing the gangplank and empty street beyond. When I don't move, he draws the bone dagger at his hip. "This is what you wanted. Now's your chance." Another second passes, and the next time he speaks, it's a frustrated growl. "So *run*, Odelia."

The shock of the word echoes through me a split second before my legs bound into action. The map, the treasure, it all leaves my mind as he calls out behind me, true to his word.

"One!"

The wood of the dock pounds under my feet, then I fly over old cobblestone.

"Two!"

The shadows of the warehouses engulf me, but it won't be enough to hide. I've got to outpace him.

"Three!"

I can't help but look back. He clears the gangplank in a single leap, his long legs eating the ground between us.

Adrenaline shoots me forwards like a cannonball, and I take the most crowded alley I can find, dodging parked wagons and empty crates. With any luck, it might slow him down.

Something explodes behind me, banishing the hope. His steps pound the cobblestone, echoing off the sleepy buildings. I swerve, taking a last minute left. Anything to get farther from the docks. Air saws in and out of my lungs, straining my barely healed throat. I haven't had the chance to run like this since I was a child, and the exhilaration mingles with fear in my veins. Fear of what, I don't know. All of it. The ocean. The past. The way my hands will never be clean and what that means for this dream that steps back every time I think it's in reach.

Rune is the least of my fears. This whole race is a game. A test—for both of us.

On the next street, there's a tavern with people spilling out the door. Some exclaim as I dart past and the shouts grow louder, making me assume they've spotted Rune as well.

I veer right, trying to find my way out of the town. There's no cobblestone here, just packed earth and small gardens rowed with green that blurs as I pass. With enough practice in my other form I would probably be faster, but it's been too long, and shifting now would likely end with me rolled in the dirt in a tangle of legs.

I dart down the space between two buildings, so narrow each step grazes my shoulder to a wall on either side. When a shadow darkens the other side, my stomach drops even as I go *up,* scaling the houses with just the strength of my toes and fingertips. The top is wood, not thatch, thank the sea's mercy. Or the land's mercy?

I don't have time to ponder the turn of phrase, because when I reach the top, he's climbing the opposite building, that damn smile still plastered to his face. The strange tattoos on his arms and neck glimmer even more now. His shirt is tighter than the last, short sleeved and hugging the kind of muscle you'd expect from a sailor or bounty hunter or whatever he is.

Back to the race, Odelia.

Before he gains his feet I jump to the next house, slipping on clay shingles. If he's not careful, he's going to break that pretty neck. Instead of fighting the fall, I let go, rolling as the ground comes up to meet me.

I come up sprinting, begging my legs to go just a little longer despite the way they protest. The silence behind me spurs me on. Maybe he decided it wasn't worth the jump.

Somehow, he's turned me around, and I've ended up moving towards the middle of town. A woman with tired eyes unlocks a door to a building whose sign I don't have time to read. She turns, face going wan, and I veer far around, hoping to reassure her that I've no interest in mugging a baker or whoever else would be setting up shop this early.

The other side of the street has another alley, and I stop, trying to figure out where I can turn around. My chest is on fire, my legs feel like jelly. The scent of badly rotting compost shoves itself up my nose and down my throat, so rancid I can almost taste it as I gasp for air. The full body experience of it has my stomach rolling. I gag, on instinct, backing away.

Into Rune.

His blade is at my throat again even as he purrs in my ear. "That was fun."

He holds my arm on the walk back, though he doesn't have to. I'm not going to run again—not when our deal has sealed itself so well. He's torn the side of his shirt, maybe from the climb? And his skin glistens alongside the shimmering symbols on the bare part of his chest peeking through the open fabric. Now that we've slowed, the novel sound of night insects join our quiet steps.

"Did I pass?" I ask. There's too much unspent adrenaline in my veins to let his steps be the only sound.

"I don't know what you're talking about." And yet he sounds satisfied.

I glance up at him, waiting for more, but he keeps his gaze forwards. "Why give me the chance to run?"

He shrugs those massive shoulders but doesn't loosen his grip. "I was bored."

"You're sadistic." I laugh, and it sounds wrong in my ears. The reflex flares to tamp it down, but it's faint.

He seems surprised too, looking at me at last. "Says the woman so eager to run."

The tavern goers watch us as we pass, making me wish I still had my hood. The line is shorter, but a few standing outside elbow each other and throw their chins our way.

I tug against his grip but he holds firm. His hand is warm, contrasting how the night air cools the sweat on my skin. "You're going to end up getting the guard called if you don't let go of me."

"Trying to go for round two?"

My stomach flips and I choke back another laugh. The thrill of the chase has settled into my bones, like the steady crackle of a lightning storm. "No."

His smile is fierce. "Liar."

Fish stench and creaky wood greet us as we enter the dock again. This time, the man with close-cropped hair who brought me food leans on the railing, but he doesn't seem surprised.

Rune is, though. "Elio! I thought you were staying in the inn tonight."

"Call it a premonition," Elio says, obviously trying to hide a grin.

Rune pulls me up the gangplank and past the man entirely. "Ah, so you were still at the tavern?"

"Funny how fast word flies in a small town."

For some reason, Rune doesn't shove me down the brig, nor does he let go of me entirely. Instead, he pushes me towards a lone door in the back of the ship. Is this—?

"Rune, what is your plan here?" The woman's voice catches me by surprise and I try to turn, but am shoved unceremoniously through the threshold. Rune spins, putting his body in the way. The woman watches me with clear suspicion. She's fae, her long white hair tucked behind pointed ears. More interesting are the dual blades sheathed at her hips.

"I'm just making it up as I go along," he quips, before shutting the door behind him and locking it, sealing us in.

There's a desk to one side, holding a massive journal—maybe a ledger or log— and stacked documents with a mix of wax seals—one I recognize as being the inland royals, and another as the Lord of one of the isles on the southwest side of the Adamaris. Friends in high places. There's a half empty mug set on one such stack that's already coated in coffee rings, and a spy glass on the lone nightstand, next to a collection of maps of areas I don't recognize.

My attention freezes on the giant bed that takes up most of the other side. Then, irritation flares hot, crawling up my neck, and itbs a wonder my teeth don't crack as I bare them, turning and looking right up into his too-smug face.

"You can't truly believe I'll be joining you in bed?" There are at least three ways I could dispatch him in this room alone. The mug looks like heavy wood, a letter opener lays haphazardly to the side, and there's a halberd secured to the wall. His friends outside might protest, but they'd be too busy trying to stop him from bleeding out to worry about catching me.

He doesn't seem offended by the accusation, merely lifts a brow. "I know that's how things are in your world, Odelia, but you'll find it's very different on my ship."

I turn away, trying to hide the flush in my cheeks. He's so big there's no way we'd both fit without touching. I don't care if I have to sleep on the floor. He might want me in here to squash my chance of running, but there's no way I'll spend each night tangled up with him, smothered by his salt and citrus scent. "What would you know?" I ask, forcing the image from my mind. "You're too busy sniffing royal arses."

"Sniffing arse is only half the job."

I struggle to look at him, so drop my attention back to the letters on his desk. "And the other half?"

"Killing pirates, of course."

Doubt is a heavy burden

6
RUNE

Soft skin—like silk—sends a jolt up my arm where my fingers brush against it. Odelia doesn't even flinch when I weave the manacles around the iron bedhead before clamping them around her wrists again. Probably too busy realising that there's no point in trying to escape.

Alone with a pirate in my sleeping quarters.

Not a position I ever thought I'd find myself in, but here we are.

The Gilded Hart rocks with a gentle sway, the motion casting the room in a quiet lull as I stare down at the woman in front of me. Her eyes have already skimmed the royal documents on my desk—drawing conclusions, no doubt. But then, what else would I expect?

Her pulse flickers under my fingertips as my gaze travels over her cream, sleeveless blouse to find her lips—so kissable despite who they belong to.

I beg my heart to still. The run still thrums in my veins, and its erratic beat threatens to jostle its way right out of my chest. If I don't get a grip on myself, I'm afraid I'll do something I shouldn't, especially because she is looking at me with fire in her eyes and venom in her blood.

Too bad she smells like rotten fish.

My hands curl around the iron chain that binds Odelia to her fate. "Impressive footwork back there."

A huff escapes her lips. "Try not to sound so shocked. It's easy when I'm running from arrogance."

I don't stop the smirk tugging at the corner of my mouth, shoving her back until the back of her knees hit the edge of my bed. She stumbles, dropping into a heap on the blankets. Her eyes widen, and her lips part slightly as I bend down, leaning closer. "Let's make one thing clear, Odelia. There is nowhere you can run that I won't catch you." I let go of the manacles.

Umber eyes squint up at me. "So what now?" With her chains back on her voice has gone brittle—cold.

I don't answer, turning on my heel to head back to the door to double check the lock is sealed. There is no way in the deepest depths of this vicious sea I'm leaving her in the brig when she's already proven she can escape, and if she thinks I've brought her here because I plan on bedding her . . . she's even more daft than she lets on.

The wooden floorboards creak as I saunter over to my desk. "You're gonna take me to the treasure."

"Like hell," Odelia huffs.

Without turning to look at her, I reach for the crystal decanter filled with amber liquid and pour two glasses. "It was your idea. And now that we've established the likelihood of you getting away, it's time we talk business."

I can feel her stare in the back of my head. Placing the stopper into the bottle neck, I slowly spin to face her, both glasses in hand. Her eyes flick to the liquid then return to me—her throat bobbing ever so slightly.

A smile tugs at my mouth as I lift one of the whiskey glasses to my lips. The burn hits hard, searing down my throat as I throw it back in a single swallow.

Silver moonlight shines through the window. Its beams spread across the bed like fingers to frame Odelia in its pearly grasp. "Why allow me to run in the first place?"

Not even I know the real reason. Perhaps I wanted to manufacture a way that allowed her to escape. Then I wouldn't have had to make the choice to either trust the curdled word of a sea scum or give up finding out why my mother's symbol is on that map. I down the second glass of whiskey, not breaking my gaze. "Like I said. So you can get any escape attempts out of the way, and we can move forwards."

The fire in her eyes dampens—like a candle flame snuffed out by a breeze, but it returns just as quickly as it left, only this time it burns brighter.

Odelia squares her shoulders ever so slightly. "I'll only give you the riddles if you let me choose the order of the islands and you swear on your pathetic life that I will get half of the findings."

I pour another drink before sauntering across the room. The green velvet chair creaks as I sit. "Map's in my hands. You're in chains. Doesn't exactly put you in the position to bargain, does it?"

She purses her lips. "Good luck solving any of the riddles."

Touche.

A steady rap against wood sounds at my door. One of Odelia's brows rise in question. She knows she has the upperhand right now. She knows I can't get anywhere with the map if I don't have the rest of the pieces.

The knock on the door repeats.

With a huff, I stand from my chair and stride across the room. Tav waits for me on the other side, her arms fold across her chest, and her hip is popped to one side as she taps her boot lightly on the deck.

"Yes?"

Her glittering green eyes run a quick check over my body. "Just making sure you're alright."

A slight huff escapes me. Surely she doesn't presume something is happening here that shouldn't be. She knows me better than that. "Thank you, but I'm fine."

Tavi isn't convinced. Her mouth presses into a thin line. "Can I bring you anything?"

"I could use a glass of something cold?" Odelia calls from the bed, her voice dripping with sarcasm and hope.

I don't bother to look over my shoulder. "We're fine."

Tavi peers around me to look at Odelia, then back. "Are you sure about . . . this?" She gestures to Odelia on the bed.

I roll my eyes, annoyed at the assumption. "I can handle *this*."

"We can set up a guard in the brig."

I shake my head. "We still don't know how she's getting out. I don't want her to take anyone by surprise. I've seen all her tricks. Plus I'm hoping after tonight she and I have come to an understanding."

Her eyes narrow, still not convinced. "Elio will check on you soon."

"Tell him to stop hovering . . . both of you go and do something fun."

The entire crew—save for a few who'd rather stay aboard—are off enjoying themselves in town. And despite the weight of my last name, I'm more than capable of handling one pirate . . . even if the blonde-haired fae in front of me clearly disagrees.

Tavi flicks her braids over her shoulder, spinning on her heel in a huff. I smile as she walks away. No doubt she'd send Elio to check on me soon enough.

Once her silhouette disappears into the shadows, I shut the door, firmly twisting the lock back into place. Odelia watches me cross the room, my strides casual as I make my way back to the desk. I pick up the clay jug, the water inside sloshes softly as I pour it into a cup.

I turn back, cup in hand, and step towards her—slow, steady. She watches me with calculation in her eyes—fear buried beneath a layer of defiance.

The iron chain clinks as she reaches for the cup I offer. Her fingers brush mine, light and quick, but there's heat in the touch. Something sharp. Her breath hitches—and for a second, I feel it too. The flicker.

"Finally, the water you promised me," she murmurs, her voice floating like the sea current.

A smile steals across my lips as I back away. A smile steals across my lips as I back away. "Unlike pirates—as I'm sure you know—I always keep my promises."

Odelia downs the water as I settle into the chair opposite the bed. I have a feeling it's going to be a long night, so I might as well make myself comfortable.

She leans over to place the cup on the nightstand. I can't help but notice the gentle rise of her hip before it dips back down to meet the curve of her waist—silver moonlight bathing her figure in a glimmer of beams.

I avert my gaze as she straightens up. "So, are you going to tell me about this map?"

She reads me silently. "Are you going to agree to my terms?"

The chair creaks as I lean back, lacing my fingers together to rest on top of my head. "You can have half of the treasure, but there's no chance you're setting the course for my ship."

Odelia's brows raise. "What about my own sleeping quarters then?"

The soft chuckle that escapes my lips catches me by surprise. "Not going to happen."

"Fine—but if you so much as breathe in my direction I will make sure you never bear children," she mutters.

"I wouldn't dare. You stink terribly of fish rot."

She huffs. "So where to first, *captain*?"

There's zero reason for the way my title rolls off her tongue to affect me so much, but it stirs something low in my core."Twin Serpents, it's the closest."

She nods. "A three day sail then."

"Two. Though I don't blame you for assuming *The Gilded Hart* is as slow as the *Sea Bane*.

Without another word, Odelia lies down, putting her back to me. For a moment, I watch the slow rise and fall of her chest. Part of me wants to let her sleep, then I can finally have some peace, but the other half of me knows I'll be up all night. Why should she get to rest?

"So does your captain keep a tally of all the people he's attacked or does he crush them under his boot without a thought?" My voice carries softly through the quiet of the room.

She doesn't move. But there's no way she's asleep already. After a stretched silence, she sighs. "Absolutely. He journals every night with vanilla scented ink," her words float towards me, dripping with sarcasm.

I stretch out my legs. "I'm sure he takes the same pains for his beloved crew. I've always wondered, who cares for injured pirates? With the amount of scars on you the *Sea Bane* must have a shit medic. Then again the inland towns would be too weary to do a better job. Of course, you could likely force them at blade point."

"Fear works just as well as kindness. Sometimes better." Her voice is quieter this time, almost sad.

Something in my chest shifts. Perhaps even the most fearsome pirates still had feelings—though who knew which ones. She did seem to hate it on that ship.

I stare out the round, glass window, watching the glittering waves shimmer under the night sky. "What's Ivor like? Or his daughter—Nisse, right? I heard she's a hard ass. Coated in that much blood I bet she's slimy too. Not enough ocean in the world to wash that away. I wonder if the navy will string them up together. Maybe I should take the honour myself. There isn't a person on this ship who wouldn't enjoy that sight."

"I'm sure," she says wryly. "Ivor's reputation isn't exaggerated. And Nisse . . . well, she's her father's daughter. I'll be glad to be rid of both of them."

Ocean water slaps the sides of *The Gilded Hart*, wood creaking underfoot. After a while, I think she's actually asleep, her breath evening to a slow rhythm. Perhaps it's for the best—not that I'll find much rest tonight. I know she can slip out of those manacles and I'm not going to risk her escaping again.

Hours pass by. At some point, I fetch myself another whiskey, making sure to take my time with the burning liquid. I need it to last me a while. Three sips in, and my thoughts travel to my father. The last time I'd spoken with him wasn't pleasant. It never is.

He thinks I should be performing my sea-given duties, like my sister Selene and my younger brother Dash, and there's never any point trying to convince him I need answers. I need to know what happened to our mother—I'll travel each part of the Adamaris Sea if I have to, cleaning away every bit of pirate filth I find on the way.

A soft breath escapes my lips as I pull the map from my other trouser pocket. It softly crinkles as I flatten it on my lap. My gaze flicks to the swirling symbol in the top left corner. As far as I'm aware no one has seen something like this in a long time. The scribes in the royal archives would be shocked.

I had little information about my elemental bloodline. Most of what I knew was what my father could tell me and what I'd searched for myself. My mother never spoke of family—didn't have any. Water elementals are solitary creatures, rare, even without the crush of other races pushing them into wilder waters. But this sort of relic doesn't reveal itself by chance.

At some point, I set my glass down. It hits the table with a sharp clink—louder than I meant.

Odelia jolts upright like I'd drawn a blade.

Back pressed to the wall, eyes wide, breathing shallow. She scuttles away, fast and twitchy, like she's expecting the worst.

Her gaze flicks to the glass. Just a glass. No threat.

I meet her eyes—steady, unflinching. I don't speak. I don't offer comfort. I just look.

She doesn't say a word.

Minutes drag by, thick with silence and the creak of the ship settling into the tide. Eventually, she stills. Tension drains slowly from her limbs, and she slips lower against the wall, chin tucked, lashes low.

Her face is so soft in sleep.

I think back to our earlier conversation. The irritation in her voice makes her edges sharp. A viper would have to be. But in sleep she could be anyone. A baker, a kelp farmer, a mother.

My fingers slip inside my trouser pocket where I still carry her necklace, wondering if she could ever have done something to deserve it, maybe before she turned to this life. I run my eyes over the salt-crusted wave of hair resting on her shoulders. How can someone so vitriolic be tied to something so precious—how did *she* get her hands on a water elemental necklace?

I could force the answer out of her, but to what end? We'll find thc treasure, and then I'll be rid of her.

And when she's gone, I'll catch up with her crew and bleed every single one of them dry.

For Otto. For every innocent who's fallen upon a Viper's blade.

Odelia whimpers, her brow knitting together. No doubt, even in sleep she's tormented by the blood on her hands.

I rub the smooth shell between my fingers, my gaze never leaving her sleeping form. I can't trust her—*tide damn me*—I don't even know if I trust myself at this point.

I'll have to answer for my decision to follow the map. Elio and Tav's doubts are heavy burdens to bear. But the grief of my mother's absence is heavier.

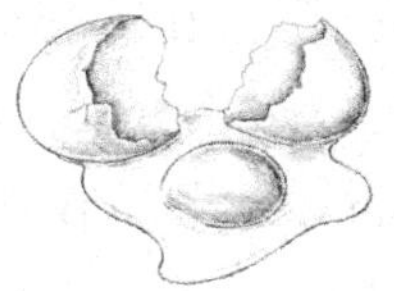

Milky pinks and buttery yellow light washes over my skin. I definitely nodded off for a few hours in the night, but when I woke I was relieved to find Odelia still fast asleep on my bed. Her position changed. No longer is she backed into the corner like a trapped deer. She's curled tightly in a ball in the middle of the bed, her walnut waves sprawling around her.

Without making a sound, I ease myself out of my chair, not bothering to stretch my aching limbs from being cramped all night. I definitely need a dip in the ocean. My skin is practically shrivelling with every passing second.

Quietly, I unlock the door and head out onto the deck, where I come face to face with both Tavi and Elio—and most of the crew. My shoulders drop, unease filling my stomach with heat. A captain's job never ends.

I clear my throat. No need to shout—they're already watching me with sharp and eager eyes. "I have decided to take us on a different course. The pirate—Odelia has a map. One that leads to a cache of the ocean's relics and treasure."

Both Elio and Tavi remain stiff. I don't look at them, but from the corner of my eye I see the way their hands twitch. This isn't the path they'd choose, but they'd walk beside me regardless.

"We sail for an island called Twin Serpents," I say. The words drop heavy. "About four hundred knots off the Emerald Coast. If the winds hold, we'll make landfall in two days."

There's a beat of silence. Then the murmuring starts—quiet, but sharp around the edges. Not all of them like the plan. I can feel it in the shift of their weight, the way a few cross their arms or glance sideways at one another.

They don't trust her—they shouldn't.

I push up the sleeves on my linen shirt. "Find the rest of the crew, and hoist the sail."

A few of the crew mutter under their breath but they step into action.

Early morning wind dances across the deck, and I turn without another word. They don't have to trust her. They just have to follow orders.

For now.

Elio takes a step towards me. "Rune—"

I stop, placing a hand on his shoulder. "You know your orders."

Tavi spins on her heel, marching away, and soon Elio follows.

As I approach my quarters again, I'm careful. There could be a chance Odelia is hiding behind the door, ready to gut me with a makeshift weapon. Yet, when I open it I find her sitting up in the middle of the bed, rubbing her eyes.

I lock the door behind me and lean against the frame. The wood groans under my weight. "Glad one of us got some sleep."

Odelia stretches, reaching towards the skies. I feel my chest tighten at the simple act. She's all doe eyed, and sleepy. It's probably a trap, a way to make me drop my guard before she launches off the bed and stabs me in the eye.

"Your bed is quite comfortable. Is the chair not?" her voice is almost a purr.

A grin steals across my lips. "Oh, the chair is fine, but the smell coming from you is what kept me awake."

Her brow knits together in the middle, eyes squinting. "Ass."

I shove my hands into my trouser pockets, as I stroll towards her. "Tavi will bring you a bucket of hot water and a change of clothes—and sheets. Once we're on the open sea, she will untie you. But if you make a problem, I'll throw you overboard without a second thought."

Odelia looks up at me from the bed. "Captain Rune—offering a pirate clean clothing? Watch out, your crew might think you're getting soft."

A huff escapes me as I take a few steps backwards towards the washroom. "Let's just say I don't need the monsters to smell us before they see us."

Keep your friends close

7
ODELIA

The fae woman brought the water bucket, unlocked my chains, and watched as I rinsed off. Her green stare reminded me of a miffed storm roc—without the feathers. Even when I'd flashed her a smile and stripped down completely, she remained impassive, standing in front of the door with her arms crossed, her warm skin flickering with the light of the lanterns.

The clothes she brought are clean and cool from wherever they'd hid in the ship's storage deck. They're an elegant, billowy linen in off-white. The sleeves are long enough to hide the viper ink on my forearm and the bottoms are long as well—overlarge in the thighs and tucked at the ankles and waist. I expect the fit to be cumbersome, but they go on well enough. Why they'd have women's clothes in this style on board beats me. They certainly don't belong to *Tavi*, whose leather pants, fitted top, and long white braids are much more "don't fuck with me" than light feminine power. Though she is gorgeous, in a scary sort of way.

No one brought a comb, so I run my fingers through my hair as well as I can, grinning as Tavi's forest eyes narrow. "Enjoy the show?"

"Just making sure you don't slip anything anywhere unseemly."

I hum quietly, pretending to think. "Are you really worried for Rune? Or is it hard to accept you won't be the most lethal killer aboard?"

She doesn't blink, but lets the silence sit for long enough I don't think she'll speak at all. "You favor your right side forwards," she says, in that haunting monotone, "but that ankle is weak. No scar, so probably an old break that never set quite right. Because of your height, you don't stand a chance at physically overpowering anyone that would be looking to kill you." Her eyes flick over me from head to toe, making me feel like she wouldn't mind spilling my insides to get a better read. "You rely on speed, or stealth, ranged weapon—since you're still alive I'd wager you're really fucking good with a ranged weapon. But in a box like this—?" She gestures cooly to the cabin. "You're stuck. Nowhere to run. To hide. Rune has twelve inches and a hundred pound of muscle on you. So no. I'm not worried for him."

I try not to cross my bad ankle behind my leg. Rather than admitting that I'm impressed, I tilt my head and blink twice, giving her perfect doe eyes. "Twelve inches, you say? No wonder his ego is the size of a sea wyrm. Or rather, his sea wyrm is the size of a—"

A sharp knock cuts me off, and I swear Tavi has to smooth an almost-smirk back into apathy as she turns to open the door.

The woman who greets us is like the first beam of sunlight after coming up from a three-day stint in the brig. "Come on!" she sings. "Don't hog her all to yourself!

"We've just finished," Tavi says evenly, then gestures me out the door.

Nerves wash through my stomach. There's no way to know how this crew will react to having me around. I'm not cowed by violence, but I sure as hell don't know how to act in the absence of it.

Outside, in the morning light, I blink longer than usual, trying to decide if I'm imagining the cheery amusement in the new woman's dual-toned eyes. She leans back and inspects me from head to toe. Her clothes are the same—voluminous and cinched perfectly, betraying an athletic build and offering peeks of deep mocha skin made richer by the midnight-blue linen she wears. It must be her outfit that Tavi gave me.

"I knew it would look great on you," she says, tucking back a few long tendrils of her hair. "Tavi, doesn't she look amazing?"

Her voice is low and smooth, and causes the tension I expected to feel to dissipate before it comes. Usually, I'd cringe away from this sort of attention, but I'm too distracted studying her eyes: one the colour of sunlight through amber, the other a dark brown that matches her locs. She turns to prod at Tavi, who remains silent, and a lightning bolt arcs through my chest as I make eye contact with Rune over her shoulder.

He's across the deck, attention locked on me, not even bothering to hide the slow, assessing sweep that sears heat over every inch of my skin. The feeling pools low in my belly. Traces up the back of my neck like the breath of a lover. There's a quiet warning in the look. We're on a truce, for now. We need each other, for now. And *seas* know he wouldn't have gotten a single riddle out of me if he kept me in chains. Neither of us will be lowering our guard, though. That's fine with me. I've got the riddles, he's got the ship to get us where we need to go, and if I try to disappear the moment we've got all the keys, I'm sure he'll have the good sense to not be surprised.

The new woman continues—distantly, I learn her name. Soraya. She's the ship's bard. She mentions something about Bear too, but I haven't looked away from Rune. *Can't* look away. Like the animal in me remembers our race. Remembers I can't outrun him. He seems amused by my attention, and one side of his mouth lifts in a smirk that heats the flame in my blood. I nurse it, let it burn into irritation. Anything but let myself be distracted by the absurd thought of being alone with him in his room all night.

If he finds out who I am, all bets are off. He hates me. Nisse. The fang of the Vipers. The ghost who ruins a ship before it knows it's been boarded. He would slit my throat if he knew. He'd string me up for his crew, like he said. And he'd do it grinning *The self-righteous, hateful, manipulating, sadistic—*

"She's not even listening to you, Soraya."

Tavi's voice rips my attention back to them. Her arms are crossed, her attention already on Rune.

Soraya follows both our gaze, twisting neatly on one foot to face him. "Ah, our fearless leader. I was just telling your pirate friend she cleans up well."

Rune walks over then, his hand fiddling with something in his trouser pocket, his gaze decidedly *not* on me. He doesn't seem to want to meet Tavi's discerning eye, either, and the lingering dregs of warmth in my belly decide to stick around.

I can hear the smile in his voice even as I turn my attention away, feigning interest in the polished deck and intricately decorated railing. "She's not so wet-dog looking, I'll admit," he says, his tone light.

Soraya admonishes him and he laughs as if she hasn't just overstepped with her captain. Suddenly, all the sky in the world isn't enough oxygen. I need to step away. Need to find somewhere else to be other than their orbit, this strange, rotating crew of the lethal and the jubilant.

"Odi!"

The name tips the world even further off balance, and my heart somersaults over itself. If we were close enough to shore, I'd leap into the water, already past the point of being on edge from the open interest and apparent friendliness. The thought of running spikes my adrenaline further, knowing Rune wouldn't let me go without a chase. Bear is trotting over, all lanky arms and legs and perfectly buttoned collar. He weaves through other crew members who pretend not to eye us, but he hesitates once he's close, and I try to wipe any trace of emotion off my face.

"It's okay if I call you Odi, right . . . ?" he asks.

Rune, Tavi, and Soraya have turned to look at us, waiting for the answer. There was only ever on person in my life that called me Odi. That version of me has been buried with her for a long time. But Bear sucks his bottom lip ring while waiting for my answer, like he's honestly nervous he's offended me. The thought makes my throat tighten in an absurd way. Again I think that he shouldn't be here, on a ship that flirts with death.

"Better than *wet dog*." I hear myself say absently, forcing my gaze up to the sail. It's full sheets and the wind is in our favour; *The Gilded Hart* slices the water like a blade. If I close my eyes, maybe I could still pretend that I'm running.

"She's not capable of making friends, Otto." Rune's tone has gone flat enough that I finally look at him. His blue hair is down in long waves. His shirt is a darker tone of the same colour, sleeves so short it would be easy to believe he'd ripped them off to make space for his arms. Every outfit he wears seems perfectly tailored and colour coordinated. He catches me looking, but when our eyes lock, the warmth from earlier is long gone. "She'd probably kill anyone who gets too close, if only to eliminate her weaknesses. Besides, once she has what she needs," he says, holding my gaze, "she'll be gone. If she doesn't try to kill us all in our sleep before then."

I clench my teeth and offer him a sickly sweet smile, ignoring Soraya's grin and the quiet warning on Tavi's face. "Don't tempt me." I turn back to Bear, trying to temper the savageness in my eyes to something soft and foreign. "I'd never kill *you* in your sleep, of course. Then who would cook?"

Bear smiles and scratches the back of his shaggy brown hair. "Ha, well, anyway, I was just coming to see if you wanted some breakfast? Everyone else already ate. Maiden Stone had fifteen different spices to choose from but"—he drops his eyes to the deck and waves vaguely in Rune's direction—"Captain says I can only pick two each time we stop or they'll weigh down the ship and we won't be able to catch pirates"—his eyes snap back up to mine—"Oh, sorry. I mean, not that you aren't a pirate but like, that we captured you. Anyway, this morning they had fresh cut octendrils in the market so I got some but we will have to salt and dry 'em because we need to save some for the trip. It's really lean but rich in protein and as long as you use salt from the east current instead of the west current, you can't even taste the octoxin. Do you like—"

Rune sighs like an exhausted father. "Otto."

Otto goes quiet, and the rest of the ship has too. A broad man with a long scar down his arm grins at our group. A woman with pale skin and razor sharp nails coils ropes, her eyes trained our way. Two men on the starboard side cast glances back at me, their faces twisted in disgust.

A slow feeling, like poison, crawls from the tips of my tingling fingers and up my arms, and with it comes a longing for my hood. Before, I could stay obscured even around others, safe in knowing that when they saw the cowl, they saw death, but never the woman beneath. Here, there's nowhere to hide. I could take any of Rune's crew one-on-one. But if enough stood against me at once, I'm not foolish enough to think I'd live through it. Maybe I should have tried harder to get away last night.

The silence stretches until Rune steps closer and sweeps his eyes over the onlookers. "Everyone back to work!"

Otto, of course, nods in a way that rocks the whole top of his body. "Right. Sorry Captain. Anyways." He turns his baby-blue eyes back to me. "Wanna see the quail?"

"I—"

Rune steps between us to catch his eye again, pressing two fingers into the younger man's chest. "Don't let your guard down."

Then he's gone, offering me his back like a dare.

The ship is gorgeous. If I hadn't seen the royal sigils in Rune's office I'd have suspected his sponsors by the elegant nature of the woodwork alone. The figurehead is a water elemental without a trace of wear or barnacles. There are no bad patches, no missing or forlorn rail posts, no cracked deck boards that leak into the lower levels. There are four rowboats in neat condition and a handful of mounted crossbows to pair with the cannons I saw below. This ship is as well equipped as the *Sea Bane*. Luckily, most of the crew carries a blade of some kind. It shouldn't be hard to steal one.

Bear leads me down a cramped flight of stairs. There's only a few bodies down here, most consumed in their own tasks, but two men and a woman hover to one side, doing nothing to hide their suspicion. My hands itch for a blade. I wait for them to follow, maybe corner us, but they don't move. Then, we're past the crew's hammocks, and all the way to the opposite side of the ship where a thin door separates an isolated set of stairs that lead back up—beneath the raised captain's quarters I assume—and to a small, tidy galley. I glance behind us before the door closes, but Bear rushes to the cast iron skillet on the counter and slaps something down into oil that sounds like it's already hot. There's a single table bolted to the floor, a wall of locked cabinets behind him, and a vent directly overhead that seems to suck the smoke up and out through some trick of the wind.

His head disappears behind the end of the counter, and when he pops back up he's holding a long, short crate that cheeps softly as he places it down. "See?" He grins, his skeleton hand earring waving back and forth as he urges me to look inside.

And I do.

Why do you care

8
ODELIA

An hour later, I return to the deck, my stomach warm and overfull of leafy greens Otto picked up while they were docked. He'd invited me to hang around, but sheltering in the galley doesn't tempt me. There's only one exit, and it requires moving through the entire sleeping quarters, where anyone might decide I don't belong.

The deck reflects light from the clear sky above and I squint until the bodies by the railing take distinguishable shape. It takes one long look from the crew to realise I'm not sure where I intend to go. Tavi's voice rings from the perch midway up the foremast, directing bodies below. Rune walks up the port side, with a man I recognize from this morning—broad, tattoo-free arms, brown hair, fair, red-tinted skin. Pretty sure he's one that wasn't happy with Rune's decision to follow the map.

I fall in step behind them, instinctively ensuring the sound of my steps is masked by theirs. I want to take another look at the map, decide how many we'll take on the island, which requires, unfortunately, talking to Rune.

"Would the king support your change in focus?" The other man's voice lifts in challenge.

Rune is cordial, but tense. He keeps his head forwards, his thumbs tucked in the pockets of his trousers. "I have reason to believe the king would be as interested in the map as I am."

The man scoffs. "And he'd trust her?"

I hop forwards an extra step and put myself directly between them. "I suppose he wouldn't have a choice, would he, Rune?"

The man spins, his brow furrowing so hard it's a wonder he doesn't pull a muscle. "That's 'Captain,' to you, pond scum."

Angry heat blooms up my neck but Rune loops his thumb and middle finger around my wrist, tugging just enough to remind me to stay my hand. The touch is there and then gone, and when he speaks, it's as if he's discussing the latest wind change.

"Reid, this is Odelia. She's new, she's feisty, I expect the two of you will get along swimmingly. Odelia, this is Reid. He thinks I should toss you overboard while I've still got breath in my lungs. Now that we all know the correct way to address each other, might we please move on?"

Unamused, Reid spits into the ocean across the railing. "Nah." He scrunches his shoulders and shakes his head. "Talk later, Captain."

We both watch him walk away, and when Rune finally looks at me I swear there's amusement in his eyes. "Any complaints you'd like to bring forwards, Odelia?"

Other than the dirty looks I can't say I don't deserve? "The captain snores. Loud." Rune snorts but looks away, like he's trying to hide it. I can't help the way my lips twitch. "And apparently he thinks I'm out to murder the cook."

He sobers—but only slightly—and begins to walk again. The ocean is calm, blue stretching out as far as the eye can see, smudged by shadows on the horizon. "The cook's heart is too big. He gives too freely."

I fall in step beside him, my hands restless with no weapons to steady them on. "Then why is he on your crew?" Bear's smile flashes in my mind. "It could get him killed one day. I know you like to think the only pirates that will ever make it on this ship will be in chains, but—"

"He's earned the right to choose." Rune's voice is soft, but unyielding. "Why do you care?"

I know he'll take my hesitation as a victory, but I don't have an answer. This crew is a means to an end. A temporary solution. And not all of them will survive it. "I don't."

We come back around and approach the foremast, and he pulls his hair up into a tie, bunching it in a messy knot over his head. "Well for the record, I don't think you'll murder him. You're too self-serving. But if you ever hurt him I really will toss you overboard." Then he flashes me a grin and leaps up the first few steps of the mast's ladder, his shirt lifting to show coiled muscles and the dip of his spine. "Tavi!" he yells.

"Aye!" Tavi calls from above.

I watch him climb until the sun forces me to look away. He's only gone for a moment before Tavi slips down with lethal grace, and he drops down beside her, his boots thudding on the solid wood. "Map meeting," he says, tossing his chin towards his room. "Tavi, grab Elio and meet us, yeah?"

"Sir." Tavi nods, not sparing me a glance.

We move to the navigation room attached to Rune's quarters. It's small, little more than a wide table with a few bolted chairs. Maps of the islands and the mainland's coast hang on each wall. Tavi fiddles with a small chest in one corner and rises with the treasure map while Rune tosses his massive body into a chair and Elio takes the seat to one side.

"Alright. We're headed for the closest island that's marked. But Tavi and Elio raised some valid points."

Tavi joins them, and they spread the map over the table. I cross my arms and lean against the curved wall, trying to act like seeing it doesn't put a lump in my throat. I'd like to believe that without it I could carve a new life. But my skills don't lend themselves to honest work. And the more entrenched I end up in society, the more likely it is that someone will learn who I am. My only real hope lay in getting this money and finding somewhere remote, alone. Trees, grasslands. No questions. No chance of the past sneaking up and pressing a blade to my throat.

"Mainly—" Elio says, running a broad, tanned hand over his chin, "why bother with the riddles at all? The other islands are dangerous. The map marks the treasure right off. Why not go and see if we can break whatever lock the key is for? Worse, what if someone has already beat us to it?"

"No one's beat us there. The island is largely untouched; it doesn't appear on any other map I've seen. When we went—"

Rune cuts me off, his eyes darkening with suspicion. "You've gone there before?"

I shrug. "Following the same logic Elio is, yes. My—captain, Captain Ivor figured it wasn't worth doing all the steps. Why risk it, when we can dig for days or blow holes across the island? Tide knows we had enough sluggar bolts for it." My father had no interest in the riddles, not when there was no guaranteed reward at the end. The thought of him has trepidation snaking up my legs and into my stomach. I swallow it down. Love is a cruel, sharp thing, and his grief at finding me gone would have been all rage, whether he'd found the map was missing or not.

They exchange looks. "And if you didn't find it," Tavi asks, "how do you know it's there? Why gamble on this map"

I shrug. "Because I found the room. All I needed was the keys."

"The room," she repeats, as if she hasn't heard correctly.

"*Yes*," I say in a rush, annoyed it even needs to be said, "there's a room under the island with a wall of solid stone and a spot for a key."

Elio's brows are pushed together, drawing out the light crow's feet that bookend his eyes. "And the bolts didn't work against the door?"

I sigh. "I didn't tell anyone I found it. Plus, lighting loose sluggar bolts underground would be a death wish, would it not?"

They don't say anything for a while, their eyes dropping to the map in turn.

Rune's eyes flick to me. "There's four other key symbols. I assume that's how many riddles you have?"

I nod.

"And you're sure you remember them correctly?" Tavi asks, ever the optimist.

"Yes." I've grown tired of explaining myself, but Rune isn't done. His attention drops from my eyes and lingers over my neck, but his expression stays unreadable.

"It's about time you gave us the first, then." He stands and sources an ink and quill from a trunk in the corner. He places them at the open space of the table, but I shake my head as subtly as I can. Writing wasn't part of my education, though I can read. Somewhat. He watches me again, like he's cataloguing the information, then pulls the parchment back to him while he sits. "Let's hear it."

We still have two days until we make it to the island, but telling them early shouldn't interfere with anything. I nod and take a quick breath before speaking.

Twin serpent's teeth, one gaping maw,
Deadly to sleep, silence a flaw
To step is to leap,
One breath to keep
The beasts are the least when nature is law.

Rune's quill scratches for a little longer after I finish. Tavi and Elio peer at the words.

"That is eerie as fuck," Rune says, sitting back, his lips pressed in a thin line.

"You knew it wouldn't be especially safe." Elio's admonishment is light, but unmistakable, and its tension coils through me. Captain Ivor may have demanded his tongue for the slight.

But Rune smiles. Not a smirk or a grin—it's almost sad. "Yeah," he says.

Tavi presses a slender finger to the map. "We'll be approaching from the west, but I'll circle around to find a sheltered spot we can anchor and row in. We won't be able to take everyone."

"I never intended to."

"Rune." Again, Elio admonishes him.

Rune's voice hardens. "We'll take volunteers. I won't put anyone in danger who isn't willing."

Elio shakes his head. "Everyone on this ship—"

Knock, knock, knock.

The man sighs and heaves himself out of the chair before Rune can stand. Natural light pours into the space as he opens the door and a brightly coloured square of parchment is thrust into the room as an offering.

"Believe this one's for you," Elio says, letting the door close behind him.

Rune glances at the parchment, his face carefully neutral, before his attention flicks to me again. "You'll have to excuse us. We won't be long." Then, abruptly, he rolls the map and gestures for Tavi and Elio to lead the way out the door.

"Hey!" I say, pushing off the wall to follow.

He pops his head back through the threshold. His hair is still up high on his head, and the wily blue tendrils that have escaped catch the light. "Something wrong, *Odi*?"

I swallow once. Twice. Pretend the purr in his voice doesn't affect me in the least. "What do you expect me to do? On the ship?"

Confusion flits over his face, then the grin returns full force. "I suppose you could find a mop."

I do look. I do. But besides the mop in the careful employ of a moonlight-skinned human man, there doesn't seem to be any. Half the hammocks in the sleeping quarters have been unhooked and traded for crate tables and barrel chairs, apparently in preparation for lunch. A few of the night crew sleep around the edges, oblivious to the commotion. Their weapons are sheathed under their heads or cradled to their chests, some are in full belt and dress, ready at a moment's notice.

It's the first time I notice they're all dressed well. Each of them wears neat clothes, like they change. And wash. Their hair may be unruly, but it's trimmed well enough. Some of the men even appear to keep up with shaving. Maybe state of dress is a point of pride for Rune. Every captain has their own way of showing they've got things under control.

But how much does he pay them that they're able to maintain it?

I startle as my gaze catches on a man watching me—the one who didn't take kindly to my interruption of him and Rune. Reid. He's brawny, with tan hair and a permanent sunburn on his nose and cheeks. I try to breeze past him on my way to the line that's forming out the galley, but at the last moment he steps in my way, gets close enough that I could sink a dagger into his spleen without overreaching.

"Now don't go thinking that because you're whoring for the captain you're absolved. It's his ship, but he can't run it on his own. He's only one man."

I keep my voice soft, my fingers twitching for weapons that aren't there. "And yet, here you are, threatening me instead of making use of those massive gonads in a more productive way. Unless you wanted me to tell him you've threatened mutiny in your stead?"

Reid's face goes impossibly redder. "We all know you'll turn the moment you get the chance."

I step into his space, closing the scant distance between us. His beard brushes my cheek as I whisper in his ear. "It sounds like we have that in common."

He explodes away from me, shoving his grubby arms into my chest to force me back. Everyone in the room stills, but none move towards us. The thirst for violence in the air makes me grin. This, I know how to handle.

He's taller, but older. Slower. Assuming he's been sailing long, his hands will be the most dangerous. If he gets a solid grip on me I won't be able to break it. Luckily, these clothes are loose, and he's already moving for the dagger at his belt. If he draws it, he may as well tie a ribbon on it and pass it over.

"Reid." Soraya's voice makes the entire room flinch. "The captain already told you to let it go." She pads down the steps and comes up beside me with all the grace of a noblewoman. "Your approval is not, and will not, be needed. If you've a problem with the captain's choices, you can get off at the next dock. No one is insisting you stay, believe me."

A few chuckles from the onlookers has Reid's hand reaching for his weapon again.

"Ah ah, look at me, Reid. *Look at me.*"

There's something about her voice that all but compels me to turn her way, to watch the deathly serious look on her face.

"You will leave the galley now. Your weapon will stay in its sheath. She'd only take it from you anyways."

The room is still, silent, except the cheery sounds of Otto clanging dishes beyond the galley doors.

Reid's jaw flicks as he grinds his teeth, weighing his options. He spits. "To the sea with all of ya." Then he stalks past, the scuff of his boots loud on the steps.

Soraya pulls me to a crate table, clutching one of my hands with both of hers. "Are you okay?"

"Never better," I say warily. I want to admit I admire her ferocity. She'd commanded the room without a single weapon in hand. Even now, as the room begins to mill about, others watch her with amusement or curiosity. They like her. But I find it hard to say anything at all.

There's so much concern in her eyes I can't help but feel awkward about its misplacement.

The night is clear.

Despite my distaste for the water, there's something about the way it reflects the stars. Where *The Gilded Hart* glides, the sky ripples, as if we sail on an ocean of light instead of vast, untamed darkness.

Soraya strums a lute and sings on the starboard bow. A few of the more adventurous crew members dance, while Bear passes around some sweet concoction he insisted we finish off, since the fruit was spoiling. I haven't seen Rune, but I haven't seen much of anyone, having taken up a perch on the bones of the foremast.

From above, it's easier to see how the crew forms into little cliques. Reid stays to one side, only approached by a few others, and always briefly. Soraya commands a fair amount of attention. Bear sits beside her as she sings something hauntingly beautiful, occasionally joining in harmony. Tavi and Elio are tucked in a half-shadow. They don't look at each other, but their pinkies are covertly entwined on the deck floor between them. Maybe the fae isn't all hard edges after all.

The drink flows, like everyone is eager to have a good time before we face the first island. I don't blame them. Most have volunteered to join us on the first island, and as much as I want to believe I know what to expect, the riddle may not be as straightforward as it seems. At the very least, we'll face creatures none too happy to have us invading their home. I can't help but think it would be easier if I went alone. In and out. But *Captain* Rune would never allow it, and I can't risk them leaving me if they change their minds.

A couple hours later, my legs and hands are numb from hanging on the ropes, and a fight breaks out on deck—a man hunches over, holding a bloody nose, while a woman advances on him again, shoving him onto his ass.

Rune's voice comes from above and to the right. "That's it! Time to pack it in! If you're not on the night crew, your hammocks are waiting!"

How had I not realised he was up here? The groans from below make me laugh softly, and that's when I spot him, on the upper frame, sitting how I am now. It's dark, but I swear I see him smile back before the expression is smoothed away.

Nearly everyone is tucked below by the time I climb down. Maybe I can find a corner, or ask Bear if I can sleep in the galley. With the quail. Either way, I wouldn't get much sleep without at least a knife in my hand. I wouldn't put it past Reid or any of those who agree with him to try and get rid of their little pirate problem while I sleep.

A few of the night crew watch as I hesitate, but a solid weight lands behind me, and their attention turns to Rune.

"You're going the wrong way," he says.

My stomach swirls with anticipation, but I'm not sure which kind. "Where should I be going?"

He jerks his chin towards the steps to his room. I can feel more eyes fall on us as we move, but Rune either doesn't notice or doesn't acknowledge their curiosity.

I follow, already uncomfortable with the amount of eyes watching, and force my tone into lightness. "The noble bounty hunter wants to share a room with the wet dog?"

His keys clink as he wiggles one into the lock. I reach for my necklace but smooth my hand back down, another pang going through me as I remember that it isn't there. "I've had to deal with worse," he says, and pushes the door open, gesturing for me to go in first. When it's closed behind him, he speaks again. "Soraya said you and Reid had a chat."

The bed is unruffled, like he smoothed the proof of my presence away. His desk is neater now, the correspondence conspicuously missing. I don't bother overexplaining what happened. "Seems I've got a fan club."

Unceremoniously, he drags the giant chair in front of the door, the sound of wood on wood likely clear on the far side of the ship. A folded blanket already lays draped over the back. "You and I both." He flashes a grin. "I'd love to say I trust everyone aboard, but I can't risk losing access to the riddles. So the two of you will have to wait a while before taking turns stabbing each other in your sleep."

The jab doesn't land, and even though I know I should be wary—in the night, in the flickering lamp light, everything about him seems softer. His eyes trace over my face. He can't know how raw it makes me feel. How intimate it is, after so long hiding beneath my hood. Despite my fame, few knew my face.

Instead of taking the chair or moving to the bed, he steps towards me, and a traitorous thrill races to my chest. The room is already filled with the scent of him—citrus and salt—and it's all I can do to lift my chin to look up as he gets closer, rather than let my attention fall away. It's less how he looks, and more his presence. The intentional, almost predatory way he stalks towards me shorts out any train of reasonable thought, making the animal in me rear her head.

"You'll take the bed," he says, reaching past me to pull down the sheets.

"I—" I turn to assess the spot, as if I'll find reason to argue with him.

Click.

The reality of the situation crashes in, and I close my eyes against the useless flush of . . . frustration? Disappointment? In myself, mostly, for not anticipating the outcome.

The manacle on my wrist is cold. He holds the other in a hand, making a motion like I should get on the bed. "Sit."

"Are you serious?" I thought we were past this.

He smiles, but his eyebrows pinch together. "Did you think I'd sleep in the same room as one of you without taking precautions?"

He already knows I can get out of the manacles, but I'm not drawing attention to it. I'm sure he thinks Tavi would have relieved me of any tools or picks while I washed this morning.

He still waits for me to move.

"I wouldn't kill you while you were sleeping," I say, more earnest than I've been in over a decade. "I'd rather test myself against you while you were awake."

He chuckles, and tugs me closer to the headboard by one manacled wrist. "Who knew there was so much honour"—the manacles snap around a chain that's bolted to the headboard, one that wasn't there this morning—"in pirates."

The length gives me little choice but to sit. *Ass.*

"So is this your plan? Chain me to your bed each night until we're done with the map?" The words alone threaten to make me laugh but I hold it back, pretend I'm not considering the duality of their implications.

Without warning, he lifts his shirt up over his head and tosses it on the desk. The shadows don't hide the rippled muscles of his torso, and heat blazes through me from head to toe, only remembering to look away when he sits to unlace his boots. "It's for your safety."

The words take a moment to settle in, since the sudden image of my legs wrapped around the V of his waist is impossible to banish. I can't look at him, but I can't look away. Maybe he won't notice the way my entire body has flushed in the dark. I should lay down and hide beneath the blanket, but the room is too warm now.

Mercifully, he leaves his bottoms on, then, even though the chair is tucked firmly against it, locks the door, making a point to stash the keys in a hidden pocket on the inside of his pants. "Don't want you running away again."

"Then why'd you give me a head start?" We both know the answer. He wanted to prove there was no hope of escaping in the most humiliating way possible.

It was fun though, a little voice in my head whispers.

He shrugs and slouches into the velvet chair, unrolling the blanket over his lower half. "A ship doesn't offer much in the way of space. I wanted to stretch my legs."

I roll my eyes and lay down, turning my body away from him. After a while, the cadence of his breathing evens out. I turn slowly, half expecting him to be watching me, but his eyes are closed, and his face is relaxed. In the quiet, I study him. He's definitely older than me, but not by too much. His lips are pouty when they aren't stretched in a smile—which happens surprisingly often. He's so different from the other captains I've met, and I've met a few. Ivor would make a game of hunting them down and strongarming them into "mutually beneficial partnerships," where he'd supply info from our contacts for a percentage of the plunder.

Rune's ambition seems forced. Like he's playing a role for the sake of others. It didn't take much to divert his attention to the map. Maybe he's looking for a way out, too. A way to leave all this behind.

The thought doesn't sit well. This ship is luxurious, bordering on cushy. His crew respects him, even if some aren't pleased with where we're headed. No, he's earned his position somehow. No one becomes a ship's captain on accident. Not for long anyway.

The venom for pirates is worth noting, though even pirates hate pirates, so it's hard to say if it's trauma from his past, or just part of his moral code. Navy parents, maybe? But this isn't a mainland navy vessel. The colours are wrong, and the navy would never allow someone like Bear aboard. They maintain the coastlines against beasts too horrifying to detail. Ocean creatures, hungry and utterly indifferent to the hopes of growing civilization.

I hold in a sigh and pull the blankets up to my chin. His eyelashes are long too, I hadn't noticed it before—

"Stop looking at me and go to sleep."

No. I twist back around, mortified. There's no way he could tell I was looking at him, right? He was asleep. Soundly.

Right?

Slowly, so slowly, I look back, not allowing a slip of sound to betray me.

He's smirking. Eyes closed.

Damn him.

The sun isn't up when I wake again. I freeze, but let my attention roam the darkened room, trying to figure out what woke me. Rune's head is tipped against the back of the chair, his mouth open. He doesn't move when I sit up, even though the chain clanks against the bed frame. His blanket is still tucked around his waist, the faint markings on his chest and arms shimmering in the scant moonlight. But my senses buzzes with . . . something . . .

What was it?

There. Something is . . . scratching . . . the sound is familiar. Recognition dances on the edge of my thoughts. Rodents? No. It's not the same wood-gnawing grind.

It doesn't click until the doorknob starts to turn.

Lockpicks.

My heart leaps into overdrive. Someone is trying to sneak inside. Rune's chair would be near immobile when combined with his weight, but I'm not risking being assassinated while chained to a bed frame.

So I shift.

Keeping secrets

9
RUNE

I shouldn't be feeling this way. I shouldn't want to touch her skin, taste her tongue on mine or dance with her on these moonlit shores, and I certainly shouldn't want to *fuck* her until her voice is raw from moaning my name.

But I do.

Odelia darts away, her bare feet digging into the silver sand. Wild, brunette waves fly behind her as she dashes through the sea that kisses the shoreline. The sound of her laughter carries on the wind, and the moment it reaches my ears something inside me snaps. I *need* to chase her. I *need* to catch her, and then I *have* to taste her.

My feet move without permission. Salty ocean mist slaps against my skin as I run after her. Brown eyes dipped in gold lock onto me as Odelia throws a glance over her shoulder, a feral grin stretching across her beautiful rosebud lips. Silently, she invites me into her orbit, and I accept willingly. Here, I can want all I like. Here, there are no consequences.

Oyster coloured silk melts to her figure, the wind pressing against the soft fabric, making her look as if she has been draped in seafoam and then stitched together with strings of pearls. Above us, the sky is littered with a thousand pin pricks, each one reflecting off the waves as we prance by.

I close the distance between us, and her scent hits me—honey and pears. Sweet, fresh, nothing like the brine and rot that cling to the decks day in and day out. It drags up memories I haven't let myself taste in years: sun-warmed orchards, overripe fruit on the breeze, meadows that stretch so far you forget the sea even exists.

It's the kind of smell a man like me longs for—something that belongs to solid ground, to land that doesn't shift beneath your boots.

The steady thrum of my heart beats inside my chest, and each time I almost reach Odelia, she seems further away. My brow pinches as I see her disappear into the bushes up ahead, her footsteps in the sand my only companion.

"Rune . . ."

I whip my head around, following her voice.

"Rune . . ."

There, in the thicket, I can see her golden highlights blending in with the underbrush like prey hiding from a predator. A grin forms upon my lips. I've caught her now.

"Rune!"

The vision before me shatters, melting away into the dark as my mind comes to consciousness. Someone shakes me back into reality. Someone who smells like honey and pears.

My eyes shoot open, hands grabbing for the figure leaning over me. Without too much thought, I yank Odelia's arms towards my body. What she's doing I have no idea, but I'm not going to take any chances.

With a muffled shriek, she falls into my lap, her palms slapping my bare chest. For a moment, we simply stare at each other, but I don't miss the slight intake of her breath as she flicks her gaze down to the pale, gold markings on my skin. That's when I notice her wrists, one with the viper tattoo, the other ink free. Neither of them are manacled. She's escaped again? How does she keep doing this?

It feels so wrong that she fits so right, perfectly perched on my thighs. The warmth of her body seeping into my skin, burning through every hardened layer that I keep trying to put between us. She's not to be trusted—ever—so why does this feel so good? I knew the moment she stepped from my sleeping quarters onto the deck dressed in Soraya's loaned clothing that I'd struggle to look away. Why did she have to become so irresistible?

The room is dark. Watery moonlight streams through the round glass window, bathing us in its silver glow. My grip tightens on her arms as I find her gaze once again. Neither one of us dares to speak, yet the thump in my chest says a thousand words. It's quiet enough that the only sound in the room—besides my heart—is the creaking wood of *The Gilded Hart.*

I angle my head to the right as I notice shadows protruding from the top of Odelia's head. Only when she sees me staring does she try to pull back. That's when the moonlight catches the stick-like limbs. My eyes widen slightly when I realise what

I'm seeing. Small antlers. Pale brown. Velvet-like, standing tall between her brunette tresses.

A grin stretches across my mouth as I tug Odelia down. Her breath hitches when her lips are inches from mine, and I can feel the tremor of her pulse under my fingertips.

"You've been keeping secrets from me, little doe." The tension in the room crackles between us. "You're a nymph."

Odelia tilts her chin a little higher. "Correction—wood nymph."

The grin on my face grows wider. No wonder those damn manacles never stay put.

Her eyes flit across my face as she races to find the words to cover her truth. "A woman is allowed to have secrets. Especially from egotistical men like you."

I allow the low chuckle to bubble up from my stomach. "I call it confidence."

"Someone is trying to break into your room." Her voice is laced with frustration.

My brow raises, as I flick my gaze to her lips. "Trying to get me out of the way?"

"No, I—"

My grip on her arms tightens. "What was your plan? Get me to open the door before you deliver a cowardly blow to the back of my head?"

"You're insufferable."

"And you're a *Viper*."

The light in her eyes glimmers then fades. I watch as the words that were meant for insult settle inside her like a truth. She doesn't fight back like I thought she would, instead she seems crestfallen. Like she knows exactly who she is and despises it.

I thought all pirates were the same—proud of their title.

However it seems that Odelia is not.

She could have killed me when she had the chance. My eyes dart to my desk, where a large silver candlestick sits. There's no reason she couldn't have grabbed it and swiftly ended my life. I would have been none the wiser.

Odelia's body shifts, threatening to send blood rushing to a certain area. I need to put distance between us before proof of what her proximity does to me becomes obvious.

With effortless movement, I stand, pushing her off my lap. She takes a few steps backwards, the antlers on her head growing smaller with each passing second. I shove my hands into my trouser pockets, making sure the necklace is still there. My gaze doesn't waver as I stare down at her. "What else are you hiding from me . . . Odi?"

She folds her arms across her chest. "I don't have to tell you everything."

"Oh, but I'm supposed to trust that you're telling the truth about attempted break-ins? You're on thin ice as it is."

"Says the guy whose crew is trying to kill him," she says, brow raised on one side.

I run my gaze over her, gathering my thoughts. "Just sit down and don't move."

She huffs, popping her hip to one side, but she doesn't move.

The wooden floor creaks under my shifting weight as I saunter towards the door and drag the chair I'd been sleeping in out of the way. It scrapes out an ugly groan—wood gouging over old boards. The thing's heavy as sin, made from rough wood and iron bands, dented and scraped to hell. I can still see the old hairline crack from the last brawl it survived. Solid enough to hold back any drunk with a pick and a death wish.

Once it's out of the way I pull a small bone dagger from my waist belt. *If* she's telling the truth then I'd be daft not to prepare myself for what I might find on the other side. The hinges on the door squeak open. Elio had tried to oil it recently but I reminded him that I liked it squeaky—the noise alone would scare off any potential assassins.

Cool, salty air greets me. I pause, the door slightly ajar, yet there's no movement, no sound of any threat. My gaze skims across the moonlit deck. In the distance, a few of the night crew are at their posts, but apart from their low chatter the night is silent.

No doubt she was just trying to get inside my head.

I turn, closing the door softly behind me. Odi hasn't moved. So she *can* follow directions. Surprising. "See? The coast is clear."

She rolls her eyes so far back I'm surprised they don't get stuck. "I wasn't lying. Someone was picking the lock."

My brow raises in question. I'm finding it very hard to believe anything she has to say. "Perhaps someone just wanted to see you in all your infamy—better yet, maybe Otto's quail had come to peck you alive." I chuckle, dragging the chair back into place.

She snorts, shifting her weight from one foot to the other. "Maybe it was *you* they were after."

I look at her, let the silence stretch—heavy as the chair pinning us in.

"Then they're welcome to try." I hold her gaze until she looks away first. Always a small victory. Small, but sweet.

"I know you're desperate to escape, so how about you tell me the rest of the riddles and I'll let you off on the next island we see."

She hesitates, but only for a moment. "No."

I slowly stride towards her. "Why? Tell me. Will you take the riches back to your crew?"

"No," Odi huffs, standing her ground.

"Typical that you'd betray your own kind. So, off into the sunset, huh?" I say with a grin.

She squints her eyes. "That's none of your business."

"Mmmm my guess is another ship then? This time your own crew? All grown up. Striking out on your own. I'm sure your mother would be proud."

Odi flinches, her brow knitting together as her hand instinctively reaches for her throat, grasping for something that is no longer there. She gets heated fast—too much bite for how small she is. She pushes right up into my space, chest brushing mine, chin tipped up so she can snarl at me properly. It's almost funny. She barely comes up to my collarbones, but she spits venom like she could bring me to my knees.

"My mother's dead. Can't you tell? she hisses, words sharp enough to cut. "No milk stains on my shirt, eh? Not like *you*. Mommy buy you a ship? Wanted to make sure you could compensate in any way necessary, I'm sure."

Her words curl around me like a sharpened blade, but I'm not laughing now. It's too easy to feel that old wound crack open like it never healed.

I look down at Odi—so close I can see the flecks of gold in her eyes, see how her throat works around her anger. I should find it amusing, how small she is under my shadow. But all I can think about is my mother—how she vanished over a decade ago. No storm, no wreck, just gone.

My father held a funeral anyway. A box of rocks in the ground. An empty coffin for show. Water elementals don't just disappear . . . not unless greedy bastards come sniffing for their knowledge of the sea and its hidden treasures.

I breathe through the anger. If she's dead—and *gods,* she might be—it's because of greedy *landsmen* like the ones Odelia calls captain. Those who would carve the very sea open just to see what they could drag out bleeding.

My gaze finds Odelia's again. She's waiting for a reaction, craving it.

The small shell carving in my pocket feels smooth between my fingers as I rub my thumb over her necklace. Admittedly, my mother would have liked Odi. The same desire for freedom I once saw in my mother's eyes is mirrored in the woman in front of me. For a moment, I feel sorry for her. There's a hole in her chest that's a twin to my own. In another life, other circumstances, maybe—no. She is everything I stand against.

Dreams be damned.

She flinches as I reach for her wrists. While I hold her, I move to the chest tucked between my nightstand and the desk, pulling out a fairly long length of thin rope.

Her eyes widen, but there's no way I'm letting her free roam around the room. She might be beautiful, but that doesn't mean she isn't trained to kill.

A loop around her wrists, pulled tight and knotted twice. Then another length runs up, over her shoulders, down around her chest—crisscrossed so if she tries to shift, her arms will stay pinned tight against her sides. I anchor it at her waist for good measure.

Honey and pear wash over me as I tug the rope at her waist, the movement causing her hair to brush her shoulder.

"Hope you remember how to untie me when you need my help." Her voice drips with sarcasm.

I ignore her, and continue to tighten all the knots.

She trembles under my hands. Anger, not fear. Good. Let her be angry—she'll live longer that way.

"Elkhorn crab got your tongue?"

I flick my gaze up, meeting her. Slowly, I push her away until the back of her knees hit the edge of my bed. She sits, tries to look away—stubborn, sharp thing—but I catch her chin between my thumb and forefinger, just under the hinge of her jaw. "My mother's dead too. Can't you tell? I'm horridly lacking in propriety. A pirate in my bed?"

There it is. That flicker of defiance, the bite of fear she's too proud to swallow. She breathes through her nose, nostrils flaring, lips parted like she's weighing whether to spit in my face or find more words to insult me. Then I flick her chin with my thumb, a sharp, irritating tap that makes her teeth snap shut.

My gaze hovers on her lips, for a moment I wonder if they'd taste as good as I'd hoped they would in my dream.

She's a pirate, yes. But perhaps like me, she longs to be someone different.

Without another word, I clamp the manacles around the rope and chain her to the bed again. Then I stride across the room, boots tapping on the wooden floor, and settle into the chair.

Neither one of us dares to fall asleep, and only with the rising sun, do I finally let my guard down.

What is with you and eating things

10
ODELIA

The shadow of the island is large on the horizon by the time the sun joins us. I hadn't slept, but adrenaline has me bouncing on my toes, impatient to see what waits. We're tucked away in the galley, which is thick with the scent of breakfast, the door closed until Bear is ready for the crew.

"Would you sit? You're making me nervous." Rune's eyes glint from where he sits at the bolted table, and I offer a look that says *good, be nervous*. He's wearing long sleeves today, but seems relaxed; the top buttons of his shirt hang open and his sleeves are rolled, offering peeks of those shimmering tattoos. I don't look. We haven't spoken about last night, but I can't help wondering if the casual dress is a subtle play—like he wants to project confidence to a nervous crew. Show our would-be attacker he isn't concerned.

Or he truly doesn't believe me.

He watches me for longer than necessary, and a flare of heat crawls up my neck, spurred by the memory of being pulled into his lap, pressed so close I could feel his warmth on my lips. It's a useless train of thought, so I look away. Try hard not to remember the strength of his grip or the power so inherent I'd nearly let myself get swept in its current. It doesn't matter that every neuron in my body had lit on fire, wrapped in the scent of salt and oranges. It doesn't matter that his desire betrayed him, or that it fueled my own, unearthing something long dormant.

I can't trust him. Can't afford to be distracted, even if I can still feel the phantom trace of his lingering attention. I hadn't been touched like that in years, having quickly realised I couldn't afford that sort of vulnerability. Still, this reaction, and my curiosity, will fade. We'd both been surprised, is all.

Tavi presses forwards, speaking over the sizzle of whatever Bear has decided to make for breakfast. "I've gone through every map on this ship. This island isn't on any of them."

Rune shrugs, finally turning away from me. "Maybe it's so small cartographers don't bother with it."

Elio's voice is grim as he leans one hip against the table, bowl ready in hand. "Maybe they're so monster infested no one has cared to see if they're still there."

Both are equally likely. Most of the uninhabited islands are overrun with creatures best left unbothered. With the growth of the mainland and trade routes to the large islands already established, there's no reason to risk it, unless you're avoiding the law.

Bear brings a few plates over and I take the opportunity to help, grabbing the food left on the counter, pausing for only a breath to slip a paring knife up my sleeve. No one seems to notice, instead they smile and offer their thanks to Otto as he and I pass everything around—oats, rehydrated fruit, and quail eggs. He chatters as he goes. "If there's monsters, maybe we'll get some components. It's been a while since we've been able to experiment."

Rune nods. "It won't be a priority, but if we can gather anything and bring it back, we will."

Bear lifts a bony arm to scratch at his shaggy brown hair. "I'd rather go. You never know what'll be useful. And I've already prepared food for those that stay on the ship."

There's a short silence, in which Elio watches for Tavi's reaction, and Tavi watches Rune.

Rune's voice is uncharacteristically soft. "If you're sure."

Bear's smile stretches wide, even though it's clear by Tavi's shuttered expression that I'm not the only one who thinks it's a terrible idea to bring him along.

"We'll land by noon," I say, as Bear moves back to the stove. "All that's left is to solve the riddle."

All eyes move to me.

"The one you ate." Elio's face is deadpan, but one side of Rune's mouth ticks up.

I cross my arms, lean against the wall, and sigh. "The one I ate, yes. To ensure no one gets any bright ideas about stranding me or using me as the ship's figurehead."

Tavi shakes her head. "That's horrid."

"No, no, she makes a good point," Rune says smirking in a way that doesn't flip my stomach like a beached fish.

She ignores him and stands, though she's hardly eaten. "Alright. Well I'll get us there. You all have fun with the riddles."

Elio watches the door close behind her. "You know she's worried," he murmurs.

Rune drums his thumb against the table, then crams another orange slice into his mouth. "He's earned the right to choose."

My attention flicks to Bear. It was the same answer Rune had given me when I'd questioned his position on the crew. The kid catches my eye and smiles, tugging at his high shirt collar. The heat must make it uncomfortable.

"Bout time for the crew to line up," he calls. The entire counter is covered in plates now.

Rune stands and sets his empty dish in a wash crate to the side. "Thanks for breakfast, Otto. Make sure you're ready by noon."

Bear nods. "Yes, Captain. Prop the door for me?"

I wait for Rune to put the stopper on the door, then follow him past the line of crew members stretching down the length of the already-transformed sleeping quarters. Every eye catches on us as we pass, but I keep my back straight. At least one of them tried to break into our room last night—

Well, not *our* room—

Rune takes the steep steps two at a time and all at once sunlight blasts my retinas.

"Slow down!"

He turns like I've surprised him, nearly catching me with an elbow. "Can't stand to be away for a moment, can you?"

I give that comment the look it deserves. "I need to see the map."

His brows lift as he reaches into his pocket. "It's all yours, little doe."

I ignore the nickname in favor of the parchment in his hand, but just as my fingers brush it, he hoists it up, extending his arm up over his head, far, far out of my reach.

I squint against the blinding sky that silhouettes the chiseled muscles of his arm and shoulders. "Very mature."

He grins again, and it's an effort to tamp the edges of my mouth down, trying not to do the same. "Seems like I matured a lot more than you," he says around the absurd smile on his face. "Your crew should have spent more time plundering food—"

I crack a boot into his shin. As he sucks in a pained breath, I dodge his free arm and use the hilt of the galley knife I stole, slamming it into his ribs.

He hisses, shooting one hand over the hurt and the other towards me again. I dance away and flaunt the parchment pinched between my fingers. "I'm touched by your concern. But I managed." I'll never admit he's right. Otto's cooking—real greens and vegetables, have made a noticeable difference already, like the animal in me had lived half-starved.

The paper is dry, catching on my skin. I unfold it as I move away, letting my eyes trace the familiar markings like an old friend. Even steps close in from behind.

"I can't let you keep that knife, Odelia."

I feign innocence, but don't look back. "Hmm?"

We're approaching from the west, and the map shows the two sharp protrusions that bisect the island. Even from a distance they were obvious. Now, they rise like sentinels, the unnaturally smooth stone seeming to absorb the light. Rune steps beside me, his attention following my own.

I glance at him, but he doesn't berate me for gaining the upper hand. "Does that look like—"

"Twin serpent's teeth?" he asks. "I guess we're in the right place."

Twin serpent's teeth, one gaping maw,
Deadly to sleep, silence a flaw
To step is to leap,
One breath to keep
The beasts are the least when nature is law.

I play the words on a loop in my head. Our supplies are packed. The rowboats are loaded. Rune stole the map back, his ape-ishly long arms an unfair advantage. All that's left is to solve the riddle—and survive. The serpent's teeth are the stones. The maw could be a cave? A pit?

The *deadly to sleep* part is obvious enough. We won't chance the luxury of staying on the island overnight. The most concerning is the line about the beasts. Whoever wrote the clues seemed to think whatever might attack will be the least of our worries.

Rune orders the anchor, and the ship groans as the weight drags the bottom. Nerves bounce off each of the crew, a mix of worry and anticipation. Those that volunteered to go are quiet, studying the sandy shore. Each holds at least two weapons—it remains to be seen if they know how to use them.

Rune's voice seems louder over the somber crew. "Odi. We're up first." He jerks his head towards the waiting rowboat and extends a hand like he's going to help me inside, but there's no way I'm going to touch him. Not when my entire body is already a bundle of raw nerves. The water churns below, eliciting the memory of burning lungs and helpless fear.

A few of the crew laugh when I ignore his hand in favor of clawing my hand around the rowboat's edge, but I'm too busy fighting the swoop of my stomach as it wobbles beneath me to care. He climbs in next and sits in front of me, more graceful than I, his attention spiriting over my white-knuckled grip on the side. Bear follows, shaking us further, then Tavi, who sits beside Rune, and uses the pulley to lower us in.

Finally, the boat settles low in the water. Rune and Tavi man the ores while I fight the urge to close my eyes, knowing the darkness would only make the fear—the memory—stronger. A larger wave lifts us, shepherding us towards the shoreline, but I gasp, waiting for the flip. For the boat to tip and the ocean to claim us. The animal in me doesn't care that we're close to the shore.

"Don't think I've forgotten that knife, Odelia," Rune says suddenly, pulling me back to the present. His focus weighs on me like a cloak, but I try not to look at him. Try to force my muscles to relax, my jaw to stop clenching so hard I'm sure my teeth will crack.

"What knife?" Tavi asks. But the accusation is thrown more at her captain than at me.

He doesn't answer. Instead, he gives a dramatic, affected sigh, like he's a rich mainland lady putting on airs for court. "I can't let you keep it."

That makes me face him. "You'd leave me defenseless on a monster-infested island?"

Again with that infuriating smirk. "One look at you and the monster will go running, I wouldn't worry too much. Besides, ask Bear what he thinks Tavi would do if you tried to pull it on the wrong person."

Otto perks up, like he's just now joining the conversation. "Hm? Ask me what?"

Rune stops rowing and reaches a hand out, effectively stranding us in the water. "Hand it over, Odi. Or I'll have to come over there and take it from you."

It's a habit to resist at this point, but he's huge. Easily half the weight in this boat right now, and my stomach already churns at the thought of him disturbing our balance and flipping us in. So with an annoyed huff I tug up the hem of my trousers and pull the knife from where it hides, wrapped and tucked into my boot.

"My paring knife!" Bear says as I pass it to Rune, his brows pinched in a way that makes him look older. "You stole it from the galley?"

"I—" I hesitate, but there's no reason. "Yes. Did you expect any better?" I shrug, looking away from the disappointment that's loud and clear on his face. It's just another reminder that they don't know me. What I'm capable of. "Can we go now?" I say to Rune, trying to keep my voice neutral. Water laps hungrily at the edges of the boat. He still watches me too closely. Those in the boats behind us slow as they near, likely wondering what made us stop.

Rune picks up the oar on his side, and the cut of the flat through the water is the only sound as we move on.

Sweat beads on his brow. The muscles of his forearm flicker as he and Tavi push and pull in tandem until, finally, we scrape against the sandy shore. Before anyone else can move, Rune leaps over the side, soaking himself up to mid-thigh and pushing further aground. His light-coloured pants cling, almost transparent now. Yet another image to banish from my mind.

Bear leaps out to join him, tugging from the front, Tavi pulls the oars in and they clink as she lays them in the bottom of the vessel before she steps over too. I rise and, keeping his attention trained on the island, Rune reaches a hand out, again.

But I can't take it.

Even though my legs feel like jelly and my stomach feels like it's one more giant-man-sized row away from emptying itself, I can't nurse the too-soft thing that's growing in my chest. Every other part of me is a jagged edge. Sharp. Better to put it out of its misery.

I ignore his offer and step out, but the silt shifts, sucks my boot down to the ankle, and I wobble, reaching for him anyways.

He pulls back just as our hands brush, leaving me reaching into open air. There's a moment of slow, unstoppable inertia, then I go down in a clumsy splash, soaking one leg in the water completely. Some of the crew that have landed laugh openly, but Rune just strides past, pulling his hair into a knot on his head, leaving me to sweep my hands in the water to remove the gummy, clay-like silt that clings to them. I deserved that one, but knowing it doesn't stop the flame in my cheeks.

The embarrassment doesn't last long. The moment my boots hit dry land, a weight lifts from my shoulders. The earth *sings*.

I feel it in every solid, unyielding step. The ground is soft at first, but I follow the others towards the tree line, relishing the way it shifts and solidifies, pulling my attention from my too-busy mind and firmly into my body, into the sensation of solid earth. This time, when my animal whispers, it's not in fear. It's anticipation. Memory. The wind whistling past my ears. The blur of green and brown and the trailing pinpricks of gentle pastels.

Soon, I whisper back.

The strip of beach is thin, crowded by gangly trees that link branches as if to ward strangers away.

"To me!" Rune shouts, drawing the group together. There's plenty of us, including Tavi, Bear, Elio, Rune, and myself. Most of the rest are from the day crew, since the others needed to sleep. Luckily, the island itself is small and we can't stay overnight, which means less supplies to carry. With any luck, it'll only take an hour to get to the centre of the island.

"We walk in pairs!" Rune calls. "We should reach the stones within the hour. From there, we'll reassess and decide what's possible before sundown. Don't get separated. If you do get separated, find and follow the shore until you see the ship. There's no point getting lost in the trees a second time." His expression is more serious than I've ever seen it, a small furrow in his brow betraying whatever worries he's shielding from the crew. Both his weapons are strapped to his belt—a sword and a dagger, both made of that same bone. His sky-blue eyes skate over each face, hesitating on me a beat longer than necessary.

"Pair up," he says, and before I can stop and watch the others ignore me, he beckons me over. "I don't need you running off."

I feign a look around. "Where would I go? I'm more concerned you might leave me here."

He lifts a brow, a bit of his usual mischief shining through. "Don't tempt me." The crew lines up, and we lead, stepping into the dappled shadows. Leaves crunch under our steps. I want to memorise the sound. "Besides," he continues, "on the rowboat I got the impression you'd suffer more if I took you back on the water."

Was it so obvious? "I all but drowned a few days ago." The way he glances over tells me he doesn't believe my casual shrug.

"Couldn't have been the first time right? In your line of work."

"My line of work?" I almost laugh. "Don't you mean being a filthy rat-infested, scum-eating pirate?"

"What is it with you and eating things?"

I can't help the choked laugh that shocks us both. To save face, I feign a cough, and when I risk a look back over he's smoothed his expression as well, sky-blue eyes trained on the dense trees that swallow us now.

"What about you? Any close calls with a watery grave?" I ask, if only to fill the silence.

"Are we making small talk now? Was dropping you all I needed to do to get you to open up to me?"

Someone stifles a laugh behind us and I whirl to find a stone-faced Tavi and a bashful Bear. "Sorry," he says. "It was just so petty."

I don't disagree. Rune sucks his bottom lip between his teeth; he obviously can't argue either.

"No," I say, turning back around. "I just think if we're going to be stuck together for the next month or so we ought to . . ." I wave a hand, unsure what it means.

"Do you think we'll become friends, Odi?" His tone is sickly sweet. Teasing.

I mask my irritation with purr. "Well I'm already sleeping in your bed."

This time the subtle cough comes from Tavi, and I don't have to turn around to know I'm right.

Rune finally grins. "Fair enough. No, I've never almost drowned in my line of work. I'm a strong swimmer."

Bear's chuckle continues for a moment, then the only sound is the chattering of whatever insects call this island home. "This is where you ask me a question," I say, keeping my attention locked on our surroundings.

"Fine. Why do you want this so badly?"

I don't need to ask him to clarify what he means. "With enough coin I could go anywhere. Be anyone."

He shakes his head. "You could do that without the treasure, without the danger."

Says the man who was going to send me into an earth prison before the map came into play. "You made it implicitly clear I wouldn't have that opportunity."

He shakes his head. "No. Before that. Before any of this. Why decide you need the map? You have to worry your crew will notice you stole it. You could have vanished anywhere. Found work. Now you have a target on your back."

"No one would allow me to work for them. Not if they knew who I was. If I was ever found out—"

"Surely the bars and temples on the mainland have seen their share of reformed pirates."

I press my lips together. He's not wrong, but they've never seen Nisse, Captain Ivor's right hand, the ocean's reaper, death's mistress, or whatever other absurd name the rumors are favoring this month. "No. With enough coin, I can find a forest, far away from any cities or towns, far away from any nooses they might hang."

"You'll be alone."

"Yes. Which means I'll be safe."

Again, we fall into silence. The crew still rustles through the underbrush, but there's no breeze to stir the canopy overhead. The chirps and trills are silent. I slow, eyes catching on a clump of yellowing leaves with veins of red caught in the light, like stained glass. I pluck just one and tuck it into my pocket. Rune watches, his face impassive enough that I don't think he'll ask about it, but I can't help but slow even more, a strange wariness blooming in my gut. The ground hums beneath my boots, but not in a way that touches my ears. It's almost like—

The animal in me freezes.

"What is it?" he asks, like the alarm is plain on my face.

I shake my head. "Listen."

His attention stays locked on me, his eyes tracing my expression. "It's . . . quiet," he says.

"The insects stopped." I should have noticed. "Do you feel that?"

The earth's rumble grows until the rest of the group is looking around in alarm. It moves through our legs, loud enough to reach our ears now. Above, birds flee, taking off in a blur of wings. Rune's blade *shinks* as it comes out of its sheath and the others follow suit, turning their backs to each other so we've got eyes on all sides. I reach for my hip, seeking a weapon that isn't there. Trembling leaves overhead shake down in a feathery rain.

Then it stops.

"The fuck was that?" Elio says, his head on a swivel, but the forest is unchanged. Slowly, the insects begin to chatter again. A bird darts past, close enough to shift the air around us. Some flinch, but I just flick my eyes to the nearest weapon. Tavi definitely notices.

"Just a land tremor," Rune calls.

All are weary as we shuffle back into our line and walk on, their uncertain murmurs rising like a wave. We haven't made it eight steps before there's a muffled shout, followed by the sound of skittering rocks.

"Corrin!"

Rune flies towards the commotion, pushing through the other bodies that begin to gather. I'm on his heels. A thin man kneels beside a barrel-sized hole in the ground, the corded muscles of his neck straining as he shouts. "Corrin!" The soil at its edges is still crumbling in.

"Back up!" I shout.

"Who the fuck asked you?" someone behind us asks.

I don't bother to acknowledge them. Rune pulls the kneeling man up by his waist and drags him back, just as a crack splits beneath him and the hole grows big enough to touch the toes of their boots.

"I'm down here! I'm alright!" Corrin's voice echoes below. The sound seems to shape the crew's panic into focus, and they break apart in a flurry of activity.

"Who's got the rope?"

"Here!"

"Everybody back up!"

"It's secure. Get it down there!"

Rune spins, sweeping his attention over the trees. "It's happening again."

He's right. The ground rumbles. Faint. Adrenaline arcs through me like lighting. It's no land tremor.

"GET HIM UP HERE," Rune commands, taking a spot on the rope, the muscles of his arms and shoulders straining as they pull. Their first heave splits the earth further, wedging the rope in a crack of its own making.

"Shit."

"Back up Corrin!"

"We'll have to break it."

"Someone get him a torch."

I step closer as they drop one in. It falls longer than I'd expected before spinning on the ground. Luckily, it stays lit and Corrin grabs it, the light reflecting off his sweaty, dirt-smudged face. He's at least a story and a half down. It's a miracle his legs aren't broken.

The rumbling grows as three men use fallen limbs to stab at the ground around the rope, trying to make space for him to get up. They're going too slow.

"Use your sword! You have to dig!" I say.

This time, they listen. Those working the ground use their weapons to chip away at it instead, slamming the blades down and twisting so the crack slowly widens. The ground shakes, the leaves and branches rattle, scraping against each other.

"Don't stop!" Rune orders. "But get a second rope secured on the other side."

"Something's coming!" Corrin shouts, his voice high and panicked.

"We're almost there, Corrin," he says, but I can see the despair as he watches the second rope get secured. The crack around the rope is only half a man wide.

"There's something—THERE'S SOMETH—"

The light in the hole snuffs out, replaced by the shine of a segmented exoskeleton.

"The hell!!" someone shouts.

It's huge. Endless. Its body moves beneath us in waves that rise and fall towards each seam. I step forwards, but a hand latches around my forearm. Bear. He doesn't say anything, just shakes his head, the skeleton hand earring bobbing away. Rune's jaw flickers as he watches the creature pass. His arms are crossed, lips pressed tight. Everyone is silent. Waiting.

The ground rumbles for ages.

When it goes, the quiet stays. The hole is empty. And even the birds are reluctant to break the tense sorrow that hangs like a shroud. The odd weight makes my stomach hollow, but I can't afford to feel it. Empathy won't help us now. Rune's face is drawn, but he agreed to this as much as anyone else here.

Slowly, we gather again. We move on. We haven't made it to the first key and we've already got one man down.

I have a feeling he won't be the last.

I NEED YOU TO JUMP

11
ODELIA

We walk, the breaks in the canopy offering glimpses of the dark, towering stones. The trees thin and all at once we break through to a grassy meadow. A flurry of fur and racing feet disappears into the woods. A rabbit or a fox or something else that's right to be afraid.

"We rest here," Rune says, but doesn't find a spot to sit. He moves to the other side of the clearing and drops his bag before pacing.

I stifle the urge to go to him, but Elio moves past me, leaving his pack with Tavi and Bear. He stands firm while Rune paces near a half-fallen tree at the meadow's edge, and I wonder how often this exact scenario has played out: Elio the anchor, Rune trapped in the insistent currents of his mind. A strange ache wells in my chest, sneaking in on the rawness that's left after adrenaline fades, but I remind myself the trust they have in each other can only lead to pain for both of them. It's not something I should want.

"Hey Odi, got any water?" Otto sits behind me, holding Tavi's forearm, where a clean slice sheets blood over her skin.

Sweat drips down Tavi's brow but she makes no move to wipe it while Bear attends to the wound. "Briar got me while I was trying to secure the rope," she says by way of explanation.

"Uh, sure, here." I kneel with them and tug off my water skin.

Bear works efficiently, washing the wound, then pulls a vial from his pack.

Elio feigns a retch as he walks back, his eyes tracing over the blood on Tavi's arm. "This stuff smells like wyrm shit."

"Smells better than infection." Bear grins, and Tavi hisses as the dark liquid coats the wound.

"What *is* that?" I ask, pulling the fabric of my shirt over my nose. The scent is something between bitter herb and gut-twisting floral.

"Mix of stuff from the islands around, and one secret ingredient." He winks.

Elio huffs a laugh, glancing at the stone-faced tavi. "It's mistleroot. Grows everywhere around Nareth. Otto here found when you mix it with herbs from the up top it's unparalleled as a wound cleaner."

"Nareth? The ocean kingdom?" I knew they had open trade with some of the islands, but I didn't know anyone who had ever actually been. The sirens were a secretive and protective bunch, often suspicious of *landsmen*, the name they'd given to all who breathe air, though I'd argue sailors and pirates would be grouped in with the *seafolk* by any other definition. The distinction seems to be more about pride than animosity, thought. I'd even heard the Sirens keep entire rooms in the upper sections filled with breathable air for land visitors.

Otto winds a bandage around Tavi's arm. His fingers are long and thin, like an artist's. "Yeah we mostly turn bounties in top side, hunt whoever's face is on the bounty posters and turn them in wherever is closest. But sometimes Rune gets requests straight from Nareth, and he always prioritizes those. The ointment was an accident. Came up with the idea because the quail. Captain knows I love new ingredients, and apparently it's popular in certain circles. I hated it. Tastes like you took a munch of this grass. So I tossed it to the quail and they loved it. So every time Rune had some he'd bring it, and once, I noticed one was sick, then it wasn't. So—"

"Bear, can you bring some of that over here?" a woman with cropped red hair calls from the middle of the group.

Otto leaps to his feet. "On it!"

"We should go too," Tavi says to Rune, standing to follow him to the others.

Elio's gaze follows them. Mostly Tavi. He does nothing to hide the way his lips tighten, or the deepening of the creases by his eyes.

"Jealous?" I ask, because I'm an ass. That ache is back again. These people care for each other too much.

He snorts. "No. Are you?"

"Unlikely." I grin at the wicked gleam in his eye, though I should feign offense. In truth, I am jealous, but not in the way he thinks. I'd never thought to miss any sort of companionship before—attachments are weaknesses, I know that better than anyone—but now I can't help but feel I'm missing something. If a Viper had been lost to that underground creature, few, if any, would have mourned. My father would have taken it as a price worth paying, if it meant meeting his goal. I would have too. It was the nature of life. Our life, at least.

Bear returns my water skin half empty and Rune calls us to continue, warning everyone to be on their guard as we approach the stones.

Rune and I lead us out. The afternoon sun is on its way down, teasing us with how little time we have before sunset. Near the top of the hill, the obelisks are weathered, leaning on cracked foundations, their shadows stretching long into the forest behind us. One is rigidly linear—sharp lines and a point that spears into the sky. The other is twisted, like its creators had chiselled a spring into the design. Hopefully, we'll find more clues once we reach them.

Water rushes nearby. A stream, maybe, or a waterfall, though the source is unclear. A natural spring? Unless the ocean has carved its way through the island. The grass gets taller the further we go. It's up to our waists before we crest the hill.

And stop.

The ground sweeps down before disappearing completely. Between the stones, there's a gaping hole twice the length of the ship that drops into darkness. Elio whistles as he and Tavi come up behind us. Bear bobs up, settling behind me to peek over my shoulder.

"This in your riddle, Odi?" he says.

"It is," Rune says seriously, and there's no reason for me to miss the playful side of him, even if the sturdiness is remarkably grounding. "We're scouting ahead. Everyone else should stay."

No one argues. The five of us move down the rapidly steepening slope, though my heart starts to gallop in protest. With the grass so tall, it's impossible to see where each step lands, what might be lurking to turn the ankle of those distracted.

In reality, it's safe, but the emptiness that stretches beyond us seems to have its own gravity, like one slip will send me tumbling into the pit. The rushing water grows louder. It falls from cracks in the walls, emptying into crystal-blue water that hardly ripples. The flooded cavern extends beneath the shelf of rock, and the realisation has fear spearing white hot through my chest. I fight the urge to turn back, and push away the knowledge that six inches of stone may be all that's under our feet.

"It's a cenote," Tavi says, kneeling at the edge like a stiff breeze wouldn't send her plummeting down.

"It's a maw," Rune says, looking at me, his eyebrows raised. I nod. But I don't know where to go from here. The towering stones bookend the cenote, pieces of chipped rock falling from the twisted side and bouncing into the cavern below. The water swallows the offering, not even deigning to move. "Come on, little doe. I know you've got some idea of what we should do."

He's only half serious, I'm sure, but even that amount of confidence is staggering. One idea does loop in my head, but it's a death wish. How could anyone complete the map if they died in the process? Surely there was another solution. Still—

More rock tumbles from the obelisk, the clattering of impact audible even over the waterfall.

I squint against the setting sun, peering up at the stone. If it collapses while we're here, it might just be a sign I should take Rune's advice. Find a job in a small town and hope Nisse stays in the past where she belongs, give up the map and the sea in one fell blow.

Instead, the column starts to move.

It unfurls, the spiral design corkscrewing down, a thousand legs scratching and skittering over the solid surface.

"Run." The word is a whisper.

Rune is still peering into the cenote. "What?"

The creature's front reaches the ground, the other half of it still unwinding, and the ground starts to rumble.

"Run!" My legs turn on their own, my knees burning with the uphill fight against the grass. Rune's long stride eats up the ground beside me, and Tavi keeps pace with Elio behind, though being a fae means she could easily push ahead. The rumbling grows, then muffles, and the vibration in the ground shifts, increases.

"It's gone underground," Bear says as we make it to the group.

"You need to go, Otto." Rune's chest heaves. He's drawn his sword, the bone wicked sharp on both sides.

"Aren't we all going?" My voice cracks. The fear in me feeds on itself now that my feet have stopped moving. The need to keep running hums just under my skin, smothering any other thought.

"No. We're staying here. It may move to the outer parts of the island." The earth's growing tremble and the way he holds his sword tells me how confident he is that will happen. "And if it attacks, it'll be the last thing it does."

My attention narrows on him, my fingers itching for a blade. "If that's your plan, then I'll need a weapon."

His jaw hardens. "No. Go find somewhere to hide with Otto—"

I've wrapped my fingers in the front of his shirt before he can finish and pull his face inches from mine. My heart trips over itself when his attention moves to my lips, then drags back up to my eyes, bringing to mind the burn of his hands on my waist and the scent of salt and oranges in a darkened room. His gaze flickers with something, there and gone again, and ill-timed heat pools low in my belly, only irritating me more.

"If you want the second half of this map," I growl, "you need me to stay alive."

"Exactly." His breath spirits over my cheek. "So go with—"

Rock shatters.

Bits of broken stone pelt us as the creature erupts from the ground, a few of its wicked-sharp legs splayed wide before it lands and begins to wrench itself out of the earth.

"Scatter!" Rune shouts, and the crew splits, staying in their pairs.

The massive centipede flips its head side to side, as if calibrating to its targets. The front of its face is flat, with a mouth of shovelling talons that whir, eager to scoop whatever is in front of it into its mouth. Rune charges like it isn't three times his height. The rest of the crew follows suit, all trying to avoid that gyrating mouth.

Elio jabs the pointed end of his sword where its legs are segmented together and the creature curls in towards the pain. On the other side, a man with one tattooed arm slams his axe into the base of one of the legs and the strike rings out like metal. In an instant, the appendage lifts and spears though his abdomen and out his back, then resumes shuffling, dragging him along as he screams.

I run for his weapon.

Rune, who obviously has a death wish, rolls beneath the skittering legs and shoves his blade at its underbelly. The shining chitin deflects the strike. It seems we won't get anywhere trying to attack the main parts of its body. The centipede drops low, shoving him to the ground, and suddenly he's on his back, desperately dodging away from the flesh-rending points of endless, blade-like feet.

I make it to the fallen axe and sprint for him, noting Elio and Tavi farther down, working in tandem, shoving their blades into its joints, the metal slick with slimy, clear fluid. They haven't noticed Rune. I leap as I near him—my height and the short axe handle doesn't give me much choice, but the jump is good, and the blade severs the surprisingly delicate connection between one part of the leg and the next.

The neighbouring feet jab towards me and then compress as the creature turns in, bending almost in half to drag its shovel-mouth my direction. The maneuver means the legs on the other side spread, allowing Rune to roll out the other way, and he disappears behind the maze of violent insect body.

There's a tell-tale whizz, and a projectile misses its face and explodes over its legs in a mess of sticky goo. The concoction hardens almost immediately, binding the bladelike appendages together, but they just lift and tuck in, and the rush of victory in me quickly evaporates as the other legs compensate and it moves as well as before.

I run, the sound of its clacking mouth close behind. Someone screams in terror, but it chokes off, strangled and wet.

I'm nearing the trees now, my only hope at this point is to give the others time to hack away at it. I can't break through its exoskeleton. And it doesn't have any eyes to—

It doesn't have any eyes.

It can't see. It's a subterranean insect. It can't use its eyes to hunt. Somehow it hunts without seeing its prey. It could use warmth, or maybe it uses some sort of echolocation, using the feedback from its rumbling to pinpoint its targets.

The meadow is ahead, and the realisation gives me another burst of speed. The half-fallen tree is easy to climb after years of ropes and masts, so I find a perch and hold my breath, waiting to see if I'll be wrong and die for it.

It doesn't slow, dodging trees and crashing through patches of underbrush, and careening right under me. Past me.

Air saws in and out of my lungs as I watch the segments pass below.

"Regroup!" Rune calls, drawing back those that are behind and those that are chasing it deeper into the forest. He spies me in the tree and flashes a grin. "Thanks for the save."

"Let me keep the axe once we're back to the ship and I'll consider it thanks enough!" I call down, flipping the weapon in my palm and lifting a brow, trying to keep the smile on his face a little longer.

His cheeks are flushed from the fight. "Don't get ahead of yourself."

The rumble grows as the centipede turns towards us. It skips, parts of it almost seeming to limp, but drives forwards without emotion or self preservation.

"It can't see," I tell them, rising to my feet on the slope of the trunk. It's almost to us now. Leaves sprinkle down, falling gracefully as the creature turns the understory into mulch. "I think it uses the vibration! Stand as near to a tree as you can. And be *still*!"

It bursts through the meadow and stones plink off the chitin scales of its face. I track the source to Bear, who sits in a tree nearby, armed with a slingshot. A series of small explosions at the creature's feet take me by surprise and Bear returns the silent question on my face with a cheesy grin. Between the slugger pods and the slime earlier, maybe I'm not giving him enough credit.

"Odelia!" Rune shouts. "Toss down the axe!"

Then he's ordering the others to back away, one eye on the creature's approach like he's got a plan. There's no time to argue, but every muscle in my body resists as I let the weapon fall handle-first to where he's standing. He snatches it from the air, then issues orders I can't hear to a group that takes off towards the stones. The centipede follows them. The others stand still, some as near to trees as possible, and it ignores them, its single-minded need to hunt driving it forwards. Rune sprints to the base of the half-fallen tree. For a moment, I think he's going to join me. Instead, he starts chopping. More of the crew join him, and the plan, the brilliant, beautiful plan is suddenly clear.

The wood beneath me jerks with every strike. The last segment of its body is nearly here, so I use the thinning limbs to heft myself as high up as I can go, leveraging my weight against the weakening break in the trunk.

"Odi! It's coming down!" Elio shouts like he thinks I should get away while I still can.

Rune glances up for a fraction of a second. His cheeks are red, his lips parted. Sweat slides down the sides of his face as his blue eyes meet mine and send a thrill to my racing heart. "I need you to jump!"

I don't ask for clarification.

I jump against the top of the half-fallen tree, using the limbs to bring me up and then back down, slamming my weight into the wood as hard as I can. Rune drives the axe into the base of the tree trunk, and we fall into a rhythm. Him axing it below while I jar it with counterweight on the top. Again. Again. Again.

When the tree falls, I leap, hoping the nymph in me remembers how. I'm still in the air when the creature screams—an earsplitting, grinding-rock hiss—and the flat of one of its legs catches me as it flails, caught in deaththrows. The swipe sends me twisting. I claw at the air, but land wrong, my weight awkward on my bad ankle, before tumbling over sharp branches. The pain flairs up my leg and something jabs into my ribs, forcing me to bite back a sob before it settles into a deep, aching throb.

A segment of the centipede twitches under the weight of the trunk. The wood had crushed a small portion of its middle, but most importantly, it anchored it to the ground. The rest of its long body lays still beyond the trees, liquid pooling where the segment sloughed away, its own momentum having pulled it apart.

Three dead, four badly wounded.

Lucky, by all accounts.

I hide my own limp. Bear has enough to tend—besides, my pulsing ankle and bruised ribs are nothing compared to the others, and I don't think anyone would take kindly to the pirate stealing the medic's attention away from the noble folk who need it more.

The sun has begun to sink toward the trees. The uninjured had returned to the ship and brought extra hands to move the fallen and wounded, and as they pack everyone up to head out, Rune lets them know we plan to stay behind to scout the cenote again.

"If we aren't back by sunset, don't come looking until the sun rises."

Hopefully, they won't need that instruction.

Rune doesn't comment on my slower pace. Either he doesn't notice because he's just as tired, or he pulls back on purpose, keeping his steps short to keep pace with me.

The white-noise of the waterfall slowly returns as we near, growing until we're facing the massive cavern again. The walls are steep, the drop long. Even if we wanted to climb down, there'd be no way back up. Rune eyes the water. It's a gorgeous, clear blue. Seaweed and water foliage float in the bottom, disguising little darting movements. Fish, maybe. From here, they look small, but the water and the distance will warp any perspective.

Rune chews at his lip. "Otto, how much rope do we have?"

"I've got fifty feet," the boy says. "There's probably a hundred more being packed up right now."

"We'll have to get it."

"We can't climb down," Elio argues. "Even if we had a good way to secure it, we can't trust the ground here. Whatever we tied the rope to could just pull up."

Rune's hands go to his belt. "I know."

I feel my eyes go wide as he shucks off his belt, then pulls his shirt over his head.

"What are you doing?" The words spill out of me. There's no way I can climb down a hundred and fifty feet of rope right now.

He throws the shirt at me, bathing me in a cloud of salt and oranges. The fabric is warm from the heat of his body. "To step is to leap," he says simply.

I again refuse to let myself gape at his shirtlessness, though the broad plane of his chest is no less impressive in the light of day. Small cuts line his arms and there's a shallow wound at the tip of his shoulder. It only takes a moment before I catch up to what he's saying.

"Rune, you *can't*—"

"—you guys keep an eye on Odi for me, yeah?" His eyes are bright as he smirks.

Then he jumps.

I lunge for him, but an iron grip chains around my forearm, jarring my sore ribs. I whimper and pull out of Tavi's hold.

"Shit," Elio says under his breath.

I drop to my knees, scooting to peer over the edge. "We have to go after him!" There's no way he'll be conscious after the impact. The height alone could kill him, not to mention the monsters that may wait below. The water still ripples with where he went down. I hold my breath, counting the seconds before he comes back up.

But he doesn't.

Light-blue scales flicker beneath the surface, surrounding him, and my heart's in my throat not knowing if the creature is curious or hungry or ready to rip the sinew from his bones for entering its territory.

A long tail breaches the water, curling up and out before splashing again. The cyan fin is gorgeously frayed, with trailing tendrils and iridescent scales. The shape is familiar, at once calling to mind the shadow in the ocean the day Rune brought me onto *The Gilded Hart.* Tavi and Elio haven't moved. They're tense, but not worried. Rune's voice floats through my head.

I'm a strong swimmer.

The pieces collide. The way he dragged me from the ocean's grasp. The mistleroot from Nareth. The royal seal I didn't recognize on his desk. Hell, even his build and bright blue, ocean wave hair.

"He's a siren?" I don't know who I'm asking. I can see him now, through the water. The clearest, most stunning blue trailing behind his powerful body. The relief weighs me down alongside pulsing pain and the absence of fear. He's okay. We're okay. We're going to live through this day.

Bear kneels next to me, clinking as he adjusts his pack full of centipede talons. "I mean. Technically? He's a siren prince."

Playing Chicken with Clams

12
RUNE

The cenote yawns open like the mouth of the earth—dark, deep, and still. Jagged, moss-covered stone walls rise high above, veined with roots that hang like skeletal fingers, sucking greedily from the damp. From the rim, small waterfalls spill over the edge, silver streams tumbling into the pool. Their constant trickle echoes through the cavern, soft but unrelenting, like breath through clenched teeth.

The water does little to hide my siren form. No doubt by the time I rise back to the top, Odi will know that I, too, can shift my shape.

For a moment I allow my body to adjust to the temperature of the water, its cooling properties doing wonders for my aching bones and dry skin. I'd been prepared for a monster attack, the riddle had warned us, but I hadn't been prepared for the sheer enormity of the creature. All those legs and feet tearing through the forest, and my crew.

I shudder at the thought of the three brave crewmen who'd lost their lives fighting for the mission that I'd thrown them into, risking it all for the slightest hope of finding answers about my mother. I'd already asked too much, so there was no way I was allowing anyone to enter this cenote and swim to the very depths and collect whatever lay at the bottom, even though I know Elio and Tavi are going to be pissed that I didn't give them a chance to follow me down here.

Being a prince has its pros and cons. Most of the time, I'm able to do as I please, but the price I pay is having someone breathing down my neck every five seconds. It's Elio's job to protect me at all costs, and Tavi takes it upon herself to protect the entire crew without the paycheck to match. Secretly, I think she likes to know Elio's whereabouts too. They've been eye fucking each other for weeks now. I don't know why they don't just get at it. There is certainly no qualms on my end.

Salty ocean water, and fresh spring water mix together, turning it a brackish green. I propel downwards, through the narrow opening that beckons at me from below. Tiny rays of sunlight pierce the murk, sending golden beams around me as I swim deeper. My eyes stay fixed on my surroundings. The last thing I need is to be surprised by *another* creature.

I grip my bone sword tighter as shadows form into mysterious shapes.

Seaweed. That's all it is.

In this form, my sight is good enough to make out the shadowed details as I near. My shoulders drop, bubbles escaping the vents behind my ears where I breathe while submerged.

The water's cooler down here, darker too. Each stroke pulls me deeper into the blue hush, the weight of the water pressing in on all sides. I've been swimming for a few minutes but I still haven't reached the bottom.

My thoughts travel to Odelia. I'd been so hesitant to allow her to carry a weapon. What if she tore through my crew—or me—or simply shifted and bounded off into the island forest without a second glance? It would have been foolish to allow it, but then she went and found an axe, ripping through the creature with the litheness of an eel through water.

And instead of waiting and watching me die, she'd saved me.

I didn't like this familiar ache that kept making itself known each time the image of wild, chocolate tresses, and umber eyes formed in my mind. Odi was making it quite difficult to hate her. Especially when she smiled. *Salted seas.* What I'd give to see her smile at me like I was more than just a means to an end. I shake my head. Light blue strands of hair swirl around me as I try to free my thoughts of a certain pirate-whom-I-despise-with-my-whole-being . . . right?

The seabed thickens with dark growth—tangles of slick, ribboning plants unfurling like fingers. Sticky, swaying things that curl up from below, reaching for skin and scales alike. One wraps around my tail. I flick hard, shaking it loose, but another brushes my side, clinging like it's alive.

I push forwards, scanning the area for something. I didn't even know what I was meant to be looking for? A chest? A key? Neither?

Perhaps I'd be searching down here forever. I shove the thought away before it can take root. That's not an option. We've already been on the island too long. Who knows what lurks out here under the blanket of darkness. I'm certainly not going to stick around and find out.

The cenote opens into a wider cavern on the sea bed. The flash of silver scales to my right draws attention. A school of minnows dart into the shadows, concealing themselves amongst colourful coral and sea anemones. I'd do well to avoid them. Sirens in the past learnt pretty quickly the sting of an anemone.

I brush past the cavern wall as I swim into the centre. Two barbed plants catch my fins like hooks, their thin, jagged spines digging into the webbing with every movement. I manage to pull them free, but not without a sharp sting blooming across my tail. Scarlet blood slips into the water—thin, dark threads trailing behind me like a warning.

Shit.

If there are any predators down here, they'll taste my blood before I see them. I need to move faster.

As I dart through the open space, the ground winks up at me. It's made of white sand, stone, and scattered shells glinting like silver teeth. That's when I see it. Nestled on the seabed, surrounded by a commune of large clams sits a tiny stone box covered in old runes that seem familiar.

I swim for it, gathering it into my hands. It's locked. Of course it is. So where is the key? I glance around trying to see if there is another box stashed away somewhere, but I find none.

If I can't find this piece then all of this was for nothing.

The box is weighted in my hands. I try forcing the lid open, squeezing the sides as I tug it apart. There's no point, it's sealed tight. Perhaps I can smash it on something? Though brute force would likely result in harming whatever lay inside, so I'd better not.

Pearl coloured clams, covered in algae and wide open mouths turn to face me. My movements trigger their senses. I float too close to one. It snaps shut with a *crack* loud enough to thrum through my chest. I jerk back, narrowly avoiding losing a fin. The thing's the size of a barrel, its ridged shell dusted in crusty sea scum.

Another to my right yawns, and that's when I see it. On its large, slime covered pink tongue rests a key. Iron. Rusted but whole. No doubt the one I'm after.

How the fuck am I meant to get that.

I *hate* clams almost as much as I *hate* pirates.

Dash and I used to play chicken with them as boys—diving down to the reef to the west of the palace, daring each other to see who could get closest before one snapped. Bravery, stupidity—there wasn't much difference between the two when we were young. Mother would scold us, but there was always a glint in her eye when she did, like she knew that we wouldn't listen to her reprimands anyway.

My brow pinches as I glance around, trying to find something to keep the clam from snapping my arm off clean through the bone when I attempt to retrieve the key. I need leverage.

Without too much thought, I place the box down, my sword joining it on the seabed as I swim around, searching for something I can use. I spot a jagged stone—sort of square in shape, heavy enough. It would have to do.

A wave of nausea passes over me, causing my vision to blur at the sides. Surely my body hasn't grown so accustomed to the world above that it's rejecting the sea. I shake my head, focussing as I lift the rock into my arms.

I ease forwards, slow and careful. The clam stirs, shell creaking as if it senses me. One wrong twitch and it'll snap shut on bone.

Very slowly, I raise the rock and jam it between the shell's gaping halves.

Crack.

It slams down with enough force to rattle my arm, but the stone holds, wedged just deep enough. I don't wait. My hand darts in, fast and sure. Cold slime coats my knuckles as my fingers close around the key.

Got it.

As I dart for the box, and my sword, something blue in the corner of my eye catches my attention. I didn't notice it before. Blue kelp, the kind my mother carried on her wedding day. I would remember it anywhere. Father used to fill the palace with it every anniversary. It only flowers once a year.

The sight of it tugs a thread in my chest. A thread that is tethered to the memory of her, but I don't have time to visit that place. I have a crew up top who are waiting for me, expecting me to come back in one piece before sundown.

As I head up towards the narrow opening, another barb from the olive green sea foliage catches in my scales, sending a sharp pain through my hip. I tug free but the barb comes with it. My hands are too full to bother with it now, I'll remove it once I break the surface.

I flick my tail into motion, forcing myself up. Thankfully the only creatures I've come across were fish. Otto would be disappointed that I didn't bring him back something he could experiment on. He'll have to be satisfied with the bag full of creatures' legs that he's collected.

Shadows melt into shapes. Ugly ones. Creatures with yellow eyes, and red gleaming teeth. Cold water enters my mouth and exits my gills as I suck in, filling my lungs with oxygen. I'm seeing things, but why?

Something's wrong.

The water pulses too loud in my ears, like a drumbeat from inside my skull. My limbs feel heavy—slow, like they've forgotten how to belong to me. Every stroke takes more effort than it should, and my vision's starting to smear at the edges again.

Seconds feel like minutes, and minutes feel like hours, but I know I'm nearly at the top. I can see the orange glow from the setting sun seeping into the thin layer of murkiness above me, so I push harder. I break the surface with a gasp that sounds more like a choke.

The sunlight above glares down, too bright, too far. But I see them—my crew, their shapes clustered at the rim of the cenote. A rope already swings down towards me, coiled like a lifeline.

From above, Odi's gaze finds mine and I swear I see her pinched brow relax.

"Grab the rope, Rune!" Tavi calls out.

I clamp the iron key between my teeth, tucking the box under the arm that holds my sword. Cursing under my breath,

I grab the rope before my strength gives out completely. Then I see it. Tentacle sucker marks ring my left forearm, the skin raised and welted, raw like something tried to taste me alive.

"Pull me up!" I manage to yell through gritted teeth.

As I ascend from the cenote, my siren form flickers, the shimmer of magic slipping like wet cloth off my skin. No one wants to see me half naked, half fish, so I let the shift happen, my trouser covered legs forming just before I'm hauled completely into the open air.

My limbs feel heavy after all that time in the water. It would take me a minute to find my feet again on the dry land. The rope jerks, and I rise. Every shift of the climb is a scream in my muscles, but I keep my grip. I keep the box. I keep breathing.

Barely.

Soon, I'm grabbing the edge of the rim, the box, my sword, and the key tumbling onto the grass. Elio doesn't waste any time, he reaches my side and drags me onto solid ground. I lay there on my back for a moment, catching my breath. A white braid, threaded with tiny bones and gold rings appears above me.

"You don't look so good," Tavi grunts, her brow pinched together.

I sit up, then shift to all fours as I slowly push off the ground to stand upright. Many sets of eyes just stare at me, wide eyed, like they know something I don't.

Water slips off my body, pooling at my feet. "I'm totally fine."

Tavi shakes her head. "No, you're not."

Elio steps beside me. "He has barbs in his skin."

I shrug them all off. It's nothing. I just need to find my land legs. "I said I'm fine, let's head back."

"Rune—"

"Where's my shirt?"

The crew that have gathered around me part down the middle as Odi takes a step forwards. The usual scowl on her face is softer. I can't stop the smile tugging at the corner of my mouth as I look down at her. She really is beautiful. Her fingers brush mine as I reach for my shirt. The thrill of it mixes with the blood coursing through my heaving chest, muffling the world around us, narrowing my focus on her lips so hard my vision darkens at the edges.

"I think you should sit down." Her voice is a gentle command more than it is a suggestion.

Shaking my head, I pull my shirt up and over. The ringing in my ears grows sharper, louder, and the figures before me blur, blending together in a heap of colours and textures. The world tilts once, then twice. After that, it doesn't bother righting itself. My knees go weak, and suddenly the ground seems closer than it was before.

"It's poison." Otto's voice is distorted. "He's going down!"

My hand shoots out, as I try to find my balance. "Fuck."

The Siren Prince

13
ODELIA

The amount of bodies inside the captain's quarters is near suffocating, but none of us volunteer to be the one who leaves.

Otto runs his long fingers over the red stains on Rune's trousers. Their captain lays, pallid and sweat soaked, in the centre of his bed. The barbs protrude a hands-width long, their tubular stems leeched of colour like whatever they intended to do is long done. The spiral of sucker marks on his forearm is swollen and weeping blood from tiny ringed circles.

Otto speaks quickly, his eyes glued to the wounds. "That one's a thrall squid. The saliva will keep him bleeding for a while. I have to go get my poultices from the galley. Can you guys get the barbs out? Don't pinch the tops, try to grab it as close to the base as you can."

Tavi just watches Rune's uneven breathing.

Elio is the one that answers. "We've got it, Otto. Do what you need to."

The boy shuffles out, leaving the three of us to decide who gets the honour of removing the barbs. I stay stock still, my fists clenched under the arms crossed over my chest, certain they won't let me touch him.

He'd gotten the key.

Or a piece of it. The box clutched under his arm had fallen when the poison took hold, though it had been promptly removed from my care the moment we'd made it back to the ship. I hadn't argued. Now, fresh anxiety swims through my veins, and I can't tell if it's for the piece that's just out of reach or the man half-dead on the bed.

Elio steps forwards with a small dagger and begins to cut Rune's pants away, being careful to avoid knocking the barbs. Rune's legs are thick and as muscular as the rest of him, but blood beads over his skin, leaking from each protrusion. I flick my attention between Elio and the barbs as he reaches a hand out like he means to reach for one, but Tavi cuts him off. For once, her every thought flashes across her face—and her hands are trembling, dancing a breath away from the hooks embedded in his skin.

"I can show you how, if you want." I don't even recognize the voice as mine. It's soft. Gentle in a way it has no right to be.

Her eyes slice across the room, her gaze landing on mine. The ship creaks as it shifts. Even the crickets had gone silent. By the time we'd limped back, it was dark, and for a breath I wonder what waits on the island in the quiet of night.

When she says nothing, I speak again. "I've dealt with my fair share of barbed bolts."

"So have I." Her eyes are tired.

Depending on the shape, barbs could do even more damage coming out than they did going in. The worst kind need to be cut out, but these are a stiff, plant-like material, a route for poison rather than the killing blow.

I step towards Rune, putting my weight on my uninjured ankle. I don't let myself look at his bloodless face before pressing a hand against his leg with my thumb and fingers on either side of the embedded stem. When neither of them object, I push in, spreading the flesh, then snap my other hand to the stem's base and yank as fast as I can.

Rune whimpers as either Tavi or Elio hiss in sympathy. There are two more lower down on his legs, but the one I'm most worried about is near his hip, leaking more blood than the others.

They say nothing as I work, and I pretend not to notice when Elio brushes the back of his hand against hers. Rune reacts less the next time, and dread pools in my gut, followed quickly by irritation. We should have waited. If we'd have made a plan, we could have found a way to go down together, my fear of the water be damned. But his over-confident ass thought he'd be noble and shoulder all the danger. He probably planned to do it the moment we found the cenote.

The last one on his leg catches, the drag of ripping flesh sending a cringe down my arm, through my aching ribs, and along every strained nerve in my body. Fresh blood coats my fingers and he groans as I apply more pressure, trying to fix the problem I caused. Otto returns. The boy's arms are stacked full of bottles and wraps that clink terribly when he dumps them on the bed. Several land on Rune, and I make the mistake of looking at his face.

My stomach swoops. His brow is pinched, his lips parted softly. Beads of sweat slip from his temples to mingle with the wetness of his hair. Slick clumps of it stick to his neck, his cheek, and my fingers itch to brush it back, but my hands are sticky with blood. The sensation is familiar enough I know how to block it out, how to push through when it feels like it may never wash away, but I doubt any of them would find it comforting.

Otto has been chattering since he walked in. Tavi has already moved to the barb in his hip. She braces, and I know my eyes are too wide when they meet hers. If this one's bleeding like this now, it hit something, and pulling wrong may kill him before the poison can.

She tugs, the movement deceptively graceful. Blood streams onto the blankets, but Otto is there, shoving some sort of fibrous material inside a split second before Rune jerks away from his touch.

"Deeproot will help stop the bleeding, but keep putting pressure on it," Otto says.

Tavi obliges, leaning in, and Otto moves to me, offering more of the red, feathery fibers. When I step back instead, he steps in, packing the wound with expert skill.

"Don't we need to clean it?" I ask.

He shakes his head. "The deeproot will help with that too. It works especially well for ocean-based poison or infection. I have a theory it works especially well for sirens too because—"

"Otto," Tavi chides, jerking her chin at the salves still waiting on the bed.

"Got it. Got it. So I don't know which of these might help but we've got a lot of areas we can test on with the way the thrall squid wrapped around him. I don't recognize the barbs, but with the amount of time it takes the squid to work I wonder if whatever it injected had a numbing element to it. Maybe he simply couldn't feel it."

Elio clears his throat. He hovers at the bed, his eyes flicking between the ship's unlikely medic and the pained expression on Rune's sleeping face. "We'll never know if we don't get him to wake up, eh, Otto?"

"Right!" Otto spins to the poultices again. Gingerly, he tips the bottles onto small squares of fresh bandage and sticks them to individual spots. First, one labeled bitter pipevines. Then another named orange bloodleaf. On and on it goes. The golden markings on Rune's arm are all but faded. It seems clear now that they're part of his heritage.

Siren Prince.

The words lurk in the back of my mind, the fearful strategist in me refusing to wait before leaping to theories. If he's a prince, why would he need treasure? Why would he be risking his life hunting pirates topside at all? Part of me whispers about vanity, but the more time I spend on this ship, the more I question that sickly confident facade I'd met that first night on *The Gilded Hart*. And the crew held their own against the beast on the island—none had turned tail and fled. No, this ship isn't just for show.

But why risk it for the map?

"His hip's bleeding again," I say, just as Otto finishes wrapping over the small bandages on Rune's forearm. A rush of nerves sends my heart racing, but I shove the feeling down, filling my lungs till they feel near to bursting before letting the breath loose again.

"Good!" Otto quips, leaning close to examine the slow drip of blood oozing down Rune's pale skin.

I blink. "Good?"

Elio sighs. "The king's going to kill us if he dies."

"Kill *you*. He loves me," Tavi says, though it's impossible to tell if she's joking. Elio's smile tells me he can see something I can't.

"Yeah," Otto says, ignoring them. "They can't be completely closed or we won't be able to draw the poison out. The deeproot filters and acts as a block while it begins to clot, but it dissolves. Now"—he leans and grabs a larger dark bottle that's buried beneath the others, then begins to mix several inside—"we can make the drawing salve. It'll have to be applied every two hours or so."

I cross my arms. "I can do it. I'll be in here anyway, right?"

All eyes assess me for a moment.

Elio nods slowly. "We'll do shifts. In pairs."

Otto lifts an arm to scratch at the back of his head. "Well, I'll have to be the one to keep an eye on him for the next several hours to check the thrall squid marks."

"And this is where I sleep," I offer.

"Then you two will pair together," Elio says. "Tavi and I will be checking in regardless. No one stays alone with him until he's stable."

Otto makes a show of acquiescing. "Yes, Captain."

"Don't—" Elio's eyes widen. "Ah, shit."

"Your greatest dreams realised?" Tavi says with a glint in her eye. "The crew will be eager for an update when the sun rises. Think you can handle it?"

Elio all but pouts. "Why couldn't he have made you first mate?"

She lifts a brow. "I don't have your irresistible charm."

"How long until we know if that drawing salve is working?" he asks, turning away from her to Otto. "If I'm still acting captain when the sun hits the ship I'm leaping overboard. I'll never hear the end of it."

Otto grins, and hope lights in my chest like a torch on a moonless night. "It'll take some time, Cap," he says. "But I think between the four of us he's got a fighting chance."

Otto is asleep in the massive green chair—his mouth half open as he snores softly—when the first light of the sun peeks through the porthole behind Rune's desk. For the first time in hours, the patterns on his arms shimmer faintly, half hidden by the bandages wrapped on one side. The sunrise means it's time to reapply the drawing salve, so I tuck one side of the blanket to the inside of his leg, keeping him covered in those intimate places that I am absolutely not thinking about as the rays through the window reach out, accentuating the hills and valleys of his upper body. The peripheral thought has heat rising in my cheeks, remembering the solid heat of him beneath me that night he'd woken and trapped my chest to his. The way my body had betrayed me by wanting to lose itself in that salt and oranges scent.

I let my attention sweep to Otto, double checking there's no one to see the absurd red my face has certainly become. Rune is infuriating. Arrogant beyond measure. And seems to enjoy finding every way to bait and confuse me. We have a plan. A deal. Our partnership is mutually beneficial. Temporary. And it *was* entirely reluctant. So why has something inside of me hummed with relief ever since the colour came back to his cheeks?

Spring has yet to relinquish the chill of night. When I've finished with the salve, I tuck the blanket back over his legs, and quietly place the jar on the nightstand next to the red-veined leaf from the island. If I was going to restart my collection, I'd need to find a safer place to store them.

Elio had brought extra chairs and mine is pulled nearly flush with the bed, keeping the captain in arm's reach and my weight off my still throbbing ankle. Rune sighs and adjusts, but there's no pain in the movement, and my heart flickers again as his face turns to me, though he doesn't wake.

His unbandaged arm splays out, putting those golden patterns on display. I'd have to ask him about them when he wakes. They're unlike any tattoos I've ever seen, but some shifters keep markings in their human forms. It's something I would have realised sooner, had I not been so focused on looking at anything *but* him.

Now, I would have to be doubly sure to keep this wayward attraction at bay. A siren prince and a pirate? It's too risky. The opposite of a low profile.

And he still doesn't know who I am.

It wouldn't have mattered. Nisse or no, if he had died and the ocean king had sought someone to blame, who better than the bloodthirsty, no good, pirate scum the prince had brought aboard on a whim? Hell, the crew would have tossed me overboard before the king had a chance, or tied me up and dumped me into the centipede tunnels. Or hung me from the bones of the sail. Or spilled my insides for the quail. And if they did find out they had Ivor's daughter?

The panic rises in a wave, cresting with all the fear and worry and lack of sleep I've ignored the last few hours. My own sleeve has torn, and the spade-shaped head of my viper tattoo peeks out. I bury it in the rumple of the blankets, my fingertips brushing his. Sensation spears through me from that small touch, and I don't pull away, trying hard to ground myself in my current reality. For now, I am safe. For now, he's okay, and my secret is mine alone.

I let my fingers wander to the art on his arms, tracing each line, watching the way the light catches behind my touch. A seed of warmth nestles deep in my chest, and for once, I don't squash it before it can bloom. His fever is gone, but his skin holds the same insistent heat as when he crushed me to him the night of our race. I let the sensation and the memory anchor me, just this once, just until he wakes up and we go back to playing the parts of the hunter and his prey.

PARTIAL TRUTHS AND BANDAGES

The wooden door to my room creaks, announcing someone's arrival. It wakes Otto, who's curled in the chair beside my bed.

Odi pulls out of my hold before she moves to the other side of the room next to my desk.

"Jellied octoblorbs—" Otto spurts out as he sits upright, his gaze snapping to mine. "Cap, you're awake!"

Before I can answer, Elio steps through the doorway, his face full of relief. He's quickly followed by Tavi.

"Rune, how are you feeling?" he asks, coming to stand beside my bed.

I try to sit up. The sheets cling, damp with sweat and salt, twisted somewhere around my legs. My body aches—but I know the fever has left me. "Why is everybody in my room?"

Elio's hazel eyes dart towards Odi. "She said someone tried to break in the other night."

I flick my gaze to Odi. She folds her arms across her chest and leans against the wall, brows slightly raised in defiance. She's still convinced of the assassination attempt.

My shoulders lift and fall. "Since when do we trust the word of a pirate?"

Usually my choice of words don't bother me, but this time when they slip past my lips they feel wrong. Odelia might be a pirate, but so far she's given no reason for me not to trust her—not since I caught her in the streets that night. A pain tugs deep in my chest, the kind that made its presence known the moment I rescued her from the water.

Tavi's brow knits together as she folds her black leather-clad arms across her chest, an evident scowl on her face. She's not pleased. "Why didn't you tell us?"

Elio pipes in, his weight shifting as he shoves his hands into his trouser pockets. "We should start an investigation."

Everyone begins talking at once, their voices blending together in a frantic hum. For a brief second, I close my eyes and take a deep breath knowing full well that Odi is standing in the corner of the room watching my crew fuss over me.

Otto stands from his chair, the legs squeaking on the wooden floor. "Are you hungry? Because I can bring you eggs five different ways real quick. I know you hate them but I did some research and I found that the yolk is really good for healing wounds internally so it would probably be really good if you ate some."

I can't help but smile, shaking my head softly before I turned my attention to them all. "I'd appreciate a moment to speak?"

"Sorry, Cap," they murmur in unison.

"For starters, if someone is trying to kill me or Odelia, we'll figure it out sooner or later. I'm not blind to the idea of someone trying to harm either one of us because they're mad she's on the ship," I say with confidence.

Elio swings his arms out wide. "But Cap—"

I throw him a look. One that tells him I'll hear his concerns later. "Secondly, I definitely could do with some food, but *by the sea* do we have something else besides quail eggs?"

Bear grins, his eyes crinkling at the corners. He heads for the door, throwing a glance over his shoulder. "I'll make you the most delicious seafood boil, garlic butter sauce included."

"Otto, wait," I call after him.

He stops mid stride, spinning to face me.

"What got me down there?"

"Thrall squid was one of them, Cap. Not sure about the barbs, but you'd be wise to avoid them in the future. Nearly took you clean out they did." Bear grins, but I know internally he's not smiling.

I can see the fear behind his eyes and all too quickly guilt creeps its way into my chest. I'd been so sure that I'd be fine when diving into the unknown, that I hadn't stopped to think what it might mean for those who'd come to rely on me—for those who were meant to protect me and I them.

Bear lingers by the door, hand resting on the knob.

I offer him a smile. "Thanks, Otto . . . for everything."

"That's what family does." He returns the boyish grin, then the door clicks shut behind him, his voice echoing through the walls as he heads for the kitchens.

My thoughts suddenly return to the reason I'm cooped up in this space. The reason why I sacrificed my body to find the answers I longingly seek. "Did you get the key?"

Elio pulls it from his pocket, holding it up for me to view. "That we did, Cap." The sunlight catches it, glinting off the side of the polished metal. It's a flat, solid circle, with a wave down the centre. I notice the way Odi's eyes light up with excitement as Elio flashes the piece around. She's just as pleased as I am to have it in our possession, even if we've no clue how difficult it'll end up being to assemble the pieces. I'll definitely be locking it away—for safety reasons.

With a gentle groan, I swing my legs over the side of the bed, being careful not to disturb the neat bandage work that can only have come from Otto's hands. As I glance down, I realise that I'm utterly naked.

Everyone in this room is about to get an eye full.

I throw a glance around, looking for the pair of trousers I'd been wearing on the island. Odi's necklace is still in the pocket.

Tavi rushes forwards, her white braid trailing behind her. "What are you doing?"

I grit my teeth as I try to stand. The pain is minimal but not absent. "Really Tavi, I'm fine. Otto's a great doctor. We need to keep moving."

She ignores my words, wrapping a sheet around my waist. Odi's gaze is on me for a second before she looks away. While Tavi holds the sheet around me for privacy, Elio slips an arm under mine and around my chest, stabilising me until I find my feet.

The bandages are firm around my thigh, hip and arm. "Otto did well with these bindings."

Elio clears his throat, throwing a glance across the room. "Actually Odi did most of the tending at the end."

Odi?

For a second, I think Elio's joking. Trying to get a rise out of me. But he's not smiling. Something burrows its way into my chest finding a home right next to my heart.

She stayed with me?

Through the fever, through the sweat and shivering and *gods* know what else—I don't remember half of it. Just flashes.

Burning. The weight of the sea pressing on my lungs. And something cool at my temple. Gentle. Steady.

That was her?

The woman I roped to a bed. The one who spits fire every time I look at her.

I turn to face her, but her gaze is locked onto something far more interesting on the floor. So I don't bother saying anything. Not yet anyway.

There's a shirt and trousers resting on my night stand. I toss on the shirt, and hot pain shoots up the back of my arm, and as I glance down, I notice the line of red ringed welts on my forearm from the thrall squid. Whatever the other creatures were in that cenote, they got me good. I take hold of the sheet. "I can manage, thank you Tavi."

She nods once before retreating.

Dense air throbs through the room. It's not the heat of the early morning, it's the eyes. Both Tavi and Elio watch me, like I'm some fragile thing that's about to fade away. I know they mean well. Yet the overprotection gets to be a little much at times.

Then there's Odi. In the corner, as silent as a shadow. She's not saying a word, but I can feel her. The way her eyes track me without moving. I need to talk to her. I also need to put on my pants.

I turn to my crew. "Is there any chance I could have some privacy?"

Elio scratches his head, his eyes darting between me and Odi. "Uhh yeah, sorry."

Tavi doesn't say a word, but I can figure out everything she wants to say by the steely gaze she throws my way. There'd be time for conversations later.

They start to file out—Elio first, Tavi close behind. Odelia lingers a moment, then turns like she means to follow.

I move before I think.

My fingers close gently around her wrist—just enough to stop her.

"You," I murmur, voice low. "Stay."

She pauses, her eyes meeting mine. Something flickers there—surprise, maybe. Suspicion. But she doesn't pull away.

Elio and Tavi turn at the door, their eyes travelling between Odi and I.

I drop Odi's hand while looking at not only my crew mates, but my friends."I'll expect a report on the other injured when I return to the main deck."

The pair nod.

"I'll make sure Otto doesn't go overboard with the scuttle crab legs," Elio mutters with an eye roll.

Tavi's green eyes give me a once over. "Let us know if you need anything."

"Thanks, Tav."

Once the door closes behind them, I let out a breath. The space suddenly feels less cramped. I wanted the room to myself to speak with Odi, but now that we're alone I seem to have lost all my words.

I turn and find her awkwardly standing in the corner again, like she doesn't know what to do with herself. "Odi—"

"I need a washroom," she says simply, already moving towards the door adjacent to my room.

No doubt she's been needing one for a while and didn't know how to ask. I give a small nod. Watch the door close behind her. The latch clicks.

And then it's just me.

The silence hits harder now than when the room was full. Louder, somehow. Heavier.

It leaves too much space for thought—and that's the last thing I want. I don't want to think about the crew I'd lost or how there's a high chance that there will be other casualties if I continue down this path.

With a sigh, I retrieve a fresh pair of trousers from the nightstand. I carefully put them on, wincing with every movement. Then I hobble around the room, searching for the trousers with Odi's necklace. They lie in a tattered, crumpled heap against the far wall. Pain bursts through my ribs as I bend to scoop them up. My hand dives into the pocket, and relief crashes over me the moment my fingertips graze the familiar smoothness of the necklace. I still can't figure out how she found it in the first place. They're rare, near impossible to find, and even more so for those that tend towards unsavory company. Could she have been chosen? I bat the thought away. A night of tending wounds doesn't change who she is. What she is.

Right?

Once the necklace is secure in my pocket again, I begin to pace, walking the length of the room as I run my fingers through my hair. The movement helps work away some stiffness, but pain is a reminder that it's going to take a while until I'm fully healed.

When Odi returns, I should thank her for helping them keep me alive, for tending to salves and bandages at the cost of sleep. Or maybe steer the conversation towards the key pieces, safer ground, something that feels less like laying my heart out for the gulls to pick at.

The door to the washroom clicks open pulling my attention from my thoughts and back to the woman I'm trying so hard not to like. That's when I notice her slight limp. My brow pinches as she makes her way further into the room.

"You're hurt," I say as she approaches me.

Dark waves shimmer in the early morning sunlight as she shakes her head. "It's nothing."

Before I can stop myself, one arm hooks around her waist, the other behind her knees, and I scoop her up in one clean motion. Heat flares through my hip, but I bite the inside of my cheek so Odi doesn't see the evidence on my face. She stiffens in surprise, her breath catching, hands instinctively grabbing at my shirt, but I don't stop.

I flick my gaze to her perfectly pink lips—just for a second. Close now. Too close.

All the ache I've been trying to bury stirs at the surface. I lean in, a hair's breadth from closing the distance. Just one tilt forwards and I could taste the silence between us.

But I don't.

Instead, I lower her gently onto the bed, careful not to jostle the injured ankle. She's still watching me, breath shallow, eyes wide.

I shift down, lifting her leg and propping it on the wooden box that someone placed at the end of the bed. My fingers graze the mottled skin just above her foot, slow, steady, deliberate. Purple and brown bruises make a patch on the outer side of her ankle. "It's badly sprained."

Odi feigns a tight smile. "I'll be alright."

I can't help the way my brow pinches as I look up at her. "Why didn't you tell anyone?"

She shrugs slowly. "No one was overly concerned about my injuries when I first came aboard *The Gilded Hart*, why would they care now?"

Guilt stabs me in the chest like a hot knife. It's true. I hadn't cared about her wounds when I'd dragged her from the ocean, but only because the thought of letting Otto within arm's reach of a Viper made my heart lurch and my hands itch for the closest weapon I could reach. Things are different now. We have a shared goal. And she's clearly got a soft spot for the ship's cook.

I slowly stand, making my way to the nightstand where Otto has left fresh bandages, no doubt intended for me. I collect a roll and move back to the chair before beginning to wrap Odi's ankle. "You only have me to blame for that, and for what it's worth . . . I'm sorry."

Her eyes meet mine, silence hanging between us for a moment, but she lets the topic drop. "So, you're a siren?" she says instead, her hand tracing absently over her neck.

I nod as I continue to bind her ankle. "I am."

Odi hisses softly as I reach the darkest part of the bruising. "And a prince?"

"Correct," I say softly, making sure to cradle her ankle as gently as possible. "Prince Rune Ahren, King Ahren's first and least favourite son, at your service."

She huffs a laugh. "Seems like you have secrets too." Her voice is soft, but not accusing. "How does a siren prince become a bounty hunter on the ocean's topside? I thought your kind couldn't stand being out of the water."

I finish wrapping the bandage, securing the loose ends together with a small knot. "Every race has their purists. Some of us refuse to leave the ocean. They might condemn my choices, but you'd be surprised at how many of us actually enjoy breathing this air."

Her brow raises, a playfulness I've not seen before dancing in her eyes. "Rebellious act then? Daddy issues?"

I release the chuckle trapped behind my lips. "I think we've had enough truths for now," I say, as I rise from my chair. "Stand and tell me how that feels."

Odi slides off the bed cautiously, but still manages to stumble when her feet hit the ground. Reflexes have me reaching out to steady her. The wall I built to keep us apart begins to crumble when she leans into my touch without hesitation, her body pliable and soft, like she feels safe.

She clears her throat, trying to hide the flare of colour in her cheeks. "Much better . . . thank you."

Part of me doesn't want to let her go, but the sensible side roars for distance. Nothing good waits if I linger. With a curt nod, I release her and retreat towards my desk. Odi smooths the folds of her billowing trousers, fabric that only teases the shape it's meant to hide. It takes everything in me to drag my gaze away.

"You know you didn't have to go diving into the cenote alone. If we'd made a plan I could have helped." Her voice is low, and if I were a fool I might say it verges on emotional.

I try to focus on the papers sprawled on the wooden surface but her words dance around me. Dropping the ink pen onto the desk that I'd picked up without thought, I glance over my shoulder. "Are you saying you were concerned for my wellbeing, little doe?"

Odi folds her arms across her chest and rolls her eyes. "I'm saying you could have spared yourself a night of fever and pain."

I turn to fully face her before leaning against the edge of the desk. "And not have you attend my wounds?" I fold my arms across my chest, brow raised. "Not a chance."

A tiny smile forms on Odi's lips, and my heart swells at the sight of it. She's smiling at *me* . . . not at Otto's chatting, or Soraya's song, but me.

I spin back around before I say something stupid. We have one part of the key now, yet there are still three more to find. And we aren't going to find them inside my sleeping quarters. So despite my still aching body, I allow a grin to dance on my lips as I pick up the treasure map, turn, and hand it to the enticing woman behind me. With a small branch of trust growing between us, I let the words tumble from my lips. "Where to next, Odi?"

You, me, and the chain you linked between us

15
ODELIA

Despite the show of confidence, Rune sleeps much of the next few days. When he wakes, it's brief, and red spots mar the sharp of his cheekbones. He eats only a little more each meal, despite Otto's attempts. Still, he is healing; The thrall squid punctures scab over. The risk for infection lessens each day. And the gleam in his eye always finds me.

I stay, guarding, careful to not get caught too close again, ignoring how the phantom warmth of his arms and the gravity of his presence make war with my willpower. I have the strangest feeling that if I were curled against him the next time he woke, he'd be pleased. The thought tempts me more than once, but I beat it back down, reminding myself of the harsh reality that spans between us—there is no world in which that sort of indulgence ends well.

A soft knock at the door floods my body with hyperawareness, but it's Tavi, carrying food.

"Otto said you like the redfin, so he put extra."

I nod, assuming there's nothing more to say. But there's something uncharacteristically hesitant about the way she sets the plate on the desk and turns back to me, though not a thread of her attire is out of place. Her unnervingly green eyes scan my no-doubt-crinkled clothes and the tangle of hair bundled on my head, as it has been every day since we left the island.

"I wanted to thank you."

Thank me? I feel my eyebrows rise. "Why?"

"For helping." She jerks her chin to a sleeping Rune, the words coming like a rope being coiled with every insistent pull. "With him. It's rare that I freeze. You didn't."

"I'm sure it's much harder when you actually care for the person you're treating." It only takes a moment for me to realise how heartless the words might sound, but I purse my lips closed, refusing to clarify with the experiences of treating those on the *Sea Bane.*

She glances between me and Rune, her eyes catching on the fork I'd rested just beneath the chair before burning into me again. I shrug. Old habits die hard. They won't give me a real weapon, and I want to have every chance of subduing anyone that makes it in here.

"I also wanted to let you know," she goes on slowly, "some of the crew are blaming you for the deaths. They plan to challenge Rune as soon as he grants a meeting. They want blood."

My mouth is dry, but I swallow, nodding. I'd expected nothing less, but it still makes any semblance of peace in me flicker and wink out. The animal in me stirs. I shake the sensation away, already mourning the food I won't be able to eat as my body braces for the chance of future violence.

When she goes, the smell of the redfin she brought overpowers the room, twisting my stomach. I can't let Otto know I hadn't been able to stomach it, so I unlatch the round window, intending to toss it to the sea. Except, when I brace to dump the plate over, a small, winged shadow darts for the fish, its sharp talons biting into my thumb.

"*Vicious seas*," I hiss, the pain sharp as a horrid bird screech sounds from above. The entire plate falls, its splash muted by the crash of the waves as *The Gilded Hart* plows on. I guess we picked up a little feathered stowaway on the last island. Either that or it's a young storm roc—as if we don't have enough trouble to deal with.

When we're two days from the next island, Rune wakes with the sun, his movements rousing me from the nest of pillows and blankets I'd arranged in his giant chair. I scrub the wispy hair and sleep from my face before I stand.

He freezes, his eyes trailing me from my bare feet to the shirt I've been sleeping in.

His shirt.

The heat of embarrassment crashes through me—at first I'd only worn it because monster gunk meant the clothes they'd given me were in desperate need of a wash, then the waist of the bottoms felt too constricting for the way I had to curl into the velvet chair to sleep. After a couple weeks being tended by the chef of *The Gilded Hart*, I was well nourished, already filling out with muscles and curves that had struggled to stay on with the rations of the *Sea Bane.*

"Your ankle looks better," he says, his voice heartachingly soft.

"You look less like you're dying," I counter, hoping the unimpressed lilt in my voice breaks whatever's trying hard to settle between us.

He just smirks, his attention tracking to my throat as I swallow. "What happened to your hand?"

I look down at the bandage. Otto had fervently insisted when he came to check on Rune and saw the gash on my thumb. *That's deep, Odi. Birds don't have the cleanest talons you know? If it gets infected you could lose it. Might be hard to use any stolen kitchen knives.*

"Nothing," I say, crossing my arms to hide it. We've more important things to discuss. "Tavi said the crew is calling for my head." I'm careful to keep my voice neutral. Both Nisse and the animal in me have learned well enough that predators can scent fear, and there's every chance Rune might come to agree with the demand for blood if they learn about my past.

Rune sobers, and he leans to the nightstand to pull out a dark shirt and slips it on. The irritated swirl of skin on his forearm disappears under the long sleeves. "They're loyal," he says. "Protective. I'll talk to them."

"And if they can't be swayed?"

He lifts a brow. "Then I supposed I'd give you a turn, seeing as how you're so personable." I blink, a jumble of words all tangled on my tongue, wrestling for purchase. His smile grows as the silence goes on. "As soon as you're decent, I'll address the crew." He moves to open the door, but pauses with his hand on the knob. "Unless you wanted to keep the shirt? I don't mind." Then the light of morning blasts into the room and he's gone, clicking the door closed softly behind him.

I dress quickly, putting on another set of Soraya's clothes and tucking the shirt into the chair. Outside, the barest shadow of the island is visible on the horizon. Rune stands near the mizzen mast, bodies already crowding nearby, vying for his attention. A few turn to me, some curious, some suspicious. What sort of bounty refuses to leave her captor's sickbed?

"To me!" Rune shouts, and all eyes find him. The weight of their gazes leave me, a few more shuffle from the bunk room, including Reid, whose red-faced glare flits to me like a moth to flame. The hatred in his eyes solidifies my shoulders and makes my hand twitch for the grip of my absent bola.

"First." Rune's voice draws me back into the moment, and I breathe deep. I can't afford to tangle with Reid. There's enough confrontation brewing with the crew as it is. "I'd like to thank Elio for standing in as captain while I was otherwise indisposed."

Elio lifts his eyes to the sky as if pleading for help, and Rune starts to clap. The crew joins in, some laughing when a sharp cat call sends red flushing over the first mate's face. Tavi's arms are crossed at the back of the group, her lips lifted into what the daring might assume is a smile.

"Second," Rune continues as the applause dies down, "I'd like to thank those that fought next to me on Serpent's Tooth. My heart aches for those injured and lost. I'll always regret that I wasn't there when they were sent to rest, but Nareth is honoured by their sacrifice."

"Honoured, and ready to see us home, right?" someone calls, to a few murmurs of approval.

Rune shakes his head. "The fight is only begun. We've faced worse and we'll face worse still, far beyond the map's challenge. Only the willing should go, but we may hold the key to some of Nareth's most precious history, and I won't be swayed by insects, no matter their size." His voice lifts in challenge. "Will you?"

Some jeer against the thought, confident, others look to those beside them, their amusement tentative. A few shake their heads, anger evident in their crossed arms and clenched jaws.

Rune nods. "We land in a day and a half. We'll make camp on shore, then send scouts to pick the best path forwards. All are welcome to stretch their land legs, but I need a list of volunteers willing to go further inland. We'll need hunters to focus on rations, and those willing to go with us for the key. We can expect the same level of risk as on Serpent's Tooth. Those that wish to stay aboard may do so without ridicule. Let every man choose for himself."

"Or woman!" Soraya calls, and Rune nods.

"Or woman. Those for the shore lift a hand and say aye."

"*Aye*," several voices reply, Soraya included,

"Those for inland, lift a hand and say aye."

The ayes are quieter, but still plenty. My shoulders drop a fraction and Rune's grin is triumphant enough to kindle something warm in my chest. Almost imperceptibly, he nods. His crew is with him, and he's with me. We've got the first part of the key.

And the next island awaits.

N*o greater beast than a man's mind, and the fear that seeks to claim it.*

It's the shortest clue on the map and already it has my legs fighting to spring. The crew tucks as much as will fit in the rowboats—tents, food, torches. This island is bigger—at least five leagues across. Even from here we can see the trees are shorter, the brush higher and more intrusive than forest on the last island. Since the map gave us so little to go off of, searching will be a multi-day affair.

"Ready to do it again?" Elio surprises me, which isn't easy to do. He clasps an arm across the deck railing and heaves a sigh, his other hand casually adjusting the shark-tooth pendant on his chest. "No telling what hides in those trees."

The wind is stronger today, but we're anchored so the sails are pulled up tight. The cloth creaks against the waxed rope that binds it. I'm not sure what to say. Half of me expected everything to go back to how it was before Rune was injured. But Tavi's glares haven't been half as potent, and now Elio is striking up casual conversation, like they think there's a wayward chance of Viper redemption just because I pulled a couple barbs out of their captain and haven't killed any of them yet.

The wind sweeps the trees in the distance as I speak, filling the air with a strange leafy hiss. "My captain used to say, 'Waiting till you're ready is like waiting to die.'"

The man next to me snorts, his head dipping over his arms like he's trying to hide it. "My mother used to say something similar, though my father would always say that 'Fortune only comes for those patient enough to bed her.'"

It's my turn to snort, and I feel the eyes nearby turn our way. "That's remarkably lewd for such sage wisdom."

His grin grows. "Just lewd enough that I've never forgotten it. Perhaps there's truth in both."

I almost ask about him and Tavi—if her subtle attentions are the reward for such patience, but there are too many bodies around and Reid has been slowly inching our way ever since Elio started talking. The brawny man stops just down the railing, feigning interest in the island he certainly didn't volunteer to explore.

"Shame about the captain, eh?" he says, his voice like grinding rock.

Elio straightens to glance at him. "Captain's in fine health now."

"Right. Thanks to the ship's new nursemaid. I mean look at her"—his brown eyes leave a trail of disgust tingling across my skin—"any flesh loving creature would be in fine health, until the venom sets in."

My nails ache from where they bite into the wood beneath them. "I'll find Rune," I tell Elio. "I'm sure we'll be the first out."

Reid turns as I pass him. "Aw, that's right. Run run, *little doe*—"

My blood sings as my fist flies towards his face. He flinches, and I pull back at the last moment, freezing the blow a hairsbreadth from his jaw. For a moment, we're both still. His face is flooding red, that rage taking over again. I know how to deal with men like him. I lean close and unfurl my hand, then tap it twice on his cheek, hard enough to sting. "Two for flinching," I murmur. Someone laughs nervously, then others join in, heckling him about the look on his face.

"Odelia." Rune's voice is neutral but firm.

I face him, turning my back to Reid. "Yes, Captain?"

He's across the deck. There's a smattering of bodies between us, but I can see something flicker over his face, gone in an instant. "It's time to go."

I follow him to the boats, waiting for him to reprimand me, but he doesn't. Tavi and Otto already sit on one side, which means I'll be on the other, squished against Rune's bulk. He holds out a hand again, but this time I take it without a second thought.

The manacle snaps over my wrist before I can lift my leg to board. I still the instinct to bolt. It's pointless to pull away—his grip is like iron, his skin burning into mine where we touch. The chains are cold, and I can't help the jagged sharp of hurt that pushes through as I look up to search his face. Does he plan to leave me behind?

Another clink of a lock finding home brings my attention back down to our wrists, and the manacles now strung between them. He's bound us, but I can't read the expression on his face. He knows I could shift. Chances are good that even if he was right there, I'd be able to slip away, so he can't expect them to actually hold me.

There are murmurs from the crew that looks on. Some nod, as if it's the most logical idea he's ever had.

I wait for the rush of irritation, but it never comes. "This is going to make rowing a tad more difficult, isn't it?"

His lips twitch. "Tavi and Otto will manage. Someone has to make sure you don't run off without us." He projects his voice over the gathered crowd, jerks his chin towards the boat, then lifts his arm up and out so I can get in. It rocks as his weight follows mine, straining the rope that secures it. When we're settled, I'm indeed squished—at least it feels that way, with the heat of his arm pressed against me. Long sleeves again today. At this point, I'm not sure if any of the other crew have seen the extent of his injuries.

"Aren't you going to ask why?" he murmurs the moment the boat settles into the water and Otto and Tavi collect the oars. Besides them, we're out of earshot.

"I've given up puzzling through the choices you make," I lie. Otto grins, but pretends he's focused on the water ahead as I go on, "As long as you don't jump into another death pit, I've no complaints being assured you won't be able to leave the island without me."

"Except that I have the key."

"For now."

He leans towards me, bracing his cuffed arm on the bench behind us so mine stays trapped as well. It wouldn't have mattered. He's half the size of the boat, his broad shoulders and chest blotting out the sun as he curls over me even as I sink back, half fearing and half anticipating his next move.

"Don't you trust me, Odelia?" His grin is wicked sharp, and I swear he's let a touch of the siren through as his voice travels directly to the part of me that aches every time he gets too close.

I couldn't stop my fingers if I wanted to. His shirt is like silk under my touch. I watch his pupils dilate, our gazes locked as I explore, brushing over the muscles of his chest, trailing over the sheer, impossible heat of him. The blood races in my veins, spurred on by my thundering heart. Curse this man and the citrus scent that envelops me now, forcing me to choose between ragged breaths and taking it deep into my lungs.

Distantly, I register that the sound of rowing has stopped. No one speaks. Time is frozen, but for the trail of my insistent, greedy fingers. "Only a fool would," I answer. Somehow, though they're soft, the words come out even as I rest the edge of his now-stolen dagger just below his exposed collarbone, quirk a brow, and press hard enough that blood beads over the blade. "Can I borrow this?"

It's Tavi who laughs, jolting us from the cocoon of swirling tension. Her radiant grin catches me by surprise and Rune swipes the blade from my hand.

"You deserved that," she says, sheathing her own readied dagger and picking up the oar again.

Rune's mouth drops open. "You *let* her disarm me."

She rolls her eyes, a smile still playing on her lips. The oars push us forwards with every slice into the water. "*You* let her disarm you."

"After," I point out, sitting up now that he's given me space to breathe again, "you chained yourself to me."

Rune scoffs, but his eyes are bright. "So it's my fault? Bear, help me out here."

Otto shakes his head. "Sorry, Cap. Saw it coming from a mile away."

"I just don't see why you haven't given me a weapon yet." My voice is dangerously close to a whine. I feel bare. The missing weight at my hip is a constant reminder of how vulnerable I am.

"You had one in arm's reach for five seconds and I'm already bleeding," Rune says, lifting a brow.

I bat my eyelashes innocently. "Then you shouldn't be so careless."

The first brush of sand under the row boat takes me by surprise. Rune hops out, getting soaked up to his thighs. His brows lift as he catches my wandering attention, a knowing glint in his eye. "But how else would I distract you from your debilitating fear of the ocean?"

We spend the first night on the shore. We circle the island twice to find the best spot, then hunters and scouts spend the entirety of the late afternoon canvasing the area. Otto gets the game salted and set over a massive fire to smoke. The crew take his direction as easily as Rune's, bringing a continual supply of wood from just within the trees. Strapped to their captain, I can do little to help. Instead, we pitch a large tent and makeshift table, where Tavi lays out parchment like it's precious glassware.

"There's been no obvious concerns," Rune says. "Arond said the game trail to the west leads deep inland, I figured we'd start there."

Tavi uses the sharp of a small blade to hone the tip of string-wrapped black lead. She's only outlined the island's eastern shore and faintly marked where the scouts reported landmarks, but it's already beautiful.

Outside, the sun truly sets just as Soraya starts to sing, the melody floating through the waxed canvas and urging me forwards. It's melancholy at first, that kind that tugs like the tide. Some of the others join, not all perfectly in tune, but the dissonance isn't out of place on this forgotten island, where yet more may find they've stepped off *The Gilded Hart* for the last time. Perhaps they sing for those they've already returned to the sea. Or those who will be gone before they go back home again. The love that has touched their lives and then vanished, leaving everything muted, colder than before.

Slowly, something hollows in me. Or perhaps the hollow is only uncovered, this wound I nurse like a babe. The one that reminds me of what life isn't. What it could have been. I reach for the necklace that's no longer at my throat, the ache in my chest flaring again. I'd lost it. After years, I'd lost the only thing my mother was able to give me before she died. The only proof that I wasn't Ivor's spawn alone. She'd said it was special. That only the ocean could choose who wore it. After she'd died, I'd spent long nights clutching it as a child, waiting for the worst to come, sure that either the water would take it, or the night would swallow me whole.

"Do you want to join them?"

Rune's voice rips me from my thoughts. I hadn't realised the way he was staring. He doesn't wait for my answer, just walks us through the tent flap and back under a sky that opens into a sea of stars. The chain clanks once as the backs of our hands brush. Everyone is gathered around a bonfire, some taking a turn roasting meat in the flame. Elio strums a lute, but the sound is nearly lost to the chorus of voices.

Tide take their souls
To the shore of the after
Shepherd them gently
In the sweet sweeping foam

Sea see them sweetly
Their sailor's souls silent
Woes buried by billows
Bones beckoned home

We find a seat in the sand, and then Rune is singing too, a low baritone that tickles the nerve endings in my neck and spine.

"I don't know the words," I say, when he nudges me to join. The admission shouldn't catch in my throat, but I have to look away, hoping the fire won't betray the mist that blurs my eyes. Pirates don't sing for the dead.

By the time it's done, I've curled my knees into my chest and stare into the flames, oblivious as they go on to dance and clap along with the next tune.

"That song always reminds me of my mother," Rune says, keeping his gaze forwards. "My father wouldn't allow it at her funeral, but I sang it for her every night, in the water, hoping my voice would reach wherever she'd gone."

He'd lost his mother too. He'd said as much, when I'd baited him before, but hearing it now reminds me there's a whole life behind him that I know nothing about. He goes quiet, and I say nothing, too torn open to push down the wave of emotion that crests over me, but too stubborn to let it pull me under.

After a moment, he sighs and leans back on his arms, tugging at the chain between us. "This is the part where you offer a heartwrenching anecdote that balances the scales of your past, before finally admitting you've fallen for my boyish charms."

I can't help the way the corner of my mouth ticks up. "In your dreams."

He leans over my shoulder, his breath spiriting over my neck. "You have no idea."

He moves out of the way before my elbow connects, then suddenly he's standing, and I've no choice but to follow or risk losing the skin of my wrist. "Hey! A little warning!" The chill nips at us as we move away from the heat of the fire and past the navigation tent, where Elio and Tavi stand outside. Rune instructs them to set a watch as we pass, but doesn't stop, instead hauling me to the string of tents farther down the shore. The sand shifts awkwardly under my feet as I try to match his gargantuan stride. "Where are we going?"

"Some were starting to notice your sad doe eyes. Figured you were attached to the whole kick ass pirate image and would rather find some privacy."

I huff a laugh, like I don't know what he's talking about. "So you admit I could kick your ass?"

He doesn't stop until we're at the farthest tent, but when he turns, the starlight glitters in his eyes. "Remains to be seen."

I furrow my brow as he gestures for me to go inside. "Aren't you going to unchain us?"

"Whyever would I do that?"

"So you can go to your own tent?"

"Oh, Odi"—he pulls us inside, and between the two of us there's hardly space for breathing—"does your optimism know no bounds?"

"Does your arrogance?" He truly means for us to share a one-man tent. Even with the entirety of the floor covered in blankets we'll still be hard pressed to arrange in a way that avoids our bodies touching. There isn't even space for a chair, just the flickering lantern tucked in one corner. The slow heat that's been curling around me flares hot, and suddenly the night isn't chill enough to temper it.

He *tsks*. "Sharp tongued thing. Tell me, do you prefer the right side, or the left?"

The irritation boils over, and I hiss in an effort to keep my voice low. "I prefer if you told me exactly what you're expecting by chaining us together. In front of the crew, sure, pretend if you must, but you know I could escape the moment you're asleep. You've even got your weapons with you, as if I won't take them and slit your throat before I go."

"I'm rather fond of your little knife habit, actually. I find it refreshing."

Words nearly strangle me trying to shove their way from my throat. "Rune!"

"Can we at least *sit*," he begs, forced to hunch over by the tent's size. "My neck muscles are seizing."

I huff and drop to my knees, and he sucks air through his teeth as the manacles jerk tight between us. *Good.*

But, when I look up at him to smirk, his parted lips and the sudden flush of his cheeks has my nipples pebbling tight under the wrap on my chest. I can't tear my eyes from his, not even to admire the light that kisses his neck and sharpens the angles of his face. He stands before me in the almost-dark, and I can see the beautiful hunter beneath, imagine the sharpening of his nails and teeth, feel the power that rivals that of the waves but, on my knees before him, I know without a doubt he would crumble for me.

"Are you going to sit?" I murmur, eyes wide, uncertain what will happen when I shatter the tension. He blinks, then drops down, sprawling over the entirety of the blankets and forcing me to lay or be pulled off balance. Our legs and shoulders press together, though I know we're both touching the edges of the tent on either side.

He sighs obnoxiously, though I'm certain he's struggling just as much as I am to take in enough air. "Must you sleep on top of me?"

"*You*"—I kick at his sprawled leg, immediately annoyed again—"are the one on top of *me*."

"I noticed you haven't tried too hard to get away."

I turn away from him, yanking our arms so I can lay on my side. The chain is cool through my shirt and the back of his hand is warm on my waist, the length of the manacles forcing the angle. I know he'll be able to feel the rise and fall of my racing chest, but it's better than encouraging the conversation any further. Every part of me feels wound tight with suffocating, raw, insistent, *feeling*. It assaults me from every side—his heat beside me, flashes of my mother, those rare moments when exhaustion and homesickness wasn't enough to temper the spark inside her. Images of my father and the kind of warmth I used to believe could be enough. The heartrending smile Rune offers his crew. Their easy laughter. The way they share their grief. Since my mother died, I've not wanted anything more than to be alone—safe.

Being alone is to be safe.

Night insects chitter, audible now over the cheer of the crew. There's no way I'll sleep. My blood sings as if a blade were in my hand, slick with the blood of victory.

When he speaks, the teasing lilt is gone, leaving his voice soft. "I need you with me," he says, and there's no way he can know the misplaced, aching warmth that blooms impossibly more in my chest as he goes on. "If there's a threat, it's likely aimed at you. I can't allow the riddles to be so conveniently disappeared." He hesitates for a breath. "And I'm not in the habit of leaving treasure unguarded."

I dream I'm dropped into the ocean, frigid cold enveloping me before the punch of a wave steals my breath and wakes me with a gasp. Rune's arms are locked around my back, hoisting me to his chest and pulling me out of the tent and into the bitter night. Breath clouds between us, but I can't tell if it's mine or his.

Something is *screaming*.

Canvas rips farther down and a grating animal sound tears through the air, drowning out the shouts of the regrouping crew. Rune draws his sword, but the creature is down before we're there. Two men and a woman are coated with green splatters, their faces twisted with varying levels of disgust. The monster leaks a similar colour, bleeding from several minor cuts and a vital wound to the bulbous neck pouch that flaps open. Whatever it is, it looks almost amphibious, with thick, meaty legs, greyish, slick skin and several eyes of differing sizes.

Its face is flat—the bottom half is mostly a hinged mouth—and the corded muscles of its thin, disproportionately long arms trail down to the needles of webbed claws.

Rune's jaw works as he studies the beast. "Who was on watch?"

"We both were," says one of the men, tossing his chin at the other. "I ran to wake the others as soon as we heard the screams—"

The other man cuts in, "But it leapt immediately. There wasn't any time."

Rune looks to the trees. "What do you mean it leapt?"

"It jumped, Captain. Two bounds brought it to us. We hardly had time to arm ourselves."

Elio sidles up to Rune. "No casualties," he murmures.

Rune nods. "Was there sign of any others?"

The watchman shakes his head. "No, Captain."

Rune looks to me, and I can only say what we're all thinking. "Let's hope it stays that way."

WHAT WORDS DONT SAY

16
ODELIA

Rune doubles the watch but no one can sleep, so we head out the next morning as the sun breaks the horizon. The stout trees claw towards us, snagging on whatever they can reach. When the game trail ends, the ground starts to squish under each step, and there's no way forwards but through. Elio and Rune take turns cutting away the underbrush, but progress is slow, and eventually we resort to simply pulling up what's in the way.

"They barely have roots," I say, tossing the long, thin foliage to the side.

Sweat has only just started to trail down Rune's temple. We've both pulled our hair up high to avoid getting it caught, and the blue tendrils haven't yet started to stick to his face. "All the better for us."

We take turns eating while we walk. The anemic shade of the thin leaves is welcome when the sun rises high, but the heat brings an impossible humidity, one that stinks like fermenting earth. Behind me, some cough, complaining that the sour burns their lungs. I keep my own breaths shallow, but seem to escape the worst of it, suffering little beyond the stench. This island doesn't offer the same invitation as Serpent's Tooth. There's no call to run, no familiar playfulness in the wave of leaves or dappled light. The soil is soaked. Suffocating.

Thankfully, the rot eases as the sun begins to sink and we search for a dryer place to camp for the night. My legs ache as much as my shoulders, which have never had to carry a pack like this before. After an hour searching with no luck, Elio starts to mutter, leaning his head to Rune. "It's like there's a half inch of water over the entire island."

Rune presses a toe into the ground, watching as a puddle rises around it. "Maybe the edges are higher elevation, so the water pools towards the centre?"

Tavi's voice feels muffled by the damp air. "Or there's ocean caves below. They might leak to the top if the island slopes in, or if there's enough pressure."

My chest clenches tight, and I have to push down the dread that rises at the thought of dark, drowned caves. The nervousness stays, clinging to my spine, ratcheting up with every snapped branch. There's a good chance we won't find anywhere to camp tonight, and if we keep moving we'll draw unwanted attention.

Rune is worried too. His brow pinches deeper the longer we walk, and I have the truly absurd urge to take his hand, as if it might ease the instinctual need to run that shoots through my legs with every step. We've fallen into a rhythm, where the chain doesn't clink as we walk, though I couldn't say when it started.

He half-turns to those behind us. "Any opposed to sleeping in the trees?"

A jarring scream plummets the forest into tense silence.

Everyone freezes, some inching their hands towards the hilt of their weapons. I swivel my head, trying and failing to see through the varying shades of shadow. Nothing moves; even the wind holds its breath.

When he speaks again, it's a whisper. "Leave nothing on the ground. Try to—"

Another scream splits the air, this one coming from our other side. It's quickly followed by a third behind us.

"It's too late." My left hand reaches through the ghost of my bola and I clench my fist tight. I'd tried to take what makeshift weapons I could before we left the ship, but none of it will stand up to the kind of creature we saw last night. "Rune. I need a weapon." Rune turns, watching my face, and I shove down the panic, willing my eyes to soften, willing him to trust me. Just for this. "Rune. *Please.*"

Another scream. Close enough to rattle the ribs in my chest.

"Rune—"

He grabs my hand, pressing the hilt of his dagger into my palm before flicking the key through my side of the manacles. Slowly, he tucks it back in his shirt pocket, his gaze never leaving my lips.

"Don't make me regret this," he says, his voice soft, and I'm not sure if he means the weapon or the fragile trust that's threading between us.

As soon as the chain's weight falls away, my spirit lifts. The manacle remains attached to his left hand, the unclasped end dangling. The dagger's hilt is smooth and steady beneath my fingers. In an instant, the panic swirling inside me turns to anticipation. Rune's sword whispers as he pulls it from his sheath and turns to watch the trees. I put my back to his, scanning the darkness on the other side.

"Pull in," Rune commands. "Backs to centre."

The others tighten their formation, facing outward. Elio is on the other side of Rune. Tavi situates herself on the far end, her dual blades nearly invisible in the dark.

The moment we still, the first creature punches through. It snaps branches as it flies, airborne till it lands on top of a man whose chest cracks under its weight.

Then chaos.

A body slams to the ground next to me—a woman that twists, scrambling back on her hands and knees until a— a *tongue*—wraps around her leg and yanks her flat. The air rushes from her lungs in a whoosh and I don't think before slicing the blade through the appendage. It springs back, painting her with bloody green, but she doesn't rise. Instead, she screams, clutching her leg where the fabric of her pants comes away in slimy sections streaked with red. The tongue spasms and falls to the ground, leaving behind a mess of dissolving flesh. She wails again, jerking her hands back as the saliva seeps into them too.

"Odi!"

I spin to find a sword tip retracting from the chest of a mottled-green creature poised to strike me, its many eyes wide and terrifyingly emotionless. With a sweep of my blade, its bulbous neck opens under its impossibly wide mouth, spilling gore with a stomach-turning gurgle. Its long arms drop, claws dragging the ground, and the frog-like upper half buckles over its thick legs.

"Their spit is acid!" I shout to Rune as the creature between us falls away.

"Then keep your wits about you!" he snips back as he pulls his sword from its body, like my surprise is a distraction. He's not wrong. He bounds away, and I don't turn back to the woman before racing after him.

We charge for the shadowy silhouette of a second creature, whose far-reaching talons shred a man's thigh before we reach him. With a grunt, the man swings hard, embedding his axe into its shoulder, but the thing doesn't flinch, just slaps him down into an unconscious heap on the soggy ground. Rune engages a step before I do, parrying its first swing and ducking beneath the second, lunging forwards enough to drive his sword backward into its leg. The move is more dexterous-thief than massive-fighter but he pulls around flawlessly, his feet faster than I'd expect from an ocean-born siren. I can't help the rush of admiration, nor the fierce, twisted glee. It's Nisse, not Odelia, that gives him a blood-splattered grin, then leaps in.

I catch it as it stumbles forwards, avoiding the claws threatening to scramble my insides. When I slash a shallow gash over its shoulder, its many eyes wink closed, but only the two largest open again, trained on me. Then the air shifts, kissing my cheeks as I narrowly avoid first, one, then two furious swings of those long claws.

My body moves on instinct, years of muscle memory taking over and narrowing my world to heartbeats and half-seconds. I'm able to sink the blade just over its hip and deal a glancing blow to one of its forearms before a fallen log does its best to tangle my footing.

A fierce burning rips through my thigh, but Rune is there, slicing at its back, green dripping off the white of his blade. I step back again, wincing at the way blood streams from the slice and down the side of my leg. It follows, its dead eyes locked on me like it knows I've lived my entire life in the body of a prey animal.

It brays in surprise when I lunge, using the scant momentum and every ounce of strength in my legs to barrel into its waist. Its thick knees buckle, and the log is there to send us both into the wet, rotting earth. I shudder at the sticky-slick sensation of its skin, then roll, trying to put myself far out of reach before it can lash out. Tavi and Rune each land killing blows—Rune to the neck and Tavi to the arteries of its inner thighs, which bleed it before it can rise to attack again.

"The last one is down, and so is Elio," she says, her voice betraying no emotion. Rune curses, breaking into a sprint the moment Tavi gestures towards where Elio lays against a rock not far away. The gash on his head still leaks blood. His face contorts with pain even in unconsciousness, likely from a trio of long, parallel slashes over his chest. The tooth on the chain around his neck is vibrant red.

"They're shallow," Rune says, ripping the man's torn shirt away and pouring the entirety of his waterskin over the wounds.

Elio groans, but sits up, wavering as Rune uses a hand to steady him. Tavi graces him with a glob of the foul smelling ointment, her mouth ticking up as he objects.

Rune crosses his arms, watching as if to ensure Elio is really awake. "You guys get him wrapped. I'll go check everyone else."

An hour later, we've tended the worst of the wounds and counted the dead. The woman with the acid-burned leg walks with a limp. Her hands are a scalded, but she nods to me at one point, offering a relieved smile as if I hadn't turned my back while she was down.

We've lost four more, and there isn't a single one of us who walks away unscathed. The forest sounds come back, wary at first, then insistent, as if they're determined to carry word of our half-victory across the whole of the island by morning. Some of our group take to the trees. Those too injured to climb fold their tents and use them as a cushion while they doze, propped up against the trunks. Rune and I stay below, quietly resting in shifts. Tavi sits next to Elio. She doesn't rest at all.

When the sun rises, Rune sends a runner to return to camp to give them the news and gather a group to retrieve the dead. Their way should be easier with the path we've cleared.

We walk on, weary and gore-spattered. The air heats as the sun rises high overhead. Unlike yesterday, there's no acrid, lung-rending scent paired with the humidity, and the faint sound of running water ahead offers an altogether more pleasant promise.

I let myself look down and grimace; the cream of Soraya's shirt is stained with a dried, slug-mucous green. "I'd kill for a bath."

"I'd kill for you to have a bath too." Rune keeps his face suspiciously deadpan, and heat flares in my cheeks, the image of water running down his bare chest and toned stomach remarkably persistent in my mind's eye. He hadn't chained me again, instead slipping the manacles off his wrist and into his pack in the early hours of the morning. Something had shifted between us, but I couldn't say what, exactly. I still don't trust him. Still expect the crew's wrath upon our return. None will take the deaths lightly, yet, here he is, forging forwards, as if it were his future on the line.

He glances over, like he expected more than my silence. "For you to wash the stink off, of course." His tone is an invitation all its own. I have to wonder if he realises how it betrays him. *Play with me.* It says. *Distract me. Fight me, if nothing else. Please.*

I straighten, falling easily into our back-and-forth despite the ache in my limbs and the way sweat burns the gashes on my thigh. "Why would I, if it's working so well to keep you away?"

He sighs, stretching his arms up high before lacing his fingers behind his head. "Actually," he says, peering down at me as we walk, "they say monster blood is an aphrodisiac."

The breath wooshes out of him as my elbow connects with his gut. His long arms swipe for me but I bound into a run, grinning as his long strides follow. A thrill chases up my spine alongside the memory of our last race, powering my legs ever faster.

The crew's shouts of surprise follow us, and so does Tavi's command for them to stand down. My wood nymph instincts bleed in, my feet sure where to land to stay near-silent, but Rune snaps branches and catches the underbrush as he goes, making both a path for the others to follow and enough noise for me to know he's struggling to gain any ground.

The inlet appears as if from nowhere, the forest ending only an arm's length from a wide stream of softly rippling water. I have to loop my arm around a tree to avoid falling in, but I turn towards the crashing behind me to find Rune barreling forwards, a feral grin stretching from one ear to the other.

"Rune!" I'm not proud that the words are a squeal. "Don't—"

He doesn't even try to stop, just scoops me up with both arms and lets his momentum carry us in.

We're airborne for a tense moment, just enough time to suck in a breath before the water crashes over us. It's warmer than I expected, but deeper too, and I flail, gripping my fingers into his shirt so he doesn't leave me stranded. He keeps one arm hooked around my waist, pulling us back to air and sunlight. Once we've surfaced, I suck in a breath and push away, slapping a splash of water his way for good measure. "*Ass*," I hiss, but the smile on my face probably dulls the insult.

"We all have our roles," he says a moment before a wave of water crests over my face, forcing itself up my nose, and even while sputtering I can't help but notice the gorgeous, trailing blue fin that slips back under the water as he laughs.

He's shifted—his teeth sharper, the angles of his face a touch sharper. His ears are peculiar too—bright-blue, fin-like. I freeze when he reaches towards me, shocked by the shimmering blue scales on his forearms and even more so by the flesh-ripping claws that are cautious as he wipes his thumb over my temple and cheek.

"I don't think any part of you isn't covered in blood," he murmurs by way of explanation, his eyes locked on mine, his touch lingering long enough for me to wonder if he can hear the way it makes my heart speed in my chest.

"It wouldn't be the first time." The words are a reluctant whisper, sticking tight in my throat. Some of the familiar grief sneaks through with them. I'm not sure there's any point in pretending I want to push him away now but, like when he spoke earlier, the words are rife with meaning that goes unsaid.

Silence that clings

17

RUNE

I don't know what possessed me to reach out—to wipe away the grime sticking to her face. Perhaps it was admiration for the way she'd wielded my blade as if it was sculpted from her very own hand, like it was a part of her. Slicing through creatures, fighting alongside my crew as if she was one of us. She might be a good head shorter than me, and a pain in my ass, but she certainly knows how to fight.

I grip her chin, tilting her head back ever so slightly. My gaze flicks to her mouth, which is slightly parted as I run a thumb over her bottom lip. She's covered in the green, mucus-like blood from the creatures that'd attacked us earlier, but even under a blanket of muck she still manages to steal the air right from my lungs.

One flick of my tail would have us chest to chest. Our breaths mingling, her tongue on mine. She doesn't try to pull away, only looks at me like she wants it too. That's all it takes for my pulse to quicken and other body parts to respond. A tremble slithers across my skin, prickling the scales on my forearms as I inch closer.

The sound of my crew cresting the hill shatters the spell around us into a million tiny pieces that wink out like forbidden stars. I pull back, sinking further into the water, and Odi does the same but in the opposite direction. We're well and truly apart when Tavi's bright white hair catches the afternoon sun as she assists Elio down the embankment. With a flick of her braid, she glances my way but quickly returns her attention to her patient, who, even though he insists he's alright, is clearly in pain.

Guilt—maybe shame—clamps tight around my chest. My crew are dying, bleeding, breaking because of choices I've made. Every path I take sends another soul back into the sea. And for what? A sliver of hope that I'll uncover something about my mother? A piece of her left behind? What her kind might find worth hiding behind lock and key? *And maybe*, a desperate part of me whispers, *the truth of what happened.*

The symbol on the map—the one that glittered on her skin—hovers on the edge of my thoughts. Mother had it marked on her chest, just below her throat. It shimmered under the light the same way my siren markings do. I shake my head, pushing the too-desperate thought away. The map is ancient. It may have nothing to do with her, but it's the first time I've seen that marking since leaving Nareth.

For this to work, I need to get wiser. As soon as we have this next key, I won't risk my crew again. It will just be me who does the retrieving. If Tavi will let me.

With the crew making their way into the stream further up, I shift back into my human form with practised ease. In the rush of chasing Odi—scooping her into my arms and diving into the blue—I'd let my true self rise, and I'll never forget the way her eyes roamed over me, tracing the lines of my siren form. Over the webbed ears. Down the scales that banded my arms. Lingering at the claws curled sharp at my fingertips like something dangerous she didn't quite fear.

She didn't flinch.

And that might be the part I remember most.

Deep, cooling waters swirl around me, lapping at my skin. Odi has moved closer to the edge of the pool where it's shallow, and even though I shouldn't, I can't help but glance back. She slips her blouse up and over her head. Beads of water roll down her honey skin, kissing her in places I wish I could.

A slender foot breaks the surface as she scrubs at her skin. The moment I catch on, I turn away to grant her privacy. Then I strip off my own clothes—they could use a wash as well. No sense smelling like the armpit of some bulbous amphibian.

Time slips by as I wash, grateful for a moment's peace. Water splashes behind me, and I know Odi is still there. A sigh slips from me at the thought of her so near. The feeling in my chest only swells when she's close—unwelcome, unstoppable. It frightens me for two reasons. First, because it feels like a betrayal of everything I've stood for. Second, because I've started searching for her in every room.

After wringing out my clothing and throwing it into a heap on the bank, I drop my head back and let the water seep through my hair, discarding any lingering blood that might be trying to cling to the strands.

I duck under the surface one more time, spinning to face Odelia as I rise. She too has thrown her outer garments onto a low hanging branch, which can only mean one thing.

Fuck . . . vicious seas take me now.

Every second near her is torture of the cruellest kind. I remember every curve of her arm and hip as I lay next to her inside the tent. It'd taken all my willpower not to reach for her and bury my face into the crook of her neck. Now, she's almost naked mere inches away.

The clamorous chatter from the crew falls away as Odi flicks her gaze up to meet me. Warmth races up my neck and into my cheeks. I've been caught. Her brow raises, as does the corner of her mouth. Silently, her eyes challenge me to come closer, but I can't. I'm too afraid of what I might do.

Water droplets hold fast to her dark lashes. "You had some impressive moves back there."

I reach up, dragging my hands through my wet hair, flexing my arm muscles. "Whatever do you mean? Aren't I impressive all the time?"

"Humble too." Odi grins. "I meant the way you ducked under that creature, and tossed your sword arm back. Seems sneaky for an upstanding man such as yourself."

I can't stop the corner of my mouth turning up. "You think I'm upstanding?"

Odi's head angles to the side, a playful grin forming on her lips. "You don't know half the things I think."

What I'd give to slip inside her mind, to trace every dark and shining path that makes her Odelia—vicious pirate of the Viper crew. A woman I have no business imagining beneath my hands, her hair wound between my claws, tugged just enough to hear her breath catch.

I need to think about something else fast.

"Learned the move from my little brother. He's always been a head shorter than me. But he's quick." I blurt out, knowing the talk of family would damper the flame sparking in my chest.

Odi stretches her arms up, fixing her hair. "You have siblings?"

I almost pass out at the sight of the supple mounds of her breast bobbing just above the surface. I'm certain she hears me swallow as I try not to gawk at her.

"Yes, two. My sister—Selene—who is the oldest. Next in line for the throne and then there is the babe of the family, Dash. He's training in my father's army. The favoured son." The words tumble out in a heap.

"No doubt he's more handsome than you too."

I sink further down into the water, so only my head is visible, and drift towards her. "You find me handsome?"

Odi huffs, rolling her eyes, but I catch the smile playing on her lips as she turns to look away.

"How about you? Got any brothers I should know about?"

She softly shakes her head, but it's her eyes that betray her. "Just me."

Silence hangs between us. Apparently, family is a sensitive topic, so I drop it. "Trust me, you're better off. Brothers can be more trouble than they're worth."

Odi smiles, but I can see the sadness that dances in her eyes.

My chest constricts. We don't have time for sadness, not yet at least. Both of us have treasure to find, and then . . . well there will be plenty of time for sadness after. "Come on, we'd best join the others."

She lingers a heartbeat longer before dipping her head. Her gaze flicks to my mouth briefly and then she turns, cutting through the water towards the shore. I swallow hard, the burn in my chest fierce enough to keep me rooted, stalling as I watch her glide away.

When she surfaces I can't tear my gaze away. First, because she's fucking perfect to look at, and then because I see a faint trail of red snaking down the side of her leg and realise that she's bleeding. How did I miss that?

Without a second thought I dart towards her, but by the time I'm there she's almost out, ankle deep in the water—thankfully she still has underwear on, because if she didn't there's a definite chance I would have lost all the feeling in my legs. "Odi, stop."

I rise and wade towards her, not caring that my naked body is on full display. She freezes, but doesn't turn. Her dark tresses send droplets back to their watery home and I have to bite the inside of my cheek to stop the flow of blood rushing to my cock.

"Turn around." My voice is a gentle command.

She turns slowly on her heel, one arm crossing her chest to shield herself, and I'm glad, because I wouldn't be able to breathe if I took in the entirety of her beautiful naked figure.

I point to her thigh which has three angry, shallow gashes running across it and a crimson trail twisting its way down her leg. "You're bleeding."

She shrugs, her lips sealed tight.

Insects hum thick in the canopy above us, wings buzzing like a chorus. The sound mingling with the voices of the crew as they washed upstream. I run my gaze over the wound again, and then my feet have a mind of their own as I take a small step towards her. "Why do you keep doing this?" My jaw locks tight, the words sounding rougher than I meant them to. I try to soften the edges by reaching out to tip her chin up to face me.

She pulls out of my grasp, taking a step back. "Doing what?"

"Hiding your wounds?"

She's already squared her shoulders, defensive. "Because packs of predators turn on the weak, since feeding them will take from the strong."

Something twangs in my chest, and my brow pinches at her words. "You think I'll turn on you if I find you injured?"

She doesn't hesitate to answer. "I think your crew would."

Her words land, settling in my chest. I glance upstream to the men and women who work aboard my ship. Most are too busy bathing to pay attention to us, but there are a few sideways glances that come our way.

She's right. Some of the crew might take a blade to her throat if they thought she was too injured to slit theirs first, but that's the minority. The majority would help her, even if they didn't particularly like it. I hadn't let Otto treat her when she first came aboard but that was fear, and pride.

"Then let me help change that," I say, offering her a soft smile.

I pivot towards the tree line, gathering our clothes from where we'd thrown them. After shoving my legs into my trousers, I stride back to Odi. Her blouse is still damp when I press it into her hands. Then I turn my back, giving her the space to put it on.

"You can look now." Her voice is soft, like the ripples shimmering around us.

With my shirt still in my hand, I drop to my knees in front of her and begin to rip it into strips. She inhales a sharp breath at the first brush of my knuckles against her skin, which is warm despite the bumps from the breeze that dances around us.

Her sun-kissed thigh is soft, softer than I should notice, and my hands are too large—too clumsy, dwarfing the curve of her leg. Otto would be rougher, more clinical but I can't bring myself to treat her like a task. Not when she's hidden her wounds, cared for her aches in silence. So I move gently.

Once I've wrapped her thigh and pulled the cloth strip tight, I tie it into a knot. Her breath is steady, but I can feel her eyes on my hands. She's watching every movement, every brush of my fingers on her skin. It floods my body with warmth, sending it down to areas that I can't hide from her even if I try. I need to hurry before it shows.

I summon a singular talon, just long enough, to slice the leftover cloth free, then will it back into me. I look up at her. She swallows, and I swear I see moisture pooling at the corners of her eyes before she looks away.

"It would have been fine, but thank you," she murmurs.

A tiny part of my stubborn heart agrees. She's a pirate and I'm a bounty hunter—a prince—but the truth is, here on my knees, I know without a doubt that I would crumble for her.

"Rune!" Tavi's voice floats across the distance, breaking the tension between Odi and I. Clearing my throat, I stand and look in the direction of my crew. Tavi beckons me, so I toss a hand up to let her know I've seen her.

"Finish dressing, and I'll meet you back at the crew," I hum quietly, half expecting some sort of quip about not telling her what to do, but she nods, then turns her back as I walk towards those already gathered on the shoreline.

Tavi tosses me a fresh shirt as I approach, not even trying to hide her smirk.

"Is this Elio's?" I ask as I squeeze my arms through the straining fabric.

"No, it's an extra. It's at least two sizes too big for Elio."

The neck line feels like it's one wrong move from tearing, but I nod, knowing well enough to be grateful for any protection from the island's insects. "How's he doing?"

She jerks her head in the direction of my first mate, who's perched on a rock further up the hill. "He'll be fine, but the sooner we get back to the ship, the better."

Her eyes settle on something behind me. I hear Odelia before I feel her presence beside me.

"Is everyone alright?" she asks, her voice genuine.

Tavi, dips her head, the gold rings in her braids catching the light. "Yes, but we should keep moving."

"Everyone to me!" I let my voice ring out across the expanse. "If you've washed off the muck, gather your weapons. We have a temple to find."

Most of the crew spring into action, leaving a few still stumbling at the water's edge while rushing to dress. Odelia falls into step as I make my way over to Elio. "Are you going to be alright walking or do you want to head back to the ship?"

Elio scoffs as he stands with a little help from Tavi. "As if I'd let you have all the fun."

A smile spreads across my mouth. "You let me know the minute you need to rest."

He agrees, and we make our way back up the hill with the crew in tow. The landscape changes over time. Sand gives way to denser areas as we slash our way through tall grasses, thick vines and swampy reeds. Light filters differently, sharper, brighter as the sun reaches the highest peak, but my eyes never leave our surroundings. I won't lose anyone else.

A shrill cry echoes through the dense rainforest to the left.

Odelia freezes, her hand finding my forearm in a light grip. "What was that?"

I hold up my fist, silently commanding the others to stop as I listen for the sound again, acutely aware of the warmth on my arm. "Didn't sound too dangerous."

I glance down at Odi, who's already looking up at me, rolling her eyes. "You'll be eating those words when a monster leaps from the trees and devours us."

My eyes drift to her mouth then back to her. "Better hold on tight then."

She quickly pulls her hand back, like she's been stung, but I catch the flush rising in her cheeks and I can't help smiling.

The screech sounds again, but this time it's followed by movement in the tree tops. My hand rests on the hilt of my blade as I take a step forwards to investigate. The branches above rustle, quick and sharp. Then they burst open with a flurry of leaves and snapping twigs.

I see scales, and pull back before the creature has a chance to snap at me.

Drakelings.

Half-lizard, half-dragon and all attitude. They're small—no bigger than a full-grown rat—but they have speed on their side. Sleek-scaled bodies in a range of colours, blues, greens, purples and reds, with two pairs of fluttering wings on their backs that hum as they move, almost like the bees on the mainland—just bigger and less friendly.

Three of them hover in front of us, and I hear the catch in Odi's breath.

I move backwards slowly until my arm brushes hers. "See, I told you it wasn't dangerous."

"What are they?" she asks, wide eyed.

"Drakelings. They aren't aggressive—not unless you spook them or try to steal the eggs from their nests."

She pauses long enough that I turn to find a strange expression playing over her face. "Why do I want to pet it?"

I swallow a laugh. "I'd avoid it if you value your fingers. They'll bite hard enough to make you curse if they feel cornered. Some of the more wealthy landsmen post capture contracts, hoping to keep them as pets, but I never understood why."

Odi takes a step back, but I catch her wrist. "Don't move. They'll lose interest soon enough."

A dark, purple-scaled drakeling creeps closer, its wings twitching. I hear the gentle clink of weapons behind me as the crew freezes, watching the scene unfold. Odelia sucks in a breath, leaning her body towards mine.

The drakeling flicks its pupils over us as if it's sizing us up for a fight. It chirrs and flits around, before deciding that we're much too boring to look at and darts back into the tree tops, the other two hot on its heels.

I exhale, tension bleeding off my shoulders as I flick my gaze down to Odi. She blinks like she's just returned to her body so I give her arm a little nudge with mine. "Nosy little shits aren't they."

She swipes a glittering drakeling scale from the ground and grins, and I feel like my heart is going to explode from my chest at the sight of her. Then I huff softly, of course the pirate would snatch the shiny things. She almost reminds me of the cliff roosting sea birds that collect treasures for their nests. I look away when she looks back at me, pretending I wasn't watching. "Like someone else I know," she says, her voice pointed.

It's my turn to roll my eyes. "With me! Move out and mind the drakelings!"

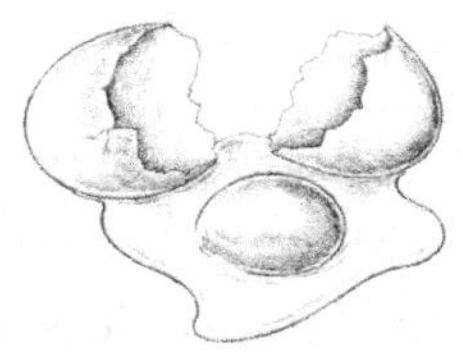

As the sun begins its descent we finally reach the tallest part of the island, and what awaits us down below is breathtaking. A forgotten temple, crumbling in places but still standing strong. It rests atop a mound, like the island has lifted it from the deep embrace of the sea and offered it to the sun.

A gentle breeze swirls around me, stirring my hair. I feel a presence beside me and look over to see Elio. His hazel eyes crinkle at the corners, squinting as he assesses the view. "Looks like that's been abandoned for quite some time."

"Like your bed."

He scoffs, folding his arms across his chest. "It gets more action than yours does."

A smirk plays on my lips. "You had Tavi worried there for a minute."

Elio sighs. It's a haunting sound, like he's fighting a silent battle and losing. "She'd never admit it out loud."

I flick my gaze to the woman who's like a sister to me. She stands tall and proud, a stern look upon her sharp features as she speaks with Odi, their attention on the temple ahead. I'd found her in a tavern five years ago, drinking alone. Two burly men had tried to pick a fight with her, but she flattened them both in seconds. I knew instantly she would be a part of my crew. There hasn't been one day since that I've regretted inviting her onto my ship.

Tavi has more stories in her to tell than I do scales. She's fierce and she is brave, but she's also a woman who longs to be loved, preferably by the male standing beside me, no matter that they've both taken more than their fair share of time coming around to it.

"Just don't go dying on her, eh?"

Hazel eyes find mine. "Hadn't planned on it."

As I look in their direction again, Tavi catches my eye, and with a simple nod we start down the side of the slope, making our way towards the ancient temple as our boots carry us through rapidly hardening ground, until beneath us is all rock.

It doesn't take us long to reach it, and as we all stand out the front, I wonder if we're at the right place. The temple is much smaller than I expected. I stare at it, unsure what to make of the place. No heavy gates. Just a crumbling structure with too much silence clinging to it.

Six statues stand on either side of the rotting path. Weather-worn figures, their features half erased by time, but not enough to fool me. Sirens. Twisting forms, cut from stone. The three on the left are male and the other three are female, all with tails and curling fins. Oddly enough they remind me of my sister Selene . . . and mother.

My heart pounds, sounding through my ears like a drum. Is it another clue? Have we stumbled on something sacred that has long been forgotten?

Footsteps crunch beside me. Odelia. She's piled her unruly locks on top of her head, exposing the delicate curve of her neck. She steps up, gaze locked on the temple. "No greater beast than a man's mind, and the fear that seeks to claim it." She speaks softly, just loud enough for me to hear.

The riddle.

I've been turning it over in my mind for the past few days, every angle, every word. It's not about claws and teeth this time. No beast in the dark. Just tricks. Illusions. Whatever this place is, it's meant to be a different sort of challenge.

"Better keep our wits about us," I murmur.

She turns to the crumbling figures beside us. "Friends of yours?"

With a light shrug I take a few steps towards the raised podiums, running my fingers over the cracking stone. "I don't know. There are a lot of older temples scattered beneath the water, most dedicated to the old ocean gods—those that drudge up islands or master the weather, like the Sotor. There are ones even older and as ruined as this, meant for worshiping the water elementals, though the practice isn't nearly as common as it used to be. They're a proud race, and tend to believe whatever the water touches belongs wholly to the sea, tribute or no. They must have made sure their treasures were well protected before they left."

Or so I figured. My mother's disappearance caused me to pour over the archives in the royal library even outside of my studies. There wasn't much but I found every scrap of parchment the archives had to offer. "What I wonder is why there would be a siren temple on land. The seabed shifts slowly, constantly. It could be that this was underwater, tens of thousands of years ago, but it would have been abandoned the moment it touched open air . . ."

Odi steps beside me to examine it, so close I can feel her warmth. Her fingers are painstakingly gentle as she runs a finger over the crack that splits the female siren's chest.

"It's all so beautiful." Her eyes meet mine across the short distance, and my heart falls from my chest, flopping about on the ground like a fish out of water.

Tavi flicks her gaze between us, and then scoffs lightly. "Alright everyone, follow me." She and the others move off towards the temple. Leaving Odi and I alone.

I gesture fowards, letting her lead the way.

She does, but speaks over her shoulder in a sing-song lilt. "Are you sure you don't want to tell me more about the riveting history of tens of thousands of years ago?"

I lift a brow at her retreating back before following, my steps much louder than hers. "History *is* important," I call, "especially to a prince. It's okay to admit you're lucky to have me along."

She tosses back a grin before we make it to the crew. "Perhaps I am."

The doorway ahead yawns like a broken, toothless mouth, carved stone giving way to shadows. I move through the crowd and pause at the entrance. "Before we head in, I need a small team of you to stand guard here at the door. Those willing, say aye."

A few hands shoot up, before the willing participants shuffle off to make a small barrier around the outskirts of the temple. "If we're not back by dawn, head to the ship. Don't wait for us."

With that settled, I turn my attention to the darkness behind me. Elio hands me a lit torch, then he gives one to Tavi. We step through one by one, boots echoing on slick stone, until the ground just—ends.

I catch myself before I go tumbling straight down. "Shit."

Elio produces another torch, smaller this time. He lights it on Tavi's before tossing it down into the darkness. I peer over the edge, thinking I'll watch the orange flames sink through the shadows for miles, but it only lasts a split second before it hits solid ground.

A pit, maybe ten feet deep, the stone worn smooth like too many leather soles have made the descent before us. Time and dampness have chewed at the edges, making the drop uneven. Cracks spiderweb out beneath the lip. Not a trap. Just ancient and forgotten.

"It's not too deep, just mind your step," I call over my shoulder.

Tavi drops down first, grunting as her boots hit the floor below. Elio starts to follow but I grasp his arm. "Perhaps you should stay here."

His lips press tight. He's never been one to stay behind. "Rune—Cap, I can handle it."

I drop my hand, biting back the words that dance on my lips. The images of him bleeding out somehow are vivid in my mind, but Elio has never been one to back down from a challenge.

I press my lips together to hold in any protest and nod, letting him move to the edge. He braces himself with one hand, landing with a soft curse.

The rest of the crew make their way down one by one until only Odi and I are left on the edge. I can see the unease in the way she fists her hands into the sides of her billowing trousers, but her face remains impassive.

"Me next," I yell down.

They make way for me, some even moving further into the shadows with their torches as they scan the surroundings.

I'm only airborne for a split second before my feet hit the solid stone. At times like these, I'm grateful for my father's height and that he passed it on to me. The top of the platform now sits roughly an arm's length above my head.

Odi paces at the lip. "It's farther than it looks."

I reach up towards her. "I've got you."

She hesitates, but only for a moment. As she sits on the edge ready to push off, I reach up and slip my hands around her waist. I feel the catch of her breath the moment I take hold of her before she bites the sound off with gritted teeth.

"I've got you," I softly remind her.

She nods once, her face hard, and then she leaps.

In one smooth movement, I swing her down from the ledge and place her feet gently on the ground. I keep my hold on her for just a second longer than necessary. Her hands grip my forearms, but she lingers too, her eyes skirting over my face. She still faintly smells of pears and honey, the scent batting away any other thought in my head.

Then she's gone, taking her warmth with her.

Good. I don't need the distraction.

The space opens up as we move deeper. The ceiling stretches higher, walls breathing wider. The stale air grows cooler, tinged with wet stone and something older—something faintly sweet, like rotting fruit.

Torchlight flickers across carvings etched into the walls. Some half-faded. Others are barely even visible. For once, not even I can make out what the markings might be.

We walk for a short amount of time before the pathway opens up. The crew comes to a stop behind me. No one dares to say a word.

Tunnels.

Dozens of them, branching out from a single chamber like ribs from a spine—jagged mouths leading in every direction, each one swallowed in darkness. No markings. No signs. Just cold, crumbling stone and choices we don't know how to make.

"Shit," Elio mutters. "Which way?"

No one answers.

Odelia stands beside me, arms crossed tight over her chest. I don't need to look at her to know her mind's already running through every path, every riddle, every lie this place might throw at us.

I scan the tunnels, one by one.

It's a gamble. But so is standing still.

And this place . . . it doesn't feel like the kind that rewards hesitation.

Two different beasts

18
ODELIA

"Everyone pair off."

Rune's voice is carefully neutral, but the fact that he wants us to split up at all makes my stomach flip. Tavi moves to Elio, and it's just Rune and me left when the others settle, passing torches to ensure each group has at least one. On the far side, someone coughs, wet and hacking, and I wince as the sound echoes off the jagged walls.

"Each group takes a section," Rune calls. "Don't go too far in at first. We scout and return with any information that might hint at where we're supposed to go." He gestures, sending them fanning across the chamber. Soon they're only visible in stark bits of torchlight across a lake of shadow.

When he turns to me, his smile is strained. "Looks like we're up."

Every tunnel in the section we take looks identical. I run the torch along the outside of the door, passing it silently to Rune so he can lift it over the archway. We fall into the routine of the movements, fingers brushing at every pass of the light, not daring to speak. The quiet here feels sacred.

Even whispers are punished, multiplied as they spirit off the walls like ghosts. Silence has always been a sanctuary for me, a hiding place. Here it's alive.

Waiting.

When we find nothing at the opening, we start with the first tunnel on one side. I count fifty paces till we turn back again, then we enter the next. And the next. It feels like hours in the dark, the flame reflecting off the runes in the walls, its smoke sitting low, clinging to my face and constricting my throat.

When we exit again, there's commotion in the main chamber. One of the men is hunched on the ground, two arrows embedded in his bicep.

"They came from the walls," his partner says.

"The arrows?" I ask. The bolts are heavy, but they look ancient, the wood splintered. It's a wonder the mechanism still worked.

"Dozens of them," the injured man grunts.

Rune kneels to check the arrow in his arm. "Someone go up top," he says, throwing his chin at another group standing nearby. "Have them make a lift to get him up."

"I'm fine," the man objects. "The wounds aren't deep. Just got stuck in the meat is all."

Rune ignores him, instead looking up at his first mate. "Elio, I want you to go back up too."

"Captain—"

"I'm not taking arguments, Elio. You're already injured. This is as far as you go. Leave the arrow spitting walls to those spry enough to get out of dodge."

I'm certain the words are meant to come out as playful, but Rune's face is too tight, and a muscle in Elio's jaw feathers before he opens his mouth to protest again. Old, familiar anticipation floods through me as the tension rises, preparing for violence. But Rune's voice just comes out quieter, as steadfast as I imagine mountains might be. "That's an order." He turns back to the men on the ground. "Which tunnel was it?"

"It—" The man hesitates, his eyes scouring the mess of identical tunnels before his shoulders fall. "I don't know."

Rune curses and stands, raking his hands through his hair as he moves away. I follow with the torch, and he doesn't turn to see if it's me before he tips his head back and speaks to the nothingness above us.

"I can't keep losing people, Odi."

I step in, trying and failing to keep my voice low enough the words won't catch on the stone and come back to me. "He's going to be fine—"

Rune finally turns, and the vulnerability in his eyes has two urges warring inside me: to step back, or to step into him, to be the tether that holds him above the raging of his thoughts. We're frozen, for a blink, the wound on my thigh throbbing with the memory of his careful hands. For a moment, I wonder if he'll call all of it off, go back on his word, ship me to Stonegallows for the trouble I've brought. Instead, he sighs heavily, resting his hands on his hips as he takes in the shadows of the tunnels.

"Captain," another pair calls from the fourth section. "We found something!"

It's a . . . frog creature. Like the ones we'd fought.

The faded etching lies just inside the tunnel, invisible from the outside.

Rune's eyebrows are pinched as he studies it, his arms glistening with the strange humidity that suffocates everything else in here. "I can't decide if it's a good sign or a bad sign."

"Is this the only one?" I ask a man I recognize as one of the night crew, Jortan.

Rune directs the others on a targeted search, and an hour later we've found only four tunnels have small carvings—an amphibious monster, a curling centipede, a vine of pinwheeled flowers—and a coral-studded sea dragon.

"So we start with them," I say, trying to hide my growing claustrophobia.

Rune nods. "It's the only difference we can tell so far, besides the dead ends, arrows, and the one that's caved in and leaking water."

"You don't think it hints at what we'll have to face, do you?" I could do without ever encountering a giant knife-legged bug again.

"Here," he asks, "or as we find the keys?"

"Either?"

He doesn't answer, his jaw feathering as he mulls over the question. My eyes rest on the final icon. Sea dragons are more myth than anything. Aren't they?

We're interrupted by those looking for orders, and he directs most to stay, selecting three other pairs for the marked tunnels, reminding them if they come across traps or get wounded to trace their steps back. I follow him towards a tunnel slightly left of centre, palming the hilt of the bone dagger that's still sheathed at my waist.

He stops and brandishes an arm, inviting me forwards in an absurdly prince-like fashion. "Since this island had the frogs, we'll start with this one."

I pass him, the wariness balanced by relief to finally be making headway. I'm not afraid of the dark, but the narrow space sets me on edge. "Last one there's a rotten sea slug," I sigh as he follows, bearing the torch high. For a hundred paces, the walls are straight and unchanging, but the ground slants down as the walls start to curve, and the air shifts. Stales.

Goose flesh rises on my arms. "How long do you think it's been since anyone has been in here?"

"There's no way to know. I supposed we'd have to wonder how old the map itself is."

I trail my fingers over the rough walls as we walk. "You think the map is as old as the temple?"

He shrugs. "I think it would be close. No one has seen an elemental map for hundreds of years."

"Will any of the ocean's temple goers be grateful it's been discovered?"

"Some." His voice is careful. "I mentioned earlier it would have been abandoned the moment it touched open air. A portion are incredibly dedicated to the old gods, so the fact that this one is above water now won't sway them. With any luck, the map's treasure will hold all sorts of relics. They would be the true prize, when compared to your glittering things."

I grin. "Well you're welcome to them. I've no use for—" The ground falls away, and I gasp, jerking Rune's arm to stop him from moving forwards. It's another drop. A sweep of the torch reveals it's about the same as in the main chamber. Rune is already lowering himself to the edge.

"Are you sure we'll be able to get back up?"

"I'm sure," he says, landing lightly and laying the torch on its side before lifting his arms up to help me down. I find it too easy to relent, bracing my hands on his forearms while his fingers wrap firmly around my waist. He sets me down so gently I don't feel it in my injured leg—then he doesn't let go. His warmth draws me closer, and without thought, I slide the tips of my fingers over the heat of his arms, firmly aware of the stone wall at my back and how it might feel to be pressed into it, the cool rock holding me steady against his relentless need.

I blink, nearly overtaken by a consuming, heady adrenaline.

His eyes are molten in the torchlight. His grip tightens for a breath, as if he can anticipate my sudden urge to flee.

"Rune—"

He yanks me closer, slamming my chest into his. His grip is like iron, and I melt for it, every part of me going limp with relief. I lift my face to his, the blaze low in my stomach greedy now, insistent.

But he twists me away, his fingers hooking painfully into my side as he whips his sword out with the other hand. The rock clangs, the steel screaming in my ears in angry echoes.

Then silence.

He picks up the torch, and holds it over the body of a reptilian creature with a stinger on its tail. It's strangely flat, the colour of dark stone. It had to have been completely silent, invisible in the dark.

"It was waiting on the wall," he says, his chest heaving.

My heart pounds too, my emotions somersaulting over themselves. "How did you see it?" The tunnel is pitch black where the torch doesn't reach.

"Darkvision,' he says. "I assumed you would have it too." His eyes sweep over the flush in my face. I don't know what else he sees. "Perhaps I should lead from here?"

I nod, swallowing, letting my face fall to hide the embarrassment that snakes up my spine.

The silence envelopes us again. The walls shine, weeping puddles onto the floor.

"Salt water," Rune says. I don't ask him how he can tell.

Time retreats, replaced by subtle changes in the rock around us. The etchings disappear, then the smooth finish roughens to natural stone. Bits of it litter the pathway. I'm careful to avoid the added noise, but Rune crunches over them, the sound like a beast grinding bones in its teeth.

"Do you have to do that?" I ask, after the third time.

"Do what?" He doesn't look at me, but his smile betrays him. He's *bored.*

"Goad me in whatever way you must in order to get my attention? Any stinging lizard within a league will know where—" I gasp. He's stopped, the toes of his boots peeking over the edge of where the floor drops away. Again. "Why does it keep doing that?"

"I have a theory. But I hate being wrong, so better hold onto it for now." He moves to sit, dangling his legs like he's going to lower himself down.

"Wait!" Something about this one does feel different. Like a weak branch, or a predator on the wind. "Can you see the bottom?"

"Yes—hmm." He sweeps the torch at his feet, peering down hard.

"No, actually." His brow scrunches. "There's a lip at about the same distance down as the others, but it drops off again after. I'll go down and check before helping you follow."

I'm already shaking my head. My limbs nearly vibrate with pent up tension. My legs want to spring, but I wrestle my voice into annoyed resignation. "Just hold on."

I take the torch and leave him in the dark as I retrace our steps, grabbing a few of the loose stones. When I return, he's laid back on the ground, eyes closed, his hands laced behind his head. The torchlight illuminates him slowly at first, then all at once. His shirt is lifted, exposing the taut strip of skin just above the waist of his trousers.

"Enjoying yourself?"

I snap my attention away and move to the edge. When he sits up, I lift an arm and arc two of the stones into the void.

One. Two. Three. Four—

My eyes widen as Rune's face twists with concern.

There's a splash below. Faint.

"At least I know how to swim?" he says to my unimpressed look. The drop has to be at least a hundred feet.

Both our faces glisten with a sheen of sweat. "You were going to a watery grave—"

"There was a lip!"

"You would have taken a single step and fallen in."

"Oh, Odi, I'm flattered you care—"

"With our only *torch.*"

He barks a laugh as he stands, but his eyes catch behind me in a way that has me spinning, dagger already drawn.

"What is it?"

"A ledge," he says. "Horrible things really. I'm not sure your borrowed blade will be quite enough to save us."

I ignore him, peering harder into the shadow. The light falls on a hint of narrow pathway barely cleaving to the wall. The light doesn't reach the other side.

"We'd be walking blind."

He breezes past me. "Let me go first. Once I find the other side I'll come back for you."

"I'm not *waiting,*" I hiss. Waiting is an invitation for things more terrible than mere reality. In my minds eye, we'd both die a hundred deaths before he could cross, and a hundred more as he returned again, the constant threat of bitter, forgotten stone giving way beneath him propelling me into thoughts more horrifying than acid-tongued toad creatures that could be banished with a well-timed sword.

No greater beast than a man's mind, and the fear that seeks to claim it.

The riddle's warning all but says if terror lies in wait, we're going the right way. "Together, then."

I pass him the torch, following close behind as he moves to the wall. His feet overlap the ledge as he stands with his back to the stone and begins to inch sideways. One misplaced step and we'll be down. Maybe we'd survive the fall, if we hit the water right, but something tells me we'd be stuck treading in stagnant darkness until our bodies finally gave out. If we were lucky enough to not get eaten.

Once he's an arm's length down, I press into the damp-streaked stone. The animal inside me panics, finally overwhelmed by the dread of the tunnels, but caught fast in the trap of my human mind. There's no time to do more than lock her down before she gets us killed. She quiets, muzzled, restrained by years of practice and the wall I've built between us.

We move, slowly, until the start of our path is swallowed by darkness, until nothingness surrounds us on all sides, the torch cocooning us in a bubble of light. The fear in me turns to deadly silence. Everything in me turns to silence. A sanctuary of unfeeling. This is where Nisse reigns. Where blood sprays warm on my face and intolerable weakness means a quick death.

Rocks tumble from under Rune's feet, and we freeze, waiting to hear them fall. A couple seconds later, they shatter over stone. "Multiple levels, then," he quips, as if both our muscles aren't on fire with coiled energy. Sweat drips down my neck, into my eyes, the air so tight in my lungs I fear I'll be dizzy soon.

"Fascinating."

For the first time since we started, he turns back to look at me, his lips pressed tight. "Watch your step here. It may be a stretch for you." He lifts his long legs across the gap easily, but he's right; I'll have to leap. On the other side, he turns and points the torch towards where the ledge has crumbled away. Even the rock under his feet is cracked and tired.

"Back up," I say, shooing him with a small wave of my hand. "This path isn't meant for giants."

"You think I'm giant, little doe?" He smiles, but it doesn't reach his eyes. He's worried, trying to distract us both.

"I *know* you're giant." Two can play at this game. For distraction. "You were kneeling naked before me hours ago. Not to mention you have a habit of wearing soaking wet pants." I leap as he laughs, not giving either of us a chance to think. Loose rock slips under the first foot that lands. The second lands true, but the damage is already done. Gravity sinks its claws into my chest, and I feel the moment of no return. Sinister darkness threatens below, concealing the death that waits in the form of concealed stone. My lungs seize, heart leaping into overdrive, sprung free from my rigid focus.

There's a moment of weightlessness.

Then an impact to my chest slams me against the wall. Pain flares through my head, sharp. Bloody iron floods my mouth. Rune's citrus scent is close, but my vision is blurred. Then the ground is moving, crumbling. Rocks fall, echoing as if it were a rain of cannon fire.

"Odi—" His grip is on me, launching me around him, pushing me down the other side. "Run!"

I blink, shuffling sideways even as my eyes struggle to focus. Blood pounds in my head in waves of pain. But the word lives in me, and my feet move like they've waited a lifetime for me to let them.

Run.

More rocks fall, but I don't stop. I feel him behind me, imagine the soaked stone giving way beneath him.

"Jump!" he shouts. But I don't see the end, not with a guttering torch and the weak vision of my human form. He should have gone first. Shouldn't have pushed me ahead where my reluctance to trust could kill us both.

The rock wavers beneath my feet and I leap, every hope and dream of freedom I've ever had suddenly small against the desperate will to live that floods through me as I'm airborne for a half second. The opposite side isn't kind when I land, full body into solid rock, catching me by my ribs and hip and sending a razor sharp pain through my injured leg.

I open my eyes to darkness.

And silence.

"Rune!"

The scream rips my throat, echoing in the inky black, fading into ripples, then into quiet again. The torch is gone. There's stone everywhere my hands can reach, but I can't see. I can't *see.*

"Here." The word is a grunt. Relief drowns common sense as I turn and scramble towards him on all fours, one hand slipping into nothingness. I gasp and pull back, then gingerly feel along the uneven edge.

"Where?"

"Just back up. Don't come this way." His voice is strained, and the pain in it ricochets through my insides, swirling the darkness into vivid nightmares.

"Fuck you, Rune." I crawl along the edge until my hands find his, the worry having turned to anger in a breath. He's hanging off the ledge, holding on with the strength of his fingers. I'm tired of his constant masochistic need to martyr himself. I'm tired of him throwing himself into danger at every turn. For saving me when I don't deserve it.

He grunts, and I hear his arm slap down on the ground. "Fuck me yourself."

I laugh, and sit back, then a pair of useless, quiet tears streaks down my face, the relief bubbling over. "I won't be able to pull you up."

"You don't have to." He pants, but another strained breath later his head is nearly in my lap. I raise on my knees and wrap my arms into his, tugging with all my might. Then his leg is up and he propels himself forwards, falling over me as we go. He catches himself with an arm, his chest brushing mine as it heaves between us. His shirt is gone, and I wonder if he can tell how my nipples harden under his weight. I can see nothing, but I don't flinch when something gentle and sharp traces the drying streaks my tears left behind.

"You shifted." It's not a question. It's instinct. The change is subtle, the difference between a kitchen knife and blood-soaked blade but impossible to miss, even in the dark.

"Half-shifted." The words spirit over my cheek, down my neck, slinking low to the heat that already grows between my legs. "It isn't easy to hold onto out of water, but it can help with strength and speed, for a time." He pauses as I strain my eyes, trying hard to see his face, then rolls off of me, to his back, sprawling on the ground. "You should give it a try."

The thought pinches something in my chest. "I wouldn't know where to start."

"We've got time."

It's strange to know my eyes are open, staring sightlessly ahead. I scan from side to side, but there isn't even a hint of light. "You mean because our way back just disintegrated?"

"I bet you got top marks in pirate school."

I kick his leg and he throws his knee back at me, but doesn't pull away, letting it rest on my thigh.

"You can still full shift. Your other form might have better sight in the dark."

Oh. Shit. It does. The moment he says it I know it's true. She'd see even better than regular animals, thanks to a brush of magic. But I can't let her out here, not when she's so prone to fear. "She won't like it," I murmur.

"She?"

"My other form."

His voice turns peculiar. "So . . . you?"

"No." I shake my head, ignoring the pain that rocks back and forth in my skull. For some reason it's easier to speak into the inky haze. Like everything else is gone. "She's not me. I can't even keep control of her now. We're . . . two different beasts."

"And . . . you never wanted to learn?" He says it like the war in me is unnatural.

Ivor's voice rings through my head as clearly as if he were here. *You keep that animal off my ship. Can you blame a starving man for his hunger? And now he's dead. We are predators, Nisse. That creature cannot be who you are. Not anymore.*

"It doesn't matter," I whisper into the darkness.

His clothes jostle beside me. He's standing, I think. "Well," he sighs, "if you decide you'd like to actually be helpful, you know what to do." His steps are quiet as he moves away, his voice turning more playful as the distance grows. "It would probably be a better idea to leave you here, honestly, since I may very well have to carry you if we continue like this."

I stand, following him blindly as his steps fade into nothing. "Rune." My heart hasn't even had time to recover from the stress of our near fall. It thunks tiredly in my chest, failing to summon enough panic to rile me. I cross my arms as I walk, testing each step before trusting it. "Rune!"

I hit a wall and feel my way along. He's still here. I know it. He wouldn›t leave me. The weight of his predator's attention is too heavy to mistake for anything else—he's watching, trying to bait me into shifting. The wall opens, and my stomach leaps into my throat as it disappears. The ground feels solid, though. Another tunnel.

"Straight shot from here," he purrs into my ear, sending breath down my neck and my heart leaps at last, adrenaline spearing to every sensitive part of me. "Are you shifting, or am I going to have to hold your hand?"

I ignore the shiver that courses through me, instead squaring my shoulders to continue past him, ignoring how impossible it feels when I can't see my own feet. The darkness eats everything. One wrong step and another hole in the ground may swallow me whole. Already, part of me fights for the shift, desperate to be able to see what lies waiting in the dark.

"*Savage seas,* Odi" Rune says from my other side, spooking me again. "Just shift already."

"Fine," I spit, frustration uncaging the panicked animal. The moment it's free, I lose every shred of control. The strange feeling of unmaking passes through me in a blink, drawing me closer to the ground, lengthening my arms and snout, and then the fear has me and I'm sprinting, seeing the tunnel in abstract shades of grey—but I *can* see. Rune curses and sprints after me, the sound and overwhelming salty ocean scent of him spurring me to flee faster, whirling around the tunnel's curve, shying and kicking out as the moving trickle of water on one side tricks me into ever more surprised fear.

"Odelia!"

The shout crashes around my sensitive ears like clamping jaws. I can't stop. I can't ever stop. There's too much behind me, things I'll never escape. Not least of all the towering male with razor claws and flesh-ripping teeth, whose voice echoes through my body in ways that it shouldn't.

There's a wall far ahead. I swing my head from side to side, looking for where the tunnel must split off. Something beneath me slips, a rock depressing beneath my hoof, but I'm past it in a blur, then the plunk of bolts hitting the rock walls clatters behind me, the air hissing as one barely misses my rump. Then the dead end ahead begins to slowly slide open.

Too slowly. I'm going to break my neck crashing into it. My hooves slip on the stone, tangling as I try to pull back.

"Odi!"

The hunter's voice sounds far away, nearly drowned out by the bolts that continue to shoot from the walls at my back.

I miss the door by a breath before finally tumbling to a stop, unable to catalogue all the aches that flare as my mind finally quiets. I stand and shake, my barreled chest heaving. I feel the strange twitch of my snout as it adjusts to the sudden scent of dust-choked stone.

This room is different—and well lit. Glowing crystals are set in the centre of each wall, bookended by rectangular holes carved high up in between. The cave feels natural, but it's unmistakable how it's been smoothed and shaped. An altar sits in the centre, bearing the same symbol on the map. It's raised, like a golden pyramid of steps, and crowned by a small box.

I startle as the stone door begins to slide closed again. Thundering footsteps pound beyond it, and Rune slides in as gracefully as I did, surprising me into throwing my head up and prancing away. He groans, laying still for long enough that I put my head down, turning one eye on him. The blue of his scales is vibrant, alternating in shades I'd never noticed before, colours that may not even have names.

"I had to wait for the arrows to stop," he explains between breaths. "You're fast." From the ground, he turns his head towards me and pokes out his bottom lip. "And *so* cute," he says, drawing out the words, as if he were Otto speaking to his quail.

I flick my ears, tempted to sink a hoof into his chest, but the wicked sharp of his claws keeps me away.

"That it?" he asks, nodding to the altar as he stands.

I swing my head up, bringing the golden steps into focus. The symbol is carved into the tier below the box, which waits for us. The next piece of the key. The thought allows me enough focus to return to my human form. Between one blink and the next, I shift, settling into my body like I've moved from the buoyancy of water to the gravity of land.

"Don't you dare," I say, taking a few quick, wobbling steps before catching myself on the raised platform. My legs feel like jelly, but I don't know if it was the sprint or the shift. The lid on the box lifts easily, and I reach in, scooping out another circular piece and stashing it in the wrap of my breasts. "I think I'll be holding on to this one."

Rune's eyes sparkle with challenge. "And you're so certain I wouldn't risk fetching it later?"

With the thrill of victory coursing through my veins, it's easy to croon, "You could try."

"I may not be able to resis—"

The top of the altar sinks into itself with a foreboding thunk and our attention shoots that way.

The tense silence is overwhelmed by a rumble. A wall on the far side grinds against the floor, pulling back like an invitation. When it stops, I look at Rune, expecting triumph. It must be our way out, but his fin-like ears are twitching, his scaled forearms rippling as he grips his fists tight.

"You know how you hate water?" he says grimly, his eyes locked out of focus.

My heart drops to the cave floor. "What?"But I hear it—a tell-tale roar. Familiar and terrifying. Faint at first, then growing, screaming louder with every heartbeat that passes.

The holes in the walls erupt, but I'm already moving. Rune is beside me, his arm wrapped around my waist like he can urge me faster than the voice that chants in my head.

Run.

Run.

Run, little doe.

The temple is filling with water.

The coffin lid

19
RUNE

Of course this *gods-forsaken* place would be filled with mechanisms of self-destruction should someone take the temple's prized possession. I should have guessed it from the start, but I'd been too busy trying to keep me and Odi alive.

Or perhaps I'd been too distracted trying to keep my hands off her.

Her heartbeat pounds against my chest. *Ba dum, ba dum, ba dum*—solid and unrelenting. I don't blame her for being afraid, I am too. Not for myself, I was born in water. No, my fear is reserved for my crew. All I can do is hope that they all made it out before the water began to rise.

The tunnel opens into another room, and Odi's breath catches beside me. "Rune . . . the water—"

My gaze flicks to the floor as I release the grip I have on her waist. The salt water is up to our knees now and quickly rising, pouring in from the top of the room as well as seeping in from somewhere underground.

I turn to her, searching for her face in the dark. My vision isn't quite as good as it might be underwater, but I know she can't see a thing. Her eyes are unfocused, her brow creased, teeth catching on her lower lip as her gaze flicks desperately around the room, searching for light. She can't even shift—her deer form would be more hindrance than help here. I have to get us out.

"We need to work together. Hands on the walls. You go left I'll go right, yell out when you find something," I call above the rising waters.

"But Rune—" Odi hisses, not bothering to mask the panic on her face now.

I lay a hand on her arm gently and squeeze, trying to offer her some sort of reassurance. "Stick to the walls. If you feel anything unusual, call out and I'll find you."

She nods, her unfocused gaze resting a little too far to the left of my face, then begins to move away, running her palms over the smooth stone surface. I move right. The walls are dripping with water, and all I can hope is I don't come across one of those lizard-like creatures we'd encountered earlier.

It feels like we search for hours, but I know it's only been minutes, if that. The water rises to my mid-thigh now, which means it will be at Odi's hips soon. We need to find a door.

"Anything?" I yell across the room as I keep searching.

"Nothing!" Odi's voice is muffled by the sound of rushing water.

Shit.

This can't be the end. I didn't come all this way, risk so much, just to live the rest of my days inside a maze of water.

Worse, I'd have to watch Odi drown.

I can't let her die. Not when she and the map are the only link I have left to my mother.

"Rune, there's something here!" Odi cries out.

I spin around, searching for her silhouette in the inky shadows. She's across the room.

Her dark brown eyes look towards my face as I wade towards her, and even though I doubt she can see me, I offer a smile. "What did you find?"

She runs her hand over the wall. "It's a perfectly cut stone sticking out. It seems to be the only one here."

I lean over her shoulder, feeling for it. "How do we know it won't open a trap door and release a whole bunch of flesh eating piranhas?"

Her shoulders lift and fall, brushing my chest. "Do we have a choice?" The strain in her voice is evident. As the water rises, so does her fear, pronounced in the whites of her eyes.

"I'm willing to risk it if you ar—"

She doesn't even let me finish before she slams her hand against the stone. It gives way with ease. At first nothing happens, we just stand there, both of us holding our breath. I almost suggest searching again, perhaps it's just a loose stone.

Then a vibration tingles my hand that rests on the wall, and travels up my arm. My shadowed darkvision allows me to catch the wall to the left of the stone shifting sideways. "There's a crack here," I call to Odi. She grips my arm as I lead us to it.

The water is up to her chest, which is rising and falling with intensity. "Will we fit?"

I measure the gap by fanning out my arm. It's going to be a tight squeeze—for me at least, but we have no other choice. "I'll go first."

Odi steps in behind me so I reach back to grab her hand. At first it's stiff, but then her fingers relax, curling around mine. Her touch sends a ripple of pleasure up my spine and my mind drifts back to that moment when I was on the ledge—fingers aching, holding on for dear life.

She'd cried.

In the dark, when she thought no one could see, she let it spill. Quiet, raw. And I can't help wondering what else she's wept for in the shadows, when the world's back was turned.

Something in my chest had cracked open then, sharp and deep, and I knew—

I never wanted to be the reason her tears fell.

We leave the roar of water behind us, but its absence doesn't mean it's stopped—only that it's climbing unseen, in the narrow crack we're wedged between. The stone presses close on either side, forcing me to shuffle sideways, shoulders scraping, careful not to let the jagged rock snag my clothes.

Odi squeezes my hand. "Can you see anything up ahead?"

"Not yet." I can't even turn back to her or risk scraping my nose.

Pear and honey wash over me as she presses closer into my back. "I hate wet wraps in my boots," Odi mutters.

A chuckle escapes my lips. "As soon as we get out of here we'll dry them by the fire. Then it's off to the next island."

"I never want to see the ocean again."

This time the laughter that bubbles up erupts and echoes off the walls, ricochetting between us. "Probably should change job titles then. Perhaps something land based?"

Odi doesn't answer, but it's too narrow for me to face her so I keep my focus ahead, and the grip on her hand firm.

The space seems endless, and the monotony of our steps allows my thoughts to dance across my mind. She'd moved so effortlessly when she shifted into her deer form, but her animal took over—controlled her, causing her to bolt. For a moment I wondered if I'd be able to keep up with her agile twists and turns, or if I'd lose her for pushing her to that point.

I'd meant well. I thought inexperience had stifled her confidence. I've met plenty of shifters, and no one has ever talked like that—*She won't like it.*

She.

It sits in the back of my mind. Gnawing. What in the *savage seas* does she mean she's *not* her? As if her beast is a stranger she's forced to drag along.

Over the trickle of water seeping down the walls, I hear Odi's sharp intake of breath. "I swear something just touched my leg."

Heat travels over me. The last thing we need is some creature taking a chunk out of our flesh. But I still don't see where the tunnel might open ahead. Her grip in mine is squeezes tighter, and my own concern manifests as it always does—distraction.

"Sorry, I can't control where it goes, these pants are too tight."

"Rune—" Odi hisses, but there's a little less strain in her voice.

I squeeze her hand back, and hers loosens, like she only just realised how hard she was clinging.

A faint flicker of light winks at me through the black. Finally. It could be the main tunnel. Could be the crew, or a way out.

"There's an orange glow up further."

Odi's warm, relieved breath brushes my arm. We push on, shuffling through the narrow throat of rock until it finally spits us out into open space. My boots slide on slick stone as we spill into the chamber.

I suck in a breath and release it, along with the tension in my shoulders. The glow is brighter now, licking shadows up the walls above us, but it isn't sunlight, or the crew. "Fuck."

Odi whirls to face me. I can see her clearer now. "What is it?" she asks, her brow pinching.

"It's the torch we dropped earlier. We made it back to where the floor dropped out, but we're further down." I mutter.

She twists, turning her attention to the glow that rests on the thin ledge halfway down the far wall. It's only slight, but I catch the way her shoulders drop in disappointment.

Not an exit.

The orange light's enough to see the rest—the dark water creeping higher, kissing the edges of the rock floor, inch by inch. The sound of it is slow, deliberate, like it knows we've only got so much time.

I finally release her hand, moving across the room towards the flame. The absence of her warmth doesn't sit well with me. I want to spin around and find my place beside her again, but I won't let this room be our coffin. "We need to get up on that ledge."

The water ripples, and then Odi is beside me. "But we've already been up there."

"Exactly, it will take us back to the main chamber," I say with as much confidence as possible.

She shakes her head. "It's the first place anyone stuck here would try to get out. You really think they didn't design this place with a trap for that? That passage is probably sealed by now."

I fold my arms across my chest, glancing down at her. "And what if it's not?"

Her brow lifts, her arms mimicking mine. "And what if it is? We waste time, we burn what air we've got left, and we're right back where we started."

I don't have the answers, but I don't want her to think I have doubts. There's no room for that here. Doubt will get us killed. "Then we'll have to come back this way?"

"And hope the temple hasn't decided to slam that door in our faces too?"

A gentle sigh escapes my lips. "I'm not asking you to like it. I'm asking you to trust me."

Odi runs her gaze over me, lingering on my mouth before she spins on her heel and walks towards the torch holding ledge. "How are we even going to get up there? Not even you're tall enough."

I glance about the room assessing my options, which are next to none. I hadn't noticed it when we first came in but now my eyes land on some thick roots growing from the cracks in the stone wall like bones from a giant tree. "We will climb them. You can get on my back."

She shakes her head. "This is a bad idea, Rune."

I spread my arms out wide. "Or . . . we can just wait until the water rises and swim up there if you like?" It wouldn't take long, but it would seal away any other options if she's right.

"Fine, just hurry up," she says, her voice doing little to hide her concerns.

A small grin rolls across my face. I didn't think she'd like that option. Though I can't help but wonder if that's exactly how the temple was designed to be used.

I move to the boney roots where Odi waits for me. "Get on," I tell her, crouching low.

There's a beat of hesitation, then her legs hook around my waist, snug and warm, her arms sliding around my neck. She's lighter than she looks, but strong—the kind of grip that says if she's not holding a weapon, she'll become one. The press of her thighs is distracting in ways I don't dare to admit right now, and in the dark, I'm glad she can't see the grin tugging at my mouth. If I recall, she had her legs wrapped around me once before, but this time she's not trying to kill me—thankfully.

We climb, my boots finding holds in the damp rock, her weight shifting with every pull upward. When we haul ourselves over the lip at the top, I let out a sharp breath. "See? Totally fine."

Odi slides off my back, her boots echoing off the stone ground as she lands. She tucks a few damp, loose strands of hair back into the pile on top of her head before she stoops to collect the glowing torch off the ground. A stone shifts strangely beneath it. "You're luc—"

That's when the sound hits—low at first, then a deafening roar. The ground trembles beneath us.

I don't think. I just grab her, swing us both towards the drop, and leap. We hit the water which is now up to my hips and I shove us under the ledge's lip just as a wall of water crashes through, pounding the chamber. The once lit torch now doused and floating away.

Through the spray, she twists her head towards me. "What were you saying?"

I roll my eyes, holding us in place against the surge. "Well, what do you suggest we do?"

"There has to be a tunnel somewhere."

The water keeps rising. And she might be right—but finding it before she drowns is another thing entirely.

I refuse to give in to that nagging pull of fear clawing at the edges of my mind. The riddle says it plain—*No greater beast than a man's mind, and the fear that seeks to claim it.*

I won't let it take me.

Not the fear of never making it out.

Not the fear of never seeing my crew again.

Not the fear of dying without answers about my mother's disappearance. And sure as hell not the fear of leaving wet wraps inside Odi's boots. With her brain, and my brawn. We can do this. But the water is rising faster than I can think. "Wait here. Hold onto the root. I'm going to shift and see if my darkvision can find us a way out of here."

Odi's eyes grow wider in the darkness, and I notice the bob in her throat. I offer her a reassuring smile before I turn, but before I can dive into the water, she's caught me by the wrist.

"Rune, wait—"

Without thinking, I reach out and brush my thumb over her chin, barely grazing her bottom lip. "I'll only be gone for a moment."

The usual determination and fierceness return to her eyes, like she suddenly remembers who she is, and she nods once. Then I'm gone. Diving head first into the swirling waters. The cold hits like a slap as I swim down, gills behind my ears filtering the oxygen into my lungs. My skin prickles, bones reshaping, webbing stretching between my fingers. Claws sharpen, teeth lengthen, and my vision cuts through the murk like it's nothing.

I push deeper, scanning the jagged walls until I spot it—a thin crack, just wide enough to promise something on the other side. Loose stones shift in the current, the edges crumbling like old bread.

A surge of water shoves past me, dragging a thick branch along. I snatch it before it's gone, jamming the end into the gap and wrenching at the weakest points. Stone gives way with a dull crunch, bits swirling off into the dark. I dig harder, faster, until the hole yawns just wide enough for me to squeeze through.

It's the way out. Has to be.

With a powerful flick of my tail, I return to Odi. I find her clinging to the roots, worry creased on her brow.

"Take my hand," I call above the rushing water.

She focuses her attention on trying to find my claws stretching for her in the dark. For a moment I think she's going to shake her head, and retreat back under the ledge, but she doesn't. She entwines her fingers in mine, fitting us together like puzzle pieces.

With a grin, I pull her close. "Now, it's not too deep yet but we're going to have to swim under the water for a moment."

Odi musters a smile into the dark, but I know it's only to distract me from the fear written across her face. "Lovely. Just don't let go, yeah?"

I pull her closer. "Wouldn't dream of it."

She takes in a deep breath, and then we dive. The force of the water swirls around us at first, dragging at the billowing fabric of her clothes, but I push through, swimming with one arm around Odi's waist until it catches us. We reach the hole, which has grown larger with the churning current. Water sucks through like the stones were the plug and I've unclogged the drain. I pull Odi tighter into my arms, shift back into my human form and brace for impact.

The current shoves us through. We're spat out into open air, tumbling blind until gravity takes over. We drop—hard.

I twist mid-fall, slamming my back against the stone floor with a bone-jarring thud. Air punches from my lungs and I grit my teeth against the pain, trying not to let it show. All that matters is that Odi's safe. She's still in one piece, sprawled across me. Drenched dark hair sticks to my face, her heartbeat hammering against my ribs.

The water rushes past, hissing into the shadows, leaving us dripping in the sudden, echoing quiet.

"You all right?" My voice is rough, half-growl, half-breath.

She nods, but doesn't move, and for a second I'm not sure if it's relief or something else keeping her pressed against me.

With a groan, she finally rolls off onto the moist stone surface, and we both just stare up at the ceiling for a moment. Odi's chest heaves in and out as she drags air into her lungs. I stay still beside her, offering her some form of stability. Only when her breaths become quiet do I suggest getting up. I was lying when I called her a wet dog before. The woman is breathtaking when she's drenched.

The chamber is sealed above us, but through the darkness I can see the outline of a tunnel on the other side of the room. Odi's attention is locked on it too. The only thing separating us from the opening . . . is the giant, glowing pool stretched lazily across the expanse.

"I'm so over water," I murmur to Odi beside me. I may be a siren, born of the seas, but even I've had my fill.

She looks up at me, a small smile tugging at her lips. "Tragic. What will the waves do without your endless brooding?"

Now is not the time to be looking at her lips, but I can't help it. "I could brood less if you stopped giving me reasons to," I say, flashing her a grin of my own.

She rolls her eyes as she takes a step towards the edge of the pool, but not before I catch the flick of her gaze to my lips. The blue glow bounces off her skin, making her look as if she's a creature from another realm. "Will it never end?"

I step up beside her. "I could carry you if you like?"

She tilts her head up to meet mine. "Thanks, but I do know how to swim."

I shrug lightly. "The offer is there."

The glow of the water is plenty that I don't need to use my darkvision, and Odi can see well enough. My eyes search the surface of the water, looking for signs of life. Danger. Anything that might think we are its next meal, yet I find nothing unusual. It's just a deep pool—too still compared to all the other chambers we've encountered.

"Shall we?" I usher my hand towards the edge.

Odi nods before she crouches down and slips her feet into the water. I don't think. I just dive head first, shifting the moment my hands break the surface. As I come up, Odi is already treading water waiting for me.

I offer her a wink. "Last one to the other side is a rotten sea slug."

She huffs, and takes off swimming, splashing water in my direction as she passes by. The loose fabric of her clothes weigh her down and get in the way, stealing her momentum, but she pushes harder. For a moment I release a breath, allowing myself to hope this is the way out.

We're halfway across when something catches my eye—a flicker of silver glinting beneath the surface. It's nothing, I tell myself. A rock. Lost treasure perhaps. Or just my mind playing tricks.

"You know what I'd like to know, little doe?" I say, keeping my tone light. "Whether that key is still tightly secured."

Odi glares at me mid-frog-stroke. "For your information, it is."

"Oh good. Can't have you losing a piece."

"It's not me you should be—"

Her words break off in a sharp scream. I spin, just in time to see the silver ripple in the water where something's nipped her leg. I grab her, hauling her tight against me and striking for the ledge, but the water ahead churns.

I focus my gaze to cut through the surface and find the predators below. Shapes circle—dozens of them. Sleek bodies, rows of teeth flashing like broken glass.

Gnashies.

Flesh eating fish with blades for fins. A species so old that I didn't even know they still existed. Last I'd heard of them they lived in the deepest depths of the ocean, preferring the darkness to any forms of light.

Odi's arms clamp around my neck from behind, her nails biting into my skin. She's breathing hard, quick and shallow, and the tremor in her hold tells me she's close to full panic. We're both treading water. I could shift to grab my sword, but there's too many, and she's too far from safety to make a break for it without losing skin.

"Rune, what are they?" she whispers.

"Hungry, unfortunately."

Something familiar stirs in my chest. Something I've not let surface in quite some time.

I know a way to make them back off. But it means opening a door I've kept locked tight, showing Odi a piece of me I'm not sure I want her to see.

A shadow slips too close, teeth snapping in the dim light, and the decision's made for me.

I draw in a deep breath and let it out as a flat hum—soft at first, then rolling out of my chest, curling through the water like smoke. I keep the brunt of it from Odi as the sound blooms, echoes bouncing off the cave walls until it's a melody—low, haunting, threaded with something older than I am.

The fish still. Jaws shut. One by one, they melt back into the depths, vanishing as if they'd never been. They know to whom they threaten with their wicked teeth, and they know what will come of them if they take a single bite.

The water's quiet again. My voice fades with it. And all I'm left with is the pounding of Odi's heart against my back, and the weight of what I just let her hear.

"What in all eight seas was that?" she breathes. The words are warm on my ear, sending a shiver down my neck.

I turn to glance at her over my shoulder. "You're welcome."

We make it to the other side of the pool in one piece. Odi clambers up the bank and onto drier ground as I shift back. When I join her, she's still looking at me like I've grown a third head.

My shoulders lift and fall with ease. "It's really nothing, shall we keep moving?"

She shakes her head in disbelief, and I can't stop the smile tugging at my lips as we enter the eerily quiet tunnel. The glow of the pool fades behind us. Odi sticks to my side as I guide us both through the dark.

The tunnel ends abruptly, my boots kicking loose stones across the ground.

"What is it?" Odi hisses, blinking into the dark.

I reach out, running my hands over the surface in front of me. "It's a doorway, but it's sealed shut."

"Alright, all of this is getting really old. I just want to get out of here," she groans, lacing her hands through the knotted mess on her head.

"There's a lever."

She folds her arms across her chest, popping her hip. "So pull it."

"What if it's a trap?" I say, not entirely mocking her concern from earlier.

Odi searches for me in the dark, her face pale in the absence of light. Fatigue has bruised the skin below her eyes and siphoned the pink of her plush lips. "Can't be any worse than what we've already been through."

I can feel the fight leaving her as easily I can sense the shifting of the evening tides. She's coldly logical, always three steps ahead, but the exhaustion is seeping in. I know battle-trained royals that would have let the water take them by now. But we've gone too far for her to give up.

"You'll have to make the choice, Odi." I speak softly, letting words settle.

She sighs as she shrugs, exhaustion rippling off her in waves. "Well there's no going back now. So pull the lever, Rune."

I grit my teeth and wrap my fingers around the cold metal. "Here we go."

The lever groans as I force it down, and the door shudders open with a deep, grinding scrape. We step inside—just a few cautious paces—and before I can blink, the slab behind us slams shut with a sound like a coffin lid.

Then I hear it.

A low rush at first, like distant rain. Then faster, louder—the hiss and surge of water forcing its way in. It pours from the seams in the walls, icy and relentless, rising around our boots, our knees—faster than ever before.

"Rune—"

"I know."

It's already climbing higher.

Fuck. Fuck. Fuck. And another for good measure.

"Fuck," I mutter under my breath.

From somewhere the water is pouring in faster and faster, but around my feet I can feel the tug of the current pulling the opposite way. There is a drain open somewhere. I can sense it. I just need to shift, grab Odi, and swim.

The water is to our waists now, salty, cold, and climbing quickly. Beside me, Odi's breaths come sharp and shallow. "It's—it's too fast," she stammers, voice fracturing as the roaring around us closes in. "We're not getting out of here, Rune. We're going to drown. *I'm* going to drown."

Her hands slap uselessly at the stone walls, fingernails scraping over the grime like she could claw her way out through solid rock.

I grab her shoulders, but she's trembling so hard I fear her teeth will rattle right out of her head. "Hey—look at me."

"I can't—I can't do this again. I can't die like this." Her voice cracks on the last words and I can feel it. That moment where something inside her folds . . . gives up.

For a split second, I'm shocked. This is not the pirate I've come to know. One so fierce and capable that she laughs while covered in monster gore. Wields weapons like she was born in a war. Sometimes I wonder if she was.

Tears stream down her face, too many for me to wipe away. I grab her wrists and tug her towards me, wrapping and arm around her waist. "You listen here, little doe. I told you I would get us out, and that's exactly what I plan on doing."

The cold water hits her ribs. Her lips are going blue. She tries to pull from my embrace, pressing back against the wall like she's trying to escape into it, eyes wide and glassy, fixed on nothing. And I know, if I don't snap her out of this now, she'll be gone before the water even wins, so I pull her closer.

"Odelia." I command her attention with my voice, but her gaze can't meet mine as a sob escapes her lips.

Without thought I shift as the water reaches her chin. I have to convince her to calm down so we can get through this. "There is a current below. I saw a doorway beneath us. We can swim through."

She shakes her head, small and frantic, the movement brushing her wet hair against my jaw.

I press my forehead to hers, forcing her to feel my steadiness. "It's the only way."

Another sob shudders out of her, the sound barely louder than the water lapping at her mouth. Our heads press against the ceiling. "Rune—"

"Do you trust me?"

The pause stretches, heavy as lead in my chest. Her breathing is fast, shallow, gulping at the last pocket of air. Then, finally, she nods, crumbling. The cry that slips out of her is raw, the kind that rattles bone, and the water catches it, air leaving her in a burst of bubbles as it surges over our heads.

Her fingers clamp around my forearms like a lifeline, nails biting into my scales. Her eyes widen, and for a heartbeat, I don't see the pirate with a sharp tongue and steel spine. I see a woman trembling against me, every ounce of fight tangled with fear, trusting me with her last breath.

So—fuck it. I do the only thing that makes sense.

I frame her face with both hands, pull her to me, and seal my mouth over hers.

BREATHE WITH ME

20
ODELIA

The ice of my limbs turns to flame in an instant. The cold gives way to glorious heat, spearing through my chest, rising hot in the skin of my neck, sinking deep into the very marrow of my bones. I'm on fire. Melting beneath the touch of his hands and the warmth of his body. The water disappears. The keys. The map.

I'm drowning. Distantly, the animal is screaming that I'm drowning.

But his mouth is locked on mine, strangely gentle despite the way his long fin loops around my waist and legs like a serpent, dragging me closer, pinning me still. He traces the tip of his tongue over the seam of my lips, annihilating any half-formed objection the fear in me tries to grip.

I've been touched before, need sated in the shadow of apathetic alleyways, unwelcome thoughts silenced by the quiet that comes with a rough hand and a willing neck. But this . . . I don't have words for this.

I'm aching. Close to tears for simple, gentle closeness. For the plump of his lips and the way he clings, like he hasn't considered letting go.

When his fingers tighten, when they thread into my tangled hair, when his tongue pushes my lips apart, filling me with a taste like stormlight, I give in.

The sun is gone. The soil won't sing for me again. The ocean will win at last, but I've traded my final breath to be here, rooted in nameless feeling.

Time stops, an eternity between now and the inevitable crush of suffocation.

I'll die here.

Instead, he *exhales.*

My chest inflates with borrowed breath, and then we're moving, flying through endless dark. Adrenaline rekindles in the pins and needles that assault my hands. Inertia drags all the blood towards my limbs. I can't see, but I can feel how fast we're going, forced to tuck my face into his chest to stop the pressure of the water from ripping open my eyelids and still-tingling lips.

He kissed me.

In the moment before he saved my life, he'd kissed me and there's no way he'll admit to it. I can see the infuriating smile already. "*You're always so hopeful, Odelia.*"

My lungs burn, refusing me the time to stoke the irritation. The water's pressure is still painful in my ears. There's no telling how close we are to surfacing. I push against him as the pain in my lungs increases. He relents, slowing, and loosens the cage of his arms, making me grapple for him as I feel myself start to drift. His hands move to my waist, warm, strong, the sudden, sweet bite of his talons taking the whole of my attention for a split moment.

I clench my teeth hard against the need to breathe. Ocean water burns my eyes as I try to communicate what I need.

"Again so soon, savage thing?" His voice is a melody in the water, its vibrations kissing along the exposed parts of my skin. My breasts tighten under their wrap, but I don't have time to wait for his teasing. I slide my hands up his arms and around his neck, pulling myself up so my lips meet his. I can *feel* his smile.

This man will be my undoing.

Despite the fact that I've braced myself, the first brush of his tongue threatens to empty my mind again—empty all of me, so that I might beg him to fill me again. My lips part, my own tongue darting out to meet his as our mouths seal together. He tastes almost the way he smells, like citrus and the intense silence that follows thunder in an ocean storm.

My chest begs for relief as we explore each other. His hands stay gripped tight, but I lock my legs around his hips, pulling us closer, tangling my fingers in his hair. At some point, it lost its tie and floats around his head, slipping like silk under my touch.

For better or worse, neither of us will be able to lie about what this is.

When I still, he breathes into me again, then pulls away. "I think it's just on the other side." His voice sends goosebumps over my arms. The hair on the back of my neck stands in anticipation. "Let's try to get there while you still have the strength to resist me."

The water slows my punch towards his chest, the fabric of my sleeve billowing between us and brushing my face in a way that sends another wave of anxiety through me. Then we're flying again—down, if the pressure in my ears is any indication. In an instant, we twist again, moving up.

Then break into open air.

I drag in a desperate breath, my lungs filling to the point of relieved pain. The room is dim, lit by spiderwebbed cracks high in the rock above. We're almost to the surface.

But the room is full of water.

Not drowned in it, but surrounded on all sides. The platform before us is a hand's width higher than a cavern lake.

"Here." His voice doesn't have the same ethereal quality as it did under the water. He ushers us to the platform, urging me to pull myself up. The effort asks for more strength than I have left, but I do, collapsing on the hard stone, sucking in deep lungfuls of wet air.

"I feel a current. I'm going to check it out, but I'll be right back."

My throat is raw, strangling my voice. "What if you don't come back?"

"I'll come back, little doe."

Then he's gone.

My body still hums, heart racing for his touch and how death came so near I could feel the brush of her fingers. I wait.

Strange sounds edge in on the silence. Dripping that echoes, clicks, rumbles I can't name. No doubt there are creatures hiding in the water—hungry fish, perhaps even the toad creatures—but I couldn't move if I wanted to, every part of me weighted to the cold stone at my back.

I startle when Rune surfaces, but my hand only lifts pathetically for my dagger and falls over my stomach.

His grin of sharp teeth is radiant in the half-light. "I found it."

"Found what?" The apprehension flares wild in my stomach.

"The way out. Come on."

I'm already shaking my head, feeling the rock beneath it as hot tears slip down my temples to itch in my ears. "I can't Rune, not again." I can't go back to the insistent press of the water—dark, patient, waiting for my surrender. The fear claws up my throat, like it's already taken me. Maybe if we wait long enough, the water will recede. Maybe it would be better to die here, rather than move towards that watery, inevitable end.

His voice is too patient. "There's no other choice, Odi. We're getting out of here. Both of us. And when we get back I'll make sure Otto rewards you with quail eggs five ways. I won't even let Tavi take any."

Tavi. Had she stayed with Elio, or taken a tunnel? Did she make it out, did anyone?

I let my head fall sideways to look at Rune. There's so much determined hope on his face, but the worry shows in his eyes. We won't know who survived until we get out of here. His crew is at stake, and here I am, being a shameless, useless coward.

"You should have let me die." The words carry all the cold logic I can muster. Quietly, I wonder if he'd have saved Nisse too, or if he'd have let me drown if he knew the truth.

He smirks. "Feeling sorry for yourself, Viper? We've got two more keys to find—unless you want to cough up the riddles? Maybe then I'll let the sea take you."

I press my lips into a line, feeling the irritation crawl its way to the forefront of my jumbled feelings. "Do you immediately piss off all the girls you kiss?"

"Only the pretty ones."

I huff a laugh, which turns to a sputtering cough. His gaze is steady as he reaches over the ledge, beckoning me closer.

"One more breath, and then it's over."

I nod, clench my teeth, then press all thought away so I have the willpower to force my aching body to roll towards him. I'm so cold I don't feel the water as I slip in, though I can feel his warmth as he cradles me to his chest.

"Once we start, we won't be able to stop," I feel the breath of his words on my cheek, "so I need you to take a deep breath. On three, ready?" He doesn't wait for me to answer. "One."

My hands tremble where they grip around his neck. *Just one more breath, and then it's over.*

"Two."

I force my body to relax as I inhale, if only so my aching lungs can take in more air.

"Three."

We plunge in and speed down, the pain in my ears growing until I'm certain they'll pop. He was right about the current.

It's heavy, the water rushing past even as we're forced to slow. It's hard to tell if we're making any progress. The thought almost grips me, but I cling to him instead, unwilling to let the little air I have left be used for more panic.

I can feel the strain of his body, the way his muscles coil against the water. For a moment, I wonder if it will win, then we break free, the flow changing, the dark behind my eyelids growing lighter and lighter until we burst into the open air of a clear blue sky.

I gasp, sucking greedy lungfuls of non-stagnant air. We're near the shore, the crew's tents visible far in the distance. *The Gilded Hart* waits down the way, gorgeous as ever.

Soon, Rune is walking us towards the shore, his fin turning to legs before I realise he's shifted. His arms are warm, his chest solid, but shivers wrack my spine as a breeze kisses my wet clothes. Not even the sun can warm the kind of chill that's settled in my bones.

The calm of the island is jarring compared to the chaos we've left below. Insects chitter and voices of the crew already call out, relieved to see Rune unharmed. I expect him to put me down once they see us, once his steps begin to splash in the shallows, but he pins me to him when I move, quietly refusing to let go until we're far, far beyond the reach of the tide.

SHE WOULDN'T WANT YOU TO DIE

21
RUNE

It had taken us hours to get back to the ship. Mostly because I'd promised Otto as much monster loot as we could carry, and he'd be disappointed if I turned up empty handed—not that he would show it.

Sucker pads, acidic saliva, organs, and even a few vials of sticky monster blood. I caught a few of the crew gagging as they bottled it up. Couldn't blame them, really. Who knew what Bear would do with all of it, but I wouldn't ask any questions—never did. The amount of times he'd found a remedy for a weird rash or someone's thinning hair was uncanny. He had a gift. So when he asked for monster bits, I made sure I did my best to deliver.

Late afternoon sun washes its orange glow over the beach, skimming across the seafoam kissing the shore. Never have I been so grateful to see the bright world around me. It was getting quite dark for a moment there—mentally and physically.

I watch as Odi loads ropes, tents and bags of monster parts into one of the row boats. She insisted on helping despite my suggestion she rest in the warm sand. *Gods* know she needs it after what we endured, but the work seemed to bring colour back into her cheeks. Her rhythm flows alongside the crew. It sparks something in my chest seeing her fit in like she's one of us.

One by one, the rowboats circle around to bring supplies and the crew back to *The Gilded Hart*, until it's only Tavi, Elio, Odi and I left to fill the last boat. We'd lost two men in the temple. It marked my heart, making it feel even heavier than before. *No more.* If I can help it, Odi and I will be the only ones to risk ourselves on the next islands.

"We're ready for you, Cap," Elio murmurs as he comes to stand beside me.

Silently I nod, moving towards the boat. Tavi, and Elio hop in on my command, though Tavi protests, saying she would push us off the sand. After a firm look, she rolls her eyes, jumps in and grabs an oar.

Just as Odi is about to step in, I reach out, catching her hand to assist her. Her breath hitches at my touch. Her head swivels in my direction, then she glances to where our hands meet, but she doesn't pull away.

"Thank you." Her voice is barely a whisper.

I offer a smile, my gaze flicking to her lips, before releasing her hand and putting all my weight into pushing the boat off the shore. I wade after it, and once it's cleared the bank, I pull myself in.

No one says anything, each of us lost in our thoughts. So much has happened over the last few days that I don't blame anyone for needing some quiet.

The pull of the oars brings us closer and closer to *The Gilded Hart.* My chest swells with pride as she sits elegantly in the water, her spruce bow bobbing up and down calmly as she floats on the Adamaris Sea.

My home away from home. The place where I feel more myself.

Father spent a lot of time with Selene, teaching her the history of our race and how to be a royal worthy of the throne, and when he wasn't doing that he was holed up in his chambers grieving mother. He knew I didn't care for the royal life, so he practically threw the ship at me when I asked for it. Told me that I had mother's adventurous spirit. Perhaps there'd been a small part of him that hoped I would find answers about her too.

The rowboat thuds against the hull with a hollow knock, the smell of tar and salt wrap around me like the embrace from an old friend. Weathered but sturdy ropes dangle down the side of my ship, swaying with the tide.

Elio's already grabbing one, boots braced on the wood as he hauls himself up and over the edge of the railing. Tavi throws me a glance and then follows Elio, her white braids swinging in the wind. The others drop the boat's braces down, and I hook them on before moving to follow.

Odi still stands, one arm thrown out to steady herself, the other gripping the rope. She flicks her gaze to the looming deck above, like she's not sure her taxed body is up for one last challenge.

I step in close, wrapping an arm around her waist while steadying the rope in her hands. "Your turn." My voice comes out softer than I intended.

She blinks up at me, hesitation obvious in her dark brown eyes. There's a question there, one I'm not sure I can answer.

Before she can voice it, I guide her forwards, the warmth of her pressed against my palm. Exhaustion evident, she glances between me and the ship one last time before her boots find the first knot, then the second. A breeze snakes between us, swaying the rope, and her entire body tenses, the ocean dark where it laps at the hull. I close the distance between us, bracing her between my body and the hull as the rowboat rocks beneath me.

"Don't give up now, little doe," I murmur, my hand sliding from her waist to the small of her back.

Her mouth forms a thin line and I swear I can hear the crack in her teeth as her jaw sets. She moves, and I follow close enough to catch her if she slips.

When she's over the rail, I plant my palm against the warm wood and haul myself after her in one motion. Odi turns, hair loose in the wind, cheeks flushed from the climb. I let my gaze linger on her face a heartbeat too long. Her lips are cracked, the whites of her eyes red from the salt that clings to the strands around her face. She opens her mouth to speak when the sound of heavy footsteps sound behind her on the deck.

"What the hell happened out there?" Reid sneers. His question is for me, but his eyes are pinned on her. Two men stand either side of him, arms folded over their chests, both carrying a scowl upon their lips.

"Reid, is there something you'd like to talk about?" I ask nicely, keeping my irritation at bay.

He jerks his head in Odi's direction, who stands beside me, all evidence of her weariness gone, her arms folded, brow raised like she's ready to gut him the moment he draws a blade.

"You're not going to let a filthy whore of a pirate influence our moves and kill more of our crew are you?" Reid spits, like Odi's presence is a stain. "You'll ruin us. Send us all to the deep on the word of a fucking viper. They're dead, Rune. Our men, our friends, are dead. And it should have been her." Reid turns his head sideways, like he's addressing the crew. "What's the bounty for a Viper, eh? Thrice that of a Headtaker. Yet she's cost us so much more. We're fucking *bounty hunters,*" he shouts, not bothering to hide his rage now. "Not treasure hunters. And not fodder for the whims of your mange-ridden bitch."

A bird screeches horribly in the space of the silence that falls, grating against my already raw nerves. It's something between a cough and the strangled laugh of a gull, only there to mock the tension between us. Across the deck, Elio and Tavi's focus is pinned on us. A few others have slowed their loading or rigging to listen, eyes skirting between the conversation and their task.

I know Odi's tired, but her body practically hums with restrained violence. My dagger sits at her waist, dull and salt crusted, but her fingers don't even twitch.

Instead, she *laughs*, the sound murderous on its own. "At least I don't have a dick the size of a shrimp."

Reid's attention narrows back on her. "You'd still choke on it."

"Yeah . . . from the smell."

His face twists. "You fuc—"

I lift a hand as he moves to step forwards. "Reid, I understand your frustrations. The losses upset me too." My voice comes out low. I already feel the guilt gnawing at my insides, and Reid's glare only drives it deeper. "But this is the risk," I remind them, more for myself than anyone else. "Every one of us knew what could happen. All who went volunteered."

"Volunteered to die?" Reid hisses, his bushy brow pinches in the middle.

Odi steps forwards before I can stop her. "Do you think I wanted them to?"

Reid's jaw works, and then he's in her face, close enough that something in me snaps. "I don't care what you want," he says. "I just want you off this ship. Preferably with weights on your legs."

I'm moving before I can think, my hand closing around Odi's wrist, pulling her half a step back. I place myself between them, my gaze locked on the male in front of me. "Back down. That's an order. Go and get a drink, we all need one."

Reid doesn't right away. "She's—"

"I said go," I repeat, my voice sharper this time.

One of the men behind Reid mutters something I don't catch before he spits onto the deck, twisting on his heel as leads the trio away.

The moment they're out of sight, I let my guard down and slowly let go of Odi's hand. Her breathing is quick beside me, the tension still evident in her frame by the way her shoulders are squared and her head held high.

She flicks her gaze to me, a silent question on her lips.

"I can't punish him for it," I tell her quietly. "He's allowed his own thoughts."

Even if they cut deeper than he knows.

Odi's gaze drifts out to sea. "Talk like that to the captain of the *Sea Bane* and you'll get your throat slit."

Her eyes glaze over, like she's reliving the truth of that in her mind. My chest constricts to think about what she might have been through that I clearly don't know about. I want to reach for her, to tuck her wild curls behind her ear, and whisper that aboard my ship, she's safe.

Clamorous laughter shatters my thoughts. The crew that stayed aboard the ship help to empty the row boats, organizing all the supplies and leaving the monster loot in a separate pile. Some of them look at the components with disgust, while others grab handfuls of flesh ribbons or amphibious tongues to brandish against the others. Maurice, a golden-skinned human man who's been with me through so many fights I've lost count, *squeals* as the man next to him jabs the green-grey skin in his direction, causing another wave of laughs. I grin, my eyes finding Odi. The withdrawn look on her face is gone now, but she just moves for the crates of sticky limbs, jaw set, and gaze focussed, ignoring everyone else.

I jog to catch up to her, determined to break the shroud of the last twenty-four hours. Anything to lighten the mood, even just for a moment. "Not your version of fun?"

She snorts, brushing away a stray lock of hair as she reaches for a crate. "That word is unfamiliar to me."

A grin steals across my mouth as I step into her pathway. "Surely there's something that you like to do." I've travelled to many islands, many parts of the mainland. I've heard and seen the weirdest things, not a lot surprises me.

Odi releases her grip on the crate, and stands tall, folding her arms across her chest. "Will you let me take this to Bear if I answer you?"

"Absolutely."

"Fine," she huffs. "I like to run."

I pause, watching her, the weight of those words sinking deeper than she probably meant them to. *Run.* A simple word, but there's more beneath it—something caged and aching. As a siren I have the sea to shift and stretch. As a shifter dwelling with vipers, she only had the deck of a ship, a creature made for speed and open ground, forced to pace behind wooden walls.

It makes my chest tighten.

I offer her a soft smile before reaching down to grab a sack of monster parts. When I straighten, her eyes are glassy. "Running suits you," I say gently.

The look she offers is soft, like a small part of her feels seen. I don't wait for her to answer as she finally picks up the crate. Twisting on my heel, I lead us towards the galley. "Especially your furrier form. I guess she doesn't get the chance very often." It's strange to talk about her beast like the fear isn't hers. All of it is her.

"You can see why," she answers, her voice low and tired like she doesn't want the others to hear. The jostling components fill the silence that follows.

When we make it past the lines of hammocks, I pause, trying and failing to stop myself from pushing her just a little further. "She's safe here. No matter what form you're in, if you go overboard, we'd just pull you back up."

She blinks her brown eyes up at me, like she's processing the thought, and I start walking again, hoping she realizes I don't expect her to respond. Her gaze drops to the floor, her lips press into a line, but she doesn't argue.

It's a start.

Otto's eyes grow to the size of dinner plates when I push the door open,

"All of that for me?" he gasps as he tugs at the collar of his shirt before rolling his sleeves up.

The sack I've been carrying squelches as I drop it at his feet. "Well, I certainly didn't harvest monster organs to give to the quails."

Otto grins. "*Vicious seas*, am I going to have some fun."

Odi drops the crate next to the sack and then perches herself on the edge of the kitchen table. Her creamy blouse is bloodstained despite our pathetic attempts at washing on the island. The fabric slips off one of her shoulders as she hunches forwards, tired from exertion, yet she smiles at Bear with such endearment, her attention focussed on the way his face lights up at the sight of monster legs. I can't help noticing the way the afternoon sun kisses the exposed skin on her shoulder, travelling across her collarbone to caress the curve of her delicate neck. My fingers itch to brush her nape, to bury my face into the place her pulse flutters with life.

Something's shifted between us. It started the moment back in the temple when I saw the fear in her eyes when the water started rising, and all I could do was taunt and tease her just to keep her fear at bay. Then she stood her ground against Reid, fire burning without an ounce of trembling in her voice. It was the way my body moved before my mind caught up—how all I could think about was getting her away, keeping her safe. The instinct hit like a wave, sudden and unforgiving.

"What will you do with all of it?" she asks Bear.

Otto holds up a green limb, breaking my trance.

"I presume that these are mudaliks due to those orange sucker pads." He points to the canvas sack. His blue eyes are wild with passion, his unruly hair messed by the ocean breezes. "There are so many elixirs I can make."

The table creaks under my weight as I lean my hip against it, grateful for a moment's rest while the pair liaise back and forth about all things monsters. Soon Odi and I would have to go back to how it was before. In this together simply to fulfil a mutual goal. Her, to pocket gold and find some lonely, land-based paradise, and me to find what I could about my mother, or the very least my water elemental bloodline. After that, I'd never see her again.

"We don't have to eat them do we?" Odi asks, her voice hesitant, like she's afraid of the answer.

Bear starts pulling out another mudalik leg to inspect before he answers. "I wouldn't feed this to my worst enemy."

My brow raises, and I inspect my nails like I have all the time in the world. "He'd deserve it."

Otto snorts, but it's true, and when I come face to face with the man, I'll shove this monster guck so far down his throat it'll come out the other end whole.

I glance across the table to where Odi sits, her hair cascading around her in soft, dark waves. She catches my eye, and for a second neither one of us looks away. Her perfectly pink lips are slightly pouted, and when I think about how it felt to touch them with mine, my lungs constrict from the absence of air.

If given the chance, I'd probably do it again.

The door to the galley squeaks open, announcing the arrival of Elio and Tavi. My gaze lingers on Odi's face for a moment longer as Elio brushes past me to drop another bag of monster goodies.

Odi offers them a worn smile and then turns back to Otto. "So what sort of elixir requires such dangerous ingredients?"

Otto's eyes glitter with joy as he starts digging through the bag of monster loot Elio discarded, kitchen knife in hand. "See, the thing about mudalik sucker pads, they're sticky as sin. Dry 'em out, grind 'em fine, and you've got yourself a powder that'll seal any cut tighter than stitches. Even works on rope burns! Thought about mixing it with honey, but that's sticky on sticky and, well, then you're just stuck." He laughs at his own joke before tumbling into the next thought.

"And their spit—oh, their spit's glorious. More acidic than a sour wine but you dilute it right, mix it with seawater, and aloe vera gel, and it becomes a potent disinfectant." His grin is wide, eyes bright, but he doesn't pause.

He flips the knife, gestures with it like punctuation. "And the skin. Don't waste it. We wash it, cover it in salt and dry it out. Then if someone burns themselves, you can re-hydrate the mudalik skin mixed with quail egg whites to the burn area and repair your skin. Maybe I should have asked for more—"

"Otto." My voice cuts through the air, but I'm sure to offer him a smile. He'd talk all day if I let him.

He blinks at me, fingers twitching against the knife hilt. "Right. Rambling again?"

"A bit." I wink. The boy's chaos has a way of bleeding into the air around him, but I'll admit, I'd rather have his endless chatter than silence.

Odi looks everything over. "It's amazing Bear, you should become a healer, not a cook."

The skeleton earring Otto wears swings softly as he shrugs. "Why not be both? It's all mixing and measuring, finding the right ingredient."

Tavi speaks up from where she's taking the bandages off Elio's leg. "Speaking of healers. Elio could use some attention." The fabric of his trousers is stained with dark red. Otto springs into action, rushing to her aid.

The sight of it hits me in the stomach. I've lost too many already, and what if Elio had been one of them? I don't think I could learn to live alongside the guilt of knowing my best friend died because I couldn't be satisfied with the quiet presence of unanswered questions. "Here, press that there—no, firmer," Otto rattles on, hands flapping as he gives instructions, then scurries off to fetch his jars of salves and tinctures. His voice fades down the corridor, leaving the room quieter, charged.

Elio winces but doesn't move, not when Tavi steps closer, not when his fingers catch her waist and tug her between his knees. She exhales sharply, cheeks blooming pink, but she doesn't push him away. Instead, she leans over the wound, fussing with cloth and pressure, her hands steady despite the flush on her skin.

I look away, then back again just in time to catch it—the briefest of kisses. A stolen thing, soft as breath, gone before it can root. Tavi pulls back instantly, red-faced and scowling, muttering something about infection. Elio just grins like the cocky bastard he is, sitting there bleeding and smug.

Like a magnet, my gaze finds Odi again, who still sits on the edge of the kitchen table. She's not looking at the two love birds over in the corner. No. She's looking at me. Warmth erupts in my chest like a forbidden flower blooming under moonlight.

I wonder if she's thinking about the kiss—or whatever she wants to call it. My weight shifts under her gaze. I'm trapped between wanting to reach for her here in front of everyone, or darting from the room and pretending like nothing happened.

I flick my gaze to the serpent tattoo on her left wrist. In all honesty I *should* do the latter. It's what's expected of me. Bounty hunters and pirates don't mix. And if I had my way I'd have her captain and the rest of her crew rotting in the deep already. Yet the last thing I feel like doing is running away from her and there's no way either one of us can deny what happened in the water, the moment our lips touched.

Her brow raises, a silent challenge to see who will look away first. I vow to myself that it won't be me—

Tavi clears her throat, and I glance her way. *Damn it.*

Both she and Elio are staring at Odi and I. Warmth unravels up my neck under the scrutiny of being caught staring at the woman I'm supposed to loathe.

The scent of pear and honey carry past me as Odi shuffles off the table. "I think it's about time I go freshen up."

I nod as Otto stumbles back into the room with an armful of glass bottles and bandages filling the atmosphere with his chatter again. Odi slips from the room like a ghost, yet the absence of her presence is felt deep in the soft part of my chest. The place I hadn't allowed to see the light for some time. My hand finds the necklace in my pocket without thought, turning it over and over. It's a habit now. A ritual. And still, the damn thing keeps its secrets from me.

Bear chatters as he tends to Elio's wounds, voice running quicker than the ship's clock. His words bounce from poultices to mudalik bile to how he'll stew something later that will taste like food from a rich man's parlor. Whatever that means. Then he starts rattling on about brewing more tonics for the few crew members who've been up late with wet coughing. Elio humours him with the occasional grunt.

Eventually, Tavi straightens, wiping her hands on a rag before she releases a gentle sigh and faces me. "I should bathe too," she murmurs, her voice soft. "We're only six hours from the next island, though I doubt we'll be ready by then?" She phrases it as a question, but we both know the answer before I nod.

"Once we're there we'll anchor and rest a couple days. No point in rushing." The marks on the map had been so close together I thought perhaps they were related somehow, but nothing in the temple confirmed that. It's strange, when all the others required long stretches of travel.

She leaves me to ponder with an injured first mate, the creak of wood, and Otto's endless ramble.

The silence inside me is loud. Too loud. The water in that temple had aimed to weed out the weak and the unlucky. Both challenges so far had required an infinitely deep respect of its power. The water elemental symbol floats in my mind again and for a moment I let the memories fall away, allowing myself to simply be the boy who lost his mother, who clings to the impossible hope he might find her, before I force myself back into the captain I'm supposed to be.

I step forwards, peering over Otto's shoulder. "You have everything you need?"

"Yes, Cap." Bear finishes wrapping Elio's leg. "Just need to keep it clean."

Placing a hand on his head, I ruffle his hair. "Good. Then make sure dinner is a feast tonight. A full one. Tonight, we remember the lost, but we also celebrate the living."

Otto's pearly white grin reaches all the way to his ears. "Aye, Cap."

My gaze moves to Elio. "Have we heard from Killian?"

He nods, and I don't know whether to feel relieved or concerned. I've been hunting Ivor's ship for so long that knowing its whereabouts on a regular basis gives me mixed feelings. He's like a specter, the thought of him haunting me. There's no way he can threaten us from so far away, but I'm uneasy all the same. I can only imagine the peace I'll feel once the sea scum is finally off my ocean.

"It arrived two days ago, but we were at the temple. The note said, '*Ivor's ship cut north past the Isles. Sails patched but holding. His crew looked mean enough, but half were drunk off their own rum. Less scary than a bull shark scenting blood. Idiots.*' his words," Elio says with a lopsided smile.

I huff, shaking my head. "They're further than I thought they would be, but until all of this is over, I'm glad for the distance."

I turn to leave when boots scuff behind me.

"Rune," Elio gently calls, pushing himself off the bench to follow me. "Reid had a point earlier. We nearly died today."

My gaze flicks to Bear, who's already busy prepping vegetables, before I return it to Elio. The words sting because they're true. With a sigh, I fold my arms across my chest. "So, as my second in charge, what would you suggest I do?"

His lips purse. "The crew . . . they need a morale boost. A break."

I nod in agreement. "They'll have one. Dinner tonight will lift their spirits, and I'll announce that no one is coming with me onto the next island. I won't risk them again."

He stiffens. "Rune that's not what I meant—"

I cut him off, steel in my voice, though it's for myself as much as him. "I have to do this, Elio. I can't rest until I know. But no one else will bear the burden."

His jaw works, but when he speaks it's softer, almost pleading. "She wouldn't want you to die."

The words cleave something raw inside me. Elio gives me the same look my sister Serene did the day I left the kingdom and took to the high seas. No one understood mother like I did. No one saw the pain in her eyes every time she talked of the world beyond our castle walls, like she feared she'd never see it again.

What kind of son would I be if I let this chance go? A cowardly one . . . that's what. And I refuse to be like my father. Ignoring everything and everyone in hopes that one day the pain of losing her will go away. I couldn't live with myself if I didn't at least try.

I look to the floor, scuffing one of my boots on the wood. "Well then, I guess I'd better live."

I KISSED YOU. IT DOESN'T MEAN I WANT TO BED YOU

22
ODELIA

The shed drakeling scale I'd managed to find on the island had surprised me when I'd gone to wash. In all the chaos, I'd completely forgotten I'd slipped it in my pocket. It's iridescent in the light, glittering like a precious jewel. I tuck both it and the leaf together on the nightstand, admiring them. I'd had a small collection of land things ever since I was a child, despite my father trying to break the habit on more than one occasion. Being here, knowing none would arrive to condemn me for it, it seems the instinct can't be helped. I adjust the scale again, watching it catch the light before moving to the washroom and scrubbing my skin raw. Whatever enchantment the ship had that allowed for running water must have cost a fortune.

I almost ignore my hunger and fall into bed, but the smell of Otto's cooking draws me right back to the second deck, where I hide near a corner barrel as others move hammocks and pull out the makeshift tables. Every bone in my body aches. My eyes are unfocused, ignoring the sideways looks and the haunted expression some of the others share, when

Soraya appears as if from nowhere and smacks her palm down on the barrel top.

"Mind if I join you?" she says, gracefully sitting before I have the presence of mind to answer. Behind her, some begin to line up at the galley door. She twists her neck to follow my gaze. "I always wait till they're done. Otto cooks as he serves, so even if you're one of the last, it's still hot."

I stop my hand before I can reach for the necklace that's not there, saying nothing. The weight of the last twenty-four hours—no, the last few weeks— curls heavy in my chest like a rock. Not grief, nothing so noble as that, but emptiness. The kind that comes when the overwhelm has taken residence for so long that its blessed absence leaves numbness. One I'd usually welcome.

"Guess Rune got the key, then?" she chatters like the silence would swallow her whole.

"I got the key." It hurts to speak, my throat raw from crying. I shove the memory of drowning down, but it lingers at the edge. "We got lucky." Without my panicked shift, we may have walked into the final trap and died riddled with arrows. And without Rune . . . well, it's becoming clear these keys weren't meant for land-dwellers to retrieve, at least not alone.

"Jortan and Maurice said they'd hardly made it two-hundred steps before their tunnel went under water. Neither are sirens or"—she gestures to a pendant at her neck—"have a breath stone, so when they couldn't get past, they turned around. Tulin and Arinna said theirs split in three."

My eyes catch on an unwelcome figure over her shoulder. Reid looks almost like he's going to come over, but he spots

I press my lips together as Soraya's eyes twinkle like stars. She looks at Tavi like they've adopted a puppy.

"I'm going to see if I can get Otto to let us skip the line," Tavi mumbles, gone from the table in a blink. I watch her go, then turn a suspicious look on Soraya. She plays with a spring of hair that's pulled from her braid.

"She can scent it. Or sense it. It's a fae thing."

Right.

I stand to leave just as Otto rounds the corner with two steaming plates, Tavi on his heels with one of her own. My mouth waters just enough to sit down and endure the embarrassment of knowing they and who-knows-who-else on this ship knows—or thinks they know—what happened with Rune. Tavi is the only fae, but I hadn't thought to ask if there were any land shifters like myself on board. If I'd spent any time at all in my deer form, it may have occurred to me that our scents may have mingled by this point.

Otto's speaking before he makes it to us. "So, I have to admit I did experiment a little more with the mudalik flesh and I really believe there's not a way you can cook it that it won't kill you. Oh! Don't look at me like that, trust me I've built up a tolerance to a lot of things but I didn't swallow, just tasted it. There's nothing that kills you that tastes *good*, you know? I could be wrong but I figured no one would want to eat it anyways. It was sort of a thick mucilage texture—"

"Bear can we not talk about the snot frog, please, and thank you." Soraya has gone a faint green. Her food is untouched.

"Oh yeah, uh. Sorry. Well, the ship bird wouldn't eat it either. Seemed like a good enough sign I shouldn't feed it to the quail."

"The *ship's* bird?"

"Well, yeah, land bird of some kind, grey, kinda plump. Probably why he's staying on the ship far as I can tell. Looked like he might have made friends on the island but decided he liked my cooking better than hunting his own." Otto beams. "But"—he scratches the back of his head—"when I offered the mudalik he pecked and screeched like a ship running aground. Wasn't too happy with me."

"If it's the same one from the the other day, it's not harmless. But I didn't get a good look at it," I say, feeling the phantom gash in my thumb. "Did it try to hurt you?"

Otto shakes his head. "Course not. He's a good bird. Just letting me know he knew it was poison is all."

A low, unbalanced feeling makes me consider the answer before I concede, too tired to do anything but shovel another forkful in my mouth. The kid can cook. "And that will be good for your elixirs?"

He nods. "Yeah but I'll probably start with some shot. I used a lot for the centipede. Is Rune gonna come eat with you guys?"

Soraya shrugs. "No, he hasn't had his daily allotment of broody prince time."

Tavi lifts a brow. "We lost people down there, Soraya."

Soraya waves a hand. "He was this way before too. It's just worse with the map."

I pause for a breath, my plate mostly clean already. "Strange that a prince would have a need for gold."

They all go quiet. Quiet enough to know there's something I don't know. A bittersweet smile grows on my face as Otto clumsily excuses himself, and the other two pin their focus on their food. Yeah. There's something they aren't saying. But Rune will be stuck with me all night, and there's no way I'll give him another riddle until he explains exactly what his aim is in all of this.

My blood warms, and the anticipation turns quickly to something else. I still feel the strength of his hands like a brand on my skin.

"So," I say pointedly, since Tavi's been so eager to chat, "how's Elio?"

"Better," she says without looking at me.

I don't back down. "I've always thought men look better with scars, and he's already a looker."

"And here I thought I'd be helping Rune write his wedding vows soon." She finally looks at me, completely unentertained. It makes me smile wider.

"I do prefer a man with a little more hair. Up top."

Soraya snorts into her eggs.

Relenting, I lower my voice. "Why do you guys hide it? Rune approves wholeheartedly, trust me—down in the tunnel he waxed poetic about dying before you came out and admitted your feelings."

"He did not."

I shrug. "He didn't. But if he had, he wouldn't have been wrong. I don't need to *scent* anything to know."

Tavi sends an accusing look towards Soraya, who puts both her hands up before saying, "I just thought some frank honesty would be nice on this ship for once. And the girl has a right to know you can tell they've been . . . close."

"I can't *tell*—" Tavi cuts off with a sigh and sends her eyes up like she's beseeching the deck above us for patience. "It's vague. Especially—"

"With the stink?" I throw my chin at the line of sailors behind her.

She nods, but her lips curl up on one side. "My bloodline mixed with humans a long time ago, so the sense isn't as sharp as it might be for others."

"Is that also why you're afraid of the dark?" I ask innocently.

"Why I—who told you that?" Her forehead pinches, just slightly.

I shrug. The line behind her moves forwards, most of the others either quiet or somber.

She breaths so deep it's almost a sigh. "Some elves are born with darkvision, some aren't. Like I said, we mixed with humans a few hundred years ago."

It's not an admission, but it's close.

"It's the same with me," Soraya says. "Human father, siren mother. Fifty-fifty shot of being able to shift, but I can't."

That takes me by surprise, but it makes sense. The voice, the allure. I almost bring up that I can shift, but the thought of talking about it has the exhaustion rushing back in. Rune likely told them the moment he found out.

The animal in me has been . . . quieter. Even with our return to the water I've yet to feel the tightly wound tension of her beneath my skin—her warnings and whispers. I should be angry at Rune for goading me. For pushing me to lose control. But the truth is, that as terrifying as that run had been, my blood had thrilled in a way that almost made me mourn how I'd shoved her down so long. Almost. I'd kept her and me both alive. I'd stopped her from taking over, from bolting, again and again.

Softer memories brush the edge of my subconscious. Older, washed in the faded watercolour of time. My mother, nuzzling me in her deer form. Teaching me the patience needed to learn the animal's drives and needs. But it hadn't been enough. The grasp I'd have would slip every time we returned to the water.

And then she was gone.

"Well," I say, standing and pulling up my empty plate, "thanks for lunch ladies. It's been . . . enlightening."

We should be close to the next island, but there's no shadow on the horizon, no matter how hard I squint my eyes against the glare of the water. Bodies churn on and over the deck, directed by Elio, who has to shout over the crash of waves that carry the ship through open water. The darkened sky behind us bodes ill, but at this time of the year, the wind should carry any storm far to the south. A few of the crew note the plate in my hands, including a swooping bird's shadow that I scowl at as I cross to the captain's quarters. The damn thing has been messing the deck like it means to. It's surprising no one has put a bolt in it yet. I shove down the annoyance, ignoring it all the same way I ignore the rising swell of nerves in my stomach.

I knock, then chastise myself. If Rune wanted privacy, he shouldn't have forced me to share a room with him in the first place.

The moment I walk in, I spy familiar rope and leather waiting on the bed. "Is that my bola?"

"It seemed time to return it." His voice is heavy behind me, and I turn to find him taking up an impossible amount of space while sitting in that damned chair.

His eyes are trained on the plate in my hands. "Otto wanted me to bring you food," I say by way of explanation.

"Otto said that, did he?" The words are teasing enough that I freeze, realizing too late that there are empty dishes on his desk.

I set the plate down on the desk and face him. He's sprawl legged in a surprising amount of captain's finery. A navy jacket with gilded buttons, dress boots, a white shirt that strains over the width of his chest. He's washed too, based on the dampness of his wavy hair and the scent of oranges that envelopes the room. For a moment, I wonder if they use scented soaps in Nareth.

I shrug, knowing neither of us will believe what I'm about to say. "This plate was left alone, and I was already on my way here. Figured it must take a lot of energy to run your mouth as much as you do."

He huffs a laugh, but it's subdued. "So you brought me food?"

"So I brought you food." I hadn't seen him grab any, and it was the least I could do after . . . I swallow, too proud to admit I'd been caught.

He says nothing. Only studies me with an aggravating, knowing look.

"Are you going somewhere?" I push on, gesturing to his state of dress as I study the dishes beside him, because the weight of the last two days is dense between us, and both walking away and looking him in the eye seem like they're each on separate lists of bad ideas.

"There will be funerals tonight. On this ship we honour our dead."

The word settles on my shoulders, the rage in Reid's words ringing in my ears again. I know it's worse for Rune. The Vipers wouldn't have spared the thought, but Rune looks like a mountain has crumbled around him, pinning him under the grief.

I should reach out to touch him. Curl in his lap and let my weight remind him the world is still beneath us. Our boundaries are tangled, blurred in places they should never have been blurred, but in this moment it's simple comfort he needs.

I'm just not sure I'm capable of it.

I feel his gaze on me like a challenge now, and force myself to meet it. He's tired. Even more tired than I am. Dark circles nest under his bright-blue eyes. There's a healing cut over his cheekbone and probably all over the rest of him, if my own small wounds are any indication. The temple had tried to swallow us whole. Had tried to polish its stones with the grit of our bones. I grit my teeth, shoving it all down again, as far to the back of my mind as it will go. I'm not capable of comfort, but we do distraction well.

"Think Tavi will let you borrow the Captain's hat?" I say.

He turns to the bottle beside him and pours the waiting glass till it's full of liquid amber, then pulls another from the wall bracket and fills it too. "Hate hats. They make my hair flat."

When he hands me the second glass, he's got the ghost of a smirk on his lips. I down it in one go, watching his eyes flick from my face to the skin of my bare neck as I swallow. When his gaze flicks lower, going molten, the air shifts. The sweet heat of the alcohol mirrors the feeling that teases my core and makes my breasts feel heavy with need for a hand or lips or the flick of a tongue. I can still taste him. Can feel the space between us charged with the friction of who we are and what we want and what we've already endured together.

He downs his, never taking his eyes off me. "Was there something you needed, little doe?"

There's something in the question. Another dare, maybe.

"I planned to sleep," I say, honestly. "Until this evening at least. You could join me . . . if you don't take up too much of the bed."

Neither of us moves, the implication thickening the air between us.

He watches me with that too-discerning look again, like he's picking the words apart. Like I don't see how the knuckles of his hands have gone white where he grips the arm of the chair. "Are you feeling breathless out of the water too?" He smiles. "Here I thought you were an honourable pirate, never taking more than you need."

My cheeks flush. "I'd argue your greed rivals my own. Unless you've chosen to forget what happened in that water?" I suppress a shiver as the memory of his taloned hands on me, his tongue brushing my lips, asking for more. Red crawls up his neck as his eyes go dark. I know he's thinking the same.

"Just because I kissed you . . ." His voice rises, rough, his body going still like a predator waiting to strike. ". . . doesn't mean I want to bed you."

I take a step towards him, drawn by the taunt in the words and by his gravity, the way his presence takes up the entire room.

"Just because I tolerate you"—I brace each of my hands on the armrests and lean over into his space, letting my voice drop to a murmur—"doesn't mean I don't want to kill you."

Fast as a viper, he hooks a hand around the back of my neck and yanks me so close I can feel the kiss of his breath. On instinct, my hand moves to the bone dagger at my hip, and I catch myself with a leg over his waist. A thrill runs up my spine at the firm press of his cock on the inside of my thigh, even as, again, I press the blade to the base of his throat.

"Do it," he says, grinning now, the metal glinting between us. His other hand embeds in my hip, squeezing hard enough I can't help the whimper of need that escapes me. "I'll wait."

I just grin back as the hand on my hip releases to peel the dagger from between us. I don't fight it. The bone clatters on the floor, and then his hand is back on me again, searching, while the other is a visce around the back of my neck. His touch moves over my leg, ghosts over my ribs, and stalls on the dull kitchen knife I'd tucked beneath my wraps. "You're a menace," he says fondly, and fire follows the trail of his fingers as they slip under my blouse to tug the weapon from its hiding place.

"You didn't really expect me to go into that forest completely unarmed, did you?" I breathe, pulse racing. I let my fingers hook and drag under the collar of his shirt, while his slip beneath my thigh, tugging me closer.

"I'm learning I've no idea what to expect from you." His hand stops, his thumb tracing circles around the sharpened duragan bone tucked low in my pocket.

Victory shines in his eyes as I pull up on my knees so he can grab it, then settle the rest of my body on top of him, molding to him even as he holds my face still. The grip wars for my focus. The heat of his body is a caress on its own. My nipples ache for attention and I'm already a puddle where his length thickens further between my thighs. Immediately, his other hand lands on another weapon—a throwing knife wrapped and tucked by my ankle. It was easy to nick from the mess of the second deck.

"Really, Odelia?" he asks, but there's nothing but amusement in his tone.

"Viper, Rune."

"I didn't know vipers could be so eager to be unarmed." The words vibrate in my chest.

I bite back a whimper as his fingers finally circle the peaks of my nipples in turn, sending an electric arc of need shooting low, then they slide up, and I gasp as they dip down the front of my shirt, snaking past my wrap to snatch the bundle secured between my breasts.

"You ass!" I spit, trying to push away, but he doesn't let go.

Instead he slips the most recent key into his shirt pocket and pulls me closer, wrapping an arm around my hips and grinding our bodies together. My breath hitches so sharply my back arches, and he takes the opportunity to nip at the taut bud of my breast through my shirt. "I told you I'd get it."

I suck in a breath, but wrap my fist into his shirt, shoving him back into the chair. He just pulls me down with him, grinning as his mouth crashes into mine.

My knees sink into the cushion as he pulls us closer, every inch of his firm chest crushed into me down to where our hips meet. I grind into the sweet pressure between my legs as his tongue slips over my lips, begging for entry. I open for him, flicking mine into his mouth, there and gone again. He groans, and the sound vibrates through my entire body.

One of his hands slips under the back of my pants to cup my ass, while the other makes it under my shirt, palming my breast over the cloth that binds my chest. His pinky finger brushes against the blunted end of his letter opener and he pulls away, his chest heaving against mine. "Fuck Odelia, where do you even keep all these weapons?"

"Keep going and find out." I pull him back into me, sucking his lower lip into my mouth to nip, letting my hips grind over him in invitation. He tangles his fingers into the fabric of my blouse, lifting it up over my head.

Then there's a knock.

We still, chests heaving. His pupils are blown wide, nothing but iris in the dim light.

"Yeah?" Rune calls, his eyes pinned to mine.

"Storms coming." It's Elio. His voice is strained, muffled by the wooden door.

Rune sighs, letting his head fall back to rest on the back of the chair. "What do you mean?" The storm should have continued far past us.

"Just come see," Elio calls, his voice fainter, as if he's already walking away.

We shift, untangling our limbs and freeing ourselves from the grip of the chair. His lips are pink, and his eyes flick over me as I reach for my shirt.

"I'll be back." He moves to leave, but stops. His voice is gravelly, but low. "You should get some rest. It may be a rough evening."

The door whines as he goes, then closes with a soft click. Then it's just me, the heat in my veins, and the knowledge that I am absolutely, undeniably, completely willingly fucked.

You bastard

23
RUNE

I am royally fucked.

Tavi knows it by the look she gave me earlier. I know it, and no doubt Elio knows it too. It's one thing to pull Odi close, it's another to have her straddled across my hips with her soft, warm thighs, her infectious lips clinging to mine as our tongues entwine in a passionate dance.

I wanted to inhale her. To drink her in until I drowned in her essence from the inside out. She was all consuming—the way her back arched into my touch as her hips rolled over my cock. Any longer and I would have come undone.

I would have torn the buttons from her blouse. Sending them across the room like tiny bone shards so that I might have complete freedom to explore her sun-kissed skin. To touch her, taste her, and watch her come apart in my hands.

Damn the seas.

Odelia is a walking ocean. Unpredictable. Dangerous. Raging. Calm. Breathtaking. And I'm drowning in her.

What am I doing? Father would rage if he knew that I had a pirate in my bed. Selene would scold at first, and then she'd want to know all about Odi. Dash would probably cheer me on . . . in secret of course.

Mother would have asked when the wedding date is.

I have this overwhelming desire to reach for Odi every time she's near. She doesn't need me to protect her, *gods* know she can hold her own. I've seen her face her fears head on, rallied her bravery against hopelessness. She's strong like she's schooled it into an art. And yet, there's something in the way she feels pressed against me, the way her breath hitches when I brush her lips with mine, the way her eyes soften when she thinks no one is watching.

All of that makes something sharp and fierce coil in my chest. I want to shield her. Guard her. Keep the world's teeth off her skin.

Little doe—you're not making this easy.

I wasn't entirely surprised by her little weapon stash, but why hadn't it occurred to me to search her sooner? She still can't be fully trusted, right?

She's still a Viper.

Pirates hunt to kill. They cling to the old tales, the ones where water elementals whisper secrets of the oceans treasures. And my mother is—was—one of them . . . a water elemental. She told us how the tales were true, how the greedy would capture her kind and bleed them until everything they knew spilled out onto the deck. The elementals keep what is lost in or taken by the sea, and Odelia has to know how precious one of their maps would be. What wouldn't she sacrifice to find a wealth like that?

She's only using me. My ship. My crew.

She has to be.

So why do I feel this need to pull her closer instead of pushing her away?

A diffused flicker of white light behind dark, ominous clouds flashes on the horizon as I make my way from my room to the quarter deck. The storm is approaching abnormally fast, yet there is still time to pull the ship round and head southwest.

Unkind winds whip around me as I step out into the open. Elio is already halfway up the ratlines, trying to get a better view. He flicks his attention to me as I approach. "That's the biggest storm I've seen in a long time."

I plant my palms against the railing's edge, straining my eyes into the distance. Soraya appears beside me. She doesn't say a word. She doesn't need to.

Boots thud on the deck as Elio drops from above. "Cap?"

"We should've been at the next island by now," I growl in frustration. I'm mad at myself, at this damned map. Whatever trick it's playing is made worse by the angry gale that promises much, much worse. "At least then we could have gotten the injured to higher ground."

Soraya twirls to face me. "You didn't know it would change direction."

My jaw cracks as I grit my teeth. "I should have been prepared."

"Well," Elio chirps, "there's no point dwelling on that now, what do you want to do?"

There is really only one thing we can do, and it's going to require all hands-on deck. We have to outrun the storm before it tears the ship apart and sends us to the bottom of the cold, vicious sea.

I push off the edge of the ship, twisting to face the sleeping quarters. "Get everyone up here."

Neither Elio or Soraya need any more instruction. With a nod, they scatter like soldier crabs.

Pear and honey wrap around me, and my chest constricts. I turn to face Odi, who appears out of the shadows that grow as the sky darkens ahead of the storm. My gaze travels from her flushed cheeks down the curve of her neck, across her delicate collar bones all the way to the swell of her breasts.

Ten minutes ago I'd been teasing her perfectly taut nipple with my lips, and if I had control over the weather, I'd still be holed up in my room with her moaning my name as I gave her every pleasure she demanded of me.

"I thought I told you to stay in the room," I say, taking a small step towards her.

Odi squares her shoulders, her eyes flicking to the mass of dark, angry cloud approaching. "Looks like you're going to need all the help you can get."

She's not wrong. Again.

At first I hesitate, then I jerk my head towards the lower deck. "Join the others, and do whatever Elio tells you."

The corner of her perfectly pink lips tugs up in one corner. She runs her eyes over my face before letting them stall on my mouth, and then she grins. "Yes, Cap."

Fire erupts in my soul, spreading wildly through my body as I watch her dash away. I genuinely need to get a grip on myself, or she will be my undoing.

"Odi!" I call after her.

She spins, her dark hair swirling around her with the wind, eyes wide with anticipation. "Tell Elio the crew needs to get their weapons ready—they'll know what I mean. I don't know what to expect with this storm."

Her brow pinches in the middle, but she nods once and then she's gone, melting back into the shadows from which she came. I run a hand over my face and release a sigh. Just when I thought I'd have a restful night.

The horizon's gone black, swallowing sea and sky in the same breath. The wind howls through the rigging, snapping ropes taut, and every creak of the hull feels like the ship's bones groaning under the weight of what's coming.

Sheet lightning continues to roll across the clouds, washing the deck in ghostly white before plunging us back into half-light. I can taste the storm in the air—iron, salt, and something sharp that claws the back of my throat. The waves are already rising, heavy swells that punch the hull and spray cold brine over my face. A storm like this doesn't just test a ship. It tests the men on it. And it's coming for us fast.

There is no time to waste as I race for my room. Thrusting the door open, I dart across for the weapon that is more part of me than my bone sword. The halberd gleams from its stand on the wall even in the dim light, its shaft carved from dark driftwood, smoothed and reinforced with strips of galanthor bone. It's etched with curling tide marks like the ones that shimmer beneath my skin.

The blade isn't plain iron—no. It's hammered from a metal with the sheen of abalone, colours shifting with every tilt. Blue, green, silver, like the skin of a fish beneath sunlight.

I strap it across my back, the weight familiar. It isn't just a weapon. It's the ocean itself, forged into something sharp and loyal.

Once it's securely in place, I double check the sword by my side, and then I leave the room, slamming the door behind me. By the time I'm back on deck, so is half the crew, looking grim as rain begins to lash at us.

Elio finds me halfway up the stairs to the sterncastle deck. His emerald eyes are filled with concern. He knows this storm isn't normal. "Everyone's headed up."

"Where is Tavi?" I ask. Our boots pound on the stairs in unison as we reach the top.

Elio glances towards the sky. "She's in the crow's nest."

"Tell her to switch places with Nico. I need her down here."

Elio nods and races off.

The storm chews at the ship, every plank groaning under the weight of the sea. I shove my shoulder into the wheel and wrench it hard. The timbers scream, the rudder dragging through water thick as iron.

"I'm not getting any purchase!" My voice is swallowed by the wind. Salt lashes my face, stinging my eyes. The wheel bucks in my grip, fighting me, the ship yawing just shy of where I need her to go.

Boots slam the deck beside me. Elio returns, dripping from the rain, his clothing plastered to his chest like a second skin. "Tavi will attend to the crew on the main deck. Need me to check the rudder?" he yells above the braying winds.

I hesitate, knuckles white on the spokes. Sending him down there in this—when the ocean's churning like a beast—feels like tossing him straight into its jaws.

But we're out of options.

"Fine," I growl. "Be careful."

He nods once, and then the change takes him. Scales ripple down his skin, catching every flash of lightning in gleaming green. His legs fuse, stretching into a long, sinuous tail that ends in fins sharp as blades, emerald bright even in the stormlight. Gills flare behind his webbed ears, and for a breath he looks half-man, half-something older, born of tide and storm.

Elio vaults onto the railing without hesitation. One glance back and a grin on his lips—then he dives, cutting clean into the chaos below.

The sea swallows him whole while I keep my grip on the wheel, holding the ship steady. She fights me with everything she has. "Hold on, girl. We're going to get out of this," I mutter to her sails.

My gaze darts across the deck below, taking note of every crew member. Is everyone accounted for? I search for dark, chocolate hair. Umber eyes. World shattering smile. Yet, she's nowhere to be seen.

Surely she hasn't slipped from my grasp so easily.

No. There is no way she would venture out into this monster.

Where are you, little doe?

of us that looks over the main deck. "I don't think this is a normal storm, Rune."

"What do you mean?" I yell above the roar of the wind, though her words strengthen the suspicion that's been growing in me as well.

She flings her gaze over her shoulder, locking on me with disbelief. "Does it look normal to you?"

It doesn't. And it pulled us in faster than any storm I'd witnessed before. Some instinctual foreboding curls low in my gut, warning of the danger approaching. Not the gigantic clouds, or the unrelenting winds that tear through the ship as if it were on a personal mission to drown us all. Something else.

"So what are you suggesting?" I yell, unwilling to be the one that voices what I fear, in case the name summons our doom all on its own.

Odi lets go of the rail, slipping on her feet as she makes her way to me. She reaches my side, holding on to the post attached to the helm. "I think it's—"

A deafening sound spears from the blanket of ink above us—high, sharp, splitting the night wide open. It tears straight into my skull, making me flinch against my will. Beside me, Odi clamps her hands over her ears, eyes darting skyward.

I follow her gaze.

They circle the storm in the near distance—shadows nearly as big as a man, wings cutting jagged through the lightning flashes. Storm Rocs. Giant seabirds, but twisted, wrong. Their feathers are slick and black against the storm, eyes gleaming white when the lightning catches them. Each cry rakes the air raw, sharp enough to make my teeth ache. These birds, plus a storm, can only mean one thing.

Odi's pupils are so wide the brown is gone, replaced by a dark circle of fear as she shoves the bola into the belt around her hips. Her attention shoots to the angry water. "It's a kraken."

My heart stutters and I let the chill of her words rattle down my spine. "It's definitely a kraken."

From above, I hear someone call. "It's the water!" says Nico in the crows nest. "There's something in the water!"

I grip the ship's wheel tighter. I won't let this happen—can't. With one hand, I reach for Odi's wrist, twirling her to face me. "Prepare for attack! I want a rope on everybody, no one goes overboard today!"

She nods and races to the railing, calling out to Elio and the crew below. At once they scramble, tying themselves to each other and to the masts. I can't hear their mutters over the heavy thrum of the storm but I see them mouth the word kraken a few times, their eyes filling with fear.

This isn't something we're prepared for.

A groan sounds through the air, wracking my body with the reverberating sound. It's the kind of sound I'd imagine would sound when the world decided to end, opening wide and swallowing us whole.

Odi whips around to face me again. "Rune—"

"What!?" My voice comes out harsher than I intend, but I'm not sure I can handle more bad news right now.

"There—" She points into the dark of the storm. The water churns under *a second* flock of storm rocs. "It's the Sotor."

The blood drains from my face so fast I feel the chill crawl over my skin. My fingers flex against the wheel, knuckles bone-white, but I keep my shoulders squared, jaw locked. I can't let them see it . . . the crew—Odi. I can't let them see the fear clawing at my throat like smoke choking my lungs.

Odi grips my forearm. "Rune, that means—"

"I know."

The storm that surrounds us hasn't given birth to a single kraken, but two. Male and female. The Sotor.

Every old tale I ever heard presses in at once. No sailor survives the Sotor. Together, they don't just sink ships—they scour the sea clean.

My heart hammers so hard I think the others must hear it, yet outwardly I hold still, rigid, as though carved from the same wood beneath my boots. Inside, though—inside, I'm a boy again, listening to my mother whisper warnings about what waits in the deep.

I force my breath slowly. Don't show it. Don't let it break through. But *gods* help me—inside, I am absolutely petrified.

Letting go of the ship's wheel, I take Odi's hand in mine. At first, she glances down then back at me, shock registering on her face. She doesn't resist when I tug her towards the mizzen mast behind us.

She only protests when I push her back up against the mast. "Rune, we don't have time for this," she says, almost breathless, her face flushed pink.

I drop her hand only to cup her face in mine. It's so small between my palms, and even though the Krakens approach and the storm rages around us, all I see is her. Water droplets cling to her dark, upturned lashes as the rain pelts her skin. I try to shield her from as much of the tumultuous state around us as I can.

"What are you doing?" Her voice is hoarse with emotion.

My answer is low, rough. "What I want."

Then I claim her mouth with mine.

She goes stiff, but only for a breath, then she melts, hands creeping up my rain-slicked shirt, curling around the back of my neck and dragging me closer. I press harder, greedier, my arms cinching around her waist like if I hold her tight enough, I can fuse us into one body and cheat the fate clawing at our heels.

Her lips part for me, soft as velvet, and the taste of her collides with salt spray and stormwater on my tongue. It's wild, desperate—a sanctuary in the eye of the tempest.

My heart sighs, loosens, like it's found the missing piece it's been raging for all these years. The kiss turns hungry. Possessive. The kind that carves itself into your soul and never lets you walk free of its shadow.

She rises on her toes, fingers tangling into my soaked hair, tugging me down like she'll drown if she lets go. The moment her hand slips under my shirt, palm flattening against my chest, my mind blacks out.

I need this more than I need air.

She won't die today. I'll make sure of it.

My hands move over her waist, up her spine, keeping her pinned—while the other works quick, silent. Rope slides through my fingers and the iron rings beside us like second nature, wrapping once, twice around her middle. She doesn't notice—too caught up in the kiss, too intent on me.

I deepen it, pressing harder, and with a quick yank of my arm the knot cinches tight. By the time she feels it, it's done. Secure.

She gasps against my mouth, realising, her eyes flashing when I pull back just enough to meet them.

"You bastard," she breathes as wet strands of hair cling to her freckle-dusted face. She's tied firm. No chance of going over, for now at least.

I grip her chin between thumb and finger, my eyes lingering on her pink, swollen lips. "Just stay out of the way. . . that's an order."

As I back away, she bares her teeth at me . . . feral, furious, every inch of her like the wrathful storm around us. She's mad, and I don't blame her. If I were in her place, I'd hate me too. But there's no room for guilt, not now. I'll ask forgiveness later, if later comes. Right now, I can't fight with one eye on the enemy and the other searching for her.

She fears the sea. And that will drown her faster than this storm ever would.

Fool me twice

the stairs ahead, aiming for a better vantage point. Rune looks to the water beyond, but the tentacle is just another shadow betrayed by the lightning that booms as it reaches its long fingers down, called by the rocs.

The woman it grabs barely has time to scream. It wraps her ankle and lifts her higher and higher, like a rod reeling in, even as her eyes flash and her body curls up to sink her dagger into its flesh. The others shout, and it's Tavi that flies to where the tendril bends over the ship's railing, slicing at it in a flurry of impossible speed.

The woman, released, falls through the air, and her rope catches low on the wood of the mainsail and she swings, narrowly missing a roc that claws for her.

The tentacle writhes on the deck, severed. In flashes of blinding white, it's a faint, murky pink edged with iridescent green, its inside riddled with haphazard suckers. The crew is on alert now, ready when the next slips over, and the next. I watch, trapped, as the kraken grips the deck of the ship with three massive tentacles.

Fire flashes, there and gone again, doused by the rain. The bolts can't do their job in this. An attack from above me all but glues the nearest tendril to the wood and I look up to find Otto, sitting on the pole of the lower mizzen mast, his eyes squinted against the assault of the storm. If this ship goes down, the ocean won't spare even the best of us.

"OTTO!" I shout, trying to catch his attention so he can cut me free and let me join the fight. He looses another slug, and the stuck tendril is peppered with exploding shot, bursts of flesh tossed over the deck. "OTTO LET ME GO!"

There's no use. The wind screams over everything. Even the bursts of slugshot are silent compared to the storm. The ship rocks dangerously side to side, water crashing over the deck in deadly waves as we rise and drop with the anger of the sea. The half-drawn sails rip in the wind, tangling in the rigging.

The rocs sweep onto the deck, pecking gleefully at the mangled tendril and the bits scattered nearby. A man charges them with a battle axe, all primal rage, but the one closest just skirts back, then leaps forwards with a push of its wings and spurs his gut open. He goes down, and they begin to eat him before he stops moving.

I flinch away as a body crashes down near me, so close I can feel the graze of his clothes. The ship tilts again and the unconscious man slips a few feet away. His arms are mess of ribboned skin and muscles. He must have slipped away from one of the rocs.

Across the deck, Rune moves like a storm of his own, jabbing opportunistic birds from the air and batting back the kraken's seeking grasp as the tentacles crack the ship's railing and reach for masts. A cut on his arm already weeps blood, but Tavi and Elio flank him, the latter in his half shift, his wounds open and seeping down his chest.

The ship tilts again, and when the body beside me tries to slide past, his sword appears from beneath him. I catch it with one planted foot. The ropes strain painfully across my stomach and wrists, but the ship rights itself again. I have the weapon, but I can't reach it, and another rush of helpless frustration sets my teeth on edge. I slip a boot off. If I can—

The ship goes sideways and the weapon slips, sliding just a hair out of reach. I stretch for it, pain flaring in every nerve.

Then a dark shadow swoops down, crunching the body's ribs with the force of its weight. The bird tugs at the strings of muscle already fanned across the wood, then one of its eyes trains on me.

Wet air saws in and out of my lungs as it cocks its head, then steps forwards. The chaos of storm and sound and death narrows to the emotionless black of its eyes and the rain that forms glittering beads over the grey of its feathers. I'm stuck. Another step. A leap, and I'll be in gutting range. No chance to fight it, no hope of grabbing the sword still trapped under my bare foot or the weapons sheathed beneath my clothes. Rune left me here to die. Pride, fear. No matter the motivation, the end is the same.

We were so close.

The bird's image blurs and I flinch away, waiting for the bite of talons, but none comes. There's a jerk of pressure at my waist, and I open my eyes to watch the ropes fall away.

"Come on!" Otto grabs my aching wrist and wrenches me down the stairs, leaving behind the roc, whose massive claws are now glued to the deck with slimeshot. He drags us past the overwhelm of shooting crossbows and arcing blood and into the captain's quarters. I yank my hand away just as he pulls me through.

"I'm not hiding," I say, my voice hard.

"Cap said you can't swim. You go out there, you're going overboard. Unless you can get a rope on you, but it doesn't look to be helping anyone else out there."

The ship tilts as if in agreement, and we plant our feet as Rune's coffee mug slips across the ground, rolling cheerfully to the other side of the room.

"I can swim. But you need to stay here."

"But the captain said—"

"I don't give a damn what your prince said, Otto," I shout as I open the door to the gale of the storm and leave, letting it slam behind me. I sweep my eyes over the deck, looking for the tell-tale silhouette of Rune's massive body. It's carnage. Some are still tied to the mast, others have cut themselves free, trying to avoid the tangle of ropes and bodies. The ocean crashes over the top in waves, washing the red of blood and sinew and bodies away in watery streaks. An oily gel leaks from the tentacles, seeping out in a purple ooze.

Another bird drops beside me, but this one is down, its feathers still being chewed away by the acidic bolt embedded in its chest.

A group loads a larger crossbow mounted to the deck, aiming for the tentacles that reach up out of the water. Two meet their mark, exploding just seconds after impact.

"I think they're retreating," Elio shouts from somewhere across the chaos. The lightning is high in the sky, sheeting across the clouds, illuminating the birds that have pulled away to circle above. The tentacles fall back until only one is left, speared high in the air, with no apparent interest in the ship or the bolts that fail to make purchase.

For a moment, I think it might be over, and the creature's retreat offers a half-second of easy breath. I see Rune on the other side of the deck, his head tipped back to watch the sky. Blood drips freely from the handle of his bone blade. I follow his gaze to the rocs above, whose circle formation has tightened, sped. Electricity crackles over their bodies, zipping in sparks and webs of rumbling light.

Then the sky erupts in a deafening boom, and white sears so bright the pain spears into my head. I flinch, blinking away the shattering cracks of light that live behind my eyelids.

The world seeps back into focus in muted shouts and blurred images. Water rushes over my feet—my boot is still missing. The ocean is chill, insistent.

"BRACE YOURSELVES."

I don't know who says it, only that the world tips a moment later, and my feet lose contact with the deck. I flail in the darkness, fingers grazing taut ropes as I slam into those that have tied themselves to the mast. When the ship comes up to catch me, it's with the railing, and my back arches against the blinding pain as the bones of my back slam into the wood.

On all fours, I look up to find the kraken has the ship curled in one, massive, suckered grip, the tentacle electrified by the roc's lightning. It buzzes and arcs with bursts of current that hit the deck. Water floods and empties away from it, turning it into an alternating hazard of loose electricity. The crew turns all the weaponfire they have, sinking bolts of bone and solid wood. Some explode, like Otto's. Others do little, the kraken's mucus layer nulling any acidity or flame that tries to stick.

Rune manifests in the middle of the chaos, halberd brandished like he thinks he'll get a chance to stab at it before the water electrocutes him. Bolts fly over his shoulders, but he doesn't flinch, his face fierce in the unnatural dusk. The tendril grips the main mast. I rise as a bird tries to fly at his back. My bola aims true, tangling its wing and bringing it down to where I can leap forward to press a blade into the space between its head and neck. He turns as I untangle the weapon, our eyes meeting between one flash of lighting and the next.

Then he's gone, lost in a flurry of ripped sails, flying shadows, and struggling bodies. I move to follow, but a force rips me backwards by the base of my tangled braid, shooting pain down my bruised spine, and it's all I can do to draw Rune's dagger as I'm yanked into the deeper shadows.

"You did this, you mangy bitch."

Reid. His voice alone makes my stomach curdle. I spin, aiming the handle of the dagger into the sensitive lower bones of his ribs. He hisses and lets go, but angles his own blade to my neck, like he thinks he could move fast enough to use it.

"I'm a little busy, pissbreath," I say, gesturing to the chaos around us.

His sunburned face is smeared with blood that leaks from a cut at the crown of his head. His eyes are wide, his grin almost manic. "We're already dead," he says, shouting over the wail of the wind. "Because of you." The words are punctuated by a swipe of his blade.

I leap back. He's taller and stronger, but it's half a thought to parry, sending the edge away. The blood in my veins is beyond boiling, but I've got bigger problems than a small man with an overinflated ego. "Is this how you want to die, Reid? Felled by a pirate? Letting the kraken take you would be a much cooler story."

He bares his teeth and swipes again. I step to one side, then leap to parry another sloppy blow, grinning now, because the look on his face might be the last pleasure I get before this ship is taken by the sea. "Harder to gut than you expected?"

A neat feint leaves him open and I snap my blade to the delicate skin above his collarbone. He freezes, arms wide, flushing redder with every passing moment. "Leave it," I say, as if he were a dog. "Let the ocean have you. There'd be more dignity."

I give him my back, irritated but not surprised when I double back to find his arm flung high, ready to bring his sword down to cleave me in two.

I dive behind him, catching myself in a half-cartwheel, wincing at the ache in my spine as I come up, brandishing my bola like a whip. It's a manoeuvre I've practiced a hundred times, more. The long end wraps his unbalanced ankle and I *pull* with the weight of my entire body until it slips, and his knee jars against the wood. Then, it's nothing to press my blade to the back of his neck too.

"Do it again, and you're dead."

His brawny shoulders shake, and my face twists as I realise he's laughing.

I step back, unsteady as seawater tugs at our feet again, but keep my blade lifted when he turns, his expression a tortured mix of amusement and pain.

"I knew I recognized you."

I feel myself go still.

"You're *her*. His daughter."

The roar of the sea compounds with the blood in my ears. "What are you talking about?"

"The bola. I've seen it. Has to have been over a decade ago. There used to be a little village along the coast of Brackbay, just a speck on the mainland." His grin widens impossibly more. "You ruined it."

"The next words out of your mouth decide if you live or die." I'm not sure if he hears me, but he doesn't miss the way I lean in, just a hair, drawing his eyes back to the blade a handsbreadth from his face.

"It was you who killed them all," he spits. "Snuck into a tired old manor, slit the throat of the lord and lady, the gardener, their only son and wife who'd come to visit while he was on leave. You ended a bloodline that night. It was Ivor that pulled your cowl back, just a little. And you—your eyes were empty, even as they set the manor ablaze. So young. Must have been born ruined, I thought. Yeah. Don't you worry, *Nisse*." The name, the memory, tears something vital away from me, but Reid just shakes his head in mock pity. "I won't tell Rune. He's had his chance."

"You won't?" Everything in me screams that I should kill him, that if Rune finds out, it's over. The map. The keys. Hell, he might string me up like Reid has always wanted. Even if I managed to get away, it would ruin any chance I'd have of starting over. Without the treasure, I wouldn't make it far, and it would only be a matter of time until someone found me. But something in me, something small and weak and soft, has enjoyed how little blood I've spilled these last few weeks. The same part that wonders if maybe Rune *won't* spill my intestines into the sea the moment he finds out how much I lied to him.

Reid shakes his head again and I lower my blade by a fraction, wary. But when he speaks, the look in his eye promises death. "I'll just have to let Ivor know where his daughter has gone. Who she's fucking. And with his map in hand, no less. Tsk. Tsk."

I blink, speaking before the words have fully processed. "Ivor would kill everyone on this ship."

The man's face shows no regret. "If they're *lucky*."

A breath. I give myself a breath to come up with a reason to let him live.

And then I jab for his throat.

He drops at the last second, and the blade slices his cheek and splits his ear at the lobe. With a manic snarl, he heaves his blade towards me, but the attack hardly registers. I'm already spinning the bola in my left hand, ready to wrap his wrist. As expected, he pulls up and back, but I use the leverage to step into his guard, and sink the narrow blade between his ribs until I feel his lung pop.

He sucks in a wet shuddering breath as the ship rises on another wave, the horizon a mountain range of peaks and valleys. I loosen my hold and let him fall over the railing as we lean. He goes like a felled tree, his body stiff, legs flipping so he hits head first and disappears. The storm swallows him.

Another secret, another lie. One I can't bring myself to feel sorry about.

On the main deck, a man screams. I sprint that way, slipping in puddles of feather-filled ooze and patches of gore.

The storm rocs that are left have retreated, waiting for easier scraps. Tavi and Rune hack away at the tendrils snaking across the ship. They've managed to dislodge the big one, but if any of them get enough purchase, it will crack the ship in half.

I duck away from the suckered tip of one appendage, spinning to swipe at it for good measure. Rune doesn't look at me when I make it to him, my blade drawn and ready to meet the kraken's blind attacks.

"Don't slip," he says, jaw set. "I don't have time to rescue you at the moment."

A Necklace Lost

25
RUNE

The violent storm tosses *The Gilded Hart* through the waves like a leaf in the wind, her hull groaning in protest. The Sotor circle further out and I fear that the worst has only just begun. My eyes dart everywhere at once, taking in the chaos around me.

The crew shouts over the wind, some hauling ropes, others diving out of the way as storm rocs nose dive from the skies. Silver white hair flies across the deck as Tavi takes two rocs down with her blades.

If the feel of the kraken ick oozing down my arms doesn't put me in the ground, the stench will. It smells of rotting meat mixed with storm roc shit and burnt hair. It's all I can do not to heave up the contents of my stomach onto the deck.

Purple, oily gel amalgamates with the crimson blood seeping from the gouge on my arm. The sharp pain has long passed, leaving me with a dull aching throb.

I've lost count of how many birds I've cut down. Each time one drops from the sky, another claws its way out of the murk to take its place. My mind is torn between a million places at once. Trying to keep an eye on Elio, Tavi, Otto, the crew, and now Odi. Plus keep the gigantic birds from tearing into my flesh.

How am I supposed to keep this ship from sinking when all I can think about is Odi not going overboard, and how see through her wet blouse has become? The moment I pulled the ropes taut around her waist I knew she wouldn't stay put. It wasn't a shock when she appeared beside me, blade ready and a vicious grin on her face, but I had to try.

Of course, now she's glaring at me. I can't say I don't deserve it. Both our chests heave as we drag air into our lungs. "Was roping me really your best plan?"

I fight my smile as lighting sheets across the sky, illuminating the lethal promise in her eyes. "I've had worse."

She swipes at a shadow that flies too close, fast as a dartfish. "You almost got me and Otto both killed."

I drop my gaze down, away from hers. I'd wanted to protect her. I didn't think it would go like this. Be this bad. I lunge, stabbing at a roc that gets too close, thankful they're growing more cautious. "If you go over, you're dead. And you want me to watch it happen?" I track the slow bob of her neck as she swallows, wisps of hair plastered to her face. Rain pelts into my chest, hard and fast. Water drips off my nose and chin, and swiping at it with the wet sleeve over my uninjured forearm does nothing to help. "At least half-shift," I say, half-plea, half-shout over the rage of the storm around us. "You'll see better. Be faster—"

"You've seen what happens when I shift, Rune!" she calls over the gale. "I can't."

She can. And if she did she'd see a hundred times better than she can right now. But she won't. I see it in her eyes, the fear that she'll lose control. There's no time for convincing. I drop it, angling myself towards where a group strikes at another thin-tipped tentacle that creeps over the railing's edge on the far side. Maybe she's right to be cautious. We don't know what her half-shift looks like. The slick deck won't be kind if she ends up with hooves.

The thought flicks my attention low enough I notice her bootless foot. I feel my brow pinch, confusion tripping my racing thoughts. When I look back up, she's smirking at me.

Before I can ask where her boot went, Elio emerges to my right, a shortsword in hand. He's half-shifted, talons flexed and incisors sharpened, with a mix of blood and kraken gore strewn across his chest and stomach. He sees me running my eyes over him and he shakes his head quickly. "I'm fine, its mainly from the rocs."

Web-like veins of lightning scatter across the heavens, followed by a thunderous boom that rattles me to the core. The rain is coming in sideways. Between that, the bird entrails scattered over the ship, and the kraken limbs leaking onto the deck, I'm surprised any of us can find our footing.

The birds dive in earnest now, screeching, tearing, snapping with hooked beaks. There isn't a minute to spare as I dart across the slippery wood. My blood curdles when a screech pierces the sky, and a roc drops down, clawing at my shoulder. I rip it off and hurl it into the mast, its body snapping with a wet crack.

My mind isn't on the birds though. It's on *The Gilded Hart*. I can't let her fall. She's all we've got between us and the black maw of the sea.

"Back me up!" I roar over my shoulder. Elio darts to my right, and not many would, but I notice the way he favours one leg over the other. He's still injured but pushes through the pain either way.

He is to my left. Steel sword slashing while Odi wields her bola or my dagger when the rocs get too close. I don't look back, I trust them to guard my spine. My focus is forwards where a tentacle—murky pink, edged with iridescent green—writhes across the deck like thick ropes of muscle.

I charge, sea brine spraying all around me, and drive my halberd in deep. The blade bites into a sucker, cleaving it clean. Purple blood sprays across my face, warm against the icy rain. The tentacle recoils with a shudder, the kraken bellowing in pain, but it doesn't retreat.

Lightning splits the sky, illuminating the chaos. Asher, one of the night crew—cries out, tangled in wings and ropes, bleeding out where he falls.

My heart hammers in my chest as he goes down. I want to scream into the void. Empty my lungs of the anguish I feel.

There's no time.

From the corner of my eye, I see Tavi swinging on ropes from mast to mast like she's on vines in a jungle. Her blades slash through feathers, dropping rocs from the sky. She's okay. She's alive. Now I need to find Otto and Soraya.

I spot them both, back to back as they fire off bolts of slimeshot. Some find their mark, others miss but ward off the birds for a moment. Both alive. Good.

That's when I notice the pulse of bioluminescence through the waters. I should have seen it sooner. Each time the lightning strikes the kraken, the ocean around it becomes electrified. It's like a conduit from sky to sea.

As I whip around, I watch a roc pin Maurice to the deck. I race for him, Elio and Odi on my heels. The beak tears into his shoulder and he lets out a bloodcurling scream. I don't hesitate. I drive my bone blade down through its skull. There's a crack, and the shriek from the bird cuts short, body twitching before it slumps lifeless beside the crewman.

The male gasps for breath, clutching at the wooden boards beneath him. "Thank you."

I yank him up by the collar and shove him towards the rigging. "Move!"

A loud groan brings my attention back to the sea. The kraken grows out of the water like an obelisk of stone. A tentacle reaching for the heavens before it bears down to wrap around a crewman on the deck.

"NO!" I roar, dashing for him. But it's too late, the kraken squeezes, and his eyes bulge from his head before I hear the sickening sound of his spine pop.

My boots skid to a halt as the kraken flings the body through the storm to the waiting female kraken behind him. Odi curses, Elio echoes the sentiment. It's too much. All of it. We're going to die.

same moment I realise I have about five seconds to get out of the water before I become fried shrimp.

White bolts of lightning stab into the male kraken. It roars, sending a pulse of electricity into the sea just as I pull myself up the rope. The electricity sparks up, restless, arcing out of the water. One of the smaller arcs catches the tip of my fin and ripples under my skin, but I can bear it. I hiss through my teeth and yank on the ropes, falling over the railing in seconds. Just as well the sword still in my hand is made with the same resistant bone we use for our bolts.

Odi rushes to my side as I shift back. "You're delusional."

I smirk at her. "Or, I'm a really good swimmer."

She huffs as she reaches for my hand to help me up. Her touch gives me life. It's enough to bring fresh wind to my lungs, though I can't help but feel quiet guilt at the thought of her necklace somewhere on the bottom of the Adamaris Sea.

"You're bleeding. Again," she gasps, oblivious to my thoughts as she squats down to inspect the wound on my thigh. My jaw clicks as I watch her delicately move the torn fabric out of the way. The sight of her on her knees before me does something in my chest. I have to get it together.

"I'll be fine." I offer her my hand, pulling her up. "We have to keep moving."

No sooner do the words leave my mouth than a tentacle slaps the deck. Elio, Odi and I sprint for it. I pull my bone blade from its sheath and drive it down with all the force I can muster. They attack it from a different angle, and white braids fly through the sky above as Tavi leaps to land on the slick planks with a thud.

She flashes me a grin. "Time to carve this tentacled bastard into chum." And then she's gone. Twin blades singing in a blur of carving motions.

I follow her lead, slashing against another tentacle that snakes over the railing. The bone blade slices the murky pink flesh, but it's like trying to hack through a rope thicker than my biceps. The cut is shallow, pathetic and the kraken recoils out of irritation more than pain.

My chest heaves, sweat and sea brine stinging my eyes. What are we doing? All these blades against limbs, and we've barely slowed it down. Every strike feels wasted.

Elio runs a taloned hand through his hair before wiping his face from the relentless rain. "I don't think any of these weapons are working."

Another tentacle coils around a mast, the wood groaning under its strain. My grip tightens on the hilt of my blade. If we keep hacking blindly, the ship will be gone before the monster is.

I nod. "I agree, stabbing the tentacles isn't doing anything."

My chest heaves in and out as I try to catch my breath. I stare out at the male kraken.

Think fast Rune.

I chew my bottom lip as the kraken's eyes drag over the body of my ship—all glorious wood and gilded trimmings thanks to my father's insistence. I despise the way the beast looks at her hull, like she's an empty seed pod in the wind.

Then I run for the nearest crossbow.

"Cap—" Elio says.

I don't answer. The weapon is already loaded, slick in my hands, blood and rain running down the stock, but I brace it against my weight and squeeze. The bolt whistles through the storm, and then sinks deep into the kraken's eye with a wet *pop*. A groaning shriek pierces the night sky, shaking the ship to the bones. Purple blood spurts from the wound, trailing down the sea monster's body. The beast recoils, thrashing, tentacles reaching for the ship, colliding with the hull.

The impact sends a shudder through *The Gilded Hart* and she groans in protest.

"Hands on your bows!" I shout, voice raw over the thunder. "Aim for the eyes!"

Elio, Odi, the crew. They scatter like crabs. Reaching for every crossbow in sight, mounted or not, and as I release a breath, bolts are loosed into the inky night. A few find their mark, biting into soft, squelching orbs. The kraken bellows, batting most away with a sweep of its limbs. The deck rocks under the weight of its fury, planks groaning as if ready to snap.

"AGAIN!" I scream.

And again the crew fires off bolts. This time many find their mark.

Beyond the shrieking male, the female waits. Not attacking. Just circling. Watching. Patient as death itself. Waiting for her meal—my crew.

Not today you filthy sea cow.

I reload fast, forcing the massive weapon steady as I aim. My heart pounds in my ears, my temples throb. I think of Odi. Of Otto. Of Elio, Tavi and Soraya. Of mother. I'd do it for them. It's madness to even try. But I steady, exhale and let the bolt fly.

It tears through the downpour and I use my darkvision to track it. My mouth splits into a feral grin when it finds its mark. The female's central eye. The ocean shatters around me with her shriek, worse than thunder, worse than the cry of a sea wyrm. Her eye bursts into a spray of milky yellow fluid, juices raining down on the waves slapping at her skin. She writhes, descending into the ocean in a storm of bubbles and thrashing limbs.

The male freezes, lets out a bellow that rattles every exhausted body on deck, then surges after her into the deep.

Gone.

The birds scatter with them, peeling away into the sky, their screeches fading into an echo. And just like that, the storm breaks. The sea is calm. The sky opens in a surreal blanket of soft light.

I feel the gentle pressure of someone squeezing my hand, and I'm not sure which of us reached for the other, but when I glance down it's Odi, gripping back like she's afraid to hope that this might be the end. So I squeeze her hand back.

The moment the sun's warm beams hit my skin, I drag in a breath that I'd been too afraid to take. And I stand there on the deck, chest heaving, crossbow trembling in my grip, soaked in rain and kraken blood, with Odi by my side.

"That was fucking brutal," I whisper.

Bloodstained Hands Comfort None

26
ODELIA

The relative silence echoes in my ears. We're still. Tense. Waiting for the storm to brew again. But the rocs are all but invisible in the distance now, and the krakens will follow, waiting for the next unlucky ship caught in their deadly, symbiotic wake.

"Gather the wounded and the dead, search the water too. I want a head count," Rune says. His voice is even as he fades out of his half shift, though he grips my hand like the world is tilting. It may as well be—the Sotor? They're a legend. A myth. A ship may survive an encounter with a young, curious kraken. But the Sotor are the breeding pair, royalty in their own right. Older than kingdoms.

We shouldn't be alive.

"We're taking water!"

I don't recognize who says it, but Rune lets go of my hand and bolts that way. I follow on instinct, pulled by his gravity. A younger man with wisps of auburn on his chin meets us at the door of the lower deck.

Rune takes a cursory glance around. There are more of us down than standing. I don't miss the way the muscle in his jaw feathers as he tracks each face. "Have you seen Merrick?"

The other man's hands are shaking as much as his voice. "He went over. I tried to—I tried—"

Rune doesn't wait for the crewman's panic to settle in, instead he clamps a hand on his shoulder, spinning him away from the carnage and steering him down the stairs. "Then you're our shipwright!" Rune says, his tone brooking no argument. I follow them into the dark of the lower deck, blinking against the sudden dimness.

"I'm just an apprentice."

"Not anymore."

The younger man sets his jaw. The stairs squeak with every step, the wood wet and swollen against their iron bolts. We reach the storage deck and step down into water up to our ankles. Down here, some sort of glowing moss radiates enough light to see that black streaks mar the hull in shattered webs of damaged wood. I hold in a gasp. I've no experience with lightning damage, and my only comfort is that if it were as bad as it looks, we'd already be under water.

The shipwright motions ahead. "It's here."

Halfway down, where the streaks of darkened wood intersect, water flows down the hull from a hole halfway up. Worse, cracks follow the lines of damaged wood, allowing sea water to seep in like teardrops.

"Looks straightforward enough," Rune says, though I suspect the cheer in his voice is solely for the new shipwright's benefit. "Where do you guys keep the plugs?" His eyes are already on a box down the way, but he lets the young man find it, then starts to pace, sloshing water around as the man scrambles for the right size.

"I'll find a bit of extra sail," I say, splashing my way to a stack of slowly-soaking fabric in the corner. My voice is raw and rough from shouting over the storm. The *Sea Bane* had been patched more times than I can recall, with all manner of plugs and fabric—usually not ones intended for the purpose.

Rune sighs, giving a cursory glance as I move away. "Just leave as much as we can. We'll need it."

"Not if we're at the bottom of the sea," I argue, too bone-weary for the words to have any bite. I bring the sail piece, trying to avoid stepping on anything sharp with my one bootless foot. It would do no good to survive the kraken, patch the ship, and then die of lock jaw. "You should go join the injured."

He ignores my pointed look at his bloody leg. The pocket of his trousers had ripped clean off at some point. "Got that plug, Stiden?" The water has risen by an inch.

Stiden nods, his brow pinched in concentration as he takes the cloth from me and wraps it around the wedge of wood. It doesn't budge when he presses it against the break.

Rune's voice remains impossibly even. "The hammer, Stiden."

I can't tell if it's sweat or seawater that drips down the shipwright's face. "I *know* I need the hammer, Captain, I just . . . I always was holding onto it before."

Rune limps forwards, like the pain is finally settling in as the adrenaline wears off. "Well this time I'll hold it, and you can have the honours of trying hard not to break my fingers."

"Yes, Captain," the man says, his voice thin as he hands over the fashioned plug and goes to the box for the sledge hammer. Rune holds it to the hole with both hands, angling his face away. A ghost of a smile flits over his face when he sees the way I'm already wincing in anticipation of a busted thumb or broken wrist.

The man swings, and I flinch when the slam echoes through the lower deck. Once. Twice.

In the silence, the stairs creak, and Tavi appears, her eyes flicking over me, then Rune and Stiden, who both examine the patch. The stream of water has stopped, though the crack webbed above and below still drips ominously.

"Alright down here?" Tavi calls, opting to stay on the third step.

Rune claps the shipwright on the shoulder again as he nods. "We're alright. I'll meet you up top, we'll see if we can't find Bear and let him know we need the resin warmed to seal this up. Then"—he says, facing Stiden again—"I'll need you to scour every inch of the hull for signs of more leaks. Our next stop will be for repairs, but we're counting on you to make sure the ship can make it there."

The man is white as a specter, but obeys, following Tavi up the stairs with Rune and I at his back. Up top, the crew is gathered, most sitting against the mast or railings, others laying down, eyes closed against the bright of the sun.

Rune's eyes skirt over the faces that turn to us, his face darkening.

"Otto's in the galley, we needed more of the poultice," Tavi says over her shoulder as if she can read his mind. She moves away to salve a man's shoulder wound. Her clothes are ripped, but compared to everyone else her injuries appear minor—a cut on the back of her hand, a bit of blood soaking through her pants at the back of her leg.

Rune's shoulders lighten microscopically, and he nods for the shipwright to go find Otto before kneeling next to Tavi, using a dark solution to clean a puckering rib wound on the woman nearby. His hands work with expert precision, flushing, salving, and wrapping. I join them, working through wounds as quickly as I can. Soraya leans against the railing, head tilted back, quiet tears streaking down her cheeks. One of her legs is clearly broken below the knee, and blood dries over angry slices on her dark-brown thigh.

"You're going to be okay," I tell her, my voice rough. She doesn't even wince when I apply the salve.

"I know, I know," she says quickly, brushing off the concern. Her voice quivers. "But Beron—" The words are choked off by the sobs that start to wrack her chest. I look to the broad-chested man that sits thigh-to-thigh with her. His tanned, scared arm rests over a wound in his stomach. His face is tipped back, up to the sky, peaceful.

He isn't breathing.

The afternoon turns to dusk before those alive start to believe they might stay that way. Tavi sets Soraya's leg, but several with electricity burns send Rune to the galley to consult

as proud and polished as ever. Moonlight gleams from her cheekbones and between her brow like an adornment. The water elemental must have been carved by a master craftsman.

"My mother used to whittle wood," I say, surprising myself. "Smaller than this, of course. My father still has a few of her figurines. Little land animals. I pretended they were my friends." Those last words come out softer. I've never admitted it out loud, and I'm not sure why I do now. Maybe it's the way he follows my gaze, looking into the face of the figurehead. His eyes are mournful, and only become more so as they seem to unfocus, lost in thought.

"Mine used to paint," he says, quietly. "There are entire murals on the castle's hallways documenting the history of her people. We'd had to drain each section as she worked, and once the paint dried and we nullified the sea stone, the flow of water and the light would warp the images, and they would look alive." At some point, he'd taken the time to change from his formal attire. He smooths a hand over his pocket, the movement habitual. "It was magic to me. She taught us to think in colours, look for the beauty in even the forgotten places of the world."

The ache in his voice settles in my chest. "She sounds amazing."

"She was."

The ocean waves churn in the silence. I want to ask when he'd lost her, and how, but I wait, unwilling to take more than he wants to give. The moment feels like standing at the edge of a cliff, a breeze away from the kind of fall you can't stop.

"She's why I wanted the map." The words confuse me enough that I look at him, my brow pinched, but his gaze is still trained on the carved woman beside us. "When I saw her mark, I had to try. A water elemental treasure trove—centuries of coin and history spilled into the sea and collected. Coveted, claimed by the ocean. Had she helped grow it? Had her kin left what they found most precious?" His voice goes high and thin. "Would I find . . . clues there? Of where she'd gone?"

Two realisations hit me at once—the map was rarer and more extraordinary than Ivor ever knew—and Rune's mother . . . was a water elemental.

They're rare creatures, and their treasure troves rarer still, according to the tales told by drunk pirates and superstitious fishermen. I'd heard horrible things, too. Of the harm done to those elementals that were captured by land dwellers who believed they'd be a quick ticket to the sea's riches. Ivor had never believed in that sort of thing, he had more efficient methods, but other pirates did, hunting them, pushing them further and further into hiding, until people began to wonder if they were ever real.

"That's why you're a bounty hunter," I murmur, the pieces clicking into place. "You think she was captured."

"I—" He pauses. "It was something I could *do*. A way I could act. While telling myself that answers were out there somewhere. They had to be. And even if I never found them, at least I'd keep the seas that much cleaner. Safer. I don't have anything else."

The words are so raw I know he believes them. "Rune—"

His voice turns sharp. "I'm done with the map." I go silent, stomach dropping to the waves below as he goes on. "We can't keep doing this. It has to be over."

I train my eyes to the sea, pretending not to feel the heat of him beside me. I'm too much of a coward to ask what exactly he means—the ending is the same either way. He's lost enough. So we're done. No map. No keys. No reason for Nisse to haunt *The Gilded Hart*.

The ship creaks, motionless but for her gentle sway side to side. The sails that are patched have been rolled tight to avoid strain. Beyond, the horizon stretches endlessly on every side. One slip and I'd go over. I wait for the fear to come, to claim, but it's muted, exhausted—or perhaps sated by the knowledge he'd go in after me, just like that very first time.

"I'm sorry," I say. The words feel foreign. My teeth clamp tight against any explanation, against giving more than I already have.

He lifts the glass beside him and dumps it over the side in one smooth motion, watching how it disappears in the sea. "Me too."

I almost have to bite back a smile. We're so different. Too different. I'd do anything to feel less—and he martyrs himself to it.

"You didn't steer us into the Sotor, Rune." The words come out soft. "You just handled what came for you. It's all any of us can do."

He shakes his head.

His grief is tangible. There's nothing I can say, not really. So I stay, half-wondering if I should go, half-wondering if

I should take his hand like before. But something in me remains stunted—these hands are too bloodstained to be any comfort. They've snapped necks. Driven blades into the soft of eyeballs and held fast as my bola choked the life from so many I've lost count. They're for violence, for sinking chipped fingernails into whatever I've needed to survive. How many have flinched away? And how little mercy were they shown?

This crew . . . they mourn together. Hold each other. Wrap the dead in tear-stained canvas and press dried bundles of flowers and herbs between the layers before releasing them to the deep, anointing them in both earth and water. It's a far cry from the *Sea Bane*, where the useless were tossed over like filth—dead or alive. I helped with that too.

Rune rests his hand on the prow beside me, inches from my own. It would take one movement. One quick surrender. Maybe the urge alone is enough to prove how much I've changed.

But he tied me to the mast. He'd kissed me and taken the key.

We can't keep doing this. The words replay in my head on a loop. We can't keep dancing around the reality of us. We can't push for a dream that claws back, that takes more than it could ever give.

It was always going to end this way.

Easy steps disturb the silence. Elio strides up, still bandaged and shirtless, but his short hair drips water.

Rune's eyes flash as he turns, letting himself back onto the deck. "I told you to rest."

"And I told you to stop being an insufferable mother hen. I get enough of that from Tavi."

I try to pretend I'm not listening, but snort anyway, the image too absurd for me to reign in the reaction. When I look back, Elio grins, but Rune still studies him, cataloguing the way he favours one side.

"Needed a swim. Wanted to check the damage from the outside."

Something in his voice suggests there's more he's not saying, and I turn to face them, my nerves already prepared for the moment it's bad news.

His eyes flick between us both, then rest on Rune. "I think there's something you need to see."

A CHILD OF THE SURFACE

27
RUNE

"Where?" I ask, as I swing my legs over and jump down to the deck. Boots thud behind me as Odi joins my side.

Elio fiddles with the white shark-tooth necklace he always wears. "Below. A little ways off. Didn't get a good long look. Square, white stone—at least it used to be. Barnacles all over it. Crumbling before my eyes—"

"Maybe the map marks more than islands," I mutter, before beginning to pace back and forth. I should have considered it before.

"You think it marked the Sotor?" Elio asks.

I shake my head, but Odelia is already speaking. "No one could survive that. It wouldn't make sense."

"No," I agree. "The Sotor go where they please. We'd hardly have been the first to see them if they lingered in one spot for long."

From where she sits on the railing, Odi tracks my every step. She looks tired, like she'd rather tuck herself away in the dark somewhere and shut out the world. Who knows . .

. perhaps I'd join her. With the weight of death on my back, it's hard to find the desire to keep chasing my mother's ghost.

I flick my gaze back to Elio. "But I can go scout it. You need to rest. And there's every chance it's unrelated."

He folds his arms across his chest and cocks his head to the side. "And the siren statues out the front? Same as the ones we found at the temple."

My brow furrows as I spin to face him.

"Why the hell didn't you lead with that? How far did you go?" I ask, trying my best to not sound too desperate.

He huffs, a smile playing on his lips. "You cut me off. And I didn't go far. Just to where I could confirm the statues."

I offer him a nod—an apology. ". . . Fair. How far down?"

"Deep enough that only a skilled swimmer would reach it."

This is it. The third key on the map. But I can't help but hesitate. I can't afford to trigger some natural disaster or awaken another slumbering sea creature that will try to tear us in two.

We barely survived the last one. The ship is a wreck, just like the crew who dwell on it. Everyone is exhausted. Morale is low. Lower than the critters who live in the shadows on the bottom of the seabed.

My bones ache from overuse. My mind aches from being in a constant state of chaos. And my heart aches for the folk I've lost along the way.

On top of that . . . I'd just told Odi we're done.

I begin to pace again. Empty whiskey glass in hand.

"So are we going to take a look?" Elio says when I pass him for the fourth time.

I don't answer. I don't know *how* to answer him.

So he presses again. "Am I missing something here? This is the next part of the map. Why are we not rushing to assess it?"

With a sigh, I stop and stare out at sea. It's barely visible in the dark as it gently slaps against the side of the wooden hull. Pinpricks of silver stars begin to appear above, sending a shiver down my spine. I need to make a decision.

"I'm just tired, Elio, and I've put everybody through so much." My voice is heavy.

Odi still hasn't said a word, so I twist to face her. Her eyes find me like a compass to true north. Her gaze holds me steady, but I can't read it. It's as if she's waiting for me to make the call. Perhaps I want her to silently beg me to continue on this journey with her. Because if I don't . . . I drop her off at the next port we find. And she knows it.

"If this is it, what does the riddle tell us?" I ask her quietly.

She tucks a strand of her loose, dark brown waves behind an ear. "*Balance the scales, feather to stone, heavier still, the guilt-sown bone.*"

For a moment I'm lost in her voice, the way the sounds roll off her tongue like a poem she's rehearsed a thousand times before. She doesn't stumble over the words, every syllable is accounted for. Like she's whispered these riddles into the dark when no one was listening. She knows them better than anyone . . . they're a part of her.

This is why I have to keep going. Odelia has made her motivation clear. She's counting on this to secure her entire future. She hadn't pushed when I'd wavered, hadn't argued or insisted. But it's her only goal. If I send her off, will I keep the pieces of the key? If I give them to her, if I give up, Odelia will find a way to keep going, with or without a crew she can trust. The thought of anyone else being with her, of her being forced to work with those that might have no qualms about letting her drown or worse, sits heavy on my chest. And so does the thought of searching for years, only to give up the only link to my mother I've found.

This is the third key. We're here now—and the riddle doesn't sound threatening. I can go. Alone. We've come too far, sacrificed too much, to give up while we're *standing* on the next piece.

My gaze travels between Elio and Odi before I spin towards the steps to the deck. "I'm going in."

"I'm coming with you," Odi says behind me.

I don't bother to turn around, slinging my answer over my shoulder. "No, you're not."

"Yes, I am," she snaps, her steps pounding down the stairs, voice sharp enough to turn a few heads of the crew. "Because I'm not about to trust you to get the key, and keep it for yourself. We're in this together."

This time, I do stop, turning on my heel to look down at her. Her words sting for a moment, falling into that soft spot that's been growing larger and larger for her each day. I thought we were past the suspicion. I've done nothing that wasn't for her own safety. True, I'd swiped the key from between her breasts, but that was as logical as it was pleasurable.

Brown eyes glare up at me. Stubborn as a barnacle clinging to a rock, she is. I loose my breath, realising quickly that I could argue with her until both of us were blue in the face but she'd sooner bite her own tongue off than back down.

I straighten, folding my arms across my chest. "Tell me, Odelia—how exactly do you plan on breathing down there without a sea stone?"

The tension between us is so thick I could slice it with my blade, yet Odi doesn't seem fazed. She squares her shoulders as she tilts her face towards me. If she thinks I'm going to—

"She can borrow mine!" Soraya's musical timbre interrupts. She limps up to Odi, leaning on a wooden crutch that Otto no doubt found for her.

"You should be resting," I reply gruffly.

I would think after all this time as captain on this ship, my crew would actually listen to me when I order them to rest.

Soraya simply rolls her eyes at me. "I'll rest when I'm dead. Besides, I won't be using it any time soon." She gestures to her bandaged leg.

A smirk appears across Odi's lips, as one brow raises. They've got me cornered and they both know I have nothing to combat with. Unless . . .

I flick my gaze to Odi's billowing trousers. "And what of your attire? It didn't do you any favours in the temple. It spooked you more than once." Even I know I'm reaching, but I press on with all the confidence I can muster. "If we get separated, you'll need to be able to move without convincing yourself something is sweeping past you in the dark."

Tavi drops down from the rigging like she's been listening the whole time, landing light despite how tired I know she must be. She leans against the side of the ship next to Elio—who still remains shirtless. "I think I can help with that."

"There," Odi smirks. "Now you can't say no."

With four sets of eyes on me, I know I've lost this fight. But for once I don't care. Odi is the riddle keeper, and without her I'll likely never find the key. And truth be told, part of me wants her there. The thought of her at my side steadies something in me. It's a comfort I've not felt in longer than I can remember—if I've ever felt it at all.

I run a hand through my hair and release a soft sigh. "Fine, but change quickly. Once that sun is fully set it's going to make it even harder for you to see underwater."

Odi doesn't give me the opportunity to change my mind. She dashes off after Tavi while I'm left standing on the deck wondering if what I'm doing is utter lunacy.

"Will you be alright to play captain while I'm gone?" I ask Elio.

He nods once. "I'll be fine. I doubt the crew will do anything more than rest tonight."

"Keep an eye on Bear, too."

Elio nods again. "I always do."

Tavi returns alone, shoulders tense.

"Everything go okay?"

She nods. "She's changing. But I think she caught a few whispering as we passed. It's been going on all day. I was going to bring it up sooner but it didn't seem like the time."

"Whispering?" I ask. "About the Sotor? The keys?" The crew's morale is at an all time low. I'd be surprised if most of them didn't have something to say about how the last few days have gone.

But Tavi shakes her head. "It's Reid."

"Reid?" I ask slowly, waiting for her to explain how the man was causing me more grief from beyond the grave. I took no pleasure in his death, but he was one of the last I'd expect the crew to grieve heavily for.

She steps closer to me, lowering her voice further. "There were no roc marks on his body. His only wound looked like he was stabbed . . . By a blade," she clarifies when I don't say anything. "It went through his ribs so clean I would have missed it if I hadn't seen the blood on his shirt."

"You think he was murdered in the middle of the storm?"

"If he wasn't, it was one hell of an unlucky accident." Tavi's expression is even, hiding her thoughts, but I already know where this is going.

The crew will blame Odelia without question. Images flash in my mind—Reid's flushed face, spitting curses at her. Her calm control, the way she'd ignored him, shamed him, cut him down with words but never reached for any number of the weapons she always had hidden on her body. She wouldn't have let that control slip, not when killing him would risk the map. But few on this ship would follow the same logic. She'll be held guilty by default.

I sigh. Just another thing to keep an eye on.

The sound of boots thudding on the deck draws near, pulling me from my thoughts.

When I see her, my jaw hits the floor, and it takes every ounce of self control to not let blood rush to my cock.

Odi is donned head to toe in black, tight leather. It's matte, like snake skin. A tiny part of me reacts to the image. A viper. Like the one wrapped around her wrist. A reminder of the crew she belongs to.

But the image is hastily replaced by the fact that she is most definitely the most beautiful pirate I have ever laid my eyes on. A long braid hangs over one shoulder, swaying with each step, a dark rope I can't stop my eyes from following.

I shouldn't stare, but I do. Curves where they ought to be, the oil lamps attached to the mast throwing a golden glow over her in all the right places. She waltzes up to me, hips swaying like she knows they're a weapon to be used against a man.

She's got me. I'd drop to my knees right here and beg her to use me in whatever way she pleases if I weren't surrounded by folk who wouldn't care to see their captain devote his soul to the woman they blame for our recent tragedies.

Heat prickles at the back of my neck, and I curse under my breath. I've faced down storms, monsters, blades at my throat, and yet one woman walking towards me in leather near undoes me. There's no softness in her stride, but there's a tease in it, too—like she knows exactly how good she looks and isn't shy about letting me drown in it.

And *vicious seas*, I want her all the more for it.

"Ready when you are, Captain," she coos, running her eyes over my frame.

I straighten and clear my throat. "Let's get to it then."

Soraya slips the faintly glinting sea stone from around her neck and loops it over Odi's. It sits close to her throat like a choker. A black satin strip to complete her look.

A twang tugs my chest at the reminder of her necklace lost to the sea. Should I tell her the truth? That I hadn't thought she was worthy but couldn't bring myself to return it to the sea? That it was lost all the same, simply because it confounded me?

Focus on the water.

When Soraya is done, Odi and I move together towards the rail, the darkening sea churning black below. I swing my legs over the side, the salty wind rushing up to meet me. I glance to where Odi should be to my right, ready to dive in. But she lingers a few paces back, her long braid shifting in the breeze, her boots still firm on the deck.

She blinks hard, chin trembling before she forces it still. The mask of certainty cracks, and for the briefest breath, I see the fear bleeding through.

"There's still time to back out, little doe," I offer quietly.

She shakes her head, but I catch the way her throat bobs with uncertainty. "I can do this."

I know she can. We've been through worse together, but something tells me she just needs a little boost of confidence.

With a grin stretching across my mouth, I offer her my hand. "Prove it."

She only hesitates for a beat longer, then her hand is in mine, and she's hopping over the ship railing to stand next to me. "Ass."

A low chuckle rattles my chest as I glance over my shoulder to Soraya, Tavi and Elio. "Try not to sink the ship while I'm gone."

I've been leaving her a lot lately, but there's no doubt in my mind that *The Gilded Hart* is in good hands. If it came down to it, there's none I'd trust more to take her over in the case of my absence—or my death.

Salt water slaps the hull, sending up a spray. I turn my attention back to Odi "On three?"

She nods and squeezes my hand gently. "On three."

"One. Two. Three," I murmur, then our bodies are diving for the Adamaris sea.

I shift the moment we hit the water. A cloud of bubbles surrounds us as we sink down below the surface. Once they clear, I point to the sea stone around Odi's neck. She watches, wide eyed as the stone pops open, releasing a pale lilac bubble that becomes more see-through the bigger it grows. It forms around her head in a wavering shape, thin as glass that bends and sways when she moves.

"Pretty impressive, right?"

She weakly nods, but doesn't answer and that's when I realise she's still holding her breath. She freezes, eyes growing wide. Her hands fly up to claw at her throat as if the bubble might split, allowing water to rush in. She shakes her head, lips clamped shut, panic pouring off her in waves.

I grab her by the arms, firm but not rough, holding her steady in the dark water. I lean close, forcing her gaze to mine. "It's alright," I say, pulling her a fraction closer. "Trust the stone. Breathe."

She shakes her head again, brown eyes wild with fear. Her chest spasms, fighting the urge. I squeeze her arms tighter, grounding her. "Odi. With me."

At last, she gasps, sucking in a desperate breath. Instead of drowning, she exhales, shaky and disbelieving as the bubble holds. Her hand drifts up, fingers brushing the edge of the magic sphere, awe softening her panic.

Then her eyes snap back to me. "Rune—" Her voice is in my ears, clear as if we were standing on deck. "I can . . . talk?"

I can't help the grin that twists across my face. "Aye," I say. "Welcome to life under the sea."

Pink flushes her cheeks as the colour comes back to it. It makes my heart swell to see her in my world. Here, where my blood thrums with the richness of my heritage. The place where my heart truly feels at home. And she's smiling . . . at me.

I offer her my hand once again. "Come on, little doe."

Odelia threads her fingers through mine. The touch of her soft skin against the roughness of my hand sends a thrill up my arm. I grip it firmly, and then we're flying. Midnight water rushes past us as we glide down deeper and deeper, towards a towering finger of jutting rock Elio advised as a guide.

The soft lilac glow of Odi's sea stone is enough to illuminate a very small circumference around us, but it's not enough to help her see very far. Shapes stir in the murk, fish scattering, drifting, sea weed tugged by the current. Then I see it.

I point ahead. "Look."

It sits on a column of jagged rock, pale stone where there shouldn't be any. Square edges too clean to be nature's work, jutting up like giant, broken teeth.

"It's definitely a temple of some kind," Odi murmurs, her eyes wide with interest.

With her hand still firmly in mine, I slow and together we drift down until the full bulk of the structure looms before us. Barnacle-crusted just like Elio said. Four siren statues that once stood proud lean at odd angles, their carved poses almost too lifelike. The space is crowded with opportunistic kelp reaching for sunlight, and the wary bodies of fish that watch curiously from within pockets of stone and coral.

Odi releases my hand and swims for the door. I follow, my hand cool from her absence. We hover before the door. It's massive, cut from the same white stone, sealed tight. No handles, no hinges. Just a smooth slab between us and what lays on the other side.

I place a palm against it and push. Nothing. Not even a budge. So I pull back and then ram my shoulder into it. The pain is minimal but existent. I don't bother to try again, but instead turn to Odi.

"What did the riddle say again?"

She runs her hands over the door. "*Balance the scales, Feather to stone, Heavier still, the guilt-sown bone.*"

We circle the structure, trailing our hands along the barnacle-crusted stone, searching for any kind of weakness. I follow behind her, trying to keep my focus trained on finding a way in, and not . . . other things. "And you don't know what that means?"

"*Feather to stone* . . . it has to do with weight." She stops mid swim, twisting around to face me. Her braid takes a few seconds to catch up, floating around her like a coiling snake. "What are the chances there are actual scales here waiting for us?"

I follow her gaze as she sweeps her attention over the overgrown sea bed. There's no telling how much she can see in the half-light. "I'll look."

She nods and we drift lower, sand shifting beneath my tail and her kicks. I lead us farther down the sloped stone, my attention glued to the ground below me. Something catches the corner of my eye—flat slabs, half-buried, their edges too perfect to be natural. I dip to sweep away the silt with my hand. A plate of stone. Another opposite it, resting lower, like an uneven pair.

I hear the sharp intake of Odi's breath. "This has to be it."

I look back at the silhouette of the temple above. "So we balance them?" I murmur. "It seems too easy."

She drifts closer, eyes narrowing on the plates, her body moving with the water like she belongs here. I let myself watch her for a moment. Down at the bottom of the ocean—wrapped in the very fears she hasn't dared name. She's steady. Her fingers trace the stone with care, sure and unshaking. Her breath stays even, the bubble around her face rippling only when the current stirs it.

She's at one with the ocean, like the animal in her is one with the land.

It's a breathtaking sight.

Brown eyes search me out, bright with challenge. "You think we just press them?"

I drift over the taller plate and coil my tail around, applying as much pressure as I can. The stone sinks slightly, but it's more reluctant to move than I expect.

Odi grips my bicep, tugging me out of the way. "Let me try."

She clambers on, flapping her arms in an upward motion to keep as much of her weight on the plate that she can. It does even less. We're too buoyant to make a difference.

"We're missing something," I say, glancing around for some sort of clue.

Odi runs her fingers over the edges of the lower plate, and a few bubbles stream out from a hidden seam. I'm hopeful for a second, watching the door, but it remains steadfast.

She looks deflated, her shoulders dropping as she returns back to the stones. "What if we try standing on the lower one?"

I nod, and we take turns. Each time the plate moves, then it resets. The siren statues flanking us seem to sneer, their blank eyes watching us fail.

"We'll have to find something heavier," she hisses. "How long do I have with this sea stone?"

"All up, an hour. I'd say we have about forty minutes left," I answer, distracted by the leaning figures higher up. She stops, turning to follow my attention. There's something about them. Something that's different than the others we've seen.

"They aren't attached," she says.

She's right. The last statues were secured to stone, crumbling, but holding fast. Any self-respecting sea dweller would realise the clue for what it was. Underwater structures have to withstand the ocean. There isn't even a plant pot that would be unsecured in Nareth.

We move as one, working together to lift the least decayed statues we can find. First, we place one on the higher scale. It depresses, sending the second scale too far up, so we haul another statue, and for some reason it sinks the second scale flush with the ground.

We hover side by side, chests heaving. Odi's brow furrows, and I long to reach out and brush the creases of worry from her face. We're running out of time.

Then she looks up at me like it's the simplest thing in the world. "The guilt-sown bone. We have to be on the scales."

I'm already shaking my head, glad the water can sap the heat from my skin. "We've already tried."

"It's balance," she insists. "Not just the weight. *Together*. At the same time."

There's so much certainty on her face that I step onto the scale, wrapping my tail around the statue for balance. My stomach dips as the slab shifts with a thunk, rattling below me before settling only a bit lower than before. It's nearly even with the other now, but still a hairsbreadth off.

Odelia ignores my dismay and steps on the opposite side, sweeping her arm up to flatten her feet on the stone.

It dips an impossible fraction.

Then locks.

Bubbles surge around us and she looks at me with an earth-shattering smile as a low gear-shifting rumble vibrates through the water. My heart stutters. Not only is this woman violently beautiful, and a badass with a weapon, she's also ridiculously smart, and I'm glad she insisted on joining me down here, because I could not have done this without her.

The temple still trembles as we approach, stone dust clouding the water.

The way in yawns before us.

Odi squeals with delight, spinning to throw her arms around my neck. I hesitate from the shock of her display of sudden affection, but then I give in and crush her to my chest, being mindful not to disturb her sea stone bubble.

After a few seconds, she pulls back, her face slightly flushed. I smile, and gesture towards the doorway. "After you."

It's dark when we enter. The only light is the soft glow of the sea stone. The room isn't overly large, but big enough that I can be fully upright without hitting my head on the ceiling. The walls are smooth stone, yet void of carvings, or windows. Nothing says *I'm the key, come get me.* There is only a tunnel to my left, leading downwards.

Odi hovers at the dark entrance, her voice hesitant. "I think if we're going to find the key, it's going to be down there."

I nod. "Want to take bets on what else is waiting along with it?"

She gives me a look, ignoring my answering grin. Then we slip into the tunnel, the walls narrowing as we push deeper, the sea pressing heavier with every stroke. The glow of Odi's sea stone casts a pale shimmer across the rock, catching on the weeds that sway with the current.

I gesture to a stretch of long, ribboned fronds drifting like banners. "Blue kelp," I tell her. "It only flowers once a year. My father cut one of its blossoms the day he asked my mother to be his queen."

Mother had told me the story countless times in my younger years. The memory ghosts through me, sharp and bittersweet, but I push it down.

Before Odi has a chance to ask another question I point at a cluster of sea plants—pale stalks with sharp, twisting ends. "That one's poison," I chuckle. "Only if you're fool enough to eat it. Otto would do good with it though."

Her eyes flick towards me, a faint grin tugging on her lips.

The end of the tunnel appears, spilling us into a vast hollow, and for a moment I forget to move. Odi is frozen at my side, both of us struck by awe at the vision in front of us.

Walls of coral rise around us in great ribs of colour. Bending and twisting like the wildflowers that grow in fields on land. Crimson fans stretch wide, waving at us with the flowing current. Pale fingers of branching coral glow faintly, tipped in gold and violet. Anemones pulse as schools of tiny silver fish dart through them like stars.

Light blooms everywhere, spilling from the living creatures themselves. Soft blues, fierce greens, threads of white that curl like wispy clouds on a summer's day. I don't know where to look first.

Above us, loops of rainbow fish turn as one, their scales catching the glow in bright flashes, a ceiling of shifting stars. Odi hovers beside me, her mouth open in awe as the mound of coral in front of us seems to rise and fall with breath. Peach, aqua, pink and purple clusters of coral grow from the mound like flowers of the sea. Some change colour with every throb of their heartbeat. Lemon yellow coral sways, their fronds falling like grass in a hidden meadow. This cavern is alive. It's a world breathing beneath the world.

"What is this place?" she whispers, drifting towards it.

I flick my tail, keeping my distance so she doesn't feel like I'm hovering. We circle around the hump of coral in the centre of the space once. And yet there is no obvious place that the key might be.

"If I were a key, where would I hide?" I ponder.

Odi drifts closer, fingers reaching for a spray of lemon coral. Her hand hovers, then lightly brushes the edge of the yellow blossom.

Then the coral blinks.

An eye. Slitted, golden, opening where no eye should be.

Odi jerks back with a sharp gasp, colliding with my chest. Instincts take over, and I wrap my arms around her, ready to shield her as the cavern shudders with a low, thrumming vibration that rolls through the water.

"Odi—"

"I'm sorry, alright?" She throws over her shoulder.

The coral mound unfolds, shifting. What I thought were branches, peel back, scale by scale until the shape uncoils. An ocean dragon—woven of coral and sea itself—stretches up to the cavern ceiling. Long tendrils of her body ripple with light, fins like flags float around her. Then there's her teeth. Glinting like crystal daggers as she opens her mouth.

I hold Odi tighter, one arm around her waist, the other reaching for the blade at my hip, half ready for the fight of our lives.

But then a voice blooms inside my head, as calm and deep as the Adamaris sea. *"Be still young ones. You stand in the heart of what is sacred. It's not often I see a child of the surface co-existing with one born of this very water."*

The dragon's golden gaze sweeps over us, not cruel, not kind—simply knowing. She is no nightmare beast, but something older, revered. Her teeth are sharp enough to tear us in half, yet her presence hums with a strange grace, a weight that makes me bow my head without meaning to.

Against my chest, Odi trembles, but she doesn't pull away. And I, for once, have no words.

"Did she talk to you in your head?" she whispers.

I nod slowly, not wanting to alarm the giant, radiant creature in front of us.

Her voice floods my mind once again. *"What is it that you seek?"*

Finally, I manage to find my words. "We seek the hidden key."

"Ahhh, I see. And what shall you give me in exchange?"

I relax my hold around Odi, only slightly. The desire to have her as close as possible is too strong, besides if her air runs out, we both know I'm going to have to . . . help out. "What is it that you wish for?" I ask the dragon, like I have everything to offer her.

Smooth timbre cocoons my mind. *"Do you know the riddle that belongs to this temple?"*

Odi straightens her back, squaring her shoulders. "I do. Balance the scales, feather to stone, heavier still, the guilt-sown bone."

The cavern trembles once again as the dragon chuckles. *"That is only the first half."*

I angle my head to the side, looking at the breathtaking creature. "There's more?"

She nods. *"Give something not given. Nor something that's made. Something to lose, forever to fade."*

Odi twist to look up at me. "What does that mean?"

"Your guess is as good as mine."

The cavern shakes as the dragon bends down so that her face—a hundred times the size of mine—is level with me. *"This part of the riddle is for you . . . prince of the sea. There is little the land might offer that would flourish here."*

My brow furrows. How does she know? Perhaps the markings shimmering on my chest, or the golden royal circlet around my right bicep has given my identity away.

Odi pulls out of my grasp, eyes wide with wonder. "Even with a sea stone I don't think this key could be obtained without the help of the *seafolk*. Whoever made the map . . . they didn't want land dwellers to be able to get to it alone." She looks to the dragon. "Or by force."

I release a light chuckle. "Perhaps we make a good team after all."

She huffs and rolls her eyes before she mumbles the riddle again. "Not given, not made . . ."

"Coin's no good. Blood maybe?" I mutter, though the thought makes my stomach knot.

She shakes her head. "Blood is made. She wants something else. Something *you* can't get back once it's gone."

The dragon's golden eyes watch us drift back and forth as we try to figure out the rest of the riddle. "We're on borrowed time too, Odi."

"I know," she murmurs.

Odi appears by my side. Her eyes are half-glazed, but I was careful to ensure the song never touched her. "Boy, do we have a story to tell Bear," she murmurs. The words are light, but her gaze lingers on me, searching. I flick mine down to her lips as I offer her a soft grin, shoving down yet another grief that will make its home in me. "Last one back to the ship is a rotten sea slug."

There's only one bed

28
ODELIA

It takes us a week to limp to the nearest harbor.

Rune and I help tend to the wounded, passing each other like specters. Whatever hope we'd gotten from finding the last key had faded the moment we agreed not to make a big announcement to the crew—not until *The Gilded Hart* was in better shape, and our prospects were brighter.

During the first few evenings, his eyes catch on the items I've stored on his nightstand, on the way I reorder them when a rogue wave knocks them about, but he doesn't ask, and we slowly fall into a quiet routine. It would be more practical to tuck them away, but hiding them in the drawer feels almost like a betrayal, and seeing them reminds me of my goal.

I still hear his voice in my sleep. His song. The words stay distant, never fully formed, but the pull of his siren's magic is undeniable. I reach for him before awareness comes to me, only finding empty space. Sometimes, when I wake, his eyes are already locked to mine from across the room, and I wonder if I say his name.

Neither of us brings it up in the daylight.

Whiterock Harbor creeps closer over the day, blotting out the horizon. Flocks of seabirds screech overhead, sending anticipation coursing through my veins. The sound is more welcoming than the screech of the ship's bird, who, again and again, has ruined the silence of mourning. Hopefully it gets off and stays off.

The crew is lively, laughing, making plans for the food they find and the company they'll seek once our feet hit shore. Otto, of course, is the most excited, and something in my chest eases as the haunted look in his eye retreats for now.

"I need to visit the alchemist and the general store, and Rune said I don't have a limit on ingredients this time if they have any suggestions for the sort of poultices we might end up making in the future. Can you imagine how much the alchemist would pay for coral dragon horns? I can't believe you guys actually saw one. The—"

"Bear." Rune approaches slowly, his gaze flicking to me and away again. "You'll need this." The bag he passes to Otto jingles heavily. "We'll spend the night at the dockside inn. Feel free to take Stiden if you end up needing extra hands. He'll be staying on the ship tonight."

Within the hour, we've been heaved in and secured. The old planks creak, bowing under my feet. The dock is alive with sounds and colour. Other ships unload wagons of cargo pulled by large minotaurs or squat donkeys. Those walking greet us with smiles and nods and Rune nods back, tossing a coin at the men who helped pull us in. This port is popular with those from the mainland, and it shows—women in summer gowns walk arm in arm down the bricked thoroughfare in the centre, heading for shops or entertainment. The storehouses are three stories tall and stretch wide, with guards and tax masters checking every shipment that's catalogued and carried in the door.

Before my feet hit the cobblestone of the road, I slow, taking it in. It takes me a while to place why it feels wrong.

No one is scowling.

None look on in suspicion. As a Viper, there'd been little opportunity—or reason—to visit any respectable settlement in the daylight hours. Even then, there was little hiding what we were, not with Captain Ivor around.

"You okay?"

The question startles me out of my thoughts. I hadn't realised I'd stopped. The rest of the crew stream past me. Even Soraya, on her crutch, walks ahead, alongside Elio and Otto. Rune stands just behind me, his thumbs tucked into his pockets. He's changed. The sleeves of his dark blue shirt are long, but rolled to show hints of his shimmering tattoos. His trousers are fitted well, tucked into polished boots I'm sure I haven't seen before. He fits right in, confident on land and sea, where I can't help but look for threat in the friendly faces that welcome us.

"Yes," I say, squinting as I let my eyes trail up to a balcony, where a fae child watches us and the rest of the crowd mill about. "Not used to such a warm greeting, I suppose."

"They don't know who you are."

The words are supposed to comfort me, but he doesn't know who I am either. Guilt worms its way through my gut. The chances are low I'll be recognized here, but the fear stays all the same. We stare at each other for a moment, the thing between us alive and fighting for breath. After a rest, there's only one more key. One more challenge for us to face together before we get what we wanted and go our separate ways. That thought is supposed to comfort me too.

Instead, I wonder if I should tell one of them the final riddle, then shift and disappear past the edges of this town, let Rune claim the treasure on his own. Then there's no risk I'll ever have to see the betrayal on his face if he found out.

"Come on."

His broad body overtakes my vision as he passes, and I follow, if only because I refuse to be alone. To my surprise, he doesn't aim for the inn with a swinging sign above it that reads "The Weathered Hull."

"Where are we going?" I ask, falling into step beside him. I keep my head on a swivel, abandoning myself to the knowledge that my awe betrays me. There are little wheeled shops selling fruits and bread-wrapped meats as they roll down the way. Tailors, general stores, trinket shops, even a spot dedicated solely to the post. Bodies fill the space, moving around and through everything.

"I don't think I've ever seen so many people at once."

Rune grins. "The novelty wears off, I assure you."

I believe him.

The eyes of those we pass seem drawn to him, catching on his face and the marks on his arms. He's taller than even the tallest of the humans, and the crowd parts before us until we step into a bakery whose scent sends a wash of memory through me. I all but choke on the emotion, the sudden clarity

"I don't despise you." His hand snakes out around my upper arm, stopping me in the middle of the crowd. He just watches my face, at first. Creaking wheels and the low buzz of conversation fill the silence and I look for an explanation in his bright eyes. My every nerve stands on end, the commotion beyond us fading. My focus narrows to his thumb, which lifts to catch whatever crumb is left on my face.

"I thought that was very, *very* clear." He pops the thumb into his mouth, already grinning like a fiend as he sucks it clean.

The entirety of me ignites in flame, burning away my ability to argue as he keeps walking. He knows I'll have no choice but to follow, completely annoyed and having failed to stop my lips from twitching into a smile. A human woman watches him go and then snaps her head back to me with an expression that's a mix of admiration and embarrassment. I avoid her eye and urge my legs to move as he steps back out towards the dockside shops.

Tavi appears and falls into step with us just as I reach him. "Most everyone has gotten a room already," she says, her eyes flicking over the bags in his hand and the pie in mine. "Some said they plan to stay at the inn on the other side of town. I told them we'll do a headcount here tomorrow at noon."

"Thank you. Stiden should be back with news about the repairs, have you seen him?"

Tavi shakes her head, scanning those that mill about on the dock.

Rune nods. "I'll go check in with him. You two go ahead."

"You're sure—"

"I can—"

Tavi and I speak at the same time, and Rune puts his hands up to halt us. "I can handle it. Order an extra ale for me once you get a table."

Once he goes, I turn to Tavi. "Elio inside?"

She nods. "We've actually already eaten. I'll have to force him to rest soon. He won't say it, but he's still hurting."

I follow as she moves into The Weathered Hull. "Maybe Otto will find something stronger for pain . . ." I trail off as I see Soraya perched by the hearth, her splinted leg resting out in front of her. A lyre sits in her lap. The memory of Rune's voice springs up again. It was less sound and more a feeling. A rattling, bone deep, sensation of melody that pulled you in. Now that I think about it, Soraya's voice tugs in much the same way, but lighter, more delicate.

Elio waits at a table near Soraya, who begins to pluck out a melody. "Rune on the way?"

"He went to go check on Stiden and the repairs."

I set my wrapped pie on the table, deciding it's better to wait until my stomach has more in it, otherwise the sweetness alone may make me sick. The inn has a long bar that's packed tight with greasy-haired sailors. Some of the others from *The Gilded Hart* are scattered in groups and pairings at the tables, many with several empty mugs before them.

Elio follows my gaze, nodding to the packed bodies. "If he doesn't hurry, he won't get a room. Tulin said the one down the way is full up, and this place is packed."

Tavi gives a nearly imperceptible shrug. A server approaches and grabs the empty plates on the table. He's tall and wiry, with scarless knuckles. "What'll you have?"

"Two ales, please," I say. "And whatever vegetables you've got, if that works?"

"You should try the lamb," Elio says, leaning in like it's a well-kept secret.

"I actually avoid meat if I can." I shrug, letting my eyes travel over the crowd of faces around us.

"Really? I'll choose it every time. I spent a long time on a siren diet, but there's something about a steak . . . it has this texture you can't find in the ocean."

"I prefer venison, myself," Tavi says and I sputter a laugh, trying to decide if it's a joke at my expense. Her eyebrows raise a fraction, like my reaction surprises her.

"Has Rune really not told you?" I ask, running through the logic in my head. I'd assumed he'd let them know at some point, if not the rest of the crew. But then—he's surprised me before. And he knows how strange I feel about that side of me. "I'm a deer shifter," I say, holding Tavi's gaze.

Elio snorts. "Damn, Tavi, how'd you miss that? You basically just said you'd like to stick a fork in her."

"I'm definitely going to stick a fork in you," she says, deadpan. "I've spent a long time away from the forest. And I can only scent so much over the stink of your boots." She kicks at him under the table for emphasis.

Elio brings a hand to his chest like she's wounded him. "Abusing your patient? You know that only turns me on."

She bites back, but their words blend into the buzz of the crowd. Rune hadn't said anything. He'd let me keep my secret. I'm not sure why the knowledge makes my body respond the way it does—with an aching warmth that settles around my wary soul.

They go upstairs just as my food arrives—a whole plate of seared mushrooms and veggies. I struggle to identify a few, but scarf them down all the same. Hopefully Otto makes it back soon, he'd probably know every one of them. When I've finished I choose a corner to lean into, uninterested in taking up the whole table for myself. I hold Rune's mug and sip mine, checking each body that comes through the door. It's strange that I don't feel that instinct to reach for my old hood anymore, but the amount of people is overwhelming all the same. I've no coin for a room, which continues to feel more and more like an oversight as the innkeeper exchanges coin for keys.

"Odi!"

Otto waves from the doorway and then moves to order at the bar. Rune follows him in, but cuts a path towards me when I brandish the extra mug.

"Things okay?" I ask as he downs it in a swig.

"Yes. It won't be cheap, but they have what we need to patch it. Once I can make it back to my father's ports, we can see about a permanent fix. Did you get a room?"

I shake my head. "I wasn't graced with any pocket change." I look pointedly to Otto, who walks up carrying three mugs in each hand.

"Good lad!" Rune says, taking two and passing them to me. "Let me go get us a room."

"Us?" I call after him.

"Rune's very protective," Otto chirps, sipping on the first of his ales before tossing his chin in greeting at Soraya, who still sings by the hearth. "Everyone else already go to bed?"

I scan the tables. "As far as I know. Most everyone is too exhausted to bother drinking this place dry."

Otto nods distractedly and Rune dodges full tables as he returns, his face pinched in a peculiar expression.

"What is it?" I ask.

"There was only one room left."

I look to Otto. Leaving him without a room isn't an option. "Well, I can—"

"Oh no, I'm good!" Otto says, catching my concern immediately. "Soraya got us a double bed before I went to the alchemist."

"Oh. Well then, it's fine." I shrug at Rune.

"It's a single. There's only one bed."

I shake my head, confused. "The cabin on the ship has one bed."

His smile grows. "But this one isn't likely to have a *chair*, Odi."

I'd assumed that, but I still take a drink to hide the heat crawling up my neck. I study a point over his ridiculously toned shoulders. "There's always the floor."

He cocks an eyebrow. "You'd sleep on the floor?"

I grin, meeting his eyes over the rim. "No. That's all yours, Captain."

When he speaks, it's a purr, sending my mind scrambling around the memory of his body beneath mine, of his pleasant surprise every time he discovered another weapon hidden beneath my clothes. “Oh, I won’t be sleeping on the floor, little doe.”

Who needs manacles when you have sheets

29
RUNE

Odi lingers behind me while I unlock the door that leads to our room for the night. She might not be touching me, but my heart responds to her nearness anyway. The air shifts when she's close, and my chest answers before my mind does, heart drumming like it knows her place better than I ever could. As if it will always find her, no matter the distance.

The knob finally gives way and I push the door open, stooping under the frame as I step inside. I hold it wide, gesturing for her to come in before I quietly click it shut.

Off-white lace curtains with a floral backing cover the window on the farthest wall, keeping the room free from prying eyes. A cluster of wildflowers in a dainty, yellow vase grace the top of a square wooden table. And two small wooden chairs sit proudly on either side.

A round rug, woven in deep blues and reds, lies across the floor—soft underfoot, a small stitch of homeliness in the otherwise plain room. No big, comfy chair.

"You were right about the chair," Odi murmurs as she glances around the space.

Her eyes are still caught on the jar. "This is too much, Rune."

The desire to reach out, tip her chin up so her gaze meets mine and then beg her to touch me the same way her fingers dance over each gift with such a softness, coils in my chest.

"No need to borrow Soraya or Tavi's things anymore," I say, shoving my hands in my trouser pockets. "There's boots too. They're probably tucked in the bottom."

Her brown eyes land on me, and I swear I see moisture gathering in the outer corners where her lashes kiss. An invisible thread snaps between us, and I want to reach for her. I want to pull her close and whisper into her hair that she is beautiful. That not every moment has to be sharp or full of teeth. Yet, my feet stay firmly planted and my mouth wired shut, because that would be past naked desire, past teasing and sharp-tongued banter.

"Thank you," she murmurs. "Perhaps I should freshen up."

I nod, and take a few steps back, trying to act like the novels on the wooden shelf next to the window hold my interest.

Odi shuffles around behind me, tucking the flower from the bakery into the jar. She'd continued to gather things, her nest of land treasures growing, though they'd proven hard to display on a ship. At least now they can be protected. I watch her longer than I should, wondering if she's not just a distraction but the reminder of everything I've been missing. I suck in a quiet breath. She makes me want things I've no business wanting. Things the life I have now could never give me.

She doesn't look at me when she leaves, shutting the door with a quiet click behind her. I begin to pace back and forth slowly, unsure what to do with myself while I wait for her to return.

The wood stash next to the hearth is piddling—only enough to last a few hours, but I get to work on building a fire, my mind lost to all the things that have happened over the past few weeks. I pace, running a hand over my face, it's actually nice to have my feet on solid ground for a short while, I almost forgot what it felt like. Even being in this inn feels like a weight has lifted, I don't need to be captain for a moment, I can simply be me. Even if it's just for the night. As soon as I get back to the ship, the duty will return. Which reminds me, I need to send another inktopus message to Killian. He should have checked in by now.

Soft footsteps in the hall reach my ears, and I turn to the door just as it opens. Odi steps through, graceful, wearing the night gown I'd purchased for her. I hold my breath as she crosses the room to hang the borrowed clothing from Soraya over one of the wooden chairs.

Then she faces me, and I finally release the air trapped in my lungs in a quiet breath. She's a vision dressed in sheer white. The shop assistant at the dress store had chosen well. I'd simply given her the size I needed and requested that it be modest, but not too modest. I didn't think Odi would appreciate the more stifling style that is popular on the mainland, but she'd probably stab me if I brought her something . . . barely there.

It fits her perfectly. Wide lace straps cling to her sun-kissed shoulders, continuing down to gather at her wrists in a loose structure. The cotton is thin, sheer when it catches the firelight, skimming over her curves before spilling into a soft fall at her thighs.

A row of tiny buttons runs down the front, stopping at her sternum. They're delicate pearls, the kind you find in oysters that dwell in the shallow ends of the sea. None of them are done up, teasing more than they hide. Every shift of the fabric hints at her figure beneath, leaving far too much for my imagination to ignore.

A smile tugs at Odi's lips. "Would you like a napkin to wipe up all that drool?"

I take a step towards her and watch the way her breath catches. "Perhaps I'll use the hem of your shift . . . it would be *much* softer."

Pink blooms up her slender throat, spreading across her cheeks in a glowing hue. We stare at each other for a fraction of time, but before I let my body respond to the look on her face, I take a few steps back, reach for the towel on the edge of the bed and head for the door.

I pause with my hand on the brass knob and glance over my shoulder. "You look beautiful, Odi," I murmur.

The communal washroom is small, like the sleeping quarters, yet it's tidy enough. The air is damp and warm from the steam that lingers. I fill the tub with fresh water drawn from the pump, the slosh echoing against the stone walls. I ease in, the warmth seeping into my body, soothing my aching muscles.

Salt and grit loosen from my skin, clouding the water as I scrub myself clean with the rough bar of tea tree soap left on the shelf. I duck under once, letting the water drag through my hair before raking it back from my face.

My thoughts travel to the woman who waits in the room across the hall. Knowing that I'll brush up against her skin when we sleep tonight has me undone. I know we share my room back on the ship and even that is difficult, but I keep to the chair and she has the bed. Tonight, it's different.

Seeing her in that gown too, has me weak.

By the time I climb out and towel off, the stiffness in my shoulders has eased, the smell of brine gone. The hall is quiet as I step out, the towel around my hips. I linger by the room door for a moment, hesitant to go in.

Only because I know the moment I step inside I'll want to ravish her, and I shouldn't. Though standing out here doesn't change how I feel. Aching. Yearning to touch her lips of silk with mine one more time.

With a slow, steadying breath, I knock, careful not to startle Odi. Soft footsteps whisper across the floor, then the door eases open. When her eyes find mine, she draws it wider, and for a moment, it feels as though she's opened something more than just the door.

The scent of pear and honey drifts out to meet me, warm and tender, folding around my chest like a memory I don't want to release. I'd seen the oil mixture in the marketplace earlier and had no choice but to buy it for her. It's the same fragrance Soraya stirs into her soaps—familiar, comforting. Yet on Odi, it is different. It's hers. The same sweetness I conjure in dreams, whenever my mind dares whisper her name.

She smiles up at me, stepping out of the doorway and into the hall so I can pass by. "I'll let you dress," she murmurs.

I flash her a grin. "I mean, I don't mind the audience."

An answer plays on her lips, but footsteps interrupt us. I turn to look over my shoulder. Otto walks the hall, all bare chested, grinning from ear to ear, and his blue eyes sparkling with mischief. The towel slung low around his waist does nothing to hide the jagged scar running from his left hip bone diagonally across his chest all the way up to his right collarbone. It's faded over time, but still pink, still puckered and pulling at his skin in angry memory. It had taken months to heal, months more for the pain to fade. Odi's eyes widen, her face going wan as she connects the scar with the human boy with the infectious grin and dangling earring.

My heart slams once, hard enough to steal the breath from me, and my gut sinks like lead at the memory of that fateful night three years ago. The sound of blade tearing through flesh, wet and final. Otto's anguished screams tearing the night apart. It still haunts my dreams.

He keeps the scar hidden most days, as if covering it might make people forget. But no one does. No one ever could. It marks him, not as someone who is broken, but as someone who lived through something that should have ended him.

Odi's kind enough not to remark, but it's evident on her face what she's thinking.

"Cap . . . Odi." Bear greets us with a toothy smile. "Just gonna freshen up real quick."

I nod. "The water's warm, don't linger too long or you'll become a prune," I say, with a wink.

He dips his head, cheeks flushing pink as he squeezes past us to enter the washroom. The door shuts behind him and the quietness returns. I glance down at Odi, who seems lost in her thoughts. "Do you mind if I dress quickly?"

She finally looks up at me. "Oh—of course not," she fumbles, then steps out of the way.

I can't help but smile as I slip by and enter the room. "I'll only be a moment."

The grey, linen trousers I'd brought from the ship are neatly folded on the end of the bed, where I'd left them earlier. I throw them on, tying them loosely at my hips. Warmth from the fire has made the room much more comfortable so I don't bother putting a shirt on.

The door shuts with a soft thud, and when I look up, she's there. Odi leans back against the wood, arms at her sides, eyes fixed on me. I drag the towel through my hair, paying no attention to the rogue water droplets that fling from the ends.

Her stare pins me in place more than any blade ever could. Heat creeps up my skin. Not from the fire, not from the bath—just the way she's looking at me.

I hold her gaze, slow, deliberate, letting the silence stretch taunt between us. She doesn't flinch, like she's daring me to make the first move.

"Thank you for the clothes and such," she says softly.

I throw the towel onto the table before threading my fingers through the damp strands on my head. "It's really nothing."

Odi stays rooted to the spot, still watching my every move. Her hair frames her figure, hanging in damp, dark brown waves, all the way to her waist. "Why don't you sing more often, like Soraya does?"

The question catches me off guard and it takes a second to evoke a reply. I shrug lightly.

"She sings all the time," she continues before I can answer. "Like she couldn't stop if she tried."

I fold my arms across my chest, leaning my hip against the edge of the table. The wood groans in protest under my weight. "Somone has to keep the bad boy image on deck when Killian's not around."

A soft huff travels across the room. Odi's gaze never leaves mine.

Every fibre of my being wants to stride across the room and take her in my arms, to forget the world outside these four walls, but should I?

She shifts her weight. "I'm sorry you had to give up your mother's song."

The image of the coral encrusted dragon flashes across my mind. I can still feel that empty space inside my chest where mother's lullaby once rested. It's hollow and cold. No longer do the words haunt me. Her lullaby in exchange for the key. Part of my heart still aches from the absence, but she would have been thrilled at the thought. The adventure. She'd say there's no better place for it than the sea.

I shrug softly. "It was needed."

Her gaze drifts over me—lingering at the edge of my trousers, gliding up my chest, before settling on my face. She reads me in silence, then finally speaks. "Tell me about it . . . your world. Who you were before all of this."

I let out a low laugh. "The pirate wants to know about the prince."

Her brown eyes spark with mischief, bright with anticipation. "And does the prince want to bare his soul?"

My gaze drifts to the fire steadily crackling in the fireplace. "Son of a king who's never been satisfied with anything I've done. A kingdom of marble halls and sharp rules. My father wanted obedience. A constant show of family unison for all of Nareth to see," my voice trails out. "I wanted none of it."

I look to Odi again. Her eyes don't waver, so I keep talking, the words spilling easier than I mean them to. "He says I'm like her. More my mother than a prince. She loved the world. Adventure. I never understood how my brother and sister could stand endless drills and study when there was so much more to see beyond our city. But when she disappeared, he refused to talk about her, to hope, to even *look* at me. It . . . broke him. So I left, searching for any trace of her. But I think I've really been running away."

If my father saw me now, he wouldn't yell or rage. He knew why I'd set myself towards empty revenge. The moment I stepped foot back in Nareth, he would look at me, defeated. *I tried to tell you*, his expression would say. No anger, no gloating, just that tired certainty that's worse than either. And maybe he'd be right. Maybe I was a fool for chasing ghosts across the sea.

Odi's eyes have softened like she might understand. She places her hands behind her back, shoulders still leaning against the door. "Are we going to go for the last key?"

I don't hesitate to answer. "Yes."

She tips her head gently to the side. "What made you change your mind?

Mother's laughter—like birdsong—rings in my mind. Her white hair floating about her as she darts through coral banks collecting shells and sea blossoms. The map holds the water elemental symbol. It holds answers about their world—and it holds a promise that no matter how far Odi goes after we part ways, she'll have what she needs to find the life she's wanted. One far, far away from the sea.

"The thought of someone else standing next to you when you found it." The words are more possessive than I have any right to, but her grin tells me she doesn't mind.

She pushes off the door and saunters across the room, hips swaying with deliberate intent, as if she knows exactly how each step unravels me. She halts just short of touching, her eyes, framed by long, dark lashes, trailing slowly up my chest before locking onto mine. I straighten, shoving my hands into my trouser pockets.

My heart leaps into my throat the moment her fingertips begin to trace the faint, gold, shimmering patterns on my skin. She starts at the ones on my biceps, before moving to the swirls on my chest. Heat coils low in my stomach. With every touch my restraint is unravelling.

Her fingers continue their journey, all the way down to the top of my trousers. I suck in a breath when she drags her nails just under the waistband, causing blood to rush straight to my cock. Just before she travels further I grasp her wrist. "What are you doing, little doe?"

"What I want," she whispers, mirroring my words during the storm.

I hold her gaze, heart trembling in my chest.

By the seas, she's infuriating. Impossible. Everything I should stay away from. Completely opposite of who I *should* fall for and yet, there's more to her than I had ever let myself see.

I can't promise her anything. Not with the keys, the map, the damned Adamaris sea hanging over us like chains. But maybe . . . just this once. One night where it's not about riddles or the weight of what waits for us. One night when I take her in my arms and forget the world.

She needs it. I need it. A release from all the grief and tension that's been weighing us down.

And damn me . . . damn every reckless part of me, for wishing it could be more than just one night.

The sun has well and truly set. The only light comes from the golden glow of the flames in the fireplace. Their shadows dance across the rug and spill over the table. Slowly I release her wrist, flicking my gaze between her lips and her eyes. "Then have your way with me . . . Odelia."

She exhales, a soft sigh spilling from her lips, and my mind fractures into a storm of colour. Hues burst behind my eyes. Wild, blinding—splintering into prisms the instant her hand grazes my semi hardened length. And the second she wraps her silk fingers around it, I'm as hard as a rock.

Her gasp cuts through the air, sharp and breathless. Eyes widening as the truth of what she's stirred takes hold. Her lips part, just barely, and the sight alone sends a brutal pulse of

At this point, my cock is so hard it could tear a hole right through the front of my trousers. It's been quite some time since anyone—besides my hand—paid any attention to it. I've had the opportunity to bed beautiful women, but it never amounted to anything more than a convenient distraction for all involved.

I drag the tip of my nose back up Odi's neck, all the way to her ear, where I nip her lobe. "Show me how you like to be touched."

She doesn't hesitate. The fire in her eyes telling me that she wants this just as much as I do. With a flick of her wrist, she pulls the front of her nightgown to the side, exposing one of her breasts. My knees go weak at the sight of her pebbled nipple under the golden glow of firelight.

"Suck it," she whispers.

With a vicious grin, I drop my head and capture her peaked nipple between my lips, sucking gently before running my tongue around it. She gasps out loud, arching her back to press her breast deeper into my mouth.

I think I've died and gone to the good place, and I truly hope no one wakes me from this pleasure. Pulling back, I see Odi's eyes roll back as her body responds to my touch, and I want to reach for my length and fist it until I'm spurting all over her legs, but I don't. I'll make sure she's writhing with bliss before I dare to finish.

Her gaze finds mine, and she reaches between us, lifting the white cotton of her gown up to her hips, until her legs are completely bare. I swallow, the heart in my chest exploding when she parts them wider for me.

"What I want," she whispers, mirroring my words during the storm.

I hold her gaze, heart trembling in my chest.

By the seas, she's infuriating. Impossible. Everything I should stay away from. Completely opposite of who I *should* fall for and yet, there's more to her than I had ever let myself see.

I can't promise her anything. Not with the keys, the map, the damned Adamaris sea hanging over us like chains. But maybe . . . just this once. One night where it's not about riddles or the weight of what waits for us. One night when I take her in my arms and forget the world.

She needs it. I need it. A release from all the grief and tension that's been weighing us down.

And damn me . . . damn every reckless part of me, for wishing it could be more than just one night.

The sun has well and truly set. The only light comes from the golden glow of the flames in the fireplace. Their shadows dance across the rug and spill over the table. Slowly I release her wrist, flicking my gaze between her lips and her eyes. "Then have your way with me . . . Odelia."

She exhales, a soft sigh spilling from her lips, and my mind fractures into a storm of colour. Hues burst behind my eyes. Wild, blinding—splintering into prisms the instant her hand grazes my semi hardened length. And the second she wraps her silk fingers around it, I'm as hard as a rock.

Her gasp cuts through the air, sharp and breathless. Eyes widening as the truth of what she's stirred takes hold. Her lips part, just barely, and the sight alone sends a brutal pulse of heat through me. My cock thickens, aching at the thought of those lips closing around me, soft and willing.

"I guess it's true what they say about big hands," she murmurs, eyes heavy with desire.

A grin pulls at the corner of my mouth. "Don't say I didn't warn you."

She pumps my length, slow and steady, a wicked smile on her lips and I'm tumbling over the edge and into the world that is Odelia.

The ship is getting fixed, and then we will chase down the last key, we'll find the treasure and then she will be gone. That's the truth waiting for us, no matter how hard I try to ignore it. So why in all eight seas, are we torturing ourselves by holding back, pretending we don't want what's already written across both our faces? It's going to tear us apart either way.

We've cheated death too many times. Every fight, every storm, every breath could have been our last. And if the Adamaris sea decides to drag me under tomorrow . . . *gods* help me, I want her to have had me first.

She's close enough that I can feel the heat of her breath, see the flecks of gold in her irises. The air between us hums, heavy with the desire we both know we crave. Then she tilts her chin, just slightly, and that's all it takes—I'm gone.

With a low, rough moan I cup her face between my hands and drag her lips to mine, fierce and hungry, all the restraint I've been carrying over the last few days shattering in an instant. She tastes of everything I've ever wanted, sharp and sweet, and I drink her in like I've been dying of thirst. Her hand pulls away from beneath my trousers, and even though I miss it the moment it's gone, I relish in the feeling of both her hands stealing around my neck, fisting in my hair, dragging me closer until there is no space left, only heat and the press of her body against me.

The kiss deepens, teeth and lips colliding, messy, desperate. Kissing her underwater was mesmerising, but kissing her when we both have the freedom of air is intoxicating. I can't get enough of her mouth, as I nip at her lips, and suck her tongue.

She sighs into me, soft and breathless, and the sound rips through me like lightning. I pull her closer—if that's even possible—as I run my hands down her back, over her perfectly round ass and cup the back of her thighs.

With one effortless lift, I place her on the edge of the table, dropping my hands to lay flat against the surface either side of the cotton gown that I long to rip from her body. Her chest rises and falls, breath coming in short gasps. "What are you waiting for, Rune? Take me."

"So, impatient," I say, my voice low.

I run my gaze over her face, softly biting the corner edge of my bottom lip, before I slowly lean down and drag my mouth across her jaw. Her shoulders drop, body relaxing as I trail kisses down her neck, each one slower, deeper, as if I can brand her with nothing but lips and breath.

When I reach the hollow where her neck meets her shoulder, I let my incisors graze the delicate skin. A warning, a promise. I bite just hard enough to claim a sound from her, then move lower, repeating as each moan spills from her mouth like it's meant only for me. Her hands grip the edges of my pants as she holds herself steady.

At this point, my cock is so hard it could tear a hole right through the front of my trousers. It's been quite some time since anyone—besides my hand—paid any attention to it. I've had the opportunity to bed beautiful women, but it never amounted to anything more than a convenient distraction for all involved.

I drag the tip of my nose back up Odi's neck, all the way to her ear, where I nip her lobe. "Show me how you like to be touched."

She doesn't hesitate. The fire in her eyes telling me that she wants this just as much as I do. With a flick of her wrist, she pulls the front of her nightgown to the side, exposing one of her breasts. My knees go weak at the sight of her pebbled nipple under the golden glow of firelight.

"Suck it," she whispers.

With a vicious grin, I drop my head and capture her peaked nipple between my lips, sucking gently before running my tongue around it. She gasps out loud, arching her back to press her breast deeper into my mouth.

I think I've died and gone to the good place, and I truly hope no one wakes me from this pleasure. Pulling back, I see Odi's eyes roll back as her body responds to my touch, and I want to reach for my length and fist it until I'm spurting all over her legs, but I don't. I'll make sure she's writhing with bliss before I dare to finish.

Her gaze finds mine, and she reaches between us, lifting the white cotton of her gown up to her hips, until her legs are completely bare. I swallow, the heart in my chest exploding when she parts them wider for me.

I drop to my knees, desperate to feel some solid ground to support the trembling that has begun to plague my body.

"Taste it," she commands softly.

The thread between us snaps, and my mind turns feral for her. I *need* her. All of her. With a soft growl, I grab her hips and yank her towards the edge of the table. She gasps, hands slapping the surface either side of her, as she finds her balance.

I don't wait for her breath to catch up as I bury my face between her legs. She cries out the instant my tongue touches her warmth. Lapping, sucking, driving my tongue between the slit so I can taste just how pleased she is with me.

"*Fuck*, Odi," I murmur before sucking her clit between my teeth. She cries out when I flick the hard bead with the tip of my tongue.

I glance up at her from my kneeled position, mouth still discovering the slickness that pools between her legs just for me. She moans, dropping her head back, hair brushing the table behind her as she slowly rocks her hips.

My hands find her firm thighs, and I grip them tighter, devouring her until her legs begin to shake, only then do I pull back. She drops her head to meet my gaze, brown eyes heavy with desire. "That's how I like to be touched," she utters softly.

A grin forms across my lips. "Noted."

Odi leans forwards, grips my face in her hands and drags it up to meet her in another devastatingly hungry kiss. I know she can taste herself on my tongue, and it makes my cock swell.

I slowly stand, not wanting to pull my lips from hers. I'm too desperate for her, and even though I'm kissing her, it's still not close enough. I possess her mouth with mine, our lips hauling into one another, fusing together until all I can taste is her.

She pulls back, dragging air into her lungs. So I take the opportunity to do the same while she tugs at the tie on my pants. They fall loose with almost no effort, my cock springing free from its fabric restraints.

Odi's eyes take me in, growing wider with every second. "Fuck me," she whispers in disbelief.

"I plan to."

She draws in a sharp breath as I pull her nightgown over her head and let it fall to the floor. Now she sits bare before me, perched on the table's edge, and the sight knocks the breath clean from my chest. Firelight licks across her skin, curling around her hips like molten gold.

A curse slips past my lips, as I take a step back to admire her beauty. *Vicious seas* help me, because I've never wanted anyone like this.

Odi slides off the table. "Come back here," she commands.

She reaches out to palm my length, pumping up and down slowly, drawing a bead of precum to the tip of my cock. I drop my forehead to hers, closing my eyes and gripping her hips as I let the pleasure rip through my groin.

The world outside ceases to exist. It's only her and I in this room, and we have the whole night to explore each other's bodies, and that's exactly what I plan to do.

The sound she makes when I scoop her up draws a smile to my lips, her legs curling around my hips instinctively as I carry her across the room. The bed creaks as I lay her down, melted chocolate tendrils spilling around her over the pale green bed covers.

She scoots further up as I climb after her, the mattress groaning under the weight of us both. My mouth is on her before I can stop myself, trailing kisses up her thighs, across her stomach and over the swell of her breasts.

Odi gasps, fingers tangling in my hair, and I don't slow, don't give her space to think. I reach her jawline, catch her mouth with mine and it's desperate, messy, all the hunger we've been choking down finally unleashed.

One night. Just her and I. That's all this is.

She tugs on my hair, ripping her lips from mine. Brown eyes wild, and hungry. "Where are your manacles now?"

A grin curves my lips. I reach behind me, fingers closing around the thin blanket I'd noticed draped at the end of the bed. Before she can draw breath to protest, I catch both her wrists, lift them high above her head, and loop the fabric around them. The knot bites snug, binding her to the headboard.

I lower my mouth, trailing kisses between her breasts. "Who needs manacles," I murmur against her skin, "when you have sheets?"

"Ass," Odi mutters, but she doesn't fight me.

Her chest vibrates as I chuckle against her skin before sucking a nipple into my mouth. I want to ravish her until she is nothing but a wet trembling heap on this bed. I want to fill her, until all she craves is the taste and touch that only I can offer.

With her hands pinned above her head, she's helpless. I can make her writhe with pleasure until she screams my name. Flicking my tongue over her cinched nipple, I grin as she arches her back, sweet moans trembling on her lips.

I plan to map every curve, every dip, every scar on her skin until I know her body better than I know my own, because *gods* know it will be the only passionate memory of us that I will get to keep.

Honey and pear scent washes over me as I turn my attention to her other nipple, lashing at it like it's the last thing I'll ever get to do.

"Rune—" Odi whimpers.

I slowly release her, kissing my way up to her mouth. "Yes, little doe? Would you like something?"

She nods slowly as I pepper kisses across her jaw.

"Tell me what you want." I murmur into the crook of her neck.

Her body presses into me, trying to get as close as she possibly can. "I want you."

I pull back, licking my lips with satisfaction. "Then it's me you shall have."

A soft groan escapes me the moment I slip my hand between her legs, parting her lips to feel how wet she is. "*By the seas*, you're perfect."

Lifting her head, her mouth finds mine and the world splits open. The kiss is wild, desperate. Teeth clashing, lips bruising. The kind of kiss you don't recover from.

She whimpers into my mouth as I slip a finger inside her warmth. She cries out when I slip in a second. Her back arches off the bed, as I slowly pump into her with gentle thrusts of my hand.

My heart is erratic at this point. Lost to the rhythm humming in the room. I'd dreamt of this—of taking her on the sand where the tide would lick at our skin, where the night sky would be our only witness. I'd dreamt of driving into her, again and again, until the crash of the waves was drowned out by her cries, until my name tore from her throat like a song.

The thought alone leaves me shaking, caught between reality and memory, between the hunger in my veins and the fantasy that's haunted me for far too long.

"Please, Rune. I need you inside of me," Odi whimpers.

Slowly, I pull my fingers out, and suck them clean while she watches. My cock twitches the moment her essence touches my tongue.

"Are you sure?" I ask, leaning down to kiss the top of her nose.

She nods willingly. "Yes."

Under the firelight, I manoeuvre my waist to align myself properly, hands pressing into the mattress on either side of her breasts. She spreads her legs wider, opening for me as the tip of my cock brushes her most sensitive part. "Would you like to moan some more?"

Odi's eyes flutter shut, her knees clamping my hips steady, then she nods.

I reach out to grip her chin. "I want you to watch as I fuck you."

Her eyes fling open, mouth slightly parted. I line myself up, and then with one sweep of my hips, the head of my cock spreads her warm lips, stretching them over me. She gasps, pulling at the restraints around her wrists and it's all I can do not to instantly spill into her.

I hiss as pleasure rips through me, though I never take my eyes from her. With another thrust I sink in another inch, allowing her to adjust to my size. She's soaking the bed every time I pull out, and push back in, over and over until I'm buried so deep inside her I can't see where I end and she begins. Her mouth hangs open, silent as I pick up the pace. Teasing her with every tug and thrust.

"Do you like it when I touch you like this . . . Odelia?" I tease as I impale her ever so slowly.

She nods, finding her words. "Yes. Right there."

Every whimper, every sound she makes as I drive her up the bed. It's just for me. I want to trap it somehow, so when this is over I can play it on repeat. Reminding me of the night Odi and I shared.

"Rune, untie my hands please. I want to feel you," she begs.

I don't bother to stop the momentum, rolling my hips into her as I reach one hand up to release the knot. Odi immediately drops her hands to my back, clawing at it while she wraps her legs around my hips, angling herself to take me deeper.

The movement has me groaning into her neck as I pound into her. A sob tears from her lips, and I'm rewarded by another flood of warmth. Every inch fills her to the brim.

My lips find hers, desperate for her taste. She's just as hungry as I am, and I give all I have, every last shred of control burning away. Her hands fist my hair, keeping me steady as if she can hold me in place forever.

We move together, in a rhythm that feels unlike anything I've ever felt before. Urgent and unrelenting. Each touch, each gasp winds tighter, coiling low in my groin. Ready to erupt the moment she does.

My hips slam into hers, and she cries out. "Rune . . . I'm—"

"Say it," I moan into her ear before pulling back, my arms on either side of her face.

I pick up the pace, thrusting faster as she gushes all over my engorged cock. She arches under me, pressing her breasts into my chest. I see the stars flicker across her irises just before they roll back into her head and the orgasm takes her.

"I'm coming," she cries out, fingers digging into the skin on my back.

Her sweet moans bounce off the walls, so I reach up to cover her mouth with my hand. "Quiet, little doe. These walls are paper thin."

I fix my eyes on her, sinking into her over and over, while she whimpers under my palm. I want her undone, until every bone in her body is limp with ecstasy. But the moment I feel her clenching around my length, I'm done. My stomach muscles constrict, and I release a low groan as I empty into her in waves. The world spins as I black out, hot pleasure spearing through me with every thrust. She moans, bucking her hips as she milks my length, draining me of every last drop.

With one last thrust, I collapse beside her, spent and breathless.

This is it, Nisse

30
ODELIA

We lay tangled together in the dark, a lone candle sending light dancing over our skin. The entirety of my body hums, drifting in a way I didn't know was possible. Is this what it's meant to feel like, after? Every thought wrung out, every ache replaced with sweeter ones, like the one that pulses between my legs. Impossibly, I want more. I'd hardly be able to move if I tried, but there's an undercurrent between us, keeping me pressed flush to his side, my leg draped over his, claiming him even when I've not an ounce of strength left.

He's on his back, one arm around me, the other tucked behind his head. His breaths are slow, easy in a way I'm not sure I've seen before. When he handed me my gifts—the clothes, the jar—I thought I might burst, overwhelmed by the simple kindness. Somehow, he'd pushed it farther, studying me, learning me, filling me until there was nothing else.

Only him.

"How come your arm band stays when you shift?"

His sleepy rumble goes right through my bones. "What?"

"I've been wondering," I say, letting my fingers trail over his skin. "Your shirt disappears even when you half shift, but the band stays no matter what."

He turns to watch me, rustling the soft pillow behind his head. "It's a royal thing. Like a land king's crown."

I trace a gentle finger over the band, then continue to the shimmering marks on his arms. "And these? Elio doesn't have them. Is it a Rune thing, or are royals just lucky?"

"They're from my mother."

His voice trails off in a way that makes my heart ache, so I hum, moving my touch to the scars that mar his chest. "How about this one? Not so lucky, I assume?" His lower stomach tenses as I trail over a long, thin line near his hip bone and I grin as he catches my hand to hold it still.

"That was a Reaver. He didn't like that he'd been caught."

"Ah. I'm sure he saw the error of his ways."

His grin is bright even in the darkness. "He saw the bottom of the sea."

I laugh softly, moving higher. "What about this one?" It's round, and slightly puckered. To my endless delight, he shivers as I trail around it in circles.

"Bladefish. I should have known it was there, but they're fast. Maybe the fastest creature in the water. I'd accidentally come between her and her nest. I was certainly lucky Elio was with me for that one."

"He and Tavi seem more like family than crew mates," I say, a strange ache seeding itself in my chest.

"They are. Them and Otto."

"What about Otto's scar?" I'm not sure why I go still, waiting for the answer. It feels like a secret, like something Otto doesn't usually want others to see. But that sort of wound—how had he survived it?

Rune hesitates in a way that has the warmth that's settled in me turning stone cold. My hands still, sudden anticipation sharpening my focus into a blade. Rune clears his throat, and keeps his eyes glued to the ceiling as he finally answers.

"That one was Ivor."

The words hang between us like a noose.

"It was early on," he continues, as if he can't feel the way my heart has stuttered into overdrive, sending roaring blood into my ears. "I'd just gotten my ship, and I was a fucking idiot. A few years of training with my father's guard meant I thought I would hunt down and eliminate the most feared ship on the Adamaris Sea. It took us weeks to track down the *Sea Bane*. She was moored, so we passed on by. I sent scouts below to track her, figuring I'd always know where she was so long as they could stay in contact. But they found us that night."

Part of me wants to beg him to stop. I don't want to hear it—I already know. How many ships had we emptied for trying to board us? How many lives had we taken, before they could take ours? But I don't remember this. I don't understand how any of them made it out alive.

Rune swallows, his throat bobbing. "I'll never know how they emptied the crow's nest, only that our man on watch was dead before we were boarded."

I press my lips together. The answer wouldn't help him now. It was likely Garreth, the Viper's hawk shifter. Ivor liked bird shifters, but while others would come and go, it was Garreth that was always in charge of scouting ahead and eliminating any warning system.

"They dragged me from my bed, planned to execute me in front of the crew, before Elio warned them that we had messengers already in the water, and if they hurt me, they'd end up at war with Nareth. And no matter how powerful Ivor was, a man can't fight the ocean."

My stomach churns as the pieces fall together. "So he grabbed Otto instead."

"He was fourteen."

Tears well in my eyes, though my own hands were coated red by that age. My soul was never as pure as his, never as bright. Of course my father chose him to send a message. He hadn't even tried to end him cleanly. "Ivor wanted him to suffer."

Rune's voice is filled with mournful venom. "Ivor wanted *me* to suffer."

The quiet tears track over my nose to meet Rune's skin. Soraya's shirts had hidden my tattoo, but there's no way Otto hadn't had it in the back of his head during every interaction. Every smile. Every glance.

I draw a finger over the inked snake on my wrist. "Everyone on Ivor's crew has one of these, whether they like it or not."

Rune reaches out to brush it with his thumb. Like the act will sweep it away. If I could, I'd carve it from my flesh and fling it into the ocean for the creatures to devour.

I catch his eye, holding back the tears that threaten. "Otto knew I was a Viper from the beginning," I say, my voice barely a whisper.

He nods. "He did."

"Then—why—" Words fail me. I don't understand. How could he chatter away, hand me food with a grin, try to protect me in the kraken fight, when I may as well have been the one to slice the blade through his chest? "He showed me his quail," I whisper, devastated, and Rune barks a laugh.

"He trusted you long before I did."

"You trust me?" The thought splits my chest wide open, and I should hate this vulnerability, knowing he doesn't know the truth of who I am. That I lied, that I share Ivor's blood. That I've killed at my father's command, over and over. It may as well have been me wielding the blade against Otto. This thing between Rune and I isn't real. Not when I know a single truth would shatter it to pieces.

His warm breath kisses my cheek as he answers. "With my life, little doe."

The words threaten to break me. "Then why did you tie me to the mast?" I ask, pulling back, trying to put my body and my mind back in order. "Did you think I'd let myself get killed, and then you wouldn't have the riddles?"

"I thought," he says, his canines glinting in the half-light as he grins, "that you're a terrible swimmer. And that I wouldn't be able to look away, waiting for the moment I'd need to jump in and save you."

I scoff but thread my arms around his neck and pull myself into his chest, tangling our legs together. "I'm a fine swimmer." The words are muffled against his chest.

"And I'm a hopelessly charismatic human man with a fish costume."

I snort and knee his leg, but it's half hearted.

A sleepy silence falls between us. His breath begins to even out, even as my mind continues to race—faces of the crew, Otto's grin, Rune's life-giving breath, Soraya's singing, the ease of all those on *The Gilded Hart.* I've destroyed all of it.

I clamp my fingers into fists until they ache, trying to force my body into stillness as quiet sobs threaten to take over. It's second nature to shove them down. I never wanted this. I wanted to be alone. Because alone and unfeeling were the only kind of safety I knew to search for. But now, in the shelter of the darkness, I can't help but wonder how different my life would have been, if I'd have been allowed to keep this, if I'd tried harder to find what I'd lost when my mother died.

"I trust you too," I whisper, when his arms are dead weight against me. The truth of it destroys me. There's no secret worth hiding now. No impossible hopes when who I am still stands between us. When this is over, I'll tell him, if only so he knows that below Nisse, there was always a girl, and he'd helped her find the path through the dark in the end.

My hands are warm and dripping wet. The dark of night is absolute. It hides me.

It always hides me.

I feel him before I hear him. I always do, and I don't need light to know he smiles at the carnage before us. His giant, scarred hands squeeze my small shoulders. I'm the only one—I'm always the only one—*who fit in the manor's window. When he speaks, his voice, his pride, it is my own. The sniveling animal in me cowers away from us both.*

"This is it, Nisse." His voice rumbles, blotting out the sound of weeping in the burning village beyond the front door. "This is your power. This is your strength. This is why men will weep before laying a hand on you. Again and again you've proven yourself to me. Proven you're worthy to share air with the strongest the seas have seen. You do your father proud.

I wake with a start, Ivor's voice still rippling in my mind. The inn's room comes into slow focus—the patterned window curtains, the colour of the bedding, the empty corners that harbor no threat.

The space next to me is empty. Rune pads to the door, wearing bottoms now, apparently to answer the knock that woke us both. When he opens it, the hinges don't squeak, and warm light squeezes through the door frame to illuminate the bed in a sharp rectangle of light. Elio stands on the other side. His face is wan, worried, and dread licks up my spine, never eager to leave me alone for more than a breath.

It must be the ship. Maybe repairs aren't going as well as they'd hoped. Surely it's not the injured we brought—they'd shown no signs of infection, thanks to Otto. But what could be so pressing as to need Rune's attention in the middle of the night?

"What is it?" I ask, and Rune tosses me a sleepy smile over his shoulder. His hair is mussed. He turns back to Elio, who ignores my question, and instead offers Rune a folded slip of parchment.

"It's from Killian," he says.

Rune's entire body falls into a predator's stillness as he reads the message. Whatever it is, it's bad.

Elio's gaze flicks to me, and his face is stone.

I barely hear Rune speak over the roaring in my ears. "Thank you, Elio. I'll be right out."

Elio's nod has barely concluded before Rune closes the door, the sharp sound enough to make me flinch. His fist crumples the message into a wad of spent parchment.

"Rune."

In a blur of speed, he throws it, hurling it to the wall where it hits with an emaciated *plink*.

"Rune *what's wrong*." I pull the blankets over my chest, too aware of my nakedness. I don't know why I beg. I don't know what could be worse than what we've already faced, but the growing tension in the room has my senses and my voice sharpening.

Instead of answering, he taps his fist on the little table, jaw so tight the muscles feather like it takes all his willpower to stay silent.

"Rune." I stand, letting the blankets fall away so I can find the box of clothes he'd given me last night. "I can't help if I don't know what's going on. Please." He still says nothing. I slip my shirt on, then the trousers, the fabric soft and clean and not enough to comfort me now. All the while he stares at the grain of the wood below his fist like it might give him answers.

Instinct keeps my steps light as I round the bed to approach him, and I surprise myself by reaching out, finally able to bring myself to offer a hand to comfort. "Rune, whatever it is—"

He spins towards me, gripping my arm before I can touch him. His fingers dig into my skin like a manacle. "You lied to me." The words are a hiss, brimming with hot anger.

I rip my arm away, a shock of adrenaline setting me on edge. I watch every shift of his body, every angle of threat. "What are you talking about?"

He laughs a manic, sarcastic laugh. "It always comes back to *him.*"

"Rune—"

"I should have killed him the night I found you," he spit. "I should have taken the chance—but it would have risked my men. And I thought you'd be the trick, give us some edge—and here we are. With most of my men dead after all. And me in fucking bed with *his fucking daughter.*"

No.

My voice wobbles, "Rune, I never—"

He steps closer, if only so he can look down on me. "I pulled you from the water. Who knew you'd be so clumsy a Headtaker could send you over. What reason did I have to wonder if you shared blood with the rot of the ocean? But here you are—*Nisse Ivor.* Scourge of the Sea. The ghost that haunts a ship before it knows it's been boarded. The child wraith. What names am I missing, *Nisse*?"

"Don't call me that," I bite out, a flush of anger drying the water in my eyes. I close the miniscule space between us, baring my teeth. "Don't ever fucking call me that."

"You used me. You used me, and you lied," he says, dismissing me, turning away and beginning to pace again. His bare feet slap the wooden floor in even thuds. There's an accusation in the words, but I can only huff a laugh.

"You *agreed* to the map. Why would I have told you anything else, Rune? So you could turn me in? Hang me? Confirm your suspicion that I was a twice-damned soulless wave viper closer related to leeches than your precious royal bloodline?"

He shakes his head. "But you could have told me before I—" He cuts himself off, and something like hurt flashes across his face before he moves for his clothes, turning away from me.

"Before what, Rune?" I press, hating the ice in my voice. "Before you ruined yourself with me?

His eyes flash, his expression now a mask as hard as mine. "I wasn't the one who was ruined last night." He shoves his legs into his trousers and buttons the clasp.

My face burns, and I don't know if it's embarrassment or anger or attraction as he pulls his shirt on and the toned muscles of his chest flex until they're covered.

Either way, I can't stand the silence. Every part of me feels unanchored. "So what now, you report me in the morning? See me hanged by sunset? Your entire crew will be thrilled."

"Odi—" he sighs.

I've never been able to control my mouth when I know I'm caught. "You'll have to torture me for the last riddle. I am the scourge of the seas afterall. My death has to be satisfying. Do you think they'll bet on how long I'll last?"

He's sitting on the bed now, boots on, his elbows leaned against his sprawled knees as he speaks directly to the floor. "Odelia."

"Have I missed the mark? Maybe you'll save everyone the trouble and gut me here instead. Might be easier. You can pretend I ran away. Then you'll never have to admit to Otto—"

"Thats enough!" he barks, his gaze snapping up to meet mine. There's something wounded in it. "I'm not going to kill you. And neither will anyone else."

"Why?" I don't know why I ask. I don't know why the word tries to catch in my throat. I should be relieved. I should bolt from this room and lose myself beyond the wild edges of this town. But the animal in me has been quiet for weeks, her fearful whispers silenced by the peace I'd found with his crew. I don't know how to explain to him what it means to me.

He clears his throat and stands, sweeping past me without a glance. "Because we've got one more key before we're done. Then you disappear. And I go after Ivor."

"*What?*" His words rip through me like a blade. "You can't—"

"I can. I've had eyes on him for weeks. I'll know where to find him when the time comes."

He flings the door open, and Elio is already there, standing at attention. Rune passes him, his voice echoing down the hallway as I struggle to keep up.

"Update the crew in the morning," he tells Elio. "I'm taking her back to the ship. I want everyone on board at noon sharp. No exceptions."

I don't care that the entire inn can hear me. "Rune you have to listen." Our steps are loud and hollow as we descend the stairs. If any of the crew weren't awake, they would be now. "You can't go after Ivor."

He throws the front door of the inn open to the darkness of night. The air is still, humming with insects. Little moths flitter around the torch on one of the front pillars, tempting fate. His boots crunch over the scattered pebbles on the stones. Mine are silent, though my breath isn't. My lungs heave too fast, pulling in air they shouldn't need. "He'll kill you. He'll kill all of you—"

He stops so fast I slam into his back. "And that would bother you, Odelia?"

"Yes, you ass." But there isn't enough air for my lungs. Rune's eyes linger for a breath, assessing the panic in my eyes. They can't fight Ivor. No one can fight him. Hardly any have even landed a blow. Prepared or unprepared, it doesn't matter. He positioned himself as the best, and he's attracted the best. The whole crew is either lethal or cannon fodder, and he uses each with intent. "You don't stand a chance. He'll kill you all. Reid—" I swallow the name, shove it down, but it's too late.

He wipes any trace of expression off his face. "So you did kill Reid." There's no doubt in his voice.

The panic and frustration wrestle for control. “He was going to—Damn it, Rune, look at me.” He doesn’t, so I follow in his wake, alighting onto the floating wood of the dock that bobs beneath our feet. “If he’d told Ivor how to find you, you all would have been dead. Every one of you. There’d have been no way for me to stop it—you don’t understand—”

He strides up the gangplank and towards the room with me at his heels. I’m not even sure he hears a word I say, but I can’t stop the way they spill out of me like a broken dam, spurred on by the fact that I know the fate of all who go after the *Sea Bane*. That I’ve been on the other side, opening the guts of those who have tried and failed.

I follow him into the room, not even giving it a second thought, not until I see the rope in his hands and the cold anger radiating from every inch of his massive body.

“Rune.” The words abandon me then. I don’t know why I didn’t run when I had the chance. He said he wouldn’t kill me, but he’s still going to tie me down like he’s my jailor. “Is this really necessary?” I hate the hot tears that sting my eyes.

“Sit,” he commands, gesturing to the bed.

I should fight on principle, remind him I’m not a dog, but I don’t.

I sit. Using my teeth to cage back any argument. Trying to prove I’m capable of being something that doesn’t bite back on instinct.

It changes nothing.

I offer him my hands. *Nisse’s* hands. He doesn’t flinch when he takes them. Instead, he’s gentle, and it twists something vital inside me.

I can't meet his eye as he ropes my wrists, then my middle. When he leaves, the door shuts like a coffin lid, and that damn bird squawks outside, its coughing screech almost like laughter.

No wonder she seems happier here

31
RUNE

The deck is quiet, bar the sound of gentle waves slapping the side of the hull. Pale, watery light washes *The Gilded Hart* as the sun makes its way to the horizon. I sit on a wooden crate outside my quarters, head leaning back against the door, my mind and body equally exhausted.

Behind the barrier is the woman I'd ravished mere hours ago. Now the enemy once again. I'd tied her to the bedhead, yet little good it'll do. If she wants to escape, she'll find a way. I just needed her to be away from me. I can't bear to look at her. Doesn't matter that even the thought of her sends my body into a frenzy of heat and desire. We had our one night. Now it's over.

The moment I mentioned going after her father, she'd panicked. Tried to stop me. But once I made it clear I didn't need her opinion, something in her eyes shifted. Her fire went out, and she hasn't spoken since. Wouldn't even meet my eye when I chained her to her fate.

Better to end it now than bleed later.

We'll find the key. Get the treasure, and go our separate ways. Her to wherever—me to avenge the innocent lives lost at the hand of the Viper captain.

Elio left a while ago to make sure all the shipments we'd ordered were arriving on time, and to double check the rest of the crew members paid up at the inn. It's for the best. Right now, I don't know who needs the space more. Me or him.

Odelia Nisse Ivor.

Her name screams itself into the darkest crevices of my mind that I don't dare give light to.

The signs had been there. Plain as day. Viper tattoo on her wrist. Good with a weapon, too good. Cunning. Clever. Making deals for her freedom. And like a fool, I'd fallen for it.

For her.

I close my eyes, my fists curling as they hang between my knees. I can say all day long that I'm mad she hid from me, but the truth is that I'm mad that I was ready to dive headfirst into the Odelia I've come to know. That I've given so much to her already.

If father saw me right now . . . well I couldn't bear to face his look of disappointment. I'd rather sail the seas for the rest of my days than admit I'd really gone and fucked everything up.

No matter how much I try to remove her from my thoughts, I can't. Every time I close my eyes all I can see is the way her head tips back, eyes dancing as she laughs at one of Otto's jokes. Her laughter—like spring breezes through wildflower meadows—plays on repeat.

Yet, the memory is quickly replaced with the vivid image of her in the storm, standing on a deck with blood-soaked hands. Crimson dripping from her bola and dagger, painting the wood beneath her red. Who knows how many she's killed. Her role and reputation suggest it's a number I'd rather not know.

I stand from the crate and stride to the side of the hull. I grip the edge of the railing, my knuckles turning white as I look out at the shadow-drenched, cobalt sea, deep and velvety, still touched by the last remnants of night.

She's saved my life more times than I can count, so where is my mercy now?

She hid her name, she'd killed Reid, but the moment his name left her lips, it all made sense. She was right. Reid would have used her name like a weapon. But to kill him? The deck groans softly as I pace, hands on hips. She could have come to me. I would have helped her.

Or would I? Look at how I'm reacting to the truth. Can't stand to face her. Can't stand how blind and hopeful I was—it was my own damned fault I didn't see what was right in front of me.

I'm a fool. In more ways than one. There is no outcome that didn't see Reid lifeless at the bottom of the Adamaris Sea. Because I'd seen the way he looked at her like he'd gut her the moment he got the chance. And if I found out that he'd threatened her, that he'd threatened my crew, in any way, I would have been the one to send him to his death.

Odelia had said she needed to get away. Go so far that none would ever put two and two together. The entire time, she'd been clear about her goals. About what *this* is.

I'm the one that can't seem to walk away.

I snap my head towards the door to my room, gravitating towards it like the moon tugs at the sea. My boots are silent, hand hovering over the brass door knob. It's quiet inside. Has she fallen back to sleep? Does someone with that much blood on their hands ever dream? Or do their sins keep their mind in constant turmoil, even in rest?

She's probably forming a plan to steal the rest of the keys the moment we find the fourth one. Do I care? Will I really just let her go when all is said and done?

My hand drops to my side, and my chest begins to collapse in on itself. I can't breathe. Can't think. How am I supposed to move forwards knowing what I know when all that consumes me is the scent of her hair. The way she fits so perfectly in my arms or the way her lips taste when she's exploring mine.

Then there's the way she whimpers when my head is between her legs, and my tongue is between her—

My cock is getting hard just thinking about it.

A viper in my bed?

Fuck.

I'm done for.

And then there's the damn complication of Ivor being docked somewhere close. Killian had said as much in the message, but I can feel it, like a thorn under my skin. My plan—*the plan*—was always to see Odi on her way and then face Ivor, settle the blood debt once and for all. But half my crew's already rotting in the sea because I thought I could play this smarter.

But I botched it.

I return to my place on the crate in front of the room. Head on the door, eyes resting.

Every move since finding her, has been me clawing at a mess I made myself. I should've gutted Ivor the moment I had him within reach. Should've cut the head from the snake and ended it clean. Instead, I let him walk, and now the bastard's shadow has me glancing over my shoulder every turn.

The thought of it makes my jaw ache, teeth grinding hard enough to crack. There's no undoing it, no taking back the chance I lost. And if the moment comes again . . . when it comes—I won't falter. Ivor's mine. For Otto and his mutilated skin, for my crew and years of sleepless nights, for anyone else that has suffered for the greed of those who think they own the sea.

Sunrise arrives. Warm, and glowing. Salmon hues, bleeding into daffodil yellow, spill across the waves like honey. And with the arrival of the sun comes the crew. They trickle in slowly, completely unaware of the troubles I keep.

I fold my arms across my chest, pretending to sleep so I can be left undisturbed for a little while longer. It's only when I hear a thud of boots a few paces from me do I crack an eye open to see long white braids, black leather, and a scowl.

Elio obviously told Tavi then.

Good. If my judgement can't be trusted, then everyone should be a little more cautious.

She looks to the door then to me, and before I can utter a word she twists on her heel and stalks away.

My chest constricts again. A crushing weight that I have no choice but to carry. Tavi is so pissed at me, and rightly so. Can't blame her. Yet what was I supposed to do? Say no to the last link I have to my mother?

Perhaps I've finally lost my mind. Perhaps all I'm chasing is phantoms of my own creation.

By the time midday hits, the remaining crew have returned, some more lively than others. And the shipwright, along with an eager Stiden, has finished putting *The Gilded Hart* back together.

The deck is alive with noise, boots thumping, ropes slapping, voices carrying over the sound of screeching gulls above. I make my way over, always keeping the door to my quarters in sight . . . just in case.

The port's shipwright stands near the foremast on the quarter deck, hands on hips and a streak of tar across his cheek like war paint.

"How does she fare?" I call up to him from below.

He peers over the railing. "If you want a perfect fix you'll have to take it to the builder, but we've done what we can in the time we had. It'll keep you afloat."

I nod before glancing up, eyes tracing the length of the mast. The patch job looks sturdy enough, but I can still see the strain in the wood where the kraken had wrapped its horrendous tentacles. We can't afford to face something like that again. We won't survive it a second time.

The crew hovers nearby, watching me, waiting for my word like it'll fix everything. But it won't. My jaw tightens. "Good enough," I say, though the words taste bitter. "To your posts. We set sail shortly."

The shipwright nods, already barking orders at a pair of dockhands as he goes. I let my gaze sweep the crew. Tired faces, more lined than they should be. My heart aches for what I've put them through.

The rest of this journey is on me and Odi. And us alone.

Footsteps sound behind me, and I swivel to find Elio. "All the crew are on deck and accounted for."

I nod. "Otto?"

"Yeah, he's already prepping lunch."

A smile spreads across my lips before I can stop it. Of course he's already in the kitchens. I have never known anyone to have the work ethic that he does. At seventeen years old, too.

He needs to know about Odi, and I want to be the one who tells him. It's my role as his captain . . . and his friend.

I flick my gaze towards my room, then back to Elio. "Watch her for me?"

He nods. "Where are you going?"

I brush past him, tossing the words over my shoulder. "I need to talk to Bear."

The scent of roasted meats, and charred vegetables hit me the second I enter the kitchen. Something simmers in a black pot hanging over the hearth, and Otto is hunched over the bench dicing herbs and tossing them into a glass bowl that has what looks like olive oil in it.

He doesn't hear me approach, too occupied with the task at hand.

I clear my throat. "Bear."

As he spins he launches a bunch of rosemary towards me. I duck just before it hits me square in the face.

"Sorry Cap!" He blurts, cheeks red as he drops the knife with a clatter against the wooden chopping board. "You caught me off guard."

I can't help but chuckle as he fetches the discarded herb. "It's alright. How's the lunch prep?"

His eyes brighten, and I know I'm in for a wild ride.

"Well, I was just thinking about how good this fresh rosemary is that I got from town yesterday. It just makes everything taste earthier you know? Like, if you put it on roasted meat it adds so much flavour, especially lamb, but if you mix it with oil like this, it's almost like—like a sauce right? And I can't decide if I want more herbs on the meat or the vegetables or both. Maybe just the carrots, see them? Look at their blackened edges, that's the best bit, like crunchy sweet, and the chicken smells mouthwatering—oh!" He snatches another bowl with some sort of gravy in it, sniffs it and then holds it out to me. "This is going to be so good! You hungry? Of course you're hungry. Everyone's hungry. I've been hungry since breakfast."

Otto finally stops to breathe and I smile.

"Lunch is going to be amazing as always"

He grins at me, his skeleton hand earring dangling off his right lobe. "Did ya need something?"

I gesture towards one of the stools at the table. "Can we sit for a moment?"

His brow pinches. "Sure, Cap."

We sit at the table, and I take in a breath, trying to steady my mind. I have no idea how he's going to take the news, and I'd really rather not tell him, but what other choice do I have?

"Is everything okay, Rune?" he asks softly.

I hold his gaze, and sigh. "It's Odi."

Concern washes over him. "Is she alright? If she's caught that cough I can—"

I shake my head. "She's healthy, Otto . . . she's Ivor's daughter. Nisse."

The colour slowly drains from his face, and I prepare myself for whatever curses or accusations he wants to throw my way.

Then, his features soften, in a way that makes him look heartbroken. He shakes his head, voice dropping low. "*Vicious seas* . . . can you imagine? Growin' up with *that* bastard for a father?" He lets out a shaky laugh, but there's no humour in it, just the edge of something sour. "Must've been hell."

It takes a second for his words to register. I furrow my brow, and I shake my head ever so slightly in disbelief. I expected anger, or disgust . . . possibly both? I wouldn't have blamed him either.

The breath stuck in my chest finally breaks free. I thought he'd hate me for knowing the truth, or turn on me like Tavi and Elio still might, but instead there's pity in his voice. Pity and worse—understanding.

"Did you hear what I said, Otto? Odelia is Captain Ivor's daughter."

"I heard." He lifts a hand to his chest, reaching for the scar under his collared shirt. "No wonder she seems happier here."

My jaw tightens and my chest officially aches as I sit and view the boy before me, because let's be honest—that's exactly what he is, but in this moment, something shifts. In a blink, the boy is gone, and what sits before me is a man, acting like someone who's lived a thousand lifetimes. A man offering kindness to those who least deserve it.

It hits harder than any blade could.

"So . . . you're alright?" I ask softly.

His big, blue eyes crinkle at the edges. "Of course! I'll get her extra vegetables tonight. She seems to like those best."

Before I can reply, he's out of the chair, shaggy brown hair billowing around him as he races to stir the stew on the fire. I rise from the table, heading for the door, turning to watch him in his element.

I hate to admit it. But he's right. Odi is happier here. She's different from the drowning thing I pulled from the sea that first day. She'd claimed that it wasn't her choice to be a Viper, that none would hire her if they knew who she was, that being alone meant safety, that her captain met every challenge with violent steel.

"I trust you too," she'd whispered, voice shaking when she thought I wouldn't hear.

Perhaps there were always small truths unearthing themselves from between the secrets she carried. But I have to remember . . . it doesn't matter now. I was a means to an end. She'd used me. Lied to me when she had every single opportunity to confess. And I'd slept with her . . . *gods*, I'd bared my soul to her. And all that, to what may as well have been a stranger. One who shared blood with a man that slaughtered indiscriminately. She, herself, had slaughtered on his command. Again and again.

Some animals are born vicious. Like the sea. And the Ivor blood is tainted. Nothing can change that. It doesn't matter what Odi wants or what life she thought she might lead.

Nisse. The ghost.

Otto might have forgiven her so easily, but I'm not sure I can. He'd only been a boy when he got that scar. His cheeks were rounder then, eyes wider. And I couldn't protect him. But I will now.

"I suppose you'll have to talk to Tavi, yeah?" Bear calls after me, ripping me from my thoughts.

I grip the door frame. "That's where I'm headed next."

He throws a grin over his shoulder towards me, and I can't do anything but smile in return.

The sound of the crew grows louder as I head out on the deck. Elio is still stationed outside my room. He straightens as I approach. "How did he take the news?"

I sigh, leaning my shoulder against the wall as I look over the crew's preparations. "Let's just say he's a better man than me."

Elio drops his gaze to the ground, scuffing the front of his boot. "He's always had a soft spot for strays."

"Do you think Tavi will let me speak with her?" I murmur.

There is a good chance she won't talk to me for a few days. She's the one who warned me after all. And like the stubborn ass that I am, I didn't listen. Tavi's fierce when it comes to Otto—always has been. She circles him like a hawk, ready to tear out the throat of anyone who so much as looks sideways at the boy. And there's no chance she'll stand for him sharing space with Odi if Otto were to decide he doesn't want her on this ship.

Elio's hazel gaze finds me. "I can always say something if you like?"

I huff a laugh, though there is no joy in it. "Thanks, but taking the easy route was never my strength."

"Don't say I didn't warn you."

It's the right thing to do. I owe it to her. She loves Otto, me, and Elio. And I fear the moment Odelia becomes a threat, Tavi won't hesitate to put her down to protect us. For better or worse, I'll do whatever it takes to make sure Odi makes it out alive, and then we can go our separate ways.

"Since I'll likely be thrown overboard, I suppose I should plan to check the inktopus system."

Elio grins and dips his head as he fishes in his trouser pocket. "Already did. Tossed the little guy a treat too. Those tentacles are quite grabby! I'd planned to tell you, but with everything going on, I thought it best to wait." He hands a small letter to me.

The parchment crackles softly as I unfurl it, scanning the words on the surface.

The Sea Bane is hugging the coastline south. Sails low. Scaring off fishermen. I'd like to slap them all with a frozen fish. Killian.

With an eye roll, I leave Elio at the door, and search for Tavi. It only takes a few seconds to see her up on the foremast deck, staring out to sea. She doesn't flinch when I approach and lean my arms on the railing beside her. We stay in silence for a while, just being in each other's company.

She talks first. "I told you there was something off about her."

Her words bite, like those silver fish in the temple with their sharp teeth. I drag a hand through my hair as the wind dances around us. "You were right, and I should have listened. I'm sorry, Tav."

Her emerald eyes flash, sharp as broken glass. "Captain Ivor's daughter. *By the stars*, Rune . . . of all the people to bring aboard, of all the people you decide to . . . you chose her."

"I know." The words taste like chalk in my mouth. "And you're not going to like this, but I'm going after the last key . . . with Odelia."

Tavi exhales, closing her eyes briefly like she's given up on the fight already. "Rune."

"I have to, Tav." I begin to pace. "We're so close. We've lost too much. I can't turn back now. Once we find the treasure I'll drop her off at the nearest island . . . I promise." I'm sure Odelia would demand nothing less.

"And what of Bear?" she asks pointedly. "How does he feel?"

I pass her twice before I answer. "I think he accepted her long before anyone else, and if he didn't—his kindness overshadows any negative thoughts he might have about her."

For a long moment she just stares at me, the only sound around us is the rigging above swaying in the wind.

"You know I'll have to put her down if she so much as breathes wrong," she mutters, lips pursed and eyes piercing like daggers.

There is no doubt in my mind that she's telling the truth. And that's what worries me. Because even though Odi betrayed me, I'd be a liar if I said she hadn't curled into a space beside my heart. There's no future with her now, but that doesn't mean I want to see her dead.

"I know, but we're not Vipers. We don't kill for sport."

Tavi sighs, turning back towards the sea. "You're a damned fool, Rune. Don't you dare go killing yourself . . . or Elio."

A small smile creeps across my lips. Grateful that she hasn't ripped my head off like my heart predicted she would.

My pacing stops. "Careful, Tav. Someone might think you love us."

White wispy tendrils curl around her pointed ears as she glances sideways at me, her voice softer. "You I tolerate, but Elio . . . I'd drown without him."

Those words earn her a look, my eyes widening with the admission.

She raises her brows as a silent warning, wild love swirling in her eyes. "You hear me?"

We all know who truly runs this ship. Tavi—fierce, loyal, and unyielding. She's the heartbeat of this deck, the fire that keeps us moving. Truth is, we'd all be adrift without her.

I lean sideways and brush her shoulder with mine. "Yes, Cap."

You can't win

32
ODELIA

I should have stolen the keys and run the moment we hit Whitestone Harbor.

I know we're moving, but the sun hasn't set yet, so we can't have gone far. Rune hasn't come back since he tied me. The ropes are a point made rather than an honest attempt to hold me. The thought makes my blood boil.

Yes, I'd hid the name my father preferred. Anyone would have. It's what I'd run from. A name attached to a cowled, blood-soaked woman I'd wanted to leave behind. And who would admit to years of crimes once they found themselves in a brig with a chance to get free? And Reid. Goddamned Reid. He'd left me no choice. Can Rune fault me for protecting his crew? Some blood needs spilling. Like any of the other monsters we've faced.

But instead of understanding, Rune turned on me. And worse, a fraction of me had hoped there might be a chance he'd understand.

Odelia Nisse Ivor.

I'll never forget the disgust. The way he hissed my name and it hit the air like a brand. Like something I'll never escape.

He's right.

I've been fooling myself. Playing nice with the good folk like I had a chance of existing beside them. Like they would never find out who I really am beneath—who *he* made me. But this is it. This is all I am. A killer that will always be caught in the end. A dagger always a hairsbreadth away from splitting flesh.

The door opens and I bare my teeth as bright sunlight bursts through, piercing my eyes. Rune steps in, and his cool gaze settles on me, empty, expressionless.

I hate him for his control, for the angry tears that try to well in my eyes. I don't deserve this. Not his anger nor his shock. He never expected better from me.

Did he?

"I thought enough time had passed that we might discuss how things will be moving forwards."

I let all the loathing show in my face, but don't speak.

"Odelia—" he sighs, like I'm being impossible, like something between us hadn't snapped when he tied me here.

"You said you trusted me." I look away then, unwilling to share the hurt I know will be clear on my face. My throat is dry as I swallow, sticking, trying to choke me. Just like before, when he'd left me without water, when I was nothing to him, worse than nothing. Filth unworthy of even the basic human consideration.

He sighs again, then sits in the chair that waits by the desk and weaves his fingers together, elbows resting on his knees. He studies me for a moment before his voice fills the room. "I did."

The words pierce me as well as any blade.

"This is why I couldn't tell you," I argue, trying my damndest to hold back the pain that's trained to turn into anger. "No one would ever trust me if they knew. This is why I ran. Why I can never stop running."

His voice is cold. "And Reid got in the way of that, did he?"

I try not to flinch at the accusation in his voice. This is exactly my point. When he sees me, he sees Ivor. Just like the mainland healers when my mother had spilled gold at their feet and begged them to heal her. They'd jailed her instead, and she died.

Ivor is a blight. And being connected to him means no one will look past the rot of his blood in my veins.

"I told you exactly what he did," I say, shoving the thoughts away. "He said he'd find a way to tell Ivor you harbored me. None of you would have stood a chance if he found us." I laugh, but it's bitter. "I gave him so many chances. So many *warnings.* I put him down, but he kept getting back up—"

"Enough—"

"No it's not *enough,* Rune." My legs bounce, bursting with potential energy, but the ropes won't let me stand. "You'll feed yourself to Ivor anyway."

Rune is a thundercloud, his body tense, his expression darker than I've ever seen it. "Tell me he doesn't deserve to die."

Another dry swallow. I can't explain the pinch in my chest. "It doesn't matter. You can't win."

A hint of that cocky smirk ghosts over his face, sending unexpected warmth barrelling into my chest. "You underestimate me."

I deflate beneath the crush of emotion. I can't convince him. He's already made up his mind.

"Odi." The name is softer than it should be. "Have some faith. I've got more than just my own crew at my disposal, if I need it. No more needless sacrifices."

The idea lifts my spirit, but the worry still swirls in my gut. "Fine," I say.

"Fine."

For a moment, the only sound is the dull rush of ocean water and the slow creak of the ship. "Remind me again why you've graced me with your presence?"

His unfocused eyes train back on me. "To discuss our arrangement moving forwards."

I pull up my tied wrists and go on in mock cheer. "Back to pseudo-brig, right? Me. Rope. No water? Discussion had. On to the key and our separate ways."

"Tavi is pissed."

The words halt the stream of sarcasm. "Good." Any self-respecting bounty hunter would be, I suppose.

He huffs a laugh. "No, not good. Not good for you. Not good for me. She's placated for now, but I need you to promise me if she gets in your face you won't strike first. I can't imagine either of you would walk away."

"*You underestimate me,*" I mock. "I'm not going to hurt Tavi. I *like* Tavi." Another ache pinches in my chest.

I have to get out of here. I have to get off this ship, away from them. I can't afford the feelings that put me at a disadvantage. I'm honestly not sure I could draw a blade on her if I wanted to.

"What about Otto?" I clench my teeth, shocked the question had made it out without conscious thought. Otto has every reason to hate me, to blame me, but . . .

Some of the darkness leaves his eyes. "Otto is . . . Otto." One side of his mouth lifts, sending butterflies to my traitorous stomach and tears once again well to my eyes. I've never allowed this level of emotion before, and I hate how powerless it makes me feel. "He sent up two plates of vegetables. I thought you hadn't told him yet."

"Otto is twice the man I'll ever be. But he isn't into holding grudges. I think he thinks he knows you too well." For a moment, he studies me curiously, like he wants to ask something but won't.

Any anger that made a home in me is extinguished, swallowed by the tide of emptiness that always follows. I know he can see the void in me, but my mouth works independently of my brain, asking before fear of the answer might stop me. "What about you?"

The silence that stretches between us could rival the bottom of the sea.

I watch him tuck his feelings away, my heart sinking deeper and deeper. His face turns to stone over his slate-grey shirt. His broad shoulders solidify. "We're headed for the last island. If you betray me, or turn on anyone on this crew in any way, I won't be held responsible for what happens next. We get the treasure. You pick an island for us to drop you on. After that, your plans are none of my business. And mine aren't yours."

The rope around my wrists is soft, fraying slightly. I keep my eyes glued there, unable to bring myself to look at him. "Thank you." The words don't taste foreign now, but the ache in my chest makes the realisation a bitter one.

Rune stays a moment longer, the air between us charged with things unsaid. Eventually, he moves, the thud of his boots too loud as he goes.

When the door slams I flinch, then let myself fall back on the bed as the lock clicks closed.

I don't count the days that pass. The light through the round window brightens and dulls in warm hues, pink, then orange, then yellow, darkening and lightening as the sun makes its rounds. Over and over I beg my body to let me fall into slumber, and for the most part, it does. I pass the rest of the time trying not to think, but for some reason it only brings the animal side of me forward. I retreat, and she's there, alert even when I'm in a haze. I don't shift, I think, but sometimes I wake to antlers on my head all the same.

Every now and then, voices rise—Rune, Tavi, Soraya, it's always the same. The words are muted by the wood of the door and the crash of the sea, but my name comes up more than once. Food appears at random. It's Rune that delivers it, and each time I see him my chest aches all over again.

Some of my dreams are nightmares, but others are of him. Of the night we shared. Of the clawing, grasping, greedy thing between us that was sated in full. I wake smiling, his song in my head, his infuriating grin still wrapped around my mind.

Then reality sweeps in, reminding me of the only truth that's kept me grounded.

This isn't the life I wanted.

I wanted land. Safety. The freedom to shift and fly through endless green. To run, as fast and as far as my legs could take me.

My mother was a soft, hopeful thing. She'd loved so hard she let a man split her soul between soil and sea. In another life, maybe I could have stood doing the same.

In another life, maybe my father hadn't carved every last piece of her out of me.

She can't see in the dark

33
RUNE

The ruin rises out of the ground, like some half-drowned beast, its gritty exterior painting a picture of old stone that looks like withered bones draped in vines thick as ropes. Bright green moss and ivy choke the decaying surface, spilling down broken arches and crumbling walls.

I flick my gaze to Odi. She stands rigid a few paces away, eyes fixed on the ancient pile of rubble in front of us.

There's no door, just a vast mouth gaping open towards the sea, daring us to step inside.

It took the two of us a few hours to find this last location, arriving just as the sun hit the highest peak in the sky. The journey had been mostly silent, and easy enough to navigate given it's just the two of us.

I hadn't allowed anyone else to join the search party.

Tavi wasn't pleased, but she just has to deal with it for now. At least everyone is safe on deck. I can handle Odi on my own.

Thankfully, we'd only crossed paths with one red, spotted botang python—as long as my leg and as thick as my arm—and a group of carnivorous apes that were feasting on something unidentified but definitely fresh. We didn't wait around long enough to find out what it was either.

I shove my hands into my trouser pockets, feeling for the smooth shell that's no longer there.

"One and one may enter," Odi recites to herself. "One and one may die. Soul the sole preventer, it and the divide."

What the riddle means is beyond my understanding, yet there is one line that has me concerned. *One and one may die*. All I know of that is I won't allow it to be true. I *can't* let it be true.

She looks at me, and my chest twists. All the fire that used to blaze in her eyes is gone, snuffed out like a flame starved of air. And I know all too well who shoved her into that box.

My dagger sits snug strapped to her thigh, glinting under the harsh light of the sun. It was the best way I knew how to offer a truce. I jut my chin towards it. "Don't go losing that. I'm going to need it back."

She rolls her eyes. "I wouldn't dream of it."

Together, we step inside. The cavern stretches enormous, the ceiling lost in shadow. The waxy vine that covers the outside clings to the walls inside too, with sporadic sprigs of tiny white berries scattered here and there.

I curse under my breath. We'd brushed past them on the way in, and I should have known better than to get close. I can still see the white dusting of their residue on the sleeve of my shirt.

The world tilts ever so slightly at odd angles. Soulberries. *Damn.* Too many and they'll rot a siren from the inside out, leaving me swimming in visions until I can't tell sky from sea.

With a sigh, I run a hand through my hair. "I might start seeing things soon,"

Odi whips her gaze towards me. "Whatever do you mean?"

"Hallucinations," I mutter.

Her brow pinches. "Rune—"

I shrug. "It's nothing to be concerned about. Won't kill me."

At least . . . I don't think so.

Odi folds her arms across her chest, squinting as she digests my words. "How in all eight seas did you manage that?"

"Brushed up against some soulberries a while back."

"Why haven't they affected me?"

I shove my hands into my trouser pockets. "Poisonious to *seafolk* only—especially sirens—land dwellers figured it out ages ago. Used them against us whenever steel alone wouldn't cut it."

"So why didn't you say something before?"

I shrug again. "Didn't recognise them until it was too late. We eradicated most of the vine years ago. I wasn't expecting to see it here."

"Rune . . ." Her voice is laced with concern, stoking the embers inside my chest that still burn for her.

"I'll be fine. Just ignore me if I say anything odd."

She doesn't respond, but I don't miss the way she looks at me. Like she wants to say a million things, but instead she says nothing.

Water laps against the edges of the cavern, black and bottomless, encircling everything but a single strip of land that cuts straight down the centre.

I take a step forwards, but don't miss the sound of Odi's breath escaping her lips as we near the edge. One wrong foot would have us in the water, and who knows what creatures lurk in the inky depths below.

Despite the undeniable tension between us. My hand still itches to reach for hers. To lace her fingers through mine so she feels a sense of peace. To assure her that we're going to get through this, no matter the cost.

But I can't do that.

I pause as I glance over my shoulder. Odi stops behind me, brow pinched. "Have you seen something already?" she asks, flicking her gaze around the eerie space.

I huff a soft laugh. "No. I just wanted to remind you, that if there's water, don't forget you have Soraya's sea stone."

Her brown eyes travel over my face, as if she's searching for what used to burn bright between us. The crimson vessel in my chest aches and my fingers twitch once again. But I force them to stay by my side. It's better this way.

Odi nods, and we resume our walking. The pathway is narrow at first, just wide enough for two feet side by side. It spreads wider the deeper we go until it broadens into a platform pressed against the far wall.

My head spins, stomach pitching, as the effects of the soulberries set in, but it's not enough to obstruct my plans. I'll push through it like I always do. Besides, it'll wear off soon.

The platform is paved with old, moss-covered stones. On the wall are symbols etched into the rock, similar to the ones on Odi's map—the water elementals. Every heartbeat sends a wave of heat through me, tipping the world on its axis. I

nothing but the darkness of the tunnel. My throat burns with the thought that she might've dropped into the deep just as I have. All I can hope is that she's remained calm, she has the sea stone afterall.

Water elemental markings are carved into the surrounding walls. The most I've seen on this treasure hunt so far. I should be excited. I should etch each one to memory, but the moment Odi disappeared from my sight, something in me broke.

I rake my hand along the marking, darting for the tunnel on the far side of the wall. It slopes ahead, deeper into the gloom. Panic presses at my chest like a weight, heavier than the body of water I'm encased in. I push myself harder, swimming down.

The tunnel is like every other siren ruin I've crawled through—ledges that rise and drop, ramps where humans would've cut stairs. No straight path, no mercy, just the sea's own labyrinth.

I shove forwards, every beat of my heart hammering her name. If Odi's down here in the dark—if she's fighting for her life—I have to reach her. It's not supposed to end like this.

The tunnel bends sharply to the right, spilling me into another room. Shadows dance across my vision. Blonde hair, blue eyes, laughter I've not heard in months. Dash? What is my little brother doing down here?

I lurch forwards with a grasp, but he slips out of my fingers. On second glance, it's not him anymore, it's Selene. Her perfectly poised hair piled high on her head. Precious stones glimmering on her ears and neck. The royal jewels.

"Selene?" I call to her, but her figure slips into the inky waters.

They aren't there, I tell myself. *Just a hallucination. Get a grip.*

I shake my head as blue tendrils wrap around me, their touch so light they can't be real either. *Right?*

The tunnel stretches ahead, and it feels like I've been swimming for hours. Nothing but stone walls with markings. Every now and then, the tunnel bends left or right, I just keep following it.

I dart into another round room. I'm seething. The water is endless, curling around me like a prison, taunting me. This ocean that I love, has become my enemy. Shadows slowly sway, teasing me with their secrets. How am I supposed to find Odi if there is no way out?

Something brushes past me. Light as a whisper, gone before I can snap towards it. My skin crawls. I grit my teeth until my jaw aches. I spin again, but nothing. It's just the berries—my own head trying to undo me.

But as I twist around, I see it. A shadow sliding just beyond the next tunnel entrance. Long. Low. Too solid to be nothing. My stomach knots as it circles me. Yellow, soulless eyes track my every move.

Whatever this is, I'm its next meal.

With a flick of my wrist, I reach for the bone blade at my side, but the creature is faster.

The thing bursts from the dark with a snap of its jaws, long and skeletal, ridges curling down its spine like broken stone. Its body is eel-slick, gator-thin, and fast—too fast.

Instinct takes me.

I catch it head on, razor sharp talons digging into the glossy black ridges of its jaw before teeth like shards of shattered glass find my throat. I yank its mouth wide, as it thrashes, spinning its body to coil its scaled tail around mine.

It tries to drag me down into the depths, but I dig my talons deeper, ripping at its flesh like tiny daggers. "No you fucking don't."

My chest burns, rage pounding louder than the groan of the ancient creature. I refuse to let this ruin be the end of me . . . or Odi. Her brown eyes flash across my mind. Dark hair tangled in the sheets with me. The way her body feels like silk under my finger tips. I have to get to her.

I snarl, twisting, teeth clenching until I manage to get an arm around the creature's neck. It snaps its maw, cold and malicious, trying to reach for me. We tussle, bubbles shrouding us as we crash through the water. I manage to wrap my other arm around its neck, every muscle straining until I hear bones crunching beneath my grip.

The beast spasms once, twice, then goes limp in my hands.

I shove its carcass aside, chest heaving, salt burning the back of my throat. My hands ache, knuckles raw, but I keep moving. No time to linger. Not with Odi somewhere in this gods-cursed place.

She stands no chance against a creature like that, even with a weapon and a sea stone.

The thought of her facing a haggard beast alone, does something to me. My heart beats so hard it feels as if my ribs might crack. Tremors skim across my scales, seeping into my fins, and I swear I'm going to bounce right out of my skin. Heat flushes through me, followed by an icy aftershock.

What if shes's—

No. I can't think like that. She's a good fighter, better than most, some would argue she's better than Tavi and her twin blades. Odi is brave. She is strong. She's a fighter.

But she can't see in the dark.

'FUCK!' I scream into the dark abyss.

The moment we're out of here, she's learning to control her shift. I don't care if she wants to. I need her to. So the image of her wide eyes in the dark will stop taunting me.

The illusion of her is in the water, hands clamped around her throat like she's drowning, the billowing fabric of Soraya's blouse dragging with every movement she makes. It's not real. Odelia wore her own clothes here, the ones I'd gifted her.

I swim past the dying vision. I hate what this woman is doing to me. I can't trust her. She's Nisse Ivor. The ghost.

She's proven that she can't be trusted right? So why do I have this overwhelming desire to protect her even though I know exactly who she is?

Perhaps I should be more concerned about protecting myself *from* her.

With a growl on my lips, I dart towards the next tunnel, leaving the image and the dead creature behind me. I swim like my life depends on it, because it does. The riddle will not lay claim to a life. Not mine, not Odi's.

I burst into another chamber, but this one is different. It's a dead end.

No. It can't be. Smooth stone walls surround me on all sides. No doors, no archways, no platforms, no stairs. Just a trap dressed up like a room.

I drag my hands along the stone, searching for seams, cracks—anything. My fingers trace the siren runes chiselled into the walls. The shapes are twisted, older than anything I was ever taught. An ancient dialect, unreadable. Mocking me.

My pulse hammers as I force water through my nose, filtering out the oxygen through the vents behind my ears. If I don't breathe, I'm going to be useless to Odi—if I'm not already too late.

The dizziness stays, but I sweep the walls again, scanning the chamber for anything I can use to dig myself out of this shit hole I'm in, but there's nowhere to go.

Grief. Anger. Pain. They slam into me like a tidal wave, driving me down until I hit the chamber floor. My tail strikes stone, kicking up clouds of sand that curl around me like smoke.

Did we fail? Is this my punishment—for chasing my mother's phantom, for dragging my crew into the deep and watching them die one by one? What if it's all for nothing? If the treasure isn't real, or there, or worth having after all is said and done? What if I never get my revenge on Ivor? What if I do? There will always be more pirates to hunt. Always. Where do I draw the line in the sand, saying enough is enough? It won't bring her back.

It won't bring her back.

My mind is too loud. Too many thoughts screaming. I let my head fall back against the wall, eyes closing as the weight of everything I stand to lose presses in from all sides.

The treasure has to be real. Odi wouldn't chase it with me if she didn't believe it was out there . . . would she? Too many of my crew have gone to the grave for this. If I stop now—if I let it slip through my fingers—what in the deepest parts of the Adamaris Sea did they die for?

No. I can't do it. Otto, Elio, Tavi and Soraya are waiting for me. I have to claw my way out of this mess. This mess that started the moment I hauled Odelia Nisse Ivor onto my ship.

The vicious, violent, unpredictable, daring, brave, breathtaking, maddening, stunning, infuriating, perfect woman who I can't stay mad at for one second longer, because the honest truth of it all is, I've never been more in love with someone than I am with her.

She matters more than any pirate, more than any treasure. And I'll be damned twice over before I die letting her think I despise her.

I *love* her.

I love the way she slips in beside Otto, serving plates to folk she's only just met, like they're family already. I love how she can read me better than I read myself—knows when to press a glass of whiskey into my hand before my thoughts spiral too far. I love that she never tries to tame me. She fights at my side instead, blades bared, standing against the likes of Reid as if my crew were hers all along.

She is the ocean to my parched soul.

I have to keep going.

My head tips forwards as I open my eyes. There in front of me—on the opposite wall—as if it's been there the whole time, is a symbol etched with crumbling lines, so faint with age that I hadn't noticed it. It's been years since sirens used them, but suddenly I find myself grateful for the hours in the royal libraries being forced to a princely level of education. I scurry for it, tracing the lines without thinking twice.

The floor answers with a trembling roar. I dart out of the way as a hole tears open beneath me, dragging everything with it in a violent rush. There is no choice given as the water rips me down in a spiralling pull, the whole chamber twisting like a gigantic, murky whirlpool.

I've gone and done it now.

Sharp pain splits my chest in half as I land with a violent thud on a stone platform, water churning on either side until it drains away in a sucking rush.

That's going to hurt later.

My fins scrape uselessly against damp rock, so I force the shift, breath wheezing through my lungs as I clench my teeth through the pain stabbing daggers into my ribs.

Gingerly, I stand. My feet feel numb, like they don't know how to carry me forwards, yet there is no other choice. It's an empty room with a dry tunnel that leads into another chamber, and I know if I keep following it I'll soon find a way out.

The walkway is narrow and thin as I stumble down the incline and into the room. Once inside I'm met with the scent of dank moss, and earth. Smells a lot like the land above. Surely I'm close. The left wall looks like it's been riddled with holes, dark little mouths gaping at me. I spin to face the right.

It gleams, sheer glass from floor to ceiling. The kind that makes you feel watched even when nothing stares back.

Something steps from the shadows on the opposite side of the glass, sending my heart into my throat. I rush for the partition, slamming my palms flat against the smooth surface.

"Odi!" I bellow.

What I Needed

34
ODELIA

"Rune!"

The door had sealed behind me when I made it in here, and though I watch it do the same behind him, the tension in my shoulders eases. We may be trapped, but it seems we've both passed the first part of the test.

From across the glass, Rune studies me and I return the favour—he looks unharmed. His hair is soaked and dripping in rivulets down his shirt, which clings in interesting enough ways to send my thoughts in directions that won't help us now. "Did it send you underwater?" I ask, clearing my throat. The space between us has been strange, strained, but his eyes are bright and pinned to mine in a way they haven't been for days.

His voice is muffled by the glass when he speaks. "Yeah. I guess it didn't for you since—" he waves his hand over the top of his head. "You shifted?" There's a strange pride in his voice.

I reach up on instinct, and find the soft antlers on my head. The tunnel had dropped to a cavern that was pitch black. I had to shift to have any hope of seeing. I'd actually managed to keep her grounded.

Mostly.

It was shaky at first, but it was easier when I wasn't in the hold of a ship or being pursued by a seven foot man with claws. She and I had eventually come to a tentative understanding, and we'd made it this far. It was more than I'd hoped for, considering the swinging boulders I'd barely avoided. Then the wall arrows. So many wall arrows.

"I guess the animal has its uses," I shrug, too relieved we're okay to try hiding the smile that spirits over my face.

He grins wide, making my stomach flip, and presses his hand to mine on the glass, the sudden softness in his eyes confusing me further. "I'm so fucking proud of you. I was worried I'd lost—"

A crunch vibrates from his side, making us both move to look behind him.

The wall is spiked.

He turns his head to me, brow pinched as if confused. It wasn't spiked before. I'd studied every inch I could while I was stuck in here. I open my mouth to speak, but in another teeth-grinding crunch, the wall leaps towards him again, closer to the glass like it would like nothing more than to crush him, and every nerve ending in my body zaps in a shock of electricity, sending my pulse sprinting and my hands over the glass, the sides of the walls. The corners—anywhere I haven't checked—but I've checked *everywhere.*

"Rune—"

He's doing the same, checking for depressions in the rock, slots in the glass.

The wall crunches again, sending my heart into my throat.

"I don't see anything!" he shouts on the other side.

"I don't—" my breath catches, because I do. The entirety of the floor below me is opening. I flip the dagger from the sheath at my side and start ramming it into the glass. "Rune!"

He doesn't look at me. "See anything?"

"Rune, the floor!" My heart can't beat any faster than it is, but it tries, stealing the air from my lungs and the ability to think.

The wall on his side crunches again. It's closer now, moving in random spurts.

He turns to where I'm looking, his eyes going wide as he realises the floor on this side is creeping away.

"What does that symbol mean?" I ask, panic strangling my voice. Where the floor opens, water laps at the walls. It's going to drop me in. On the far wall, beneath the water's surface, a symbol glows—wind overlaid by a circle and a diagonal line.

"Rune—" when I look back at him, the expression on his face sends another wash of dread through me.

"Odi," he says, almost gently, ignoring the wall snapping behind him again like jaws. "It's a rune. One we use in Nareth; its magic will nullify the sea stone. It means you're going to have to hold your breath." I'm already shaking my head but he goes on. "It must be part of the test—"

Words don't form. This can't happen. We didn't make it this far for this to happen. The water is pitch black, endless. It's death. It's taunting me with death.

"Look." He points to the centre, where the floor still moves, its insistence pushing me into the back wall as my feet move against their will.

But I see it. A light glows at the bottom, faint.

"I think this is it, Odi. I think this is what it wants. You have to swim."

The wall crunches again. It's almost halfway to him now.

"I can't—" but the words won't leave my lips, because there's no other option. It's Rune. And if I don't do this, he dies for nothing.

He presses his forehead to the glass, his bright-blue eyes clear even through my smudged handprints. "I have watched you face the Sotor. I've watched you grin while gutting acid-tongued monsters. You're braver than me. Stronger than me. You held things together while I broke—you—you made Tavi *laugh*. You can do fucking anything, Odelia." The wall screeches again. "But you're going to have to jump. Please."

Everything in me screams to keep my feet on the ground. The animal, the little girl tossed in to sink or swim. But I won't let him die for this. I lock my eyes with his—they're so blue, impossibly blue, shining with confidence I know he doesn't feel. I shove down the fear one last time, but fail to steady the trembling in my voice. "Count of three?"

He nods. "Count of three, little doe." He takes a few steps forwards, angling so he's in front of me. I follow until my toes overlap where the floor retreats.

He offers a smirk that doesn't quite reach his eyes and crosses his arms, tilting a shoulder into the glass like he doesn't have a care in the world. "One."

I wonder how many would hear the tightness in his voice. Would recognize the faux optimism for what it is.

"Two."

I swallow and pin my attention to the wavering glow in the water. One more time. Just one more time. *Live or die*, I promise myself, *you will never have to go under again.*

"Three."

I leap. Headfirst, arms splitting the icy water before it swallows the rest of me. It takes every ounce of willpower to stop from gasping. My eyes burn against the salt, but I won't lose sight of the glow at the bottom. I won't be the reason we don't make it out of here—the reason he doesn't make it out of here.

It takes me a moment to realise the pressure doesn't feel like suffocation. And as I settle into a rhythm, the darting shadows make me wary, but not the dark of the sea itself.

For years I've flinched from the ocean, certain her touch meant icy death. I've watched her take many, felt the crush of her fury. But now the water slips past, and it reminds me of glittering blue and trying not to smile. Of the way he cradled me with his taloned hands. Of gentle offerings and long nights of wondering when he'd finally let himself sleep. It touches my skin—and all I can think of is him.

My lungs start to burn too soon. I really am a shit swimmer, but I push harder—I can still hear the grind of the spiked wall in my head. How long does he have if I fail? One minute? Two? My muscles protest and my lungs beg, but Rune will be crushed any moment. This is the only hope we have.

My hands brush into something trailing around my wrists and I flail away, but as the glowing light below me wavers again, I realise it's seaweed of some kind, nearly as thick as both my hands put together.

It's dense too. I push through, trying not to think of how wrong I may be, how the light may be a clever trick for a hungry maw. The fire in my lungs grows the harder I heave through the growth. Even if I tried to swim up now, I wouldn't make it.

But I'm nearly there.

It's slowing me, tugging me back as I press forwards. I reach, lunging my arm out as deep into the mass as I can. One more heave, and I'll be in range. The spikes will stop, Rune will be free, and the key—

The key . . . I fight the sudden urge to laugh as the realisation hits me. The key doesn't matter.

Not the key or the treasure. Not my dream of lonely peace. Neither of those hopes are what I swim for now. They were never what I needed. What I needed was proof that there was another way to live. That my mother's love wasn't the last I'd ever feel. That a crew could sing together, grieve together. That even the most fierce are fiercest for love. That a big-hearted cook can adopt all those that adopted him. That loyalty is born not of fear but of trust. That a captain can lead by example, and choose to shoulder every burden alongside those that die for him, even if that means offering his drink to the sea.

I needed proof that a smile can be gentle. That my hands can be a comfort.

Before now, I'd never owned new clothes that weren't stolen. I'd never had things that were mine before they were anyone's. Not my mother's necklace. Not Ivor's sharp edges.

And then there's Rune, handing me a package like it's the least he can do, announcing he's going after Ivor like he knows he'll win, like he doesn't see how he's taken everything I know about the world and tossed it, skipping it far across the water, nevermind the ripples that grow. He is confidence where I am fear. He is bold where I tend towards the shadows. Considerate where I've been nothing that wouldn't help me survive. We're opposites, fire and kindling. The earth, the moon, and this tide between us.

It doesn't matter that he hates me. Or, he wishes he could. The map, the fear, the anger, I shove it all to the back of my mind as I reach the last of my breath.

One more kick. And one more again. Because if I don't make it, he'll die wondering if the fear won in the end.

I want him to know that it didn't.

I want him to know that I love him too much to let it stop me.

The keeper of my heart

35
RUNE

With a shuddering groan, the spikes halt, mere feet away from me. There's no sound, bar the constant dripping of water seeping down the crevices in the stone. I drag a breath into my lungs, trying to steady my racing heart. It doesn't last long though because the wall spikes might have stopped moving towards me, but Odi hasn't surfaced from the pool on the other side.

I press my hands against the glass. "Odi!" I yell, waiting to see the bubbles rise from the depths so I know she's okay. But there's nothing.

I pound the glass with my fist over and over, but there's nothing I can do. It doesn't budge. I'm stuck here on one side while she drowns for me on the other.

Rock grinding on itself sounds behind me. I swivel to see a small door made of stone swing down like a draw bridge to reveal a hidden alcove. I rush for it and shove my hand in to reach the shining metal inside—the last key. My heart is pounding. This is it. We can get the treasure. Success after everything we've gone through.

Yet I don't have Odi, and at this point it's all I care about.

I slam the stone door shut, pocket the key, and start pounding at the glass partition again. When it doesn't budge, I grab the sword at my side and begin to smash the hilt on it repeatedly. Something has to give.

Odi . . . little doe. I'm coming.

A groan sounds through the room, making me bounce away from the glass, caught off guard. I throw my gaze to the roof to see the wall begin to sink. A heavy breath escapes my lips. "Thank fuck!" I shout to the void.

The entry door on my side opens as the glass that bisects the room descends. For a single breath, I hesitate. Is it another trick? The instinct that pulls me towards the water could be wrong. She could have found another way out. She could be waiting for me outside the temple, swept to safety once she'd made it down, but it doesn't make any sense. Really, there's only one reason two ways would open at once.

It's a choice. An opportunity for anyone on this side to take the key and escape, or leap in to save the one in the water. Every temple so far has ensured that a land dweller couldn't make their way through by force. Even with coercion involved, this one guarantees the siren—or elemental—had the choice to make it out alone.

I turn my back to the door and sheath my blade, then I shove myself up on the lip of the stone that sandwiches the glass together. As soon as there's room for me to squeeze over the top, I take it. Every second that Odi is down there is a second closer to losing her forever.

My boots slam against the small ledge of stone flooring that is left on Odi's side of the room as I land, and without a second glance I'm diving head first down the circular looking well of black icy water.

The shift takes me in seconds, my darkvision kicking in as I frantically search for the one who has stolen my heart . . . my breath. But it's impossible to see anything. It's a forest of kelp down here, and not the nice kind.

It's thick, brown and as wide as an oar. If I can't even see down here properly, how will she? I grab the stem of some, and tug myself through the tangled web of foliage. "Odi!" I call. I need her to know I'm here, and I'm not leaving without her.

"Odi!" I call again, darting through the masses of kelp that curl around my fins. "Odelia, where are you?"

It's not like she can yell back to me either. The moment she opens her mouth it'll fill with this salty sea. Fear grips my chest. We're so close. We made it through the first part. I have the key. I just have to get her out of here.

But how?

Not even the glowing beacon of the button can assist me now. It's gone. Like she is.

I reach out, spreading my arms wide as I feel for her . . . for anything. Stone brushes my fingertips, I must be at the edge of the wall. I need to head back into the centre where the button is.

"Odi!" I scream her name as loud as I can, but the only sound that bounces back is my own voice.

What use am I as a siren, if I can't find someone in the ocean? I stop and drag my hands through my hair, wracking my brain on how I can get out of this mess—with Odi breathing. Because without her isn't an option.

As I pause, I feel the current shift. I drift towards it. A small tunnel opens up in front of me—the way out. There's every chance she found it and has already swum to the surface, but I can't leave this room until I know for certain that she's not in here.

She won't die . . . not for me.

I spin around, facing what I hope is the centre of the room, and I force my breath to steady, and my mind to focus. Then I part my lips.

With every ache, with every heartbeat, with every hitch of my breath from the moment I laid eyes on her as she sank into the depths of the Adamaris sea all those nights ago, I release my song. It spills out, pulsing through the shadows, calling to her, beckoning her to me like the old sailor's tales of sirens.

Low at first, raw and rough from the ache in my chest. The notes ripple through the water, carrying farther than I ever could. The sound isn't just heard—it's felt, vibrating in bone and blood, threading through the dark.

I pour everything into it. Her name. My fear. My need. The promise that I won't let the sea keep her from me. My voice wavers, almost breaking, but I force it steady, stronger, until the cavern itself seems to hum. Her name tumbles from my lips, willing her to me.

If she's anywhere in this cursed black, she'll hear me. She has to.

From the corner of my eye I see something pale flash against the darkness. A hand. *Her hand.* A wave of relief washes over me, and I choke back a cry.

My voice pulls taut. The song silences as I dart for her. The moment my fingers curl around her wrist I yank her towards me. She crashes against my body, losing bubbles of air from her lips as I wrap my arms around her waist.

She hardly has the strength to cling to me. The water closes around us, heavy, merciless. Her eyes flutter closed. My gut twists, no time left to think. My hand dwarfs her face as I pull her lips to mine. The instant they touch my chest bursts with life as I breathe into her. Delicate but firm fingers dig into my forearms as the colour comes back into her cheeks.

There's no time for pleasantries but by the *seas* I want her.

She pulls back, tugging her lips from mine, and nods to let me know she's okay.

I brush the pad of my thumb over her cheek. "Let's get out of here." With a sweep of my arm, I scoop her up to cradle against my chest and then we are gone.

The chilling water whips past us as we barrel through the tunnel, leaving the forest of kelp behind. It's warmer now and the light has shifted. We're almost at the surface. Odi's face is tucked into my chest, her wild brown hair billowing around us. With a powerful flick of my tail, the water spits us out of the hole and into undergrowth. I shift just as our bodies collide with the land, and I've never been happier to be in my human form. Odi claws for the edge, fingers digging into moss and dirt as she drags herself half way out. She gasps, ragged and raw, the sound wounding my chest.

I haul myself after her, legs scrambling at the soil, clumsy and burning with strain. Once I'm free I grab her waist, and drag her the rest of the way until she collapses against my chest.

"We're safe," I whisper into her soaked tendrils.

Her chest shudders, dragging in fresh air into her lungs.

A rush of emotion washes over me. I nearly lost her down there. She'd risked it all for me, facing her fear, and nearly died because of it. We lie there, sprawled in the damp earth, both of us sucking in lungfuls of air.

"You alright?" I murmur, voice horse. My hand finds her back, steadying her breaths against mine. "Breathe with me."

"I thought—" She breaks off, shuddering, turning her face into my shoulder. "I thought I was gone."

"Not while I've still got you," I rasp. And I mean it more than I've ever meant anything.

When we finally manage to stand, legs shaking, I glance back to the hole we clawed our way out of . . . and it's gone. Just the forest floor. Roots and ferns tangled together as if it had never been there at all.

Odi grips my arm, wide-eyed. "Where—?"

I shake my head, jaw tight. "I don't even want to know."

Her eyes find mine. "Did you get the key?"

I nod once, my heart still hammering in my chest. "It's safe."

We both stand there, hands hanging by our sides as we lock eyes, saying a million things at once with our silence. Then I can't hold back anymore, and neither can she as we leap for each other. Her hands tangle in the hair at the back of my neck, while mine grip her face. I crush my lips to hers in a kiss so heated it could set the world ablaze.

Teeth, tongues, lips. All of them together. Biting, sucking, tasting.

With a low growl in the back of my throat, I walk her backwards until she slams into the trunk of a tree. The bark is rough against my hands as I pin her there. The kiss is sharp, hungry, all want and need—vicious love poured out in a single breath. I drag my hands from her face and grip her hips, grinding into her with mine. For a heartbeat she matches my energy with fire, as she drags her fingers up my back, nails biting my skin.

Then she melts—just for a moment—her body softening against mine, her mouth yielding under the force of my desire. Her fleeting surrender undoes me. I'm lost in her, and I never want to be found.

Odi rips her lips from mine, chest heaving and eyes dancing with venom. "I can't believe you made me do that!"

I hate that she's not in my arms, so I reach out, curl my fingers around her wrists and tug her back into my chest. "Sorry, but I really didn't feel like getting impaled today."

My head drops down and claims her mouth once more. She whimpers softly as my tongue brushes the seam of her lips. She opens for me, and I feel my knees weaken.

She shoves at my chest, tugging free again. "Rune—I nearly died back there."

"But you didn't," I mutter, leaning in, lips brushing her jaw before she can dodge. "You're still breathing. Proof I was right. You can do anything."

Her hands slam against my chest again, but they don't push as hard this time. "That's not the point! I thought—I thought I was gone. The water, the dark—"

I cut her off with another kiss, gentler this time, lingering. "But you're safe now." I whisper as I pull back.

She exhales, shuddering, torn between fury and something else as she runs her eyes over my face. "You can't just kiss me every time I'm frightened."

"Why not?" I murmur against her lips. "Seems to work."

The corner of her mouth ticks up in a smirk, then she grabs the damp collar of my shirt like she might shake me. "You're infuriating."

"And yet," I grin, pulling her in again, "you're still standing here."

She reaches up to brush hair from the side of my face as she flicks her eyes to my lips. "Can we go back to the ship now?"

Looking up at me isn't the vicious ghost of Nisse. It's not the violent pirate who shares the Ivor blood. It's not the wet dog that I dragged spluttering from the sea. No. It's Odi . . . little doe. Fierce, loyal and brave. The keeper of my heart.

I huff a gentle laugh. "I thought you'd never ask."

I WANT TO WASH YOU

36
ODELIA

By the time we make it back to the ship, the sun is set. Tavi drops the ropes down as Rune rows us to the hull of *The Gilded Hart*, which sits high and proud on the dark, quiet water. At the top, Elio stands from where he was sitting with his back to the main mast.

"We were starting to think we'd have to go after you," he says. His eyes are tired as they flick between Rune and I, then to the dagger still at my waist.

Rune doesn't pause to chat, and we all fall into step as he moves towards his room. "We got lucky. There were only two tunnels this time."

"Oh goody." Elio still limps but the pain doesn't colour his voice. "And what sort of beastie was it? Giant bird? Basilisk?"

"Flesh-eating monkeys," I answer, which turns his wry grin to more of a grimace.

Rune's smile is brighter than I've seen it in days, and it cracks my heart wide open. I can still feel the burn of his song beneath my skin, like a magnetic pull between us. "The important part is we got the last key," he says. "Expect to wait for any other juicy details in the morning." He opens the door to the captain's quarters and gestures for me to go in first.

Seeing the blanket bundled on the chair, breathing the faint, lingering scent of him makes my heart ache with need. As soon as the others go I'm dragging him into bed and not letting him go for a week.

"Right now, we're in sore need of sleep," he says.

Elio says goodnight but Tavi hangs back. I dig through the clothes in my bag as Rune sits to unlace his boots.

"Otto left food ready for when you got back," Tavi says. "Do you need any bandages? Salve?"

"Both, please," I say, turning as I toe off my soaked boots.

Rune's head whips towards me. "Are you injured?"

"No, but you are."

He follows my attention to a scrape on his forearm. It's long, but shallow. "It's not even bleeding."

Tavi offers me a nod. "Odi's right. After those barbs, it's better we don't take any chances."

"She would have brought them anyways," I say, sitting next to him on the bed. "There's no way she didn't notice."

"Ah, princehood." He tugs his shirt up over his head and tosses it into the floor before brandishing a smile. "The sweet and constant illusion of choice."

I bark a laugh, mainly because my face flames from the heat and proximity of his bare skin. "You should let people take care of you too, once in a while."

"In that case"—he stands and presses a kiss into my hair—"I'll wash so all of me is clean and ready for you. We can't let Tavi do it, or I'll lose circulation in this arm by morning."

I shake my head and try not to listen too hard as the washroom door closes and the water begins to pump. One part of me wants to lie down, the other part wants to see the look on his face if I decided to join him.

A knock jolts me from the thought. Soraya grins wide when I open the door. "Hey! Tavi sent me. Well. Actually, I insisted." The cheer of her greeting takes me by surprise. She carries two plates on one arm, with two rolls of bandages and a tin of salve tucked in the other.

"Thanks." I can hear the washroom water turn off, so I close the bedroom door as close to closed as I can and bundle everything into my arms. I'm fairly certain Rune hadn't taken clothes to change into, which means at any second he might walk out in only a towel. Or less.

"Odi—" Soraya stops me just as I turn away. "In case we don't get the chance to talk alone again before the treasure stuff is over, I'm . . . glad I got the chance to know you."

The words sink deep before I can fully register them. She nods at my speechlessness, her parting grin a star in the night. I thought for sure there'd be none on the ship willing to offer me a soft word, but a warmth tucks itself away in my chest. For once the hope isn't unwelcome. Nothing stands between us and the final island. We've got all the keys. All that's left is to make the trip.

When I turn back into the room, Rune stands in the washroom doorway with a towel across his waist. The sight stops me long enough that a self-satisfied grin spreads across his face.

I press the edges of my smile down and move to set everything on the desk. I keep waiting for him to remember my other name, the one he hates. When we walked into the ruins, he'd been cordial, but aloof. Cool enough to chill me with a look. But ever since it spit us back out, he's clung to me. Not his hands, but his awareness, like if he looks away too long I might disappear.

Heat follows me, and I know he's watching my every move. "Washroom is all yours, little doe."

"I still have to wrap your arm." I turn, bandages and salve in hand. I should eat too, but my heart races too fast as I meet his eyes. "Sit." I toss my chin to the bed, daring him to argue.

He obeys, settling down and resting his forearm on his knee. I avoid his gaze and kneel in front of him, immediately surrounded by the scent of salt and sweet oranges. Anticipation thrills through me, but I temper it as well as I can. The scrape on his arm cuts through the swirling shimmers of the marks on his skin. He doesn't resist when I reach for it, keeping my touch light as I dip my middle and ring finger into the salve and apply it in short circles.

The air grows more charged as I move, slow, feeling the weight of his unwavering gaze. The sound of his song still drifts through my head, the memory enough to make me shiver. Next is the bandage. I cut a length and make sure to wrap it just tight enough, watching the muscles of his arm flex against the pull, ignoring the need that aches between my legs.

There's so much we still haven't said. What this is. What's changed. And if the end will be the same.

I work. All the while, the call of his voice plays in my head. Haunting and lovely and life giving. The strength of his power is undeniable. It wove itself through me until I needed it as much as I needed the blood in my veins. With it, he could command legions. Command the sea.

But he'd called me through the dark.

He found me when I was lost. Gave me breath when I had none. I'd given up, willfully this time, but when I heard him . . . my very soul was called back from the brink. His voice, his grief, had tethered me. Tethered us. If there were any chance of resisting this before, it was left behind in that water because—

"You sang to me." My heart stops as I speak. Finally, I let my eyes meet his. There's no hiding how I'm feeling now. My voice trembles too much. My sight is blurred with tears. He reaches his big hands around my face, catching the first tear to fall with his thumb.

"I didn't know how else to find you," he says softly.

He doesn't understand. I try not to let my voice crack. "Every time you sing, it's like the magic of it stays in me. I hear it in my sleep. I feel it calling me to you, even when you're silent. There's this constant pull. I can't . . . I can't get it out of my head, Rune. I've never wanted anything more than I want you." He goes still. "But what if the feelings I have are influenced by your power? How am I supposed to know—"

"Little doe," he says, shaking me slightly to halt the words. "Mine is not a magic that lingers. I've no real power outside of the water. When the song ends, it ends. I did sing for you. I had to. I poured every ounce of power I had into that ruin.

If I hadn't, you would have been gone. And what would I have done then?" His blue eyes bore into mine. "What would I have done then?" he repeats, softer, before sliding his grip on my shoulder down past my elbow, lifting my arm to plant a soft kiss on the inside of my palm.

"But . . ." My mind reels, trying to make sense of how his lips press into the skin of my hands like he doesn't see the blood that stains them. "I'm Nisse."

He reaches down to pull my other hand to his lips, this time, kissing the knuckles. "Not anymore."

Relief crashes over me at the tenderness, but his giant hands pull me in. "Come here," he says, and though I move to kiss him, he scoops me up and carries me to the washroom, his towel falling on the way in a rustle alongside the soft footfall of each of his steps.

"What are you—?"

"Shhh." He pulls me up so the words brush my ear. "I want to wash you."

There's an oil lantern flickering in the corner, joining with the brush of light from a full moon that ghosts through the window.

"I hope you plan to make it quick," I say lightly, even as something in me weeps for the idea.

He sets me down beside the tub, his lips brushing the sensitive skin below my ear. I shiver as he speaks. "I don't." Sensation zaps from where his breath skims my neck all the way down to where I'm already slick for him. "Take off your clothes, Odi." I tug at the hem of my shirt and he helps it over my head in one motion, revealing the scars on my body and the viper-shaped ink on my arm. Slowly, he slips gentle fingers under my wraps, loosening them until they fall away. As I go for the tie on my pants, he steps around me to get into the tub, and I realise it's filled with clean water and the aroma of salt and oranges. Like he'd already planned to coat me in his scent.

Once the cool air kisses my bare legs, he reaches out to beckon me in, but there's no way we'll fit. He takes up the lion's share of the room, but I take his hand, and somehow we do, with my back flush to his chest, half in his lap so the hard length of his cock rests between my legs. He reaches forwards to thread my fingers, then holds both my hands to my chest with one of his own. I suck in a breath as the first brush of contact drips water down my stomach. It's warm, but the touch is too gentle. Intentional. Like it's meant to prove to us both we're still here.

All is quiet as he dips the sponge in the water again, and it splashes in drips over my thighs. "Rune," I say as he runs it over my shoulders and across my back, tightening his grip on my hands, like he thinks I might try to bolt away. He's right. I don't know if I can take this. The water tracks down my skin, slips down my spine. "Rune." My voice cracks, sounding strange in the empty air. I'm not sure what I intend to say.

Just as well he doesn't answer.

Instead, he lifts my hands up over my head, pulling me up on my knees, and runs the sponge down the bottom of my arm, then scrubs slow circles beneath my breasts. Everything in me feels painfully exposed, like he's washing away what's been there too long. Like he already knows what he'll find underneath. I can't help the part of me that wants to shy away. Not the animal this time, but me. The woman whose body has only ever been a weapon to tend to rather than . . . this.

He trails his lips up my shoulder as he lowers us down, planting slow kisses down my neck. I dive into the sensation, using it as an anchor. My hips move on their own, seeking friction, slipping against the length of his swollen cock. "So impatient," he says. But I'm already trembling. The water below splashes again, and he sits back before squeezing it over my hair and using his fingers to scrub at the roots.

"Prince."

"Hmm?"

"Let me touch you."

"I'm not done yet." Then he's wrapped each of his hands around my wrists and pushes me forwards so my hands grip the side of the tub, his chest grazing my back. A thrill of adrenaline beats through me with every pump of my heart. "Don't move," he says. His voice rumbles, and my stomach swoops as I watch talons grow from his fingers on either side of mine.

Besides my chest, which moves with every quick breath, I'm still as he sits up on his knees behind me. The water sloshes, and I gasp as one warm hand grips my thigh, then he pulls my legs out wider.

"Fuck," he whispers as he trails the sponge over my ass and down each of my legs. The murmur goes straight between my thighs. As if he knows, he glides the sponge between them, favoring one side and then the other, barely grazing where I need him most. "You're so perfect."

My fingers clench the tub's wooden sides. The water splashes again, then goes quiet as sharp, languid talons graze down my back and around my hips. Every inch of my skin erupts in goosebumps. There's a wet smack as he slaps my ass, and a spark of pain flares through me before I jolt at the feeling of smooth, untaloned fingers slipping in teasing circles around my clit. Heat immediately starts to burn low and build, and I arch into the friction, reaching for more. He grips my hips, keeping me still, and when he finally sinks a finger into me, he speaks. "I want to watch you break on top of me." Another finger joins the first, working in and out, growing slicker with every pass. "But that will require us to move to the bed."

"Please." I can't take it anymore, but he doesn't stop, just keeps his fingers moving in slow strokes. I continue to beg, my voice is needy and breathless, dangling on the very edge of my sanity.

Finally, he stands and steps out of the tub, splashing water over the floor as he goes. The sight of him sends a fresh wave of arousal dripping down my legs. The light catches every dip and cut of sharp muscle. On the glittering scales that shine up his arms and in patches on his face. He could be a statue. A god of the sea. His cock twitches, and my eyes lock on the movement. It strains into the air, already dripping from the tip. Rune glides his fingers over the head, then fists his hand along the length and pulls in one slow stroke, his attention glued to the way my eyes widen.

"Don't stop," I say, crawling over the lip of the tub. The floor is cool on my hands and knees, but his eyes are heavy with heat, the high points of his cheeks are flushed with red, and the groan he gives as I rise to catch the beading precum with my tongue, makes power sing through my veins.

"Odi." His talons thread through my hair, and I respond by swallowing him down in one motion, as deep as he'll go. His hips jerk and his hiss sends another thrill of victory through me. I bob up and down in time with his hand, swirling my tongue over his head and flicking the sensitive triangle of skin at the bottom. He begins to move with me, rolling his hips, meeting me for every stroke, fucking his hand and my face. "Fuck, Odi."

I groan, urging him on. I'm growing wetter. My nipples ache from how taut they are against the cool of the air. I need to take more of him, but the grip in my hair tightens, then pulls me off with a wet pop. I suck in a sharp breath and then whimper as he brings my body up, lifting me off the floor. My nipples brush against his chest as he pins us together with a single, massive arm. I wrap my legs around his waist and lock my lips with his, still needing to taste him. He responds in kind, sweeping his tongue against mine as he moves us to the bed.

He lays back on the blankets, never breaking the kiss. The wood of the bedframe protests at the added weight, but the mattress is soft beneath us and he uses one hand to line himself up and the other to hold my hips as he eases in the tip of his cock. I press back into him, greedy for the way I know he'll fill me, and he takes my cue, easing out and back up, working deeper, stretching me to the point of sweet sting.

"Too much?" he asks when my breaths grow shorter. I shake my head no, unable to pull in enough air to speak. The world has narrowed to this moment—the strength of his chest pressed to mine, the way his arms engulf me, how he peppers my shoulder with light kisses, so soft I hardly feel them as he rolls his hips, reaching deeper and deeper.

When he's finally seated all the way, he stills, waiting for me. It doesn't take long before I sit up, letting my nails dig into his chest, feeling another rush of wetness at the predatory way his eyes travel over my parted lips and peaked breasts. He nearly takes up the whole bed. I'd never noticed it before, but with him beneath me now, in his half-shift, it's undeniable. My hands look small compared to his shoulders, and when he wraps his hands around my hips, his fingers nearly touch.

The thought has me moving, working myself up and down. He watches, keeping that intense gaze on me as he holds back. I can tell because his fingers flex where they've gripped me, as if it's an effort to keep his touch light. I grin, slowing, tightening on him as I trail two fingers around my breast, down my navel, and to my clit.

His groan is nearly a growl as he traces the movement with his eyes. My breath hitches at the first light touch, and his hands tighten, but I don't go faster. I want him in a frenzy, and I'm close, judging by the way his attention flicks to my fingers, to my face, to my bouncing breasts.

"Odi." There's a touch of warning in his voice, and it sends a thrill of sensation up my spine. I toss my head back at the feeling, arching as I move, basking in the feel of him, in the slow swirl of my own fingers. But instead of taking control like I dare him to, he loosens one hand to tease and pinch my nipple, and I nearly collapse right then. Intent leaves my mind, and all that's left is this feeling that finally drags us under.

"Yes," he says, his voice like gravel. "That's it. Just like that, little doe." I speed up at his encouragement, chasing the way his voice vibrates through my body. "I want to watch you break for me."

The tension levels to a higher, needy baseline and I cry out, my breath coming in groaning pants now. Finally, his hands wrap my hips with all the strength in them, and suddenly he's moving with me in perfect rhythm, grinding us together with all the fluid power he has.

"Rune, I—" My breath hitches as he cants his hips at the perfect angle, pushing me higher with every stroke.

"I can feel that," he says. He doesn't waver. Doesn't push for more. He works the angle till I'm soaking him. Until there's no thought left in me. My cries are wordless, formless, and my legs are shaking before he has mercy and speeds the pace to near punishing. All I can do is hold on while a wave of building heat spirals from my core and wraps up my body like a vise. Every part of me burns. I'm lost to it. The bed begins to creak, the bolts that hold it to the ship loosening enough that the bedhead begins to rock against the wall. If Rune is worried the crew will hear, he says nothing, only thrusting harder while he holds me still, my knees buried into the blankets on either side of his hips

"Look at me," he says. I do, and the fierce need on his face sends me over the edge. I cry out as it takes me, sweeping the world away for white-hot bliss. Rune doesn't stop. He rides it out until I've returned, and then his talons thread into the hair at the base of my neck and pull tight, sending my face up and the rest of me arching for him. "Again." The growl settles somewhere in my bones. Air isn't enough as the command pulses through my core and the pressure starts to build, as if he alone can sway it. His chest is sweat-slicked beneath my fingers, but he doesn't vary, just presses his thumb to my clit and rubs in tight circles. "Again, Odi," he groans as I begin to tighten for him.

"Yes—" I say to the ceiling, breathless, trying to let him know I'm rising fast. Trying to let him know that between his cock, thumb, and the grip in my hair I didn't stand a chance. "Don't stop, Rune. Please—"

I may fracture apart this time. I may break into a million little pieces and never form together again. The sensation builds fast, and goes higher, then higher still. I grit my teeth, crying out as he hits a stride that tells me he's past the point of no return.

"Rune."

"Come, Odi."

"Rune—" My voice cuts off as the orgasm barrels through me, taking my breath. Rune cries out as I clench around him, and delicious heat fills me as he comes. We ride the sensation together, then slow to a stop.

His grip in my hair falls away, and I let my head drop forwards. His broad chest heaves beneath me. For a moment, our gazes lock, something vulnerable and impossible threading between us. Then he smirks, eyes glinting, and I can't pin down the edges of my smile. My entire body thrums, alive with something I didn't know existed. His attention skirts down over the sweat on my skin, and he starts to harden inside me again.

"Still thinking you'll get rid of me after we get the treasure?" I croon.

He pulls me closer, burying his face in my hair. "I think I plan to spend the next few days convincing you to stay."

You're not him.
You'll never be him

37
RUNE

Warm sunlight pours through the round window beside the bed like molten gold. It runs over the rivets in the fabric, pooling around our bodies. Odi's soft breath caresses my chest in her peaceful sleep. She's been in my arms since sundown. Spending a night of bliss exploring each other's bodies hadn't been at the forefront of my mind when we first came back to the ship, but the moment my feet hit the deck, I needed sleep and to have Odi wrapped in my arms, and I have no intention of moving from my bed any time soon. I don't even remember when I fell asleep, only waking when the sound of that wretched bird became too loud to possibly ignore.

Soft, cotton sheets mould to the shape of us entwined together. I can feel the beat of her heart against my chest. It's slow and steady. Like the ocean gently lapping at the side of *The Gilded Hart*. I can't recall a time that I have ever felt this relaxed. I feel as if I could lay in bed forever . . . and that never happens.

I lightly trace a finger up and down her arm, watching goose bumps appear on the surface of her skin in my wake.

How did we get so tangled together? And what do I do now, tell her I love her, only to let her go?

Dark brown waves of hair sprawl over her sun-kissed skin. Glistening like melted chocolate. With a soft sigh, she nuzzles into the crook of my arm further and I catch a waft of her scent. Fresh spring blossoms in a fruit orchard, mixed with the scent of my soap. She reminds me of a meadow I saw once on the mainland. The rolling green hills were covered in low growing wild flowers bathed in dappled sunlight.

She feels so lovely in my arms that I can't help but slowly shift my weight so I'm on my side looking down at her. Then I begin to trace faint kisses across her collar bone until the skin melts into the mound of her supple breasts that lay bare in the sun, beckoning me to nuzzle my nose into them. Odi stirs gently by the time I reach her navel.

Her hand finds the top of my head, then I shiver as her fingers dig into my hair, nails dragging across my scalp. "Why are you awake?" she softly moans. "It's too early."

I smile, pressing another kiss to her stomach before moving my attention to her face. She giggles softly as I pepper more kisses over her eyelids, and down the tip of her nose. "Hard to sleep when there's a viper in my bed."

She pulls back, attention caught on the words. Her lips part, but before she has time to respond I claim them with mine, pulling her closer into my chest. Once I've kissed her soundly, I pull back. "Only because you're cool to the touch, and being with you feels dangerous . . . and exciting."

Her umber eyes squint, but a smile dances on her lips. “Ass,” she murmurs before pushing me flat so she can lay across my chest, resting her chin on her hand.

The sun gleams behind her, dusting the edges of her silhouette in gold. With one hand behind my head, I reach the other out to tuck loose strands of her glossy hair behind an ear. I’ve memorised the shape of her now, but there are still so many parts of her I’ve yet to discover. “Tell me about your mother.”

Her brow pinches. “My mother?”

I nod once. “Yes. I know enough about your father, but you don’t talk about her.”

She sighs softly. “What do you want to know?”

A small grin dances on my lips. “Everything.”

“Nobody’s ever asked me that before,” her voice trails off, laced with emotion.

Internally, I wince. I asked her with humour and she answered with pain. The echo of it pushes against her tongue looking for an escape, and perhaps she just needs somewhere for that pain to go. Someone to hold the weight of it for a while. Someone to gently prod the barrier of grief she uses to protect herself. “I’m asking.”

Her jaw tightens, and for a moment I think she’s going to refuse, then a soft sigh escapes her lips. “She died fifteen years ago.”

The pain in her voice mirrors my own. Grief calling to grief. So I reach for her and gently squeeze her hand. “I’m so sorry.”

Odi is silent for a moment. Thinking. Her mind taking her back to a place she probably told herself she'd never visit again. I brush my thumb over her velvet cheek, letting her know I'm still here. "What was she like?"

"Too pure for this world. A wood nymph that fell in love with a pirate." Her eyes glisten over. "Torn between land and sea."

The words are raw, and I think I'm starting to understand. "Was she a deer like you?"

She nods, and I catch my breath at the way her hair spills over her shoulder to brush against my ribs.

"When I was seven. She gave me a necklace. Told me that it was so special only the ocean could offer it as a gift," she murmurs, instinctively reaching for her neck. "I wish I still had it. It's the only thing of her I had left."

Dread coils in my gut like a snake. All this time, I thought she'd stolen it—like any pirate would. That's what made sense to me. But it wasn't stolen. It was her mother's. A gift. And then hers. And the ocean let her keep it. How do I tell her I carried it in my pocket for weeks, not understanding, only to lose it to the deep when the Sotor came?

I can't tell her—I can't. Telling her would only cut her twice—believing she'd lost it, and then hearing the truth from me. That I'd kept it. That it confounded me. I'd believed it could never belong to someone like her. That shame sits deep in my chest.

But it's mine to carry. I can't hurt her to unburden myself. Not now.

I gently graze my knuckles across her forearm. "How did she pass?"

Brown eyes map my face. "She was sick, but it wasn't the visible kind. The moment she married Ivor, the moment she left the mainland, she grew ill. Ivor says it was because she had me but I think . . . I think it was grief. I think becoming so detached from her shift made her waste away. They knew she needed a doctor, but who treats the wife of a pirate?"

Something in my chest tightens, gripping my heart with a grasp so tight it threatens to crush it. My tongue presses against the back of my teeth, words clawing to get out, but I swallow them down. Better to keep quiet. Better to let her speak first.

"She insisted on going to the mainland alone, said she'd have a better chance, but it didn't matter. They locked her up, and she died behind bars while I was stuck on the *Sea Bane*. I never got to say goodbye," Odi continues.

Tears well in the corner of her eyes, and I can't stop myself. I reach for her, wrapping my arms around her waist and pulling her tight. "*By the stars*, Odi," I whisper into her hair.

She rests her cheek on my chest. "After that, father swore land would never touch us again. He tried to make me hate it too. Taught me to take what I wanted, to cut first and never ask. Said it was the only way to survive."

I drag my fingers up her spine, offering some sort of comfort, if that's even possible. "And you believed him?"

"When you're a child, all you can do is believe," her voice is barely a whisper.

The words punch a hollow out in me. There's the child I used to be too—beleiving. Straining for a voice that meant home, the woman who vanished back into the tide and left me clinging to the wreckage of her absence. Even now, I can taste salt in that memory, the brine she always carried on her skin. I still believe that she's out there somewhere. My chest tightens, for the small, desperate boy who once cast his wishes into the waves, hoping the sea would answer.

Odi traces the shimmering patterns on my chest with her fingers. "I love my father for who he was when I was a little girl. But he hasn't been that man for a very long time. And I'm never going back."

I know what it's like to run from a parent. Yet Ivor is much worse than my own father. Mine might scold me or strip away *The Gilded Hart* when I return, but he'd never hold a knife to my throat. The thought leaves a cold taste in my mouth. It morphs to others.

Protect her. Don't let him touch her. Don't let her think she's alone in that fear. The fear that if her father finds her, all her hope of freedom will be lost. That she would spend the rest of her days on his ship believing that she'd never be anything more than his bloody shadow. I won't let that happen.

Odi moves her head to look up at me. The fire in her eyes is shadowed by unrelenting, feelingless pain.

I reach out to brush her cheek. "As long as you're here with me, I won't let him take you. And when we meet again, well, he'll find I bite harder than he expects."

With a soft groan, she straightens. Head shaking and jaw tight. "That's what I'm afraid of. You getting hurt because of me. You, or anyone else here."

A soft smile tugs the corner of my mouth. I can't help the way my body responds to her gentle confession. I pull myself up into a sitting position, leaning my back against the headboard. Then I shift her so she's straddled across my lap, my hands resting gently on her thighs. "That's not your fear to carry, little doe."

Her shoulders lift and fall with ease. "It's not something I can put down easily."

I brush my thumb over her skin. "I'll take the weight."

For a brief moment she just stares at me, like she can't trust my truth. Like it's too hard to swallow when all she's known is carrying every burden alone. I pull her closer, wanting her to feel my steady embrace. "I have an apology to make," I murmur.

Her brow raises, a faint smirk dancing on her lips. "Finally admitting that I can wield a blade better than you?"

I huff a soft laugh. "No. That's never been a question."

"What then?" She grins, leaning down to brush my lips with hers.

The act is so pure that my body melts under her touch. She pulls back, but I reach up to catch the back of her head, holding her in place so I can feel her warm breath on my face. "I wanted to say sorry for assuming you would be like *him*—your father. But you're not him, Odi. You fight . . . but not the way he does. There's a difference."

She shakes her head as she looks at the palms of her hands. A single tear spills from the outer corner of her eye, tracing down her cheek to die upon my chest. "There's enough blood on my hands to drown in . . . and his still runs in my veins—"

Her voice trembles. Her hands tremble. My body responds. Hatred for her father and what she's had to do to survive rears its ugly head, but she needs grounding. She needs to feel safe.

I clasp her hands in mine, bringing them to my lips. "I love your hands. How they tend the wounded. How they offer food to the hungry. I especially love them when they trace the patterns on my skin. These hands are brave, and strong, but they are also soft and gentle."

A fresh wave of tears pour down her cheek. I reach up to brush the moist trail away. "Ivor's blood might be part of you, but so is your mother's. Don't forget that."

Odi's brow pinches, like she's trying to fight the truth of my words as another tear falls to its death. "I've spent my whole life trying not to end up like him. What if I've already failed?"

I move my hand to cup her face, and she leans into the touch. "You wouldn't be here with me if you had," I whisper.

Her gaze locks onto me, then she crumbles. Crushing her lips to mine in a fiery kiss. One that I feel in the very depths of my soul. I pull her closer as my tongue dances with hers. Gentle hands find their way around my neck, sending heat spearing through my body. At this moment I realise I'm not just lost in everything that is her . . . I'm fucking drowning.

She slowly pulls back, resting her forehead on mine. We sit in silence together, the early morning sun stretching further into the room. Boots on the deck announce that the crew is up, tending to the ship's needs. I'd told Elio and Tavi not to let anyone bother us until I was ready.

Looking at Odi now, her naked body soft from orgasms and sleep, I'm definitely not ready to go back to reality. And perhaps I never will be.

I trace lazy patterns over her thigh, and she moans softly, tipping her head back as the sun kisses her bare neck. Heat pools low in my stomach when I imagine raking my teeth across her pulse.

She threads a hand between us, looking for my cock.

I gasp when she finds it. "Keep doing that and I'll have you whimpering in seconds." I say, my voice hinting playfully.

Odi's eyes light up. She leans forwards, a hairsbreadth from my lips, and pumps her hand again. "Maybe that's what I want."

I moan against her mouth. "Come here—"

A solid knock sounds at the door.

"Who is it?" I demand.

"Cap," Elio says, sounding on edge. "There's a message from Killian. Ivor is on the move."

I turn Killian's message over in my hands, studying the words once again.

The Sea Bane is headed in the direction of the mainland.

It had been four days. The wind had stayed in our favor, and we'd nearly made it to the last island, but something about Killian's words had kept the scrap of kelp parchment in my pocket. That Ivor is moving at all makes my stomach curdle, and I'd already responded, telling Killian he won't be keeping tabs on the Vipers much longer. We're headed for this last island. And then we'll prepare ourselves to take on Ivor.

But the more I study the words, the more vague foreboding worms its way into my thoughts. Killian is rarely ever so straightforward. I tuck the message back into my trouser pocket, but the unease doesn't leave with it.

The shadow of a bird glides over the deck. I glance up to see its silhouette pass across the warm, afternoon sun. It's big enough that I furrow my brow. Is it a roc, or the same one that has been pestering the ship? It screeches, sending a shudder down my spine. Definitely the same one. Salt spray settles over the ship as the bow plows through the Adamaris Sea. From the stern castle deck, I can see all around us. Up ahead an island looms. Large, and jagged, like a sea creature floating on the waves. Odi leans on the ship's railing just in front of me, her eyes focused on the comings and goings of the crew below, hair tangling by the wind. There's something in the way her foot bounces up and down on the spot that has me itching to reach for her. She's nervous.

I know she's been to this island before. Spent hours digging, but her father and his crew never had the keys that we have in our possession, so this is new to her and I.

Boots clatter on the stairs. Otto bounds up, grinning wide. "Cap," he says, giving me a quick nod before turning straight to her.

The ship's wheel hums under my hands, steady as the tide. I know I shouldn't eavesdrop, but something warm in my chest shifts when I see Otto sidle up to Odi's side. For once he's not all restless energy. It's the first time they've had a chance to talk quietly since Nisse became known.

Odi glances at him, and when he softly bumps her arm with his shoulder, her body relaxes. "I should've told you," Odi says quietly, so low I almost miss it over the creak of the rigging. "About my father. About who I am."

Bear shakes his head fast, dark blond shaggy hair whipping about him. "There's nothing to forgive, Odi," his voice carries easy, unburdened. "You're not him. You'll never be him."

My admiration for the young man only grows deeper as I witness the patching of open wounds between two people. Odi's shoulders ease, but I've yet to see her smile.

"How can you be so sure?" she says quietly.

Otto reaches out and squeezes her hand. "Because you're too good at looking out for others to be anything like that bastard."

With a flurry of limbs, Odi throws her arms around Otto's neck and pulls him into her embrace, her shoulders shaking. Otto's face turns beet red, but he wraps his arms around her just as fiercely.

I grip the wheel tighter, fighting back the tears. I didn't think I could be prouder of the passionate cook in front of me, and then he goes and speaks truth, folding her in his arms while she chokes back the pain she's carried her whole life.

"Land ahoy!" Tavi shouts from the crows nest.

The crew scramble to the side of the deck to peer over. We're close enough to the island to sink the anchor and gather the row boats.

Bear scurries off back down to the galley, but not before he winks at me. I shake my head with a grin as Odi comes to stand beside me. I wrap an arm around her waist and pull her closer. "Are you ready to get this treasure?"

She looks up at me, fear and excitement swirling in her eyes. "I am, if you are?"

I lean down, brushing her cheek with a faint kiss. "Let's go together."

An hour later, sand crunches under my boots as we make landfall. The island is small, but wild. Roots from vivacious green trees claw up from the ground, wrapping around jagged stones. Gulls cry overhead, like a warning. The air here tastes different, heavier, like it knows the treasure it hides.

I split the team up into two groups. The first group stays on the shore with the boats, keeping watch and the second sticks with Elio, Tavi, and I. Odi leads the way.

After walking for a while, she turns to me, her brow pinched, hands on hips, viewing the surroundings. "I swear it was around here."

"Cap!" Elio's voice cuts across the tension in the air. "There's a cavern here—runs under. Looks like it leads somewhere."

Odi and I glance at each other before going to meet him at a rocky rise where the ocean carves at the island. The drop isn't far, but it's steep, and at the bottom, water flows under the rock

I glance at Odi who is already staring at me, her dark hair whipped by the salt wind. "The tide must have flooded it. When I was here last, I was able to wade in."

Aqua water laps at the decline, stones turning slick with the sea. We'll have to swim under. It's an inconvenience, but not for me. I'll happily take any opportunity to take Odi into my arms.

Elio and Tavi hover beside the edge. I throw them a glance. "Watch the crew."

They nod in unison, and then I leap the short way down, landing in water up to my chest. I raise my hands up for Odi, letting her know I'll catch her. She sets her legs over the edge before pushing off and gracing me with a splash. With a low chuckle, I scoop her up into my chest. Her arms loop around my neck and I fight the urge to bury my face in her hair. "On three?" I murmur, walking us deeper.

She nods, the grip around my neck tightening. "One, two . . ."

I press a gentle, but quick kiss on her lips. Something to distract her. "Three."

We plunge. The noises outside muffle into silence as the cold water takes us whole. I shift, propelling into action with the flick of my tail. Its crystal-clear blue water. Nothing lurks at the bottom in the shadows, and for once I'm glad I don't need to be looking over my shoulder.

Odi's sea stone hardly has time to bubble up as light blooms ahead, shimmering pale as we break into a hidden cavern. With another powerful flick of my tail, I haul us up towards the surface. Together we break it, and Odi draws in a deep breath, rivets of water spilling down her face.

"Well done, little doe," I say, grinning down at her like a smitten schoolboy.

She rolls her eyes, but her cheeks are flushed pink.

A rock ledge protrudes out of the wall in front of us. We swim for it, and I shift back to help Odi up and out of the water. The cavern ceiling is covered in tiny specks of blue and green, glowing like a sacred tomb. A place where the sea meets the sky.

Odi sucks her breath in. "There it is."

I spin towards the wall up ahead, to a door, massive and unyielding. And in the heart of it, plain as day is a familiar shaped keyhole.

My eyes find her, wide with wonder. "The treasure."

She is me

38
ODELIA

The rock is wet and solid beneath my feet. Water drips from my braid and clothes, darkening it in specks as we approach. It's quiet. Like we've stepped into another world. The cavern is exactly as I remember—smooth stone peppered with pillars that reach towards the ceiling. Nerves swirl in my gut, equal parts excitement and trepidation.

This is it. After everything, we've made it.

The door ahead is framed with stone, sealed tight, with an impression in the centre. Rune slips the key from his pocket. The pieces had fit together easily once we had them all, each slipping onto the next. It's round, like a compass, with a pattern of waves on one side and the imprint of a nautilus shell on the back.

I let him take the lead as we approach. If there are connections to his history, his family, he deserves to find them. He deserves everything. Island after island, we fought for this. Saved each other's lives for this. Went in by ourselves and only came back out again because of the trust that was forged in each trial.

I can hardly get enough air in as my heart picks up speed. I watch him, looking for the same tumultuous nerves. Only, he stops. I step to his side and find his brow pinched hard.

"What—" I follow his gaze, and realise the problem at the same moment he speaks.

"We're missing something," he says.

My stomach bottoms out. He's right. The shape of the key is perfect, except the one cut out of the door has an extra line that protrudes from the centre. We're missing a piece.

No.

"But that doesn't make sense," I say, a weight settling over my heart and shoulders even as I deny it. "We went to every island."

Rune presses the key in the recess, to no avail. "You're sure we addressed all the riddles?"

"I'm sure."

He's a calm, windless sea while I am rising panic. "You're absolutely certain?"

"Yes!" I try to keep the bite out of my voice, but I know the riddles like I know the stars in the sky. "Can I look at it?"

I hold my hand out for the key, though I know it's useless. Rune hands it over without question. The metal is warm. The wave pattern on the bottom matches the door. It's the right size. There's no way we stumbled on the wrong island with a perfectly hidden, locked door. We've done everything we were meant to.

I run my thumb over the nautilus shell recess on the other side of the key. I hadn't missed a riddle. There's no way. But we're definitely missing part of the picture.

"Maybe it's another puzzle," I say, but there's nothing else in here, no scales to balance or accidentally slip through. If there are any secrets here, the cavern isn't giving them up.

Rune sighs. "Let's head up for now. Maybe the secret is somewhere else on the island. We can set up camp while we figure out what to do next. Check the map again."

I almost object, as if staying here might change the fact that there's no clear way forwards. We're so close, but failure already tries to envelope me in its bitter weight, smothering even my frustration. This can't have been all for nothing. Rune deserves to make it to the other side of that door.

I hand the key back to him and move to the water, my heart sinking with every step, my mind running though every flooded cavern and abandoned temple. I shouldn't have let this take me by surprise. Nothing has been as straightforward as it seemed. Rune scoops me up from behind, and I gasp, but settle my head against his chest as he cradles me close.

"We'll figure it out," he murmurs into my hair. For just a moment, I let his strength ground me. Warmth and the scent of salt cling to his skin, reminding me of the nights I've spent with him.

Then he slips us back in the water, and the sea stone hardly has time to activate before we're on the other side again.

The chitter of insects follows us as we find the others and let them know we plan to stay a while. A few take the rowboats back to *The Gilded Hart* for equipment or supplies.

Tavi finds us hovering at the rise of the tree line, watching bodies weave back and forth on the shore setting up tents. Otto disembarks from one of the rowboats and drops an overstuffed bag, then begins to drag a massive pot towards a slowly growing stack of wood.

"Any update?" Tavi asks, her eyes caught on Soraya, who also limps through the chaos.

"We're working on it," Rune says.

"There's a piece missing," I clarify.

Rune shrugs. "We could have put it together wrong."

I shake my head. We missed something. I can feel it. "I'll need to take another look at the map. I know we hit every riddle, but maybe there's something hidden that we didn't know to look for before." My thoughts stray to the nautilus marking on the back. It's a common enough design, but it feels like a clue. "If we end up leaving without the treasure, I'd rather leave no stone unturned."

A familiar foreboding ghosts over my body a breath before a rumbling voice speaks behind us in the trees, the sound like an unwelcome memory in the night. "*Without* the treasure?"

Alarm spears through my every limb, sending my body moving. I spin, dagger in hand, dread already having wrapped my chest in a tight fist. Rune is slower to react, but only by a moment. He hasn't had years of muscle memory trained into avoiding that voice taking him by surprise.

The towering figure materializes as if from nowhere, only barely distinguishing itself from the trees. "You mean we wasted all this time, for nothing?" He moves, his boots crashing through the underbrush. Panic snakes up my spine, every pump of my heart fueling the icy chains that I can already feel tightening on my wrists, as if he's already won. He steps into a spear of light and stops.

Ivor.

The trees continue to move. The Vipers smirk as they flank him, their weapons already drawn.

It should be impossible; if they were tailing us we would have known. "How did you find us?" Somehow, my voice doesn't shake. Beside me, Tavi's knuckles are white on the grips of her swords. The very air is drawn tight around us, like the next fallen leaf might send blows flying.

Ivor crosses his arms. His massive sword is still secured to his back, his posture relaxed enough to keep mine tense. "You think I wouldn't know you'd make your way back here? You're my daughter. I know you better than you know you. And a lot better than this guppy if he's really allowing himself to be alone with you near a cache of treasure." Some of the Vipers laugh and cat call in the trees. "Oh," he goes on, as if in afterthought, "there's also this."

One of the larger shadows behind him drags a gagged man forwards. His short, curly black hair is clumped with dirt and blood, but he straightens up on his knees, keeping his shoulders straight and proud.

"Killian," Rune says, his voice pained.

"Killian!" Ivor guffaws, the giant expanse of his chest rumbling with laughter. "That's really your name, son? And yet you hardly put up a fight. That's a name you have to earn, not one worn by shitty spies." Ivor lifts a boot and plants it into Killian's back, throwing the bound man face first into the dirt. "Of course, even without him"—Ivor shifts to press his weight into Killian's back—"I would have known, Nisse." He gestures to the trees, and a pair of selbies swoop down, their bodies blurring and growing until they stand as a man and a woman with steel-grey hair and eyes.

Then there's a jarring, familiar screech, and a larger bird swoops over our heads, morphing into a man on Killian's other side.

I shuffle through memories, trying to remember if I'd seen the feathered stowaway with my own eyes, but all I remember is the hair-raising screech. It takes too long for my mind to catch up. "Garreth." I look between him and the other shifters, and all at once I'm shocked by my own arrogance. I thought I could get away. I thought I knew every move Ivor could have made. But the whole time. . . "You made them stalk the ship. Too chicken to do it yourself?"

The hawk shifter spits. "Do you think I'm that stupid?"

I ignore him. "You used them to follow us." The accusation is low, but I know Ivor hears me.

He grins, finally taking his boot off Killian's back. "I didn't have to follow you. I know you'd find a way to the treasure, clever girl. All I did was wait."

His approval sits sour in my gut. I can feel Rune look to me but I don't dare look back, afraid of what I might see on his face. This is my fault. I led them all here. I thought I could get away. But no one gets away. And now I'm dragging them all down with me. I never wanted to be like Ivor, but I risked us all for a bit of coin. Rolled the dice with lives on the line and still lost in the end.

My hands shake, but my shoulders are square as I unhook the bola from my side and step in front of Rune. I don't need to ask what's next. I don't offer a bargain or beg. The rest of the Vipers have their eyes set on the shore behind us, watching the crew of *The Gilded Hart* with violent interest.

Ivor slowly pulls his sword from his back, making a show of widening his stance before beckoning me over. I throw one apologetic look over my shoulder at Rune, hoping he can see the grief in my eyes. He nods, looking so unphased it almost shocks me into a smile. A sharp whistle pierces the air and I look to Tavi in surprise. Her attention hasn't moved from the Vipers in the trees, but I can hear shouting start up behind us. It's Elio, calling the others to arm themselves and find us.

A flaming bolt rewards my hesitation. It lands between my legs and I leap forwards, rolling before it explodes and heat licks up my back.

Before I'm on my feet, trees erupt in whizzing arrows and screaming steel.

Ivor meets me as I rise, tossing a few playful swings with his sword. I duck and roll, dancing away from the gleam of the blade. His reach is impossibly long, and it takes every desperate burst of speed to keep distance between us.

"You're doing well," he says, as if they were training. "Glad to see you haven't gone soft."

The edge of his sword cleaves through the space where I just was. "Odd to compliment someone while trying to kill them."

"A fair share of men have died for underestimating us both." He swings again, and the trunk of a tree catches it, its dry bark bursting into smaller chunks of kindling. "I won't make that mistake, Nisse," he says as he rips it free.

I take the half-moment of hesitation and whip my bola around his wrist, but instead of faltering when I pull, he just lifts his arm into the air, dragging me before I have the sense to let go. Angry tears blur my vision as I jump away from another attack. I've spent my entire life fighting in one way or another. I operated mostly in shadow, but the man before me ensured I could out fight every disposable body that made it onto our ship.

But I could never beat him.

Something about his size, or the disappointment so often in his voice, caused my fear to override the frozen calm that shepherded me through these moments. He always seemed to know my next move before I did. Even now, I'm left dodging and ducking behind trees, feeling the underbrush claw at my pants, hearing wood rend and scatter. If I can just get him tired enough, I might stand a chance. But I'm too slow, trapped on the other side of his impossibly long reach. He isn't even trying.

When I pop up to face him after my next roll, my eyes catch beyond him to one side—to Rune, Elio, and a freed Killian exchanging ringing blows with three of the Vipers' best. There's a splash of red over Rune's bare chest, but I can't tell if he's wounded. Killian's wrists are mottled with bruises, but he moves with lethal precision. They're all half shifted, ears finned, talons sharp, arms glittering with scales from wrist to elbow.

The image gives me an idea, but it disappears as my father steps in the way, blotting everything else out of my vision. Taking it like he's taken everything else.

The rage starts, then, and I know it's his. I am his legacy. His right hand. My father's daughter, through and through. There isn't a life here I wouldn't take to make sure we live through the mess I've made. I thought I wanted to be alone. At ease. To find the kind of peace I thought was only found in isolation.

What I really wanted was rest. A break from the fear. Peace at last. And maybe, deep down, a father who would protect me from monsters, instead of turning me into one. Instead of tossing me into the deep with the call to sink or swim.

"How could you do it?" I ask, breath heaving as I skip back, trying to angle us back towards where he'd left my bola on the ground. "How could you gut your own daughter and call her a weapon?"

He spins as I circle him, then drops his broadsword to block as I swipe the dagger at his stomach. "I gave you a purpose."

"I was a child." I roll again, adding more to the leaves already clinging to my hair.

He points the tip of his sword at me like a finger. "You were too soft for this world. You needed to learn."

"I needed my father!" He hesitates, so briefly I wonder if I imagined it. "Instead I got a butcher." I back away, gripping the hilt of my blade so hard it hurts as he lets the space between us grow. "You stunted me. Taught me to cage my shift. Hacked away at me and then forced me to hate the only part of mother you couldn't take away."

Something itches under my skin as I say the words, spurred by my anger as the chaos goes on around us. There are groups fighting on all sides, cries of fear and pain. Those from the beach had rallied and thrown themselves into the fight.

Then a beast screams, and the world slows as a kelpie crashes through the brush and into a group of Vipers in a storm of hooves and flesh-ripping teeth.

"Eithne!"

I'm not sure who shouted, but I try my best to call a warning as it angles towards Rune and Killian. They just watch with bright eyes until the beast flies past them and Killian launches onto its back, his sword in one taloned hand. Together, they run Garreth down, Killain wounding the man as he shifts too slow, and the kelpie rearing to trample the bird under its hooves.

"Odi!" Rune catches my eye. A thin streak of crimson runs down his neck and over the muscles of his chest. I can see him warring with the urge to go after Ivor, but I shake my head. I can't let my father near him, and the others need him more. Leaves rustle and fall between us in a slow drift, and I glance up at the familiar movement in the trees, suddenly feeling the need to hide a proud grin.

"Odi . . .?" Ivor twitches as he looks between me and Rune. He says my name like he can't place it. Like he's pushed my mother so far out of his mind the nickname was lost to him.

My attention flies to the odd expression on his face. Something so close to pain. Every time he looks at me—really looks at me—it's the same. I think it's why he made me wear the cowl, to hide me. Not to conceal Nisse's face, but to bury the reminder that she's gone.

He'd rather forget. If it were his choice, I'd forget her too. But it's not, and I refuse. She's all that stops me from being him. The memory of her love and light and joy convinced me that life wasn't all survival and fear. Because of her, I knew something *else* existed—if she left the land for the sea, then I could return, and carry her memory back to where she belonged.

I'm his daughter. But I'm hers too.

Ivor watches me, his eyes widening as something stirs under my skin again. The sounds of the battle grow louder, the smell of blood and forest and burst shot grows stronger. Then his face pales, like he's seen a ghost.

"*Wildflower*," he breathes, stepping forward as the tip of his sword rests on the ground by his feet.

I feel the way confusion twists my face as he blinks out of whatever memory has finally broken through—and in the same moment realize the change in my body.

Spotted fur runs from my wrists and all the way over my shoulders and chest. My shirt is gone. A weight settles on my head as my antlers finish forming. My ears, now long and turned down, flick in reaction to the amplified sounds. The forest sharpens. Scent nearly overwhelms me and I can feel the way my face has pulled into a slight deer-nosed snout.

I blink at the realisation—the half shift.

Ivor pulls his gaze away, like he can't bare to look at the animal he refused to know.

Me. She is me.

"Put that beast away, Nisse," he growls, as the tip of his giant broadsword sword leaves the ground.

"My name," I say, raising my blade even with his, "is Odelia."

He lunges, splitting the air with a jab, but something fast impacts the back of his head. The shot makes him flinch, then his eyes widen as the venom pod bursts down his neck and back. Otto grins from a branch high above, as if he hasn't just attacked the person he should fear most in the world. I do grin this time, meeting his eyes.

My father's rage ignites, then, his eyes wild as he charges, swinging recklessly. Broken branches crack apart under his boots, but I hold my ground, my heart in my throat. As he lifts for his next blow, I sweep under his arm, fast as a dartfish now, and toss my blade hand back to land a glancing blow to his ribs, the way Rune said he'd learned from his brother. The moment I reach the other side of him, I snatch up my bola and roll forwards, expecting a blade to follow me at any moment. Instead, I see Tavi ahead, and a man aiming a bolt at her back.

"Tavi!" I shout, tossing the bola with half a thought. It wraps the man's crossbow and pulls it off aim. The shot goes wide, embedding in the leg of a Viper nearby. Tavi turns, hands blurring as she aims a throwing knife first at him—then at me. My stomach drops as the steel flies. Surprise keeps me still for a blink too long, but it slices by the flap of my ear, landing somewhere behind me with a wet thunk.

I turn as the body hits the ground—a Viper with the blade in his eye to the hilt—but I keep turning, because Ivor's crashing step has me diving for the downed man's sword.

We trade blows, my new speed evening out his strength. Each strike sends shocks of pain up my arms, rattling the joints of my shoulders. My instincts flare, helping me put anything I can between us, rocks, trees, brush. Some he tears down, others he kicks away, his face that familiar shade of red. It's life or death now. He's lost to rage, to grief. And I've gone too far, pushed him too much. It'll be a loss for him, but not the kind it should be.

I twist, almost dancing away from the hits I can't block as my arms lose strength. I wait for the fear, but it doesn't come. The realisation emboldens me, and I risk stepping in rather than leaping away, and feel the flesh of his shoulder open under my blade.

He roars, backhanding me with his sword hand. I'm only on the ground for a moment before I pop up, ready to leap under his next swing to get behind him—but he won't let me get away with it twice. He spins, too nimble for a man his size, then I feel the air shift as the blade sweeps above me, and fire blooms in the back of my ribs. I hit the ground hard and roll onto my back, feeling briars snag on my fur.

"PUT HER AWAY," he roars, stabbing the ground with every word. I'm barely able to avoid them, each strike hitting closer than the last as I crab walk away. Air saws in and out of my lungs. My body is soaked in sweat and warm blood. My back hits a tree, and he lifts his sword high, his eyes frenzied with frustration. Red and oozing green drips down his shoulders and to the front of his neck from where the acidic venom has gnawed through his skin. Burned patches mar his jacket, and Otto shoots another pod that hits his back and bursts into short-lived flames.

Ivor roars and swipes his sword down. Even with my shift I'll be too slow, but I smile at him. I've won in the only way that matters.

The ringing sound of steel on steel obliterates the world around us for a moment, and when I look up, Rune and Elio stand over me, their blades caught on Ivor's own. Together, they overpower him, shoving him back until I can gain my feet. They work in beautiful tandem, one stepping in when the other steps back, taking turns catching the heavy strikes of his blade. For the first time, hope blooms through my chest. They're gaining ground. Maybe we can win this. Together.

"Otto!" Tavi screams, her voice breaking. She's caught against two others, trying to fight her way towards the three Vipers that swarm the tree Otto is in. One shifts, a selbie, and flies up to rake at him with savage talons.

"Go!" Rune shouts to me as Elio catches a strike, but I don't need the order.

Otto's cries already have me moving.

Your mercy will be the death of you

39
RUNE

She did it. Odi half-shifted into her deer form, and she's magnificent.

She's bare from the waist up, but her breasts and chest are covered in golden fur with white spots. My breath had caught at the fire in her eyes, the way she moved with such elegant speed and precision.

With her shiny black nose, velvet skinned ears. I'm in awe. There is no version of this woman that I'm not obsessed with, and when we are done here I plan on showing her just how attentive I can be.

I just have one thing to finish first. I narrow my focus, until there's nothing and no one but the male in front of me. Grey eyes, haunting and empty. A pale jagged scar running from his right eye to the middle of his cheek. His grin wicked, like he made a deal with death and plans to fulfill it.

The chaos around me slows. I've been waiting to take down Ivor for three years. Putting all my pent up anger, and fury into finding him and dealing the deadly blow that he deserves. For years he's evaded the navy, taken lives without thought, poisoned my ocean with his greed and bloodlust. He mutilated Otto, stole peace from my crew—yet as I stand in front of him, blade in hand, I see the father of the woman I have fallen for. Viper or no, he's all the family she has left.

Can I end him?

My chest heaves, dragging in air as my blade slices through the space between us. The sound of sword against sword rings out, the chaos around me becoming a whirlwind of madness once again. Through it all, my gaze finds Odi across the sand. She's tearing through men like waves in a storm crashing over rock, one after another, unstoppable as she races to protect Otto. To balance the scales of her father's existence.

I set my jaw, chin tipped up slightly. She is nothing like him, and she never will be. There is not a single particle of doubt left in my body. Odelia Nisse Ivor isn't just a Viper, she's a fierce, loyal, kind, beautiful woman.

She's a weapon. And she's mine.

Elio is at my side, moving like he can read my thoughts. I duck, he strikes high. I drive forwards, he covers my back. To one man, Ivor might seem unassailable, but none of us are alone, and together we wear Ivor down. The man shuffles on his feet, swinging his blade through the air. Fury is carved into every line of his face. Grey eyes bloodshot, wild, the veins crawling red like a spider's web as he takes in the carnage of his crew around him.

For a moment, the bastard looks less like the beast legends claim him to be, and more like a man.

He bellows, a sound that rattles the air, and swings his ridiculously huge broadsword with the kind of strength that could split me in two. The blow jars through my arms as I block, teeth chattering, the impact shoving me backwards a step.

Elio darts in, fast as a striking barracuda, blade catching Ivor across the ribs just barely.

Ivor snarls, jumping backwards just out of reach, not even fazed by the thin trails of red seeping through his shirt. "Couldn't leave well enough alone, could you, Captain? I thought I taught you your lesson. This time I'll make sure I finish the job."

I spit blood into the dirt from a blow to the lip I'd received earlier, raising my sword again. "I'm flattered you remember me."

Elio and I circle the captain, eyes tracking every twitch, every shudder, every movement that could end us. A feral grin steals across the Viper's lips, assessing us like a predator does just before it consumes its prey.

"The prince and the pirate. She'll slaughter you in your sleep you know," he growls.

His statement is meant to unnerve me, make me feel unsafe around his daughter. To drive a wedge between us, but it doesn't.

The corner of my mouth picks up, and I offer Ivor a confident grin. "Then I will die a happy and *satisfied* man."

Ivor's eyes grow wide, his mouth turning into a sour snarl. Elio flashes me a grin, sharp and quick, and together we move again, blades hungry for the bastard's throat. Ivor swings first. His broadsword, a massive slab of steel that hisses through the air.

I twist out of the way just as it slices down, missing me by a sliver. I bring my bone blade back up just in time, swinging towards his chest but he's too fast for a man of his size, twisting just out of reach.

Elio grunts, clutching at his upper arm. Crimson stains the fabric of his shirt. I hiss under my breath, pushing forwards with my teeth bared. Ivor charges, and my blade scrapes against his as we clash. All around me is a sea of red. A bloody mess of carnage as crew members hit the sand left and right.

Killian is free, steel blade in hand as he slashes through bodies. Eithne is a blur beneath him, skin shimmering like wet obsidian, hooves and kicks driving men back in a scatter of grunts and choking curses—one after another sent reeling like driftwood. Odi, who has red stains across her side, is still on her feet, back to back with Tavi and her twin blades as they take down more crew who burst from the trees.

I feel the heat of rage crawl under my skin, a hot coal in my chest at the sight of her injury. This won't be the end of us. Ivor will not win today. We've paid too much, bled too much, to let him take anymore than he already has.

My boots shuffle through the sand as I race for Ivor again. Then dirt flies. A fistful right into my face. It burns my eyes, blinds me, and before I can clear them, he barrels into me. The air cracks out of my lungs as I hit the ground, his weight crushing me. His fist slams into my jaw once, twice—pain sparks white behind my eyes.

Ivor brings his fist down for another hit, but I block it, trying to get a leg between us so I can kick him off.

"Elio!" I grunt, twisting, trying to free myself.

Steel whistles and Elio is there, blade carving across Ivor's back. The bastard roars, rearing up just long enough for me to drive my knee into his gut and shove him off.

We scramble, Elio's breathing ragged, my lip is split in a second spot and bleeding down my chin. Ivor rises like a storm, fury red in his eyes, sword already swinging again. He's all brute force, but *gods*, the ocean scum is fast. Too fast.

A sharp snap whistles through the air. Otto's sling. Ivor jerks back as a venom pod explodes against his shoulder. Acid eats through the fabric of his coat, hissing against his skin. He bellows, clawing at the wound as the venom chews into flesh.

It's all the distraction I need as I run and leap, bringing the hilt of my blade down on the opposite shoulder with a solid thud. Ivor rages, spinning away from me, and into Elio who slams into his side, striking with his fists again and again, every blow buying me a heartbeat.

Blood coats my tongue, dripping down the back of my throat as I choke on my spit. This needs to end. I've lost too many already. I won't allow the loss of those closest to me, but Ivor refuses to go down. He fights on, eyes wild, bloodshot, filled with fury. "You're holding back."

I squint, feet planted firmly on the sand. "I'm not going to kill you in front of her."

Ivor glowers, his yellow teeth gritting before he spits blood onto the ground. "Your mercy will be the death of you."

It's true. It could be. But not by his hand.

"And the saviour for you," I mutter, pointing my blade towards him.

Ivor begins to pace back and forth in short steps, eyes never leaving me. "Is she worth it? Chasing treasure, but losing your crew? Garreth told me everything. She's still a thief and a killer—a bloodstain given shape. She won't change . . . a tide never stops turning."

I huff a laugh. "Sad thing is, you fathered her and still don't know her."

Ivor takes a step towards me, teeth barred and dripping blood. "She is born of my blood, boy," he hisses.

The words fall flat—full of menace but empty. His grin is a false victory that tastes like ground up bones. I lift the blade until the steel glints in his face. "She's of your blood," I say slowly, thinking again of the necklace I'd lost to the waves, the one that still clung tight to Odi for years, "and of her mother's. And her mother's goodness drowns any of your cruelty. Odi will *never* be you."

The world narrows as Ivor loses all control. He's a mountain of muscle and fury, his massive blade cutting arcs through the air. Every swing drives me back, every clash rattles my arm to the bone.

Elio tries to approach from the right, but Ivor dodges him, spinning out of the way and charges for me again. One of our men cries out, falling hard to the sand. My head whips around—just for a breath. It's all Ivor needs. His sword comes screaming down, and Elio slams into me, shoving me clear. The blade bites the ground where I'd been standing. Pain blooms across my ribs as I scramble up. His strike caught me just enough to leave a shallow line burning across my side.

Blood trails down my skin like wet ribbons, hot and sticky, but I'm alive.

Elio isn't so lucky. Ivor kicks out, brutal and fast, catching him square in the knee. I hear the impact before Elio cries out, dropping to the sand. The sun beats down on us, sweat beads on my brow as I dash to place myself between the sea scum and my first mate. "You're a dirty fighter."

"And you're weak," Ivor snarls.

I spit blood, blade ready as Elio manages to get on his feet again, favouring one side. Together we face Ivor, dancing with death. All three blades clash, a calamity of steel and bone. There is no room for finesse, no elegant footwork, just dirt under our boots and sweat in our eyes.

Ivor barrels forwards, jamming his shoulder into my arm. The sudden impact sends my blade flying from my hand and into the sand. With a roar, I spin and swing my fist around, connecting it to his jaw. His head cracks to the side, but it doesn't put him down, and we're shoved into hand-to-hand combat.

He smashes his forehead into mine with a sickening crunch, stars burst behind my eyes, pain throbbing through my head, all the way into my teeth. Elio cries out, scraping his blade across Ivor's side, catching the captain off guard. I take the opportunity to dart inside his reach despite my blurry vision.

With the jerk of my elbow, I jam it into Ivor's jaw. His teeth snap shut as he roars. For a moment he's all fists and fury, but I block him, twisting and kicking out my foot to trip him as he lurches for me. With quick reflexes I dash for my blade, reaching it, and turning to face Ivor. At the same time Elio rolls behind him, slashing at the back of Ivor's knees with his sword.

Ivor cries out, the cut deep enough to bring him crashing to his knees. His broadsword flies from his hand, and I rush to kick it from his reach. I flick my wrist out, chest heaving as the tip of my blade digs into his bare throat. He snarls as I hold him there. Elio stands behind him, his blade pressed to the back of Ivor's neck.

Grey eyes cower up at me. He's trapped. The moment he tries to get up, I'll take his head from his shoulders with one fell swoop and he knows it.

I push the blade harder, leaning forwards as a bead of blood spills down his throat. "If I'm weak, then what does that make you? Beaten, bleeding, and abandoned by the only soul who might have saved you, if you only took the time to love her."

Until I must be still

40
ODELIA

The remaining Vipers are tied up and left under guard on the beach. Those with life-threatening wounds are bandaged, but we don't take any more risk than necessary. Instead, several of ours stand guard while a few row out to the *Sea Bane* to dump or confiscate whatever weapons the rowboats can fit.

Otto scurries along the tree line of the beach, tending to the crew's wounds. Some pull him close to ruffle his hair, their bloodied faces grinning wide. Others tease about his mudalik pods. There's an undercurrent of proud relief. Like though his high-collared shirts hid the brutal scar on his chest, none could ever truly forget. Their booming voices carry down the beach.

We got him, Bear. It took long enough, but we got him.

I help where I can, tending to those whose wounds aren't as bad. Killian watches me carefully as I bring fresh water and salve for a slice on his thigh.

"You must be the spy Rune sent to watch Ivor," I say, figuring it's probably better to get introductions out of the way.

"And you must be the Viper's prized bloodletter."

His tone isn't unkind, so I offer a curt nod, avoiding his pale-blue eyes. All he can know about me is what he gathered while stalking the *Sea Bane.*

"Can I just say I'm glad you're on our side?" He grins, then, wide and almost mischievous as he takes the salve from me. "You move like the water. I'd hate to be on the other side of that bola."

My cheeks warm, the words taking me by surprise. "You're not bad yourself, that Kelpie had grown men wetting their pants."

The air between us eases and he nods, rinsing and slathering a few smaller wounds on his forearm before gesturing to the water, where the kelpie lays in the shallows. "Eithne is as savage as they get. She fights for her own. You know the kind," he says, meeting my eye.

"I know the kind," I agree, deciding I like Killian.

Eventually Otto catches me and demands I sit and pull my shirt up over my ribs.

"This should have been seen sooner, Odi," he says, his tone fatherly enough I can't help a grin.

"We were busy." I try not to hiss as he washes and salves the slice. If it were truly serious, I wouldn't be walking right now. "There are worse injured than me."

"Yeah, until it gets infected." He laughs. His hands work quick, wrapping four passes of the bandage before tucking it into itself. "You'll need to wash it again tonight once we're on the water."

"Yes, sir. And I'll be ready to help the others tonight too." It's strange how little he talks when he's in this role. It makes me wonder what's going through his mind.

Further down the beach, someone calls for more bandages, and he stands to go, but hesitates. "And Odi?"

"Hmm?" I stand too, casting my eyes around for Rune.

"Thanks for saving me." He scratches the back of his head. " I was a little worried there for a minute."

"I was a little worried there too," I answer honestly. His face and neck are lined with scabbed red where the selbie attacked him, but he grins brilliantly and nods before heading down the beach, his earring waving farewell as he goes.

Rune is walking up the opposite way and stops him to point at who needs supplies before catching my eye. He's unshifted but shirtless, most of his torso and arms wrapped in bandages. My stomach flips, thinking how differently this day could have gone. He catches my eye and my heart nearly leaps from my chest to meet him. All I want to do is fall into his arms, but there's so much to do here. Relief washes through me as he angles my way.

I meet him in the middle, and he pulls my hand into his and tugs me away from the commotion, away from the captive Vipers, and down towards an untouched part of the beach, where warm white sand stretches into the water. He sits, and I lower myself beside him, trying not to stretch the skin of my ribs any more than I have to.

"What now?" I ask. We came for the treasure, and we found the Vipers. But we don't have enough space to keep them all in the brig. My heart aches at the thought of leaving empty handed, after everything. I expect Rune will want to take Ivor to the nearest port, but the thought of being aboard the same ship as him again makes my insides crawl.

"Once we're aboard, I'll send word to some friends of mine, let them know where they can find the infamous Viper Captain."

"You'd give up the bounty?" I say, surprised.

He shrugs. "I could discuss a share, but I'd be surprised if any of the crew want coin for him. It would feel tainted. Plus they've waited as long as I have to get him off our ocean."

A short silence settles between us. He keeps his eyes on the water, watching the waves sweep in and recede.

"I can't believe you won," I say quietly.

"I didn't beat him, little doe. We all did. None of us could have done it alone."

The words cleave through me. I'd been terrified, but he and Elio had moved like dancers. Tavi and I fought to keep weapons clear of Otto while he'd used his slingshot from above, yet none of Ivor's men had gone to *his* aid, well aware of how easily his blade slipped while he was enraged. Loyalty was irrelevant so long as there was victory.

And Ivor had been on the losing side.

"I just . . . didn't think it was possible."

I wait for some kind of emotion to sweep in, but all I feel is steady. Quiet. Like the animal in me rests. Like Nisse might sheath her blade. Both parts of me, making way for something new. Something . . . hopeful.

But guilt creeps in at the edges of my relief. We should have been safe. Those that fought today hadn't expected to. "I'm sorry he was here. I should have—"

He shakes his head and tips his head sideways to peer at me with those bright blue eyes."You couldn't have known, little doe."

"I should have."

"So should I. I knew something was off about Killian's last message. But we won. We're safe. I was always going to take Ivor down, he just pushed up our timeline." Rune loops his arm around my waist, drawing me to lean into his chest. I try to keep my touch light, but he squeezes us together, no matter how it must hurt. "I'm sorry about the map," he says. "The treasure."

I shake my head. "I'm sorry we'll be left wondering if there's anything of your mother behind that door." I'm not sure it's the right thing to say, but he was counting on answers. He gave up so much for us to make it to the end with pieces missing. The key doesn't fit. And I don't know where to go from here.

"I'm done chasing ghosts," he murmurs, tracing his fingers over my back, the touch combining with the warmth of the sun and the sand. The words are soft but not mournful, and my heart seems ready to claw out of my chest to meet his. "She would want me to let go."

I say nothing, just trace a finger over his forearm, following the scarred, twirling pattern left by the thrall squid. Sunlight glitters on the water, tricking the eye with shapes in the sea foam. Down the beach, Tavi returns from disarming the *Sea*

Bane and shouts for the crew to gather. She'll need help if she's to begin ferrying the injured back to *The Gilded Hart.*

He sighs, the sound so affected that my lips turn up a smile before he speaks. "The real tragedy," he says, holding me tighter as if he knows I plan to stand, "is that you won't have the coin to start that new life." I laugh and shove at his chest. He smirks at me, and as always, the look pins me to the spot.

I give him my best doe eyes, softening my expression into pure innocence. "Oh that? Turns out I won't need it after all. I'm sharing a bed with an incredibly handsome, entirely humble ship's captain—"

His lips crash into mine and we go down in a tumble of sand and laughter. The world disappears as he rolls us so his hips rest between my legs. Slow heat builds low as he pins my hands over my head with one of his own, but the twinkle in his eye tells me he's thinking of the last time he held me like this.

"Oh, look," he says, brushing the sand by my head. He pulls up a shimmering piece of smooth sea glass. "For your collection."

My heart swells, but I cock an eyebrow. "Keep that in your pocket for me and I'll make sure to get it later."

He slips it into his pocket with a wink before leaning down to nip at my lips. "I love you, Odelia," he says, blotting out the sun with his massive body. His hair has come free of its tie, hanging loose to drag the sand as he looks down at me.

My heart beats hard, almost painful with the strength of the feeling that's near to bursting free. He loves *me*. All of *me*. He'd coaxed out parts I'd smothered, and run his fingers over my sharpest edges without a fear. Somehow, that fearless, impossibly gentle man saw through every lie I'd told myself to survive, and fought for the woman I am underneath. I would endure a hundred temples to get where we are now. To love him with everything I am. Free. Together. "I love you too," I finally say. "I think . . . I think part of me has loved you since you caught me that day. Since you ran with me."

He grins, then presses a soft kiss to my forehead. "Then let me run with you again, Odi." He murmurs, moving to press a kiss to my eyelid. "Let me chase you, forever." He kisses the other, his hand cupping the back of my neck. "Until I can't run anymore. Until I can't walk anymore." Water wells in my eyes and spills towards the ground as he presses his lips to a new spot with every pause. "Until I must be still. And then, let me lay with you, in a meadow, where wildflowers kiss your cheeks as eagerly as I will, until the end."

No space for hidden truths

41
RUNE

In all my years, I have never known the peace I feel like I do in this very moment. Odi sits beside me, her head resting on my shoulder as I wrap an arm around her waist. The ocean stretches wide and endless before us, sapphire waves rolling in slow rhythm, each crest catching the last of the sun and scattering it in shards of light. Ruby and ripe orange bleed across the horizon, spilling into streaks of liquid gold that ripple over the water's skin like fire poured onto glass.

The sky is a living canvas, billowing clouds shifting with every heartbeat, colours deepening, softening, melting into one another. Salt lingers in the air, and even though I can't take my eyes off the sea, I'm very aware of the woman in my arms. She's warm, and soft in all the right places.

Ivor and what's left of his crew are bound and gagged under the watchful scowl of Tavi. I breathe deep, dragging in silent but salty air. My body aches in places I didn't know existed, but the immediate threat of dying is over now, and the moment I get back to *The Gilded Hart* and my crew are safe, I'll be sleeping for as long as the sea will let me.

I lean down to press a kiss to the top of Odi's head. Her dark brown waves are silky against my mouth. She burrows into my side, her left hand resting on my thigh. Behind us, with its still sealed door, sits the cavern leading to the treasure. My chest twinges at the thought of never opening it, of giving up that last shred of hope. Yet, this time when I put those feelings aside, they don't hurt as much.

Perhaps I'll never have answers. No clues, no solid tie to the elementals I share blood with. And I need to accept that. I do accept that.

I slip my free hand into Odi's, weaving our fingers together, holding on like she's the anchor in the waves. Treasure means nothing—relics, foolish hopes, any of it—if she's not by my side. She outshines it all.

Grains of sand dance across the shore as the wind picks it up, taking it on a journey into the sea. Odi tips her head to look at me. "Where to, Captain?

"To *The Gilded Hart*," I murmur.

She offers me a soft smile, returning her gaze towards the ocean. "Would your crew accept someone like me, if I stayed?"

Her question lingers between us, soft but heavy. She says she's happy to be on the water, but I wonder if it'll be enough. The sea took much from her, yet it's still in her blood. No matter how far she runs, I think a part of her will always belong to the tide, but I know what her soul truly longs for.

"You mean someone who is fiercely brave, and knows how to put a monster down?" I pull her closer. "I think they'll be just fine."

Gentle waves crash against the shore, one after the other, hissing as they fall away, when something on the surface a little further out draws my gaze. My brow pinches as I try to make out the shape. A hallucination from all the adrenaline leaving my body . . . surely.

Yet, I find myself standing before I realise.

"What is it?" Odi says, standing too.

Something stirs in the surf. The swell thickening, rising higher and holding its shape when it should have broken.

I turn to her, squeezing her hand once. "Wait here."

Then I'm walking towards the figure like my feet have given me no choice. My blade clinks at my side with every step, matching the thud in my chest. The sea climbs into a form I know isn't possible, and yet it happens before my eyes. A woman, born of water, her body rolling and shimmering with every surge. Her hair tumbles about her like strands of tiny diamonds, her limbs nothing but flowing current. Her eyes. Deep sapphire blue. Fixed on me.

Mother.

My chest constricts. Bones aching as my ribs wrap around my heart in self protection.

She's here.

For ten years I've searched for her. Clung to the hope that maybe if I sailed the seas long enough I would find her again. And each year that passed that hope grew into something hard, and painful. But as she hovers in front of me, every wall I've built to keep myself safe falls away.

She drifts close enough that the ocean spray cools my face. A hand of foam reaches, fingers sculpted from the tide itself. She cups my cheek with a touch that's both there and not. Salt and brine burn through me, the scent a core memory blooming to life. For a breath I forget the battles, the blood, the weight.

"Mother," I whisper.

Her eyes say a thousand words but her mouth makes no sound. I choke back the sob forming in my throat as her thumb brushes against my skin.

Then as quickly as she formed, she slips back into the ocean, and I'm left staring at the sea with a different kind of ache in my chest. Wondering if I've dreamt the whole thing.

When the tide pulls back, it leaves behind two items on the shore. My breath hitches as I lean down to scoop them up. A bottle with a letter, and a necklace. *Odi's.*

I grip it firmly in my hand, taking a second to breathe, as I focus on bringing my hammering heart to a steady thud. Emotions crash through me as I glance over my shoulder to Odi who waits patiently back up the sand. But one soft smile from me has her on the move. I turn to face her when she reaches my side.

"Are you alright?" she asks, voice laced with genuine care.

I nod softly, holding out the necklace on my palm. "This is yours."

Brown eyes grow wide, as she reaches for it, gently brushing my skin with her finger tips. "You found it," she murmurs.

"I lost it." The confession feels heavy on my tongue, but it needs to be said. Odi deserves to have the whole truth, not pieces of it.

Her brow pinches as she looks up at me. "What do you mean?"

My shoulders drop, head hanging lower. "I lost it in the kraken attack."

"You had it all that time?" Her voice is barely a whisper.

The truth hangs heavy between us. A wall building brick by brick, but I won't let it stand. I can't. Not after all we've been through. I love her, and she loves me. I reach for her, pulling her closer. She doesn't hesitate and my heart rejoices in the small win. "I did. I'm sorry Odelia. When I first found it, I didn't think it could be yours."

She huffs softly. "Why? Because I was a Viper?"

My head dips lower. "Yes. But things changed—once you told me that it belonged to your mother, I wanted to give it to you. But it was too late. The ocean had claimed it once again. And now it's returned it to you. In the end I was the one that got in the way. I'm sorry."

Her eyes soften. "Thank you for being honest with me."

I lean down to press a kiss to her forehead, lingering there for a moment. "It's you and me now, little doe. No space for hidden truths."

She pulls back. "Who was that? In the water before."

My eyes search the horizon. Golden waves glitter as the sun sinks deeper. The question digs into my chest. I swallow hard, salt thick on my tongue, and finally answer. "It was my mother. She left me this."

Odi's breath hitches as I hold up the small blue bottle with a rolled up piece of parchment inside. I work the cork free with trembling fingers. The paper slips through the neck easily, tumbling into my palm.

Carefully, I unfold it. The edges are worn, but it's untouched by water. It has a faint scent of the yellow blossoms that grow on the rocks by the ocean. I can't help but smile. Mother always had a way of making everything so beautiful.

Odi leans in closer as I begin to read aloud. My voice wavers, but the words carry.

My son,

Words cannot express how I have mourned for the family we should have been. Your father always warned me I wandered too far, trusted too much—and when the worst happened, it was all I could do to hold onto the love tucked away in my memories.

By the time I escaped, you were older, and I was more ocean than woman. Existence as an elemental is . . . complicated. Parts of my mind had retreated to endure things I'll not waste space burdening you with now.

For years I've been formless, and the sea has cradled me. She has shared your journey, your persistence, your hope. I know every league you have sailed. Everything you have fought for. The grief you have spilled into the sea. I cannot be with you in the flesh, but I am with you, always.

And I am so proud to call you my son.

This necklace is for Odelia—it belongs to her. I have known few who are worthy, and believe fewer still could capture your heart. She is the land to your ocean.

Mother xx

P.S. Tell your father the blue kelp will bloom early this year.

P.P.S. I'll not have the strength to reach out again for some time. If you find yourself with little footprints by yours on the sand, be sure to let them wander into the water. I'll do my best to say hello.

The letters blur as tears well in my eyes, stinging sharper than salt. I bite down hard, but it doesn't stop the single tear that slips free, tracing a hot line down my cheek.

She's alive.

Not whole, not unharmed, but alive, clinging fast to her memories the way I've gripped onto hope. How long had it taken her to write this letter, wrestling against her weakened shift? Had someone helped her? Where has the ocean kept her, and why can't it bring her home?

I'll not have the strength to reach out again for some time.

More hot tears threaten to spill over, the joy and ache twinning together as I read and reread. There are no more answers in the words, so much that's gone unsaid.

Alive.

And she'd watched me, knew me. I may not have all the answers, but I know this whole time she believed in me as much as I believed in her—and for now it's enough.

Odi's hand comes up, gentle, brushing my tear away with her thumb. Her own eyes glisten with emotion, and it's enough to keep me grounded, reminding me that I'm not alone at this moment.

I close the letter against my chest, breathing in deep, letting the tide crash and fall around us. For the first time in a while, I feel seen . . . by the sea, by my mother, and my heart aches at the same time it feels whole.

My arm finds its way around Odi's waist, tugging her closer into my side as we stand on the shoreline. She fits beside me like she'd been created to. I glance down and watch her fiddle with the necklace in her palm. Then she pauses.

Before I can blink, she's twisting to look up at me. "Rune, the necklace. It's—it's the shape that is missing from the key!"

I feel my eyes widen at her discovery. Shoving the letter and bottle into my trouser pockets, I take it gently from her grasp to view it closer. "We have to go back."

Time blurs by in our race for the cavern, wild grins splitting our faces when we realise exactly what this means. The cavern yawns before us as we head down the slope. The tide is out, so there is no need to carry Odi through the water. I doubt she'd want me too since the injuries she sustained in the fight are still fresh, especially the slash across her ribs.

I hold my breath as she fits the necklace into the key. It glints faintly under the lowlight, sliding into place with a soft click, belonging there all this time. As soon as it settles, an arm extends from its rounded edge, a puzzle box finally completed.

She meets my eyes, brown and gold, steady with fire. Together, we guide the completed key towards the solid stone door. The ancient lock groans as we press it in, a shudder rolling the ground under our feet.

I offer Odi a grin. "On three?"

She smiles so big, I swear a dimple appears. "Always."

"One . . . two . . . three."

We twist.

The door trembles. Stone groaning against stone. I step back, pulling Odi with me. Just in case there is a trap we haven't accounted for. The great slab parts slowly, the weight of centuries grinding away.

Odi gasps softly. Then my heart swells with awe, spilling onto the cavern floor.

SOMEWHERE WE
CAN RUN

42
ODELIA

The island is a speck in the distance.

We'd left my father behind. He and his crew lay bound and prone on the shore, waiting for either luck or the mercy of whoever Rune had invited to collect them. For a blink, Ivor's acid-gnawed skin and the new, soft thing inside me had made me hesitate, but he hadn't been interested in final farewells, instead accusing me of being a dog at heel.

Tavi had introduced *her heel* to his ribs with what seemed like all the stress of the last several weeks, reminding him he'd be leashed at Stonegallows soon enough.

I'd walked away. I've waited to feel something, but there's a void where the fear of him used to be and nothing has rushed to fill the open space. A weight in me has shifted. Balanced. It feels like . . . acceptance.

I trail my fingers over the intricate, splintered railing of *The Gilded Hart*, quietly reassuring her she'd done well. She creaks in response, her bones worn and weary, but not yet quiet. Despite the extra weight, she slices through the waves, gaining speed as we reach open water. Elio shouts orders from the sterncastle deck while Tavi strides through the chaos around me. Bodies work in eager coordination, moving crates of coin and relics to the storage below. Rune picks through them all, collecting old, sealed kelp scrolls and the brittle art stones.

He's tied up his hair, showing off the sharp line of his jaw and the muscle of his neck and shoulders that flex with every movement. He catches me watching and flashes a smile, and I already know it's pointless to try and hide how my stomach flips. I would have laughed had someone tried to tell me I'd end up here, preening under the attention of handsome siren royalty.

As if he can read my thoughts, Rune's eyes turn from playful to invitation, and heat wraps my spine, traveling to my cheeks and to a place considerably lower. The hope that has settled over the crew buzzes under my skin alongside the sudden anticipation, and I laugh, drawing grins from those around me. The treasure held a fair amount of wealth. Even split evenly it'll be enough that those who step away will never have to sail again, if they choose.

Rune gathers his things and heads to his room, tossing a look over his shoulder that has me caught in his wake.

The door closes before I make it, and the moment I step through, he slams it behind me, careful of the wrapped gash on my ribs as he cages me with his arms and locks it behind us. My back presses into the cool wood. My heart rate spikes as his leg slips between mine and his hands bracket my hips, giving me just a taste of the sweet friction I already ache for.

"I've been ready to take you since the beach," he says.

"We were a little distracted."

He laughs softly, his breath kissing my cheeks as he nuzzles my hair. My hands go for his belt but he pins my fingers with his waist, pushing me harder against the door. "So greedy," he says, the words laced with approval.

I tilt my chin up, stomach flipping as his cock, thick and heavy, strains against my stomach. His pupils are already blown wide, the black consuming nearly all of the blue.

"You aren't the only one that's been ready," I murmur. "Let me touch you."

He swallows, then steps back. My skin pebbles as the air replaces the heat of his body, but the sensation doesn't last long because he sweeps his shirt up over his head, revealing the white of bandages and the shimmer of his siren markings. The scars from the thrall squid haven't yet faded, alongside a dozen other nicks and scratches he'd gathered on the islands. I move close again, drawn by his warm citrus scent and the need to map his body with my hands.

"I suppose I should be gentle with you," I say, brow pinching further with every mark I touch.

"And I, you." He scoops the knuckles of his fingers up under my shirt, brushing them along my skin until I shiver. He slowly lifts it over my head. I try to hide my wince as the skin of my ribs pulls, but he shepherds me to the bed gently, quietly folding the covers aside and urging me in.

"I'm fine," I insist as he joins me, cupping his body with mine.

"I know." He feathers kisses over the back of my neck, his fingers tracing the hem of my pants with heart-aching care.

"But from this point on, I want you to be much more than fine, little doe."

I reach a hand behind me, gripping his cock through the fabric of his pants. He sucks in a breath through his teeth and slips his hands lower, slicking a finger in the arousal that already waits for him.

"Fuck, Odelia."

"I need more, Rune," I breathe. I don't want him to go easy on me. I'm ready to give whatever he wants to take. He doesn't hesitate, instead plunging the finger inside me and palming my clit. I can't help but rock my hips with each slow, agonizingly delicious curl of his touch. He adjusts, finds the spot that unravels me, and doesn't let up. I'm too lost to the feeling to note when his pants slide down, but his hard length ends up free, and I circle my thumb over the leak of precum that waits for me, coating my hand before I pump once. Twice.

"I need to be inside of you," he all but growls into my ear, trailing his hand out of me, tracing a quick flash of claws up my stomach, there and then gone again. "I need to feel you wrapped around me."

"Yes, Captain." I scoot and he sits back to kick his trousers down, then hooks mine and drags them off my legs.

The look in his eyes is pure fire, but he's too far away, so I sit up to catch my arms around his neck and open my legs so he can settle on top of me, though he supports most of his weight on one arm. I cant my hips as he kisses me in languid brushes of lips and tongue. All I succeed in doing is driving my own need higher, teasing us both as I slick the head of him with the arousal that drips between my legs. I ache, anticipating how well he'll fill me, in awe of the way our shared breaths feel like a promise.

"I love you, Rune."

"I love you too, little doe." The words vibrate low in his chest, racing to tangle with the growing heat between my legs. He slips one big hand beneath my ass, angling me so we're in line before sinking in with slow, rolling strokes of his hips, all the while deepening our kiss. He's so gentle it almost breaks me. Will break me. Being loved by Rune Ahren is a study in consuming. In being swept away, caught in a current I don't want to fight.

By the time he's fully seated, I'm in another world, overwhelmed by the impossible fullness and the light brush of his skin on my clit. Without conscious thought, I start to rock my hips, and I feel his smile through the euphoric haze of our slow kisses.

"You're torturing me," I half-whine, half-moan, meeting each of his thrusts with one of my own, urging him faster.

He trails his lips off the corner of mine, across my cheek, working his way to my ear. "And you fucking love it." He punctuates the words by drawing all the way out before sinking back into me. When I cry out, feeling another wet wave reward him, he moves his hand from my ass to clamp the back of my leg, where my knee meets my thigh. He presses up, sinking impossibly deeper, holding me still while he increases the speed of his thrusts.

"Rune—" The growing heat steals my words. My thoughts.

I clamp myself tighter around him, urging him on, begging him for more with my body, while trying and failing to swallow down my wordless cries. I sink my fingers into his lower back, pulling him into me, chaining our bodies together as we move. The bed protests beneath us, fighting the bolts that anchor it to the floor. I tip my chin down, watching the way his body moves over me, dragging his cock out before sheathing back in one smooth motion, over and over. The sight of him fucking me already has me teetering on the edge. He groans, the sound like a touch on its own.

"I feel that," he murmurs, as my ecstasy skyrockets. "Look at me, Odelia. I want those eyes on mine when you flood my cock."

I do, and that's all it takes to send me over the edge. His shoulders glisten. The cords of his arms flex as he moves. His lips are parted, his eyes glazed with the intensity that drew me to him from the day we met.

My orgasm slams into me hard and slow, the build up drawing it from somewhere deeper, as if it's latched onto my very soul. I'm lost as Rune follows me over, thrusting deep with every wave of pleasure that clenches me tighter around him. His groan grinds out from behind clenched teeth as he comes, and I nearly go over again as he spills into me in waves. I roll my hips until he's shuttering over me, our chests heaving, our breaths mingling as he rests his forehead on mine. Every inch of me is limp, my legs tingly with weakness, and just as I've decided there's no good reason for us to get out of bed, someone knocks on the door.

"Captain." It's Elio.

Rune falls to the side, his breath coming out in pants. I huff a laugh. "Do you think they heard us?"

Rune's answering grin is wicked enough that I blush, unable to meet his gaze. He cups my chin and brings my face to his, planting a chaste kiss on my lips. "With any luck, all of the Adamaris Sea heard you. It's good for my pride."

I bat him away, laughing, but he grabs me tighter, and I don't gain an inch.

He tips his head to the door, speaking louder as he responds to Elio. "Yes?"

"We're in open water. The crates are loaded." Elio pauses. "Figured it was time you decided where we're going."

Rune looks at me, and, for no reason at all, I want him to say the mainland. It's selfish, and the fierce hope takes me off guard. To love him is to love the sea. And he will want to go home, dock at an ocean-held island where we can unload the relics we've gathered and return them to the siren kingdom where they belong. I tear my eyes from his, hoping he won't notice the way that answer will weigh down my spirit. It's unfair to him how the animal in me rears its head, sending a thrill of adrenaline through my veins, as if we've already touched endless soil. But it's not where my heart is. There's nothing for me on the mainland now. Nothing but fertile ground and nodding wildflowers.

"The nearest port on the mainland," Rune calls, settling in to curl his body into mine, as if he doesn't know how the answer sends my pulse fluttering and the world tipping beneath me.

"Where are we going?" I ask, snapping my attention back to study his face, my heart in my throat as Elio confirms and leaves us to our tangled silence.

Rune just nuzzles his nose to mine, then tucks a stray lock of hair behind my ear as the silence swells, making space for that foolish hope. For once, I don't squash it down. He threads our fingers together, and when he speaks, the words nestle in me, slotting in for a piece I always knew was missing.

"Somewhere we can run."

A SHORT WHILE LATER

EPILOGUE
RUNE

The sweet sound of Odi's moans carries through the bedroom. Hearing it sends a fresh wave of pleasure through me like an electric current as I sink into her again. My hands grip her hips, teasing her with slow, sensual thrusts. She's on all fours, head buried into the sheets, back arched perfectly for my viewing.

I shift my hips, watching my cock slide out, slick with her wetness. "Is this how you like to be touched?"

"Yes," she says, releasing a sigh.

A grin spreads across my lips, and I grip her harder as I push back in, inch by inch. She moans softly again, arching into me further. I can't drag my gaze away from the hypnotic way her ass ripples each time I pound into her. It's a perfect arc, as if sculpted for my hands alone.

The sight consumes me, a *want* so sharp, a *hunger* that can't be sated.

Warm sunlight pours into the room, washing across the floor, coating Odi's collection of leaves and shiny things displayed so lovingly on the dresser. It sends rainbows up the other side of the wall, filling the room with an ethereal glow. We've been entangled in each other's embrace for days now. The only time we stop is to hydrate and replenish ourselves. Even then, we end up coming back together, on the table, on the balcony outside, under the stars. Wherever our hearts desire.

I can't get enough of her.

"Rune—" Odi murmurs.

Her warmth gushes over my length as I pick the pace back up. Her pants become quicker, harder, our bodies slapping together as we find our pleasure. Release builds inside me, coiling tight with every thrust. Her thighs blush red beneath my touch, each sharp collision singing through us in waves that leave me trembling for more.

The bed creaks with a steady cadence, blending with my moans and Odi's whimpers. She's close too, I can feel it. I lean down—not slowing the pace—and grip her hair, gently tugging her head back. She gasps, pushing up onto her hands.

"I love the way my name rolls off your tongue," I whisper against her ear.

Her breath catches. Lips parting slightly as her eyes flutter shut. I pull out, and thrust in again. I do this over and over, like a ritual. A sacred joining together of two souls destined to find each other across the sea.

She gasps.

My cock swells.

We repeat.

The rhythm builds until I can't hold on any longer. "Say my name when you come. I want it to be the last thing that tumbles from your lips before you scream."

Her body trembles, legs shaking as I feel her warmth clamp around me. Then she shatters. "Rune Caius Ahren, *fuck me*!" Her voice splinters through the halls of my mind. Bouncing around like a fallen star looking for a place to call home.

Behind my eyes, the galaxy splits open.

It hits like the sea in a gale, wave after wave, my body seizing, every muscle drawn tight until there's nothing left but the crash, the flood, the drowning bliss of giving in. "Odelia," I groan her name, voice breaking, forehead pressing between her shoulders as if I can anchor myself there.

After a moment, I sit back up, easing out of her slowly as I savour every inch.

The world softens, our bodies slick and heaving, the aftermath of our ecstasy lessening. My chest rises and falls, breath shuddering with uneven bursts. I let myself collapse onto the bed, wrapping her close.

She's trembling, but not from fear. I smooth my palm over her hip, grounding us both. The aftershock fades, leaving only the quiet thump of her heartbeat, and the ache of knowing I've never felt so undone, so alive, as I do in her arms.

I close my eyes, content and boneless. Odi shifts in the sheets, twisting to face me. I softly smile when she traces her fingertips over the shimmering markings on my chest. "How many times is that for today?" she teases.

My eyes crack open, settling on her face. "Four if you count the one on the stairs earlier, where I tasted you, and then you tasted me, and then I came—"

Odi giggles, reaching up to place a hand over my mouth. "I know how that ended. I can still taste it."

With a sigh I tug her closer. "I hope it won't be the last for today either."

"Aren't you sick of me yet?" she says, surprised.

I offer her a grin. "Never."

Eventually, she stretches, a delicate hum leaving her throat as she sits up. I follow, dragging myself from the safety of our bed. A gentle breeze blows through the open window. Filling the room with a mixed scent. Warm soil, and salt. Land and sea.

Odi drapes a slip of dress over her frame. Oyster-coloured silk. Her dark, glossy hair hangs down her back in waves, releasing a burst of pear and honey. I slip on some loose trousers, never taking my eyes off her. My thoughts flick to the memories of pleasure we just spent together and already my cock is half hard. I groan softly, padding across the room to pull her into my arms, nuzzling my face into her silk strands. "Do we have to leave this room yet?"

She spins in my arms, reaching up on her toes to thread her hands around my neck. "It's been two weeks of our love bubble, we have to leave at some point."

I lean down to press a kiss to her nose. "Says who?"

By the sea, our cottage has become a sanctuary. A haven where we can belong only to each other, free from prying eyes, from leering gazes, from the shadow of a map hanging over us.

Odi peels herself from my arms, taking my hand as we head into the kitchen. It's simple, but spacious. Bowls of brightly coloured fruits and fresh greens adorn the counter tops. No quail eggs in sight. And the air smells of wild blooms. As soon as Odi saw the flower fields that run parallel to the ocean she'd run straight into them, picking armfulls. Every flat surface in the house now holds a vase of blossoms.

As I sit at the counter on a stool made of driftwood, she plucks a fig from the bowl, tearing it down the centre before offering me half. "Have you heard from Tavi and Elio?" she asks, her voice soft. "Did they decide who wears the captain's hat?"

I swallow the fig down before answering. "Not yet. They'll work it out. Elio will say Tavi should be Captain, but I think she likes her freedom too much. *The Gilded Hart* is in good hands either way."

"Do you miss her?"

"I do. But more than that I miss the crew." I shrug, wiping my hands on a cloth. "But Otto will love that spice we found him in town last week."

Odi's smile is small, like she's afraid to fully let go and allow herself to have happiness and love. Like she's afraid I'll long for the waltz of a ship and her song so much that I'll sail away from the shore once again. I know it's going to take time for her to see that she can trust me. My words. My promises. My embrace.

I reach across the bench and wipe my thumb across the corner of her bottom lip, catching the drip of juice from the fig. "I wouldn't want to be anywhere else though."

She grins wider, nipping at my thumb playfully "Not even Nareth? With your family?"

I huff softly before sucking the juice of my thumb. "Father and I might have patched things up when we visited, but I'm certain I don't want to live under his rule."

Odi and I had visited the siren kingdom over a month ago. It was more healing than I expected it to be. Selene couldn't stop fussing over Odi, and Dash couldn't wait to show her all around the palace.

I'd shared my mother's letter with my father. He would deny it to anyone who asked, but he'd shed a tear. Then he offered my mother's ring to me. It was a band of gold, carved to look like coral, with different blue shades of glittering stones wrapped around the band. I'd pulled him into an embrace, and he swore that I would always have a place beside him in Nareth.

We married under a canopy of shimmering pearls. Odi wore a dress that captured every essence of her. The bodice had clung close, shaped from silk the colour of sand. Delicate vines and tiny white blossoms were embroidered into the fabric, every stitch glinting faintly. From her waist the fabric shifted. Layer upon layer of sheer gauze and smooth satin flowing down in waves. Pale blues fading into shades so deep it looked like sapphires stitched together. She'd worn a veil, the colour of seafoam, with pearls scattered over it. And her hair had hung down in loose waves.

The moment we'd said *I do* was the happiest I'd ever been.

Odi saunters around the counter to wedge herself between my legs. "Are you going to show me what you've been hiding downstairs? Every time you vanish I know you're down there."

I huff a laugh, standing from the stool. "You've been very patient, and I've finally finished." I hold out my hand. "Come."

Her palm slips into mine, and I lead her down the narrow stairs into the lower half of the cottage. The shift is instant—the light dims, cools, until we step into a room walled in living ocean.

Odi gasps. Her eyes wider than a sea urchin. "Rune . . ."

Through the glass-like walls, the sea glimmers. A large sea stone bubble keeps the water at bay, clear as crystal. Beyond the barrier, shoals of silver fish dart through forests of rich green kelp. A pink and purple manta ray glides past, its colours so vivid it's glowing. Its shadow spills across the stone floor, disappearing around the bend.

Inside, the space is inviting. A large rug fills the centre of the room, covered in plush pillows and blankets. Plenty of room for . . . activities.

I glance at Odi. Her eyes are still fixated on the school of fish swimming past. She walks towards it, pressing her palm to the surface. "I've been so worried that you gave up the ocean for me."

Three strides and I'm across the room, pulling her back into my chest, leaning down to murmur in her ear. "I didn't give it up. I found a way to have both. The sea for me, and the land for you."

She turns to look up at me. Her smile hits me square in the chest, knocking the wind from me harder than a weapon ever could. "It's beautiful."

I kiss her then. Slow and tender. The kind of kiss that sears into a soul. Never to be forgotten. When my lips leave hers, it's bittersweet. "Are you up for round five yet?"

Her eyes darken in the way that makes my cock twitch, then they flick towards the stairs. "Only if you can catch me."

She's gone before I have time to grasp her. Slender, powerful legs bounding away from me. A feral grin spreads across my face, and I half-shift. Incisors, talons and scales. All of them on show. I become the hunter, and she is my prey.

"You'd better run fast, Odelia," I hiss, lingering on each of the letters that spell her name.

She giggles, but it's barely there the further she gets from me. With a low growl, my legs are moving. The wooden stairs creak with every leap. I catch her dark hair disappearing through the doorway that leads outside just as I reach the top level of the cottage.

My heart rate accelerates. Blood pumping to all areas in my body, the thrill of the hunt coursing through my veins. I'm outside, feet hitting the deck as she darts onto the sand, throwing a grin over her shoulder. "You're getting slow, siren."

The laughter on her tongue makes my heart sing. Never did I dream there would be someone out there for me, as perfect as she is. My chest aches with the love I have for her, and I plan to show her every day for the rest of our lives.

I go faster, feet pounding against the wet sand as I run through the waves that kiss the shoreline. "I'm just giving you a head start," I call after her.

She laughs, pushing her legs harder. But she could never out run me. I'd find her in every lifetime, under every moon, across every ocean.

The waves curl against the shore, spraying salt across my legs as I run, muscles burning. Each time she flashes her brown eyes over her shoulder, it only drives me faster. She is radiant in the morning sun. Oyster coloured silk dancing in the wind, hair knotted by the chase. It reminds me of a dream I once had.

A few more strides and I'm inches from her. She shrieks when I finally catch her around the waist. We tumble together in the waves, cool water breaking over us as I pin her to the sand. "Caught you."

Her breathless giggle mixes with my own ragged breath. She's grinning up at me and I can't keep my own smile at bay. Reaching down, I brush strands of sand-crusted hair from her cheek. "How shall you have me, little doe."

"Like this," she whispers, shoving the arm that is holding me up, so she can twist and roll onto me, straddling my hips.

I moan when she drags my cock free, positioning herself to sink down on it. My mind fractures when she slowly rocks her hips. All thoughts are gone. My brain is completely empty.

She places her palms on my chest and arches her back, moaning to the skies as she grinds against me. I need to taste her lips. It's been too long. I sit up, place one hand on her hip, the other tangles in the back of her hair, dragging her closer. Her eyes glitter with pleasure as my mouth hovers under hers.

"My prince," she whispers, pressing a soft kiss to my lips. "My peace." She kisses me again. "My husband." On the third kiss I'm drowning, and the only soul I want to rescue me is her. How did I get so lucky?

I grip her hip harder, fingers digging into her pliable skin, eyes locked on her as we move together. "My sea," I murmur, kissing her back. "My heart." I kiss her again. "My wife."

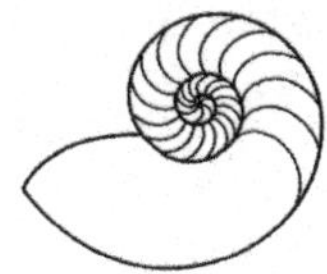

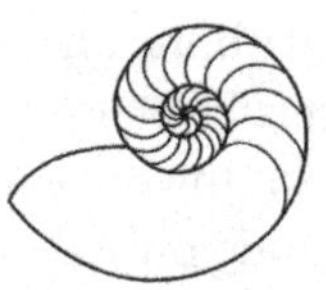

Acknowledgements

Megan

First and foremost I'd like to thank my wonderful co-author for striking out on this journey with me and making it a thousand times more fun. Because of you this book is more beautiful and romantic than I could have made it on my own. Your structure made sure we never lost momentum and your talents means this is the most gorgeous book I will have at my author table for a long time to come.

I'd also like to thank Niki, our editor, and Noelle, our PA, for their invaluable insights during revisions. You both helped make this book stronger and I will always be grateful.

As always, I'd like to thank my husband for his help with brainstorming and endless worldbuilding ideas. Finally, thank you to my son and daughter, for being patient and encouraging as I dove into the world of Rune and Odi.

Sarah

It takes a whole team of people to make a book happen, and without these people This Vicious Sea wouldn't be as amazing as it is. I want to take a moment to personally thank all those wonderful people.

Megan. You waltzed into my life like a ray of sunshine, burying your way into the soft places in my heart and making yourself at home. This book wouldn't be as beautiful, magical or fearsome as it is without you. I am so grateful for your friendship, support, encouragement, wisdom, love, creativity and our endless conversations. Thank you for taking a risk with me and writing—what I hope—is the first of many co-written books together.

Noelle. The PA of my dreams and the friend who has cosied up beside me and supported me ever since I started writing. Your attention to detail when beta reading is amazing, and the love you have for books is inspiring. I can't thank you enough for all the encouragement you have shown Megan and I, and how you helped get This Vicious Sea out into the world. You are a treasure.

Sarah continued...

Jared. My love. My heart. My husband. Thank you for always loving me and encouraging me with every new book idea I have even if I haven't finished writing all the other books I've started. I love you forever and always.

My children. I love you. I'm so proud of you, and I hope that you always chase your dreams.

A big thank you to **Niki** from Muse & Margins for editing This Vicious Sea alongside Megan. Your knowledge and wisdom is so appreciated.

My street team. Noelle, Meg, Ana, Erin, Letitia, Kirsten, Amarie, Alex, Erin R, and Brittany. Thank you all so much for all your love and support for me and my books. I truly appreciate each and everyone of you.

To the This Vicious Sea ARC team, and all the readers, thank you for your endless support and encouragement for this book. Without you, there would be no point in writing magical stories.

Newsletters

If you loved This Vicious Sea and want to read a bonus chapter, then sign up to our newsletters! The first part will be in Rune's POV from Sarah's newsletter and the second half will be in Odelia's pov and from Megan's newsletter. There are some easter eggs in there for the second book we have planned for this world so you don't want to miss out!

We also promise not to fill your inbox with anything boring. It's only good times from us.

Megan G. Mossgrove

https://www.mossgrovewrites.com/

Sarah C Davies

https://subscribepage.io/087Gke

Books by Megan G. Mossgrove

Books by Sarah C Davies

From the kingdoms of Lucius & Oscuro

Releasing Mid 2026

Fables from Sapphire Vale

Socials we love

@fixtionaddiction

@museandmargins

@pebbles88dlg

@mikel.melwasul

@atlas_creed

@readingrabbitbookshop

@booklovebyelle

@bookishwitchreads

@fantasybook.adventurer

@heyerinsreading

@electicbychoicereads

@eddyroseauthor

@starsxdust

@cozyreadsbykirst

@alexs.magical.library

@lexloganauthor

@talesandtomes_bookstore

@flowersandparchment

@indieauthorfanclub

@brittanyreads

@madeline_g.author

Made in the USA
Coppell, TX
11 February 2026

71727765R00341